THE SYNNER

WEAVINGS OF FATE

(VOL. 1)

NOOBURAI

Copyright © 2024 by Nooburai
All rights reserved.
No portion of this book may be reproduced in any form without written permission from the publisher or author, except as permitted by U.S. copyright law.
ISBN (Paperback): 979-8-9920739-0-4
ISBN (Hardcover): 979-8-9920739-1-1
ISBN (E-book): 979-8-9920739-2-8
Cover art by: Glofernwolfe
Book design by: Tracy Brauer

DISCLAIMER

This book is a work of fiction. Any similarities to any person, living or not, is purely coincidental and should - for numerous and obvious reasons - not be compared to anything in real life. Any opinions expressed in this work are those of the characters, and should not be confused with those of the author.

Also, there is plenty of blood, guts, swear words, and difficult or triggering topics present in this book. This is NOT a book for children.

PREFACE

This book began as a passion project born from my deep love for immersive storytelling, initially inspired by the richly woven worlds of *The Witcher* and *The Lord of the Rings*. What started as a simple fan-fiction evolved over time into something entirely my own—a story with its own characters, world, and heartbeat.

The journey to finishing this book has been anything but linear. The first year and a half were consumed by world-building and writing, pouring every bit of imagination and energy I had into crafting a narrative that felt alive. And then, for five years, I let the story rest. I knew that to give it the justice it deserved, I needed to grow—as a writer, and perhaps more importantly, as a person.

Returning to the manuscript after that time was like meeting an old friend, familiar yet somehow changed. As I refined the story, I realized that many of the main character's experiences were reflections of my own—shaped by my personal struggles, triumphs, and the lessons I've learned along the way. These connections gave the story a depth and sincerity that I hope resonates with readers.

In these pages, you'll find a world shaped by intricate destinies and struggles for meaning. It's my hope that you'll come to know these characters as I do and find a piece of yourself reflected in their journeys.

Thank you for stepping into this world with me. May the threads of fate woven here speak to you in unexpected ways. Now buckle up, chuckle-fuck, 'cause we're going for a ride.

Sincerely,

Nooburai

DEDICATION

To my mother, siblings, and close friends who have always challenged me and pushed me to be the best version of myself.

To you, the reader, who decided to give my humble book a chance out of all the others in the "Fantasy" row of the bookstore.

To the many authors who inspire countless others to pursue their dreams of writing via their incredible stories.

To those of you who doubted whether I'd actually do it (Git Gud, fuckers).

CONTENTS

DISCLAIMER III
PREFACE V
DEDICATION VII
PROLOGUE 1

CHAPTER 1
Thoma Fayren 7

CHAPTER 2
Eve of the Expedition 23

CHAPTER 3
The Road to Coltend Castle 41

CHAPTER 4
Coltend Castle 67

CHAPTER 5
Valdis 99

CHAPTER 6
The Return to Codrean 115

CHAPTER 7
Queen Leona 139

CHAPTER 8
The Undergod 175

CHAPTER 9
The Master 193

CHAPTER 10
The Rhydian Pass 215

CHAPTER 11
Athar.. *233*

CHAPTER 12
The Elven Emissary *249*

CHAPTER 13
Of Kings and Outcasts *273*

CHAPTER 14
Dissonance *297*

CHAPTER 15
Codrean... *319*

CHAPTER 16
The Duel *335*

CHAPTER 17
The Journey North.. *351*

CHAPTER 18
Mourtis *399*

CHAPTER 19
To Fate and Coltend *417*

CHAPTER 20
The Library... *441*

CHAPTER 21
The Portal Stone... *455*

CHAPTER 22
Traitor *473*

CHAPTER 23
Unexpected Company *483*

CHAPTER 24
The Battle for Coltend *499*

CHAPTER 25
Weavings of Fate *521*

EPILOGUE
Aftermath.. *541*

AFTERWORD
Author's Notes.. *561*

THE SYNNER: WEAVINGS OF FATE

PROLOGUE

I heard my mother's voice grow increasingly distant, her features much less defined now than only a moment ago. She walked through the main entrance to our house as my eyes began to blur and my heart began to pound.

"Where are you going? Why do you have to leave?" I shouted. Tears streamed down my face and snot fled from my nostrils as I called out after her. I couldn't have been much older than the age of five when I saw my mother for the last time; her steel-colored hair was stuck close to her body from the rain as she walked out into the twilight.

There was no warning, no sign of anything being wrong, or of anyone at fault. I wept, but I didn't know for how long. It felt like an eternity, though, as I didn't know what was going to happen to me. The only thing I did know was that my life was about to change forever.

An older man with a scar on the left side of his face and silver hair walked in the door, but I didn't recognize him at all. For a few moments, he argued with my father, who was a plump piece of shit, though all I can recall is their stuttering silhouettes bouncing off the walls just as angrily as their tones of voice.

"That *monster* of a mother of his is finally leaving, and you think *you're* going to take care of him better than *I* will?" my father said, his jowls were shaking just as much as the light bouncing off the wall. "Absolutely. You've already sent his older brother to me out of spite for *her*, and yet you have the gall to believe that I'm going to believe you will take care of this child?" the scarred man asked. His face was twisted and angry, but that wasn't what I was focused on.

It was his eyes.

They glowed like twin suns against the darkness of the room that the fireplace's light couldn't touch. "W-well yes," my father said, his voice beginning to tremble as the scarred man growled before speaking. "You've done enough already. You've gone against her will and done the unthinkable, and yet you expected her to forgive you for it?" the scarred man asked, his anger was evident and almost tangible in the thickened air.

I could feel a sort of *pressure* emanating from him, like the world was itching to bend to his will. I wiped the tears from my eyes, trying to make sure it wasn't just the light of the fire being blurred in my vision, but it wasn't.

What is that glowing stuff? Is that fire? I thought, trying to understand what I was seeing.

Oh, how wrong I was.

The scarred man looked at me. He couldn't have been much older than my father, or at least, he didn't *look* like he was. There was, however, something with the way he carried himself that told me he was strong.

Extremely strong.

He was in the middle of saying something I either couldn't understand or chose to ignore; I don't know which. I reached my hand out, and these odd hair-like strands of this aura that surrounded him came towards me. I felt it gathering in my palm and around my hand like a warmed glove.

He stopped mid-sentence and stared at me more intently.

Whatever it was I was doing had certainly drawn his attention. I remember laughing as the warm cloud of golden... *whatever it was* began to circulate around my arm and chest.

Suddenly, it halted all movement, and a sharp pain riddled my body that started in my chest. I couldn't figure out what in the realms had just happened, but whatever it was, my father had clearly taken some delight in seeing me suffer.

I blinked, and I immediately saw a smokey arm materialize in front of me. It grabbed my father by the neck, and pinned him against the wall, making sure his feet were off the ground.

"What the *fuck* did you do to him?" the scarred man growled through clenched teeth as spittle flecked my father's face. "I did the only reasonable thing *to do* to him," my father said through his tightened throat. He began to chuckle, though the sound wasn't a clear and cheerful sound. Instead, it was more like a wet gurgling, as the large, smokey claw tightened even further.

With a heavy sigh, he tossed my father aside, slamming him into the wall. The scarred man walked over to me, and after having seen that display of power, I could only wonder what would come for me next.

"Hello there," he said in a much warmer voice than he had used when he first arrived. "You're Thoma, right?" he asked with a smile, wrinkling the scar on his face. I could only nod out of fear of saying something that might anger him. "Gods above, he's done a real number on you, hasn't he?" he said, glancing over his shoulder to make sure my father was still unconscious.

"Yes," I said, the only words I could muster in my confusion. "*Yes* to what, exactly?" he asked, keeping the same, warm tone as if he'd somehow forgotten I was only a small child. "I-I'm Thoma," I said bashfully. He chuckled lightly and tousled my hair. "Yes. Yes, you are. So, can you do me a favor, young Thoma?" the man asked.

I nodded my head.

Just as I did, my father groaned in an apparent regaining of consciousness. The scarred man sent another fist of what I could only describe as hardened smoke smashing my father's face into the ground without him even bothering to look, keeping the same, warm smile on his face.

"Like I was saying, I need you to do me a favor, Thoma," the scarred man said. He paused, almost as if he was choosing his words carefully, and I thought I almost saw his smile fade for a moment, but he recovered before any significant change was made. "I need you to grab some of your things, and grab your best raincoat," he said.

"But why do I have to go? Are we going after my mother?" I asked. The man shook his head. "I'm sorry, but we can't go after her right now. Things are... *complicated*, and she's going somewhere we can't follow right now. I'm sorry," he said dejectedly.

I sniffed back some snot as the tears began to well in my eyes again as his words set in.

The man seemed unsure of what to do, but he resorted to conjuring a swirling sphere of light in front of me. It looked a lot like the fire that was dying down behind me, only far more controlled and compacted into a sphere not much larger than an apple.

"Do you know what this is?" he asked. "N-no. Is that like the shining stuff that I was playing with earlier?" I asked, almost reaching for it. "This... *stuff* is called *mana*," he said softly. He began to mold it into a few different but easily recognizable shapes.

"All things have mana in them, Thoma; you, me, your mother. Some of us even go so far as learning to control it with special powers," he said, turning the sphere into an arrow-like shape.

He sent the arrow barrelling through the room, turning sharply and avoiding all kinds of objects in the room, then coming to a quick stop in his hand, where it turned back into a sphere. "*Ooh*! That was so cool! Can you teach me to do that?" I asked, rubbing my eyes to see it better if he decided to do more with it.

"I can, but remember that favor I asked you to do for me earlier?" he said, dispelling the mana and putting a hand on my shoulder. I nodded my head quickly. "Good. Go grab your things. I'll deal with your father in the meantime," he said.

I raced upstairs and grabbed the items he asked for, failing to notice the note left on my pillow, and ran back downstairs. When I came down, I saw that my father was being loosely tied up to a chair. Not so tight that he couldn't have escaped on his own, though it was more to hold him upright than anything else. The scarred man had sat him down on a chair that was near a smaller table with an open bottle of wine on top of it.

"Ready to go?" he asked me from over his shoulder. "I'm ready," I said, still unsure of what to call him or even who he was. He merely grunted a response and jabbed something into my father's leg. I could hear the drops of blood hitting the ground from where I stood, and when I noticed it, I saw the letter attached to the cheese knife my father always used, which was now embedded in his upper thigh.

"Sorry about that," the man said softly, turning my head away. "Your mother said I should do what I can to protect you, and this is my version of it," he continued. "Why couldn't she do it herself?" I asked. "That's a difficult question that I can't answer right now, Thoma," he replied, looking down at the floor. "*Oh*... okay," I said, feeling my facial features slump a little more.

"Come on. We need to get going. I know it's dark and rainy

outside, but we need to leave tonight," he said, ushering me out the door. Just before we stepped outside, he bent down and made sure that the small notch around the neck of my cloak was clasped correctly, then patted me twice on the shoulders.

He grabbed an iron cage with small panes of glass embedded into it from just outside the door. He opened one of the glass panels that had a small knob on it, and pushed a sphere of pure mana inside, and closed the door. The cage sealed shut with a sheen of a blue, translucent mana, allowing the light to shine through cleanly.

"Where are we going?" I finally asked. I'd trusted the man until this point, but that was more out of survival instincts than anything else. I didn't know much about him, but something felt familiar about him that I couldn't quite place. He helped me onto his horse then mounted the beast behind me, making sure I was secure in the saddle before kicking his heels into the horse's sides.

"We're going to my home in the North-Western corner of Coltend," he replied, having to use a bit more of his voice since the rain had gotten worse. We rode for a few minutes in silence, as I tried to piece together everything that happened until this point. My chest was hurting a little bit, but I couldn't tell if that was from all the crying I'd done, or something else entirely.

"What's your name?" I finally asked. I'd spent the better part of an hour trying to figure out what it might be, but when nothing of the conversation that I recalled held the information I was looking for, I decided I *had* to ask that question myself. In response, the man chuckled and patted my shoulder again.

"You can call me *The Master of Codrean*," he said warmly.

CHAPTER 1

Thoma Fayren

Cold, piercing rain fell from the sky.

It was late in the afternoon, and I stood at the entrance to the stables of Codrean waiting for someone, who was supposed to present me with a gift for my eighteenth birthday. After about an hour of waiting, I finally saw who I had been waiting for: Bernar, my older brother. He was wading through the newly muddled path towards me, with a wry grin on his chiseled face.

Bernar and I have an age difference of about five years, give or take a few months, but he is much stronger and fleshed out than I am. Granted black hair like a raven's feathers, golden glowing eyes, and a generally athletic build, he also wore a pendant around his neck which he often kept tucked away. The black, leather jerkin, with hose and boots to match, was shrouded by a rain repellant cloak.

The heavy downpour made it a little difficult to see whatever it was he had behind him, but as he approached, it became evident that it was, in fact, a *very* large horse.

I would be lying if I said I didn't immediately become ecstatic with the gift.

"Gods above and below, this thing is massive," I said, not

bothering to hide the excitement in my voice.

"Yes, he is! I figured it would probably be a good gift to get you for your horse-caster certification today. By the way, what kind of psychotic turd decides to do something like this on their birthday, *huh*?" he asked, his voice sounded a lot like mine, if not a little higher in pitch, making us rather difficult to tell us apart by just hearing our voices.

"*Haha,* well, about that…" I trailed off as I rubbed the back of my neck. "He also cost me three months' worth of my salary, but I'm glad you like it," he chimed in, cutting me off slightly. Seeing as I was a little too short to get my foot in the stirrup, Bernar dragged a nearby shodding stool my way. I crawled up onto the horse's back with difficulty, as the size of the damned creature was much larger than the one I was previously used to. This, in turn, also meant I struggled to get my right foot to the other side.

Bernar let out more of a maniacal cackle than a regular laugh while watching me fumble-fuck my way about the giant quadriped. Infinite mocking was his prerogative as the older brother, after all. "I should have thought this was a possibility. It's true that you're a fine sword-caster, but if mom had seen you struggle like this, there is absolutely *no way* she would have let you try to become a horse-caster," he said, between laughs.

I felt my mouth grimace and squinted my green eyes. "*Oh,* just lay it on thicker, you derisive *thundercunt*. It's my first time trying to mount a horse this large. My old horse was much shorter than this one, and that's not even mentioning the fact that you put the stirrups a little too high," I replied with a sardonic sneer.

Bernar shook his head, still chuckling a little to himself. "That's because our rotund father had used this saddle for decades until it was passed down to me. I'm not sure if you remember much about him, but he used this saddle often and ended up tearing through the leather straps that were used to buckle it in the right spot," he replied.

"After having kept it in storage for so long, I had forgotten about the tear. I've since had to compromise with them being a little higher up until I can get them repaired properly, as the horse alone already drained a lot of my savings," my brother continued, giving me a shrug.

I recognized that my brother did, in fact, spend a lot on this present; it was a beautiful horse, after all. "I'm not saying that I'm ungrateful, brother," I began. "I do appreciate the gift a lot. I'm just trying to figure out how to get into it smoothly. So, give me a minute, will you?" I continued. Bernar merely shrugged in response, continuing to watch me struggle a little longer before finally getting into the saddle.

After finally settling in and readjusting the stirrups as closely as I could to my liking, I patted the horse's nape. "There, that's *much* better," I stated proudly, pushing a lock of mid-length walnut hair away from my eye. "Is it comfortable at least?" Bernar asked, eying the stirrups to make sure his younger brother hadn't made his situation *worse*.

"Well, Father, being the oversized shit-nugget that he is, has *definitely* broken this saddle in," I spat. Bernar let out a snort, but immediately cleared his throat. "Good. I hope you're ready for your horse-caster certification. If worse goes to shit, at least you'll have a horse that could belong to a god. Just, *uh*… make sure your spell doesn't backfire, okay? That would *suck*," he said with a grin.

A spell was the simplest form of magic we Synners used. We're a group of warriors who gained improved mana-based abilities through the consumption of a plant known as *Gwynn-leaf*. While this wasn't the only reason we *could* control mana, it certainly aided the process. We'd earned our moniker of *Synner* due to the Church of Mideia branding us such, as we *opposed the natural order between gods and men*, or so the priests and leaders of that *cult* said.

"And what if I *do* pass this certification? Do you think the Master will finally train me to become an all-caster?" I asked, openly displaying my hopes and dreams for the future. "Well, you're still missing your spear and bow-casting certifications, and that's not to mention reaching the next stages of mana manipulation, so I can't say for sure. But, in the event he *does* accept you for all-caster training, I would suggest you dig deep and dedicate yourself to succeed," my brother began.

"All-casters are rare enough as it is, and we Synners are likely to become a dying breed. Some have even become outcasts of society for having done some ill deed that would hinder the betterment of humanity. However, we must *always do our best to avoid following in their footsteps, because when all is said and done, we were created for ridding the world of evil*, or so the Master says, anyway," he continued, giving his best impression of the Master he could.

I couldn't help but chuckle at the impersonation, but I also knew the depth of what my brother meant from his history lessons over the years. Tales of Synners turning their backs and betraying their own kinsmen over conflicting ideals or other such reasons had reached the far corners of the Continent - deeming them outcasts and traitors to their own kind.

"In any case, let's begin," Bernar said with a wave of his hand. I nodded and stuck my heels into the horse's side. Hoof-fall like rolling thunder whipped up a splash of mud, and I could feel the strands of my hair flowing in the wind. I held onto the reins as tight as I could, focusing on breathing in rhythm with the horse's gallop, relaxing my mind to focus on the challenge ahead.

Casting from a solid stance is relatively simple, but this is a whole new devil I'll have to manage, I thought.

I was closing the distance between himself and the target quickly, and knew I had to begin gathering mana. The enchanted ring - which all junior Synners wore - served as a magical ward that helped to stave off, but not entirely block the heat produced by the condensed mana just before casting a spell. I focused on the one I had to produce, and reviewed the training I'd had since I was only five years old.

First decide, transfer, then conduct, and finally, release! Never mix the order up or the spell won't work, the Master's words echoed in my head.

I, for whatever gods-forsaken reason, decided it would be fun to try to impress my brother with a bolt of lightning that could be cast from one's fingertips in any direction desired. The target was well within striking range for the spell's effect, and I took a deep breath before the channeling process.

This process required anyone who wished to use a spell to draw mana from the Ethereal; The invisible realm surrounded all things, both living and inanimate, which was the origin of mana itself. I began to focus as intensely as I could manage, while still maintaining my posture in the saddle.

I forcefully closed my eyes for an instant, using all my will-power to divide my attention, sending my consciousness into the other realm. My eyes reopened, as the familiar feeling of my dilating pupils covered the olive-green irises and the whites of my eyes *as my consciousness went from the Between into the immaterial world.*

A realm of pure and plentiful power where bright, colorful shafts of light circled a bright sphere of pure power in the sky, while stars of all sizes wheeled overhead and meshed together with the shafts.

The merging of a star with a streak of power, which was a magnificent sight in and of itself since it released a blue and orange flare whenever they merged.

I looked around me and observed the ongoings above me as I did every time I wished to draw from the realm. I never had any need to rush this process, as time was not something the realm took into consideration - the only one of its kind to have such a characteristic. It was filled with life forms that roamed the vast forest of magnificent trees. The shimmering lake that was a stone's throw away shimmered and reflected the light produced from the sphere above it.

The river that flowed from it constantly changed its shape and color, according to the merging stars with the tendrils of power. I outstretched my right hand towards the sphere, spreading my fingers as wide as I could. The mana began to flow in tendrils towards my hand, warming the air around it wherever it went.

They wrapped around my fingers, and the connection began harnessing the shafts of light and transforming them into a nebula of raw mana that encased my body like a flowing, gaseous cocoon, which began to show itself in the Between.

I exerted my will, absorbing the mana into my body and mind quickly, where it could be shaped and molded into the spells I'd already learned. I condensed what I had gathered into my hands, proceeding to cast the spell out just in front of me.

The mana cloud surrounding my body suddenly condensed, and moved with the fluidity of a river towards my right hand, warming what little armor I was wearing and making the hairs on my arm stand on end as it went. The warmth gathered into an indigo, opaque sphere that glowed in the palm of my hand. The heat it generated grew rapidly, and was beginning to seep through the small ward from the ring on his hand.

Time to cast. Otherwise my ward will fail and my hand will melt from the heat, I thought, feeling the heat begin to seep through my measly protection measures.

I locked onto my target and whirled my arm the same way I'd practiced so often in the late hours of the night - a clockwise circle with the casting hand, followed by a pull-push motion with my arm. I made quick work of it and released the spell, its heat going along with it like removing my hand from a campfire. It all happened in a fraction of a second as the bolt of indigo lightning shot out from the fingertips of my glove.

The mana-bolt, now traveling through the air and any falling drop from the sky, vaporized anything and everything as it went. With the massive differential in temperature between the bolt and the air around it being as drastic as it was, the resulting boom from the rapid compression and decompression of the air was so great, it sounded as though the hammer of the thunder god had struck a mountain.

It quickly met its target, leaving it in little more than shards and splinters with an explosive reaction. Charred bits flew everywhere – a few of them passing him by a little too closely for comfort. The unfortunate chicken who pecked at the ground behind the target, was, unsurprisingly, turned into little more than a pink, feathery mist.

Bernar's jaw dropped as he looked on in astonishment. "Haha! You've done it, you lanky, little bastard! Well done!" he shouted in excitement. I looked over my shoulder as I turned the horse. "Did you have some kind of wager with Roburn as to whether I would've fucked it up?" I asked sarcastically. "N-no, why would I have that?" Bernar chuckled nervously. "On the contrary, I was actually hoping you would be able to do it. Some of the *others*, however..." Bernar replied, his words trailing off with a shrug.

I rode up to my brother's side and dismounted with more grace than I'd had when I tried to mount the large horse. Bernar embraced me, and patted him firmly on the back. "Finest use of the Kyr spell I've seen in awhile," he began, smiling brightly. "Well executed, but dangerous," he warned. "Horses get spooked easily, and most horse-casters recommend using *quieter* spells while riding. Luckily, this one's well-trained and kept his composure," he continued.

"So I've heard," I muttered under my breath. "Although I'm sure that the Master will be surprised once he hears what I've accomplished," I said, hopefully. "I don't doubt it, little brother," Bernar replied, patting my shoulder. "I know for a fact I wasn't pulling these kinds of stunts at your age. Hell, he might train you to be the best all-caster of all of us. After all, he *does* sense that you have much more power than most of the other boys here."

"I really hope you're not just saying that to make me happy, brother. You know damn well I would do my best to be the best he's ever seen," I said with ironically little self-confidence.

My brother smiled and put a gloved hand atop my shoulder, tilting his head down a bit and looking at me from beneath his dark eyebrows. "I'm sure you will be, and I'll help you in that endeavor wherever I can," he said warmly. "Does that mean you'll let me kick your ass during sword training?" I asked.

Bernar laughed heartily. "You're more than welcome to try, but I guarantee you won't land a blow if you don't pack on some muscle and learn a few new tricks. Your arrogance far outweighs your flagpole build as it is," he said. "I might not have your strength, but I'm at least twice as fast as you," I replied.

"Sure, sure," Bernar said sarcastically. "But what is speed when your legs are sore, arms are tired, breathing heavy and all that after only 10 minutes of having it out with one of those damned-ugly creatures outside?" he asked. "No, little brother.

You'll need both to survive out there. Being good with mana manipulation will only get you so far," Bernar said with a seriousness that, until this point, I had never seen in him.

I began to think about the reality of the world outside the fortress' walls I was yet to explore.

He never explained why *I haven't been allowed to go on expeditions yet, has he?* I thought, trying to remember any conversation we'd ever had about the topic.

"But, enough about that for now. We should head back to the dorms and celebrate your accomplishment today," Bernar said, flicking the back of his hand onto my chest. "It's colder than a witch's tit out here, and pissing more than the sea goddess herself can muster. We still have some time before supper, so we should change our clothes *before* the Master rips us both a new one," he continued. "I guess you're right," I agreed reluctantly because I loved the rain and cold.

"I'm *always* right!" Bernar exclaimed. "Not always…" I said, grinning slyly. "If you're going to mention that incident with the Dawn Nymph…" Bernar began. "I didn't say anything!" I raised my hands placatingly. We chuckled lightly and continued on our way. "I suppose we could try another horse-casting, or perhaps spar with each other tomorrow?" I asked my older brother.

Bernar shrugged and displayed a one-sided smile "I suppose we could do some sparring tomorrow, but we'll have to deal with whatever the Master has planned first. I hear he wants to give us his version of a *surprise test* tomorrow," he replied.

I held a pensive expression for a few seconds, but quickly dismissed any ideas that came to mind. "You don't happen to know what that might be, do you?" I asked. "I do, actually," Bernar began. "But, due to certain circumstances, I'm not allowed to talk about anything coming from the Master that he doesn't clearly state himself," he spat. "I'd rather like a challenge," I said cheerfully.

Granted, I *was* blissfully unaware of the reality outside the fortress.

"I'd love to show him the new spell I've been working on. If I'm able to do it under pressure, with the off chance that he doesn't know some variation of it already, I think he'll be pleasantly surprised." I said, to which Bernar simply shrugged. "Perhaps. Nevertheless, we should go back to the dorm to get a change of clothes before he kicks both of our asses. You know how he is when it comes to being late for the evening debriefing," he said. I replied with a nod, and placed my new horse in an empty stall, patting its neck as I closed the gate.

A fine horse if ever I've seen one, I thought as I returned to my brother's side.

Half an hour and a change of clothes later, we arrived at the mess hall. A long wooden house, with well-thatched roofing where two massive pillars supported the front of the roof above the main entrance, both engraved with tales of past Synners and their heroic actions. We walked under the tall doorway, and were relieved at the sight of the feast before us.

Normally, the food we would eat during the majority of our days at Codrean tasted little better than watered-down nasal mucus, which held all of the necessary nutritional value we needed. The feast that awaited us was certainly a surprise to be remembered for the next few months.

On the tables, there were slaughtered pigs with apples in their mouths, deer and lamb haunches. There was more than enough vodka and ale to go around, and the Synners, both seniors and juniors alike, were just going in for their second round when we walked in. Many of the Synners acknowledged our presence, as Bernar was one of the few there who had been recognized by the Master at the age of eighteen, and I hoped to match it.

Since our daily training often consisted of various different types of exercises, sword and spell drills were modified to fit each Synner's own style, while still honing the core basics. Some preferred more flashy styles, whereas others would take preference to the more conservative movement types. Bernar was one of the few who had mastered over four styles of blade-and-spell-work, leading him to be recognized as a prodigy by the Master.

Although we would all spend hours each day, training, polishing and perfecting our techniques for our preferred weapon systems, we would also have to face the rigorous physical conditioning part of it all; league-long runs in minimal amounts of time, lifting and tossing tree trunks, and endless weapon swing repetitions to name a few. This all had to be done in full gear, so that there wouldn't be a difference in performance when the time to do battle came. In turn, it made us formidable warriors that were nearly unmatched in our physical capabilities.

Usually, there was no such feast waiting for us at the end of a long training day. The habitual gruel we would eat sufficed to supply their bodies with nutrients. However, today was a day unlike the rest. Our eyes glistened at the sight of the feast before us. We walked towards the long hearth running down the center of the barracks, which heated the general area to a fair temperature, and chose some empty seats their comrades had saved for us.

"*Ah*!" the Master, who now stood at the far end of the hearth, exclaimed. His voice rang out across the mess hall like a tidal wave of sound. Everyone's hearts skipped a beat, and sat still with eyes peeled. He was not a man any of them would have liked to have annoyed or anything of the sort. Rumor had it that he had killed a Synner a long time ago for insubordination in the mess hall. At other times, he was known to beat future Synners, or *new bloods* as we called them, for being even a single minute late.

The scariest part was that no one had seen him come into the hall.

"I'm glad to see you're all enjoying yourselves, and you aren't wrong to do so," he said in a voice much warmer than most were used to. His audience was quiet and attentive, holding their breath as the white haired, glowing-eyed master spoke. "I believe everyone present heard the sound of a single thunderbolt strike near our home this afternoon. I thought the thunder god would have brought more with him, given the amount of rainfall we've had today," his piercing gaze fell upon the two of us.

Oh, fuck! We've been had, I thought.

Surprisingly, the Master didn't dally on the subject, but a thin-lipped grin managed to escape the corner of his mouth, wrinkling the scar on his cheek. He waved his hand, and decided it was better to move on to what was most important. "But I digress. I expect you all know that at the end of every day, we have our debriefing for the following day. Now, I know that many of you have more than obviously noticed that something is very different from any other day up until now."

Here it comes, we thought, glancing at each other.

"We're having this lovely feast for one reason: tomorrow we're going on an expedition," he said, and watched carefully as some of the younger Synners shifted in their seats. "I expect all of you to be looking sharp as ever at first light. We're going south-west towards Coltend Castle to take part in a war council we have received an invitation from King Truls himself to attend. As things currently stand, I will be the only representative of our section present at the meeting. If any of you have any questions, now would be the best and only time to ask them, otherwise keep your shit to yourselves," the Master said.

A few of the young ones grew uneasy; some with a certain anxiousness to go on their first expedition while others were uneasy out of pure *fear*. The fear of knowing what they may encounter on the road there made even some of the seniors shake in their hardened leather boots.

I abruptly raised his hand, and in the same instant, the Master raised an eyebrow. "Yes? What is it, young Thoma?" he asked. "I've never been to Coltend, Master, and I was just wondering what sort of beasts or monsters we may encounter on our way there," I said with a slight tremble in his voice.

I know others have similar questions, but hopefully I can get enough out of him right now to help them out, I thought, assuring myself I hadn't just made a mistake.

The Master must have sensed that I was as nervous as a whore in church, and wrinkled the scar on his cheek once more. "I've only ever been there a few times myself, and I still don't know every monster or beast that lies on the path towards it." the Master said in a nicer tone than he normally carried. "The one thing I can tell you, however, is that if we do encounter any threats along the way, you'll need all the skills you've learned until now," he said with an air of caution.

"So, you're suggesting that the likelihood of us engaging one or more creatures is more than probable, Master?" I asked the moment the last word left the Master's mouth. The Master looked at me with a look I could only assume was a nostalgic one; eager to get into a battle and show my prowess as a Synner. He chuckled lightly through his nose in response to whatever he was thinking.

"In case any of you forgot, the creatures we have long since trained to deal with are rarely ever alone. I wouldn't count on there not being in a skirmish at some point along the way," he said. "In any case, be prepared and remember your training. You'll do well enough from what I've heard, Thoma," he said and everyone in the room sat in awe.

The Master had not - in recent years - given a compliment to any of the other juniors, and while I couldn't read minds, their expressions showed they instantly felt jealousy stirring in their hearts. "Thank you, Master. I'll do my best," I said with more excitement than I had originally intended. "I know you will," the Master said calmly, and sent a small chill down everyone's spine.

I, for one, almost froze solid.

"What do you think he meant by that?" I quietly asked Bernar after we'd left the mess hall as we headed back to the dorm that was in the main fortress of Codrean. "Fucked if I know," he shrugged. "The Master's been awfully strange these days and I'm not too keen on finding out what's been eating him. Besides, it's not like he'd let us figure it out anyway, right? I mean, the bastard's creepy as hell, smart as can be, and meaner than my friend's ex-wife when she's on those days of the month," Bernar said with a short chuckle, scratching the back of his head with a shit-eating grin strewn across his face.

I smiled, and felt a little calmer as the last comment was aimed to cheer me up and remove the chill that rolled up and down my spine.

"*Ah*, screw it," he blurted out. "At least we'll get to truly see what you're made of if we do face any creatures along the way," he said excitedly. "I'm sure that if you can prove yourself to the Master, then you'll soar up the ranks," Bernar said with confidence.

I sure hope so, I thought, averting my gaze slightly.

"Well, we should get some sleep, little brother. Got a long day tomorrow, and not enough sleep or women to keep us company through the night," Bernar said briefly. "I have to review the spell I've created. It's best to always keep it fresh in mind," I said.

"*Oh*, you mean you practice *that* thing every night? Very well, then," Bernar replied as they reached the entrance to the large, stone fortress - pushing the wooden door open. "Just don't stay up too late, you mischievous little turd," he said, scuffing up my hair. "Alright, alright! I won't!" I replied with a smile from ear to ear. My brother looked down and raised an eyebrow, as though expecting something more.

"Okay, I *promise* I won't," I said in a murmur. "Better not," Bernar said. "Otherwise, I'll make you drink a bowl of goat's piss," he said, pointing his finger right at the tip of my nose. "Rest well, brother. Tomorrow's a big day... for both of us," he continued.

Bernar patted me on the shoulder, and turned down one of the stone hallways that lead towards his own quarters. I, on the other hand, proceeded down the opposing hallway, reaching one of the rooms where he found the others in a drunken sleep on their beds. I removed my clothes, avoiding a bucket of someone's piss along the way, and got into my sleeping attire. I did my best to stay quiet as I tucked myself under the covers and lay awake. I stared into the dark shadows of the thatched roof above me, and wondered what sort of things I might encounter the next day.

As my imagination ran freely, I pictured myself in the middle of a flat, grassy meadow at twilight to review my new spell; calculating how powerful it might be, and how much mana I would need to cast it. Obviously, I knew of the dangers of casting an untested spell in battle, as they were frequently addressed during training. I just hoped that whatever happened the next day wouldn't force my hand to use it, but that answer would only come the next day.

When, at first light, I'd depart on my very first expedition.

CHAPTER 2

Eve of the Expedition

Ugh, this sucks, I thought as I writhed beneath the covers of my bed.

The thatched roof above me, saturated from the rain earlier in the day, hung lower than usual, and the distinct *drip-drop* from it was helping me keep track of the sleep I'd lost.

I closed my eyes once more, and held them shut for a few minutes before giving up and smacking the cold, stone wall behind me. It had hundreds of individual scratchings on it. Names, dates, and drawings of all sorts had turned the plain granite wall into a canvas by the ones who came before to express themselves however they saw fit.

Doesn't look like I'm going to be getting much sleep tonight anyway. I should probably use this time to review my spell, just in case, I thought.

It was one of the most mana-demanding spells I had created, and I knew it would be devastating if used correctly, to say the least. I lay there, calculating and recalculating every movement to the single-digit degree, the amount of mana needed to condense the spell, how it would react with the ring's ward and whether the ward would hold. As time passed, I continued tossing and turning, probably more times than a dung-beetle would roll a turd-ball back to his home.

I absolutely hate having to wait to try this out. Although, if I go out and test it now, my energy levels for tomorrow will be severely drained, and I'm certain the Master will pick up on the mana it will disperse because of it, I thought.

I decided against going outside and tugged on the woolen blanket I was using to keep warm in the cold night.

Gods above and below, this new blanket is a bit itchier than I thought it was going to be. I can't seem to find a comfortable spot around my neck for it, I huffed, nearly giving up on the idea of sleep entirely.

Since it had rained all day long, the ground was saturated with near freezing water, which made the air even colder and more difficult to stave off. The gray, cotton pajamas I wore to sleep did little to keep the cold off my skin, and what little hair I had on my limbs stood up on their ends as gooseflesh riddled my skin, causing me to shiver.

It's absolutely freezing here. I wonder if I can use that spell I had seen Roburn cast earlier this morning, I pondered through chattering teeth.

Roburn was another one of the Synners who had graduated some years before that fateful night. He often liked to show off his abilities with mana-cloaks and masterful sword-casting techniques. Although I had never used a mana cloak before, I had read about them in the dark hours of the night, and decided to try one for myself.

What's the worst that can happen? I thought as I reached into my memories of past late-night adventures, and chose the Pyrus spell.

There. This should do the trick. I remember Roburn using it to keep warm during winter training last year. Now, if I can just condense the mana properly around me, I should be just fine, my thoughts trailed as I began to focus on the next steps

My eyes darkened once more, coating my sclera black as I *stretched out my hand once again to draw from the sphere in the sky. I knew I only needed a little and used my will to control the flow from the spiraling rings of light above me, even though I wasn't fully attuned for just how much was* actually needed. *The mana tendrils wrapped around the tip of my finger, down my arm, and onto the rest of my body, encapsulating me in a cloud of mana. I severed my connection to the realm, and my consciousness* of the world around me lurched as it returned.

I could still feel the pulsating cloud of mana around me, warming the air around my entire body like the heat of a small hearth.

Hmm, *It's still not hot enough. It's helping, but not quite there yet,* I thought, smiling warmly with the small amount of newfound warmth.

In truth, I was entirely unsure of exactly *what* I was doing, but whatever it *was* seemed to be working and, thus, thought it would be alright.

Oh, how wrong I was.

I condensed the mana that was lining my entire body and creating a small barrier between myself and the blanket. I, stupidly, flicked my index finger against my thumb, as though I were lighting a flint and tinder kit. The result, as one might have already guessed, sent sparks of mana from the inside of my palm towards the barrier.

As soon as the sparks touched the barrier, it began to burn like the coals at the end of a wood-fire's life. However, instead of dying out, it quickly gained copious amounts of heat in such a short period of time that I could feel the heat coming through my pajamas.

Ah, there it is! The Fuckening has begun, I thought, accepting my inevitable death.

The heat from the barrier rapidly set the blanket ablaze, forcing the protective coating to disappear about as quickly as it was formed.

Shit, it was too hot! I can't just lay here and die! I have to do something! I thought, knowing I wouldn't withstand the heat for much longer.

My eyes darkened once more, *as I drew more mana to shield myself from the ever-intensifying heat.* The mana surrounded me once more and acted as a shield between myself and the blanket. I tried to swat out the newborn flame with my hand, but to no avail. The fire engulfed the blanket and I threw it to the floor beside my bed.

Shit, shit, shit! That was too close for comfort, I thought.

The fire spread onto my bed and he began to panic even more so than before, given the fact that he had just lit something on fire at an hour when he should not even have been awake. The fire continued to spread, as he desperately searched for a way to extinguish the flame.

This is probably the second worst idea I've had today, I thought as I noticed a piss bucket next to one of the other boys' beds.

I raced over to it, proceeding to throw the musky liquid onto the fire. A pungent steam immediately filled the air, and I began to choke on the stench I'd just created.

Well, that was dumb. Ten points to the dumbass of the day for thinking that would work! If I can't stop the fire itself, I can at least prevent others from getting burned, I thought.

"Fire!" I shouted. The three other young Synners in the same dorm abruptly woke up and, after having noticed my mistake, displayed little more than pure, unadulterated panic. The flame that had now spread to the bases of their beds. The three were just as - if not less experienced - than I, and they all mimicked my shout sporadically.

The fear in their eyes was real enough, for none of the three had ever seen a fire-based spell in such proximity, as they would only begin to meddle in such matters the following year. Meanwhile I, now heavily influenced by the panicking trio, felt my stomach churn.

Oooooh, this is bad. This is really bad. Bernar will have my head on a platter, and there's no telling what Master will do, I thought.

The three youngsters desperately attempted to douse the flames with their blankets, however, since the flame had been mana-borne, it spread to their blankets as well.

You're a fool, Thoma Fayren. You could probably have a more intelligent conversation with a rock than with me, I thought as I shook my head. The three boys were wailing, but through their desperate cries, I heard a distinctive command. "Keep away from the door!" the voice shouted.

It was the Master.

The others and I hurried and pressed our backs as hard as we could on the wall adjacent to the doorway, assuming the door would have swung open the other way, leaving us untouched.

What kind of technique does the Master use that even I can feel him drawing mana? I thought, feeling the hairs on my arms and neck standing up once again.

The pulse stopped as quickly as it began, allowing a split second of pure silence. As the air became still and its pressure grew, it compressed their bodies as though they had reached the bottom of a lake. The pressure was released, and the resulting sound was that of the largest war-drum being hit by a giant. The pressure bent the door inwards, releasing screws and nails from their positions, as a violet wave smashed through the door, obliterating it entirely.

Our ears popped from the release, and our chests felt like they had been trampled by a herd of wild horses, though, at least the flame was gone.

It... it extinguished a mana-fire? How the...? I stopped, trying to piece it all together in my head.

As we recovered from the shockwave, we noticed all of our bedding now redecorated our room like some scary story a parent would tell their child. Overturned bunk beds, mattresses, pillows and sheets were strewn about the room, and the palpable smell of charred piss didn't help the situation either.

We stumbled back from the doorway, looking back in awe. In all honesty, I don't think any of us had ever seen such destruction inside the living quarters before, and knew that whatever came next would not be anywhere near a pleasant experience.

We all coughed due to the pungent steam and smoke from the now-charred blankets, making our eyes tear up as a result. The Master's silhouette stood in the doorway, backlit by a wall-lamp that caused the figure to flicker. Two pairs of yellow eyes glowed in the frame of the doorway - one pair his, while the other was Bernar's.

The Master was wearing a loose white shirt that had laces around the chest and neck, with his sleeves rolled up to the middle of his forearm. His gray, cotton pants were tailored perfectly to his height, not dragging any of the material on the ground as he walked. He also wore leather-soled slippers that muffled the sound of his footsteps.

He moved forward, and his hands clasped behind his back. He held his head high and straight, like a statue. We looked up at him in fear, not knowing what came next. Bernar, his right-hand man, stepped in behind him with a noticeable amount of less grace and fluency than the Master; nearly knocking over a cup that had been on a bedside table nearby. He was wearing the same style of clothes as the Master, though they were a little dirtier. The thick, smoky air was filled with the sounds of our heavy breathing and coughing. I caught my brother's eye, but he only shrugged subtly in response. The Master flinched his right eye at the sound coming from behind him, but decided to not turn around.

"Boys," the Master's voice rang out. "I understand the common mischief youngsters find themselves in more often than not. However, I would like to know who was the one who attempted the Pyrus spell," he said.

Ahaha... shit, I thought, since I knew the Master had already traced the residual mana back to me.

The boys gazed at each other, bug eyed and shaking nervously. "It was me, Master," I finally admitted. "I was the one who attempted the spell and lost control of it," I said with my head bowed, staring at the ground beneath me. The Master gave a small grunt after turning to look at Bernar, who shook his head as subtly as he could. The Master raised an eyebrow, then turned and faced the boys once again.

"That was very foolish of you, Thoma, however, I won't give you a lecture here. Follow me to my quarters," he said. The moment the word *quarters* left his mouth, I knew I was in for it, shuddering at the thought. "Yes, Master," I quickly replied. As the Master turned on his toes, I looked over at the others who were just as shocked as I was.

This is how I'm going to die, I tried to transmit with a thin-lipped smile, which earned me a few salutes in response.

I looked at my brother who shot back mixed emotions of awe and shame. I took a step forward, and followed the Master and my brother through the destroyed doorway, avoiding the small splinters in my path. The stone hallway was cold and barely lit, with large corner stones at every angle. Torches made of wood, cloth and liquified troll fat hung on the walls with iron supports, dimly lit the cold corridor. The sound of their footfall was nearly inaudible on the cold stone floor, due to the heel-toe technique they used when they walked.

On a real mission, one could walk silently across almost any surface while moving quickly. Our leather-soled shoes aided in silencing our steps, although it didn't help much to keep the cold from the stone floors from reaching the soles of our feet. As we walked, Bernar shot a glance back at me and sighed inwardly.

I know what I did was wrong, but why do I feel like I'm going to be executed over this? The knot in my stomach feels large enough to send the remnants of supper back the way they came, or perhaps toward the other end at this point. Either way, I just have to calm down. I'm sure things will work out... right? I thought, feeling guilty enough as it was, with my heart beginning to race as we climbed the flight of stairs that lead to the Master's chamber.

There it is. That's where I'm going to die, I thought as I saw the heavy cedar door that marked the entrance to the chamber.

My mouth was dry and could swallow nothing but a cotton ball of spit. The heavy door creaked open, and I hesitated to go inside. Bernar, however, put a reassuring hand on my shoulder and led me into the room, following closely behind the Master as I caught my brother's grin out of the corner of my eye.

As soon as we crossed the threshold of the doorway, torches seemed to light themselves in a clockwise circle around the room, revealing the interior in a fantastical fashion.

Did he use mana to light those? A bit dramatic, but still impressive to say the least, I wondered.

The room had six walls, four of which had bookcases taller than the average man, all fully loaded with countless books and scrolls. Some were old, dusty, and covered in cobwebs, while others appeared to be newer, or at least more frequently used. I noticed a green banded book that was on the third shelf from the ground, near the border of the bookcase itself. It was surrounded by other weathered books, and yet it seemed to have been used recently. Bernar gave me a light shove forward as we walked to the fifth wall, where the Master's desk was.

"Sit down, young Thoma," the Master said. I shot my older brother another questioning glance, but he simply nodded, and urged me forwards towards the carved, wooden chair before me. The maple chair had been hand-carved in Hjalfar, far to the North, by an old boat maker who had given it to the Master as a token of his gratitude for slaying the Mother Ochelon of the town.

The ochelons were tall, humanoid creatures, whose thick fur and skin helped keep it alive during the winter months in the Northern Countries. Their sharp claws were excellent for hunting, and they generally resided in deep caves near bodies of water. This posed potentially hazardous conditions for anyone who decided to settle near such a place.

I sat in the carved chair, analyzing the carvings themselves. They told the story of the battle between the Master and the Mother Ochelon in intricate detail. From stances to displaying movement, the carvings had almost appeared to come alive as I read over them.

It was at that moment, I realized, that my feelings were mixed, and couldn't decide whether it was awe or fear of the Master. After all, I *had* just followed the Master to his chamber to have what I knew to be more than a little midnight chat.

"Do you remember how the Synners first came to be?" the Master asked calmly. I slowly shook my head. "I vaguely remember the legend, but no specific details, Master," I replied. "Then allow me to refresh your memory," the Master replied. "A little over one thousand years ago, when monsters first slipped through the cracks of the Underworld, the gods descended from the heavens. They came not as angelic beings, but as humble beggars to avoid unwanted attention. The six who descended found themselves close to a town near ruin, with only a few formidable warriors remaining after the monsters had razed it to the ground," the Master began.

Bernar shuffled. "I had always heard it said that one of the monsters was so heavily encased in mana that it blew into little red chunks after it had been struck by an arrow," he said. The Master pursed his thin lips and tilted his head towards Bernar. His brow furrowed and his irises went from a strong yellow to a flaming orange for an instant, and Bernar was taken aback.

"Please do not interrupt me while I'm schooling a young pup who just so happens to be your younger brother, Bernar," the Master said, relieving the sting with a small smile that caused the scar on his right cheek to wrinkle a bit. "Forgive me, Master," Bernar instantly replied, bowing his head and taking a step backwards.

"Now, where was I?" the Master asked himself. "*Ah*, yes, the town. So, the gods found themselves at the ruined town, where the remaining survivors found them wandering outside the few standing wall stones. The leader of the warriors went out to meet them in the low grassy field just outside the town. The eldest of the beggars bowed as low as he could to the tall leather-clad warrior, and the man responded by picking him up off the ground. The beggar didn't quite seem to understand what had just happened, after all, what warrior would have a beggar stand as his equal?" he asked.

I simply shrugged. "Anyone with half a brain and heart would have done the same, I'd imagine," I said as if stating the obvious. "That is where you are wrong, Thoma," the Master shot back. "For this was no ordinary grunt you'd find on the battlefield. He was the Lord of Codrean." the Master said in an honorific tone.

I raised my eyebrows. "The Lord of Codrean, Master?" I asked. "I thought lords weren't supposed to do battle. They generally sit in their comfy, little castles and large rooms surrounded by whores and wine, while the lowly soldiers get thrown into the shitstorm that is the battlefield," I said bitterly. I had known a lord once before, but that had been a few years before I was recruited into the Synners.

The Master simply nodded and said nothing, agreeing with what I said.

"This lord, however, was well known for being able to see the true nature of people. While he didn't know who they were, exactly, he could tell they were no ordinary beggars. From the moment he saw the first bow lower than anyone had ever bowed before, he knew something was different about them," the Master continued. "Wish I'd been born with that skill," I muttered under my breath.

The Master heard it, but said nothing. "In any case, he invited the beggar and the other five who'd been standing in awe just a few feet away to join them for supper. The disguised gods agreed, and the warrior led them to the makeshift lean-tos they constructed after the attack," he continued.

"Food was scarce, but they happily shared the little supplies they had left. The following morning, the beggars decided to leave the small settlement, but they wanted to speak to the lord first. He revealed that they were in fact gods, and that for his altruism and kindness, each one would bestow a single gift to him and to five of his other warriors. The Lord of Codrean was taken aback at the news, and instantly took a knee, bowing his head. The god who had been speaking to him told him to rise and that he needn't kneel. He then summoned the other gods to bring their gifts," the Master said, taking a breath.

"What were those gifts? Surely, they must have been unparalleled by anything we know of," I said, hoping he would give me the answer to that question sooner rather than later. The Master simply nodded in agreement, and folded his hands on top of the desk.

"To the Lord of Codrean, the leader gave the *Realmwalker Blade*, capable of cutting through the fabric of reality if one were to infuse some mana into it." he began.

"To the largest and strongest of them, the second goddess gave the *Fate-bearer Shield*. She had forged it from the bones of a great serpent, it negates all magic used against it. It could even use the negated spell's mana to heal the bearer and those around him." he continued.

"The third god gave the *Night-kissed Mantle*, to the woman who had been an assassin for the Lord for over a decade. This mantle coated the user in mana, making them virtually undetectable." he grinned with the last word.

"The fourth goddess approached the archer, and she granted him the *Nethersong Mask*. It allowed for a vast improvement in eyesight, as well as produced an autonomous beast-claw made of pure mana for offensive or defensive purposes." he continued.

"The fifth god took pity on the most severely wounded of them, and, after healing his wounds, granted him the *Dreambinder Jerkin*. It would allow the wearer to phase through any physical attack not infused with mana." he said with a slight tone of jealousy.

"The sixth goddess noticed one of the warriors wielding dual-blades, and thus produced the *Benevolent Ring*. It could populate items already acquired out of thin air after being stored within the ring," he said.

"However, the leader of the gods decided to bestow another gift, not just for the warriors but for everyone. He moved towards the warlord with a plant in bloom and a parchment with writing on it," the Master said.

"A plant, Master?" I asked, entirely bewildered by what I'd just heard. "Naturally, after hearing about all of these magnificent weapons and such, one must wonder what a plant has to do with all of this," the Master said. "A plant?" I asked again, still in disbelief.

"Y-yes," the Master replied curtly. "As unlikely as it seems, that plant is what helped make us what we are. The plant and the parchment were the gifts the leader brought, though one is useless without the other," he explained.

"The plant had been blessed by the gods, and if properly prepared using the instructions on the parchment, it allowed the user a greater affinity to tap into the Ethereal realm. If incorrectly prepared, the user could suffer a fate worse than death, being neither living nor dead," he said, and I felt a small chill go up my spine.

"That said, it is not *impossible* for one to connect with the Ethereal without the plant's blessing. It simply speeds up the process. This gift is what sets us Synners apart from other warriors, as we can train with mana from a young age as opposed to the decades of learning normally required. The ability *can* be passed down through direct bloodlines of those who have consumed the plant, but one must never take this gift lightly. It was bestowed upon us by the gods to help us defend our homeland. Do you understand, Thoma?" the Master asked. "I do indeed, Master," I replied. "Good," the Master said.

"Now, I want you to listen to me very carefully," the Master said in a voice that made the hairs on I's arm stand up like a wooden palisade. "I have two things in store for you, but only after we visit Coltend, as I would not have you do anything tonight. I would like to give you a choice," The Master said seriously.

What the hell is that supposed to mean? I thought.

"I want you to know that I will have to either punish or test you for your insolence tonight. However, since this was more of an accident as opposed to a willful happening, I will tell you the two options," the Master said.

I felt more scared than I ever had in my life. Both the Master and Bernar, who was standing two paces behind my chair, sensed it, but showed no sign of doing so. "One is to spend a week in solitary confinement with only bread and water as sustenance, and the other is to hunt down the creature in the cave that lies just outside our fortress," he said methodically.

I still couldn't understand the reason for a hunt being considered a form of punishment. "So, which will it be?" the Master asked.

I, once again, looked at my older brother, who simply shrugged and upturned his bottom lip. I thought for what seemed like an eternity, but eventually came to a decision. "I'll go with the creature, Master," I said with as much determination as I could muster. "Are you sure? Do you even know what you'll be fighting?" Bernar asked. "Well, I've studied the bestiary a lot, and I don't think the Master would send me on a mission he didn't think I could accomplish," I replied. The Master looked at me inquisitively, then glanced over to Bernar to whom he nodded.

"Very well, then. Study up on what you have to take with you, be it knowledge, spells, or otherwise. You'll need your sword well sharpened, mind well rested, and don't forget to be mindful of your surroundings," the Master said. "I will, Master," I replied. "Good," the Master said, nodding briefly.

"Once we've returned from Coltend, Bernar will aid you with preparation for your first solo hunt."

I gulped another dry spit ball that lumped in my throat. "That is all for this evening, young I," said the Master dismissively. I rose from my seat. "Very well, Master. With your permission, I shall take my leave," I bowed deeply, then turned on the ball of my foot and was proceeding towards the doorway when the Master called out. "*Oh!* Thoma," he began.

I was wondering when the air was going to sour, I thought.

The color fled from my face as I turned back around to face the Master slowly as I could. "Find yourself another blanket, and do try not to set this one alight," the Master said. "I'll do my best to keep it from happening again, Master," I replied nervously. I walked out of the chamber and proceeded down the steps with my older brother just behind me.

I almost died, I thought, feeling a bead of sweat drip down his cheek.

"You got lucky, you lanky little bastard," Bernar said, nudging me with his elbow. "Don't think I've ever seen anyone actually given a choice of punishment before tonight," he said pensively. I shrugged in response. "Now, don't get me wrong, I know just how frightening it is to go on your first hunt, especially if your first time is going in alone," Bernar said. "Most junior Synners don't get to go on their first hunt alone. That's only allowed for senior years," he continued.

I shrugged again "I just don't understand why he'd even give me the option between solitary and a solo hunt. It simply doesn't add up," I said, shaking my head.

"*Ah*, don't go getting your hose in a knot over it," Bernar replied. "I've been to solitary before, and believe me, that was anything but a pleasant experience," he continued. "Worms and maggots are everywhere, there's naught but a pile of earth that serves as a bed. The walls are covered in scratchings of past *visitors* and the small confinement smells like years of accumulated piss and shit," he said.

I felt a wave of relief knowing I wouldn't be going there.

"Well, at least now I know what I should expect to happen the next time I fuck up," I said with a chuckle that Bernar joined in. "Well, should that ever happen, I'll be sure to leave you a nice, runny present," he said with a wicked smile. "Besides, it's been awhile since anyone's been sent to solitary, and by *awhile* I mean a few days," he said.

"That still doesn't answer my question, though. Why would he bother giving me a choice?" I asked. My brother shrugged. "Beats the hell out of me," Bernar replied with an indifferent shrug. We walked down the corridor towards the dormitory once more, seeing the destruction caused by the fire and the blast from the spell.

"Seeing as how things currently stand, or don't for that matter, I suppose you could sleep in my room for the night," Bernar suggested. "Guess I'll have to," I replied. "What of Irun, Batch, and Edryd?" I asked, noticing they were nowhere to be found. I was concerned about my roommates whom I'd almost just killed in an accident.

"I'm sure they're alright. Tough little bastards, and quite possibly tougher than you," Bernar replied with a grin. I looked up at my brother and tilted my head. "Is that so, big brother? Do you remember that time when I pinned you to the ground for five seconds?" I asked, prodding him with an elbow.

"I had passed the fuck out because I tripped on that stupid *meditation stool* of yours and hit my head on the floor," Bernar shot back with a laugh while I scoffed. "My *stupid meditation stool* is what got me recognition for my casting abilities," I returned mockingly. "It helps me to think and focus better than ever," I explained, but Bernar only squinted his eyes and pursed his lips.

"Uh-huh," he replied sarcastically. "Whatever, let's get some sleep. It's already the second hour of the morn and we're to be up and out the gate at first light," Bernar suggested.

We walked softly and quickly, as though we were the shadows we left behind in the torch-lit hallway. We soon arrived at Bernar's dorm room which wasn't unlike my own, though perhaps with less charring and fewer bits of the door laying strewn across the floor. I fashioned myself a bed of fallen straw from my brother's bed and an old potato sack for a pillow. We bid each other good-night, and Bernar stretched out his hand to put out the bedside candle by absorbing the small flame into his hand. I saw it happen, and was anxious to try it.

I think I've had more than my fair share of fire for one night, I thought.

Soon after, I rolled onto my back, into the same position I was in when all of this began, closing my eyes, and returning to the grassy field in my dreamscape once more.

CHAPTER 3

The Road to Coltend Castle

Three and a half hours later, I was being shaken awake by my older brother.

With dark circles like a fighter's black eyes, and a drowsiness that could kill a moose, I rose out of my makeshift bed and began getting into harness. My brother, of course, needed far less sleep than I did, what with being a fifth stage and all, so he was in much better shape than I was.

The black, leather jerkin, hose and boots I was attempting to put on hadn't fully dried from my horse-casting certification the day prior. This made them heavier than usual and, compounding that to the lack of sleep, brought my regular pace to little faster than a child's crawl. Bernar, on the other hand, had used the rainproof cloak to stave off the rain, leaving most of his equipment unsoiled. He got into his jerkin and hose easily, though his boots were still caked in mud and smelled of horse shit.

"You look like hell, little brother," Bernar said. I, who was *far* too tired to give the slightest amount of a shit, lazily rolled my eyes in the direction of my brother, slowly turning my head and saying nothing in the process. "Never mind, I'll take that back. You look *worse*," he jeered. "I feel worse than I look to be honest. It's like my entire body has been encased in a heavy metal," I groaned as I bent over to get my foot into the boot.

I moved at half speed that morning, and finding my equipment in what remained of the charred, piss-smelling dorm was easier said than done. I found my equipment chest under a large piece of the door, a stark reminder of my fuck-up the night before, and lifted the piece with some effort. I opened the oaken chest, and was relieved to see that my equipment had not been reduced to ash.

I began by pulling out my sword and belt, and laced it to my waist though loops in my hose. I buckled it tightly so it wouldn't jolt around as I walked, and patted it twice. He turned my back to the door and walked towards the opposite end of the room. As I was looking out of the charred window frame, I heard light footsteps coming at what sounded like a run.

Edryd, my best friend and one of those I had nearly killed the night before, stormed into the room, tripping over the bucket that still lay on the floor. He wasn't usually clumsy, but this time, it seemed, he was in too much of a rush to be cautious.

"Thoma!" Edryd cried out from down the hall. I lazily turned to face the boy now standing in the doorway with excitement clearly showing on his face. He had deep, brown eyes that could pierce even steel, and dark brown hair tied behind his head in a short ponytail. He had a toned jawline and a slightly upturned nose with the first few whiskers of his beard beginning to sprout, which for a boy of seventeen, was widely respected.

"Thoma," Edryd said again. "Hullo, Edryd," I returned. "What is it? Why are you in such a rush?" I asked, curious as to why my friend's brow was sweaty. "Don't you know?" Edryd asked. "We're about to head out towards Coltend, and our scouts have returned saying that they've seen a few monsters on the prowl about a league out on the road," he said.

They've never come this close to home before, I thought.

"*Hm*, that *is* odd. I wonder what they're doing here," I said, lightly scrunching my cheek with the corner of my mouth. "In any case, it's a chance for us to show our skills! That is, of course, contingent on there being anything *left* for us to kill," he said with a smirk and a gleam in his eyes. "I know I might sound like a psychopath, but I can't wait to finally kill my first monster," Edryd began. "After all, it's what I've been training for for most of my life," he spread his arms wide as he finished his sentence.

"I don't blame you," I began, chuckling lightly. "I, for one, have been itching to try out a spell I created, but I haven't even tested it out of battle, yet," I said, lowering my head a little in dejection. "Oh, I wouldn't worry too much about that," Edryd said. "There's not a shadow of a doubt that you're the most adept caster of our age group," Edryd began. "Even if you're not the most physically strong," he added after a short pause. We both laughed at the final comment, and stopped when we heard a blaring noise coming from outside.

The Dragon Horn. It was carved from a dragon's tooth, and passed down through the generations to signal that it was time to leave. While it was felled by one of the first Synners, there haven't been many sightings of dragons since then, making the one we had *especially* rare.

We looked at each other and both knew exactly what that meant. "Time to go. Do you have all of your stuff?" I asked, grabbing the last of my things and bundling them under my curled arm. Edryd nodded his reply just before we both took up our gear and headed out the door, making our way down the hall that led to the outer courtyard.

The sun was just beginning to show the tip of its face over

the distant Frellen Hills, the warmth from the few rays that slipped between the peaks greatly contrasted with the cold of the previous night. The birds began to sing in the nearby oak and cedar trees, while the other creatures were slowly crawling out of their holes and dens to greet the sun as if it were a long-lost friend. The cold morning wind began to blow, gently swaying the trees in all directions.

I couldn't have imagined a more beautiful morning even if I'd dreamed about it for a hundred years, I thought.

I shifted my gaze from the tops of the trees down into the courtyard where all of the other Synners, the Master included, had gathered; tightening harnesses, checking stirrups, feeding the horses their morning apples, and checking equipment against a list. I walked over to my horse, Celer, which I had so adequately named due to his speed that had been proven the day before, and checked my saddle. I tied much of my equipment onto the left side of the saddle, making sure the loop I'd made wouldn't end up hurting my mount in the long run.

He's all decked out, I thought.

"Listen up, you lot," Bernar yelled while standing on a beam that the Master's horse was tied on. The Master was sitting on his horse, idly fiddling with a chain around his neck, but as Bernar's words left his mouth, he suddenly jumped up and stood on his horse's saddle, getting a better view of the group of Synners. He stood there for a few moments, without movement, waiting for everyone to quiet down. He did a headcount; twenty Synners with himself, Bernar, and I included.

"As I am sure you all know, we ride South-East towards Coltend Castle, to answer King Truls' summons," he began. "I expect nothing less than exemplary behavior from all once we arrive at the castle, for they are not so lenient as I am over insolence," he said, shooting a glance over at me.

If he's lenient, we're all fucked, I thought, lifting my eyebrows in unison with Edryd, who was probably thinking the same thing, since he stared back at me with widened eyes.

"I believe these summons to be but for a trivial matter, of which shall be dealt with quickly and thoroughly. Although, I suspect we will stay within the castle walls for at least a day or two," the Master said.

A few of the older Synners looked at each other smiling, and each knew exactly what that meant - whoring and drinking. "On this most auspicious of mornings, bear in mind that there are very real dangers out there, and one must always be watchful and attentive, understood?" he asked. "Yes, Master!" the Synners in front of him roared. "Good. Now, mount up!" he shouted.

We got into our saddles all at once starting from the left side, throwing our right legs over the horse. After adjusting our seating and gathering our reins we silently awaited the Master's signal. My anxiety must have bled into Edryd's, since he was showing mild signs of either unease or excitement. Perhaps it was both, but I couldn't tell. We glanced over at each other with wide, nervous grins and nodded.

It's time for us to show them we're ready, I thought.

"We ride!" the Master called out, and everyone stuck their heels into their horses' sides. Our horse's hooves rolled over the cobblestone floor like thunder, making it seem as though we were an army of a *hundred*, not twenty.

The sword-casters, myself included, carried two swords: One was a hand and a half sword that was mainly used when on horseback, the other a longsword for ground combat. They clanged about on our backs and sides respectively, but were otherwise fairly secure.

We all wore thick, leather jerkins, with thicker seams at the joints than there would normally be to lessen wear and tear. Our boots were mostly made from elk or bear skin, and the few, more experienced sword-casters had glick or ochelon-skin hoods and riding cloaks. The younger, less experienced sword casters wore regular, weatherproof cloaks and were usually located in the middle of the group, surrounded by the more experienced ones to avoid unnecessary losses.

Edryd and I counted ourselves amongst their numbers.

The few bow-casters, who could infuse their arrows with mana drawn from the Ethereal, were on both sides in the middling ranks. Their bows unstrung, hung from hooks and tied down with a singular, leather strip for easier access on the side of their saddles. The vast majority of them wore woodland green cloaks, attached with many different kinds of brooches and hooks. Some more intricate than others, although it usually depended on the bow-caster's rank.

Under the stone overpass and between the great wooden doors we went, facing South-East and moving at a steady trot. The Master was at the head of the group, closely followed by Bernar to his right, and Garett, the master bow-caster, to his left.

Garett was a quiet man of eighty winters, who didn't very much enjoy the company of others. Rather, he would often spend his time in the woods, tracking deer as opposed to dealing with *blundering idiots* as he liked to call nearly everyone. He wore a griffin-hide cape, with its feathers still attached even after years of use, a griffin talon-skin jerkin, with boots and gauntlets to match.

The road the Master decided to take to leave was well worn. Over the years, it had been used to transport both supplies and Synners to their contract destinations, and within the las few hundred years, it had proved to be ever more useful than before, since the road was wide, flat, and held few rocks for wagon wheels to break upon.

Edryd, Batch, Irun, and I were two horse-lengths behind the trio, and wondered what sort of things they might discuss whenever they thought no one would be eavesdropping.

"I'd wager they're talking about all the whoring they'll do once we get to Coltend Castle," Irun said, hoping no one else had heard him. "Shut up, you red-headed dolt. If one of them hears you, it'll mean both of us being discharged from the Synners for spreading false accusations," the rider beside him shot back. "Well, well, Batch, I'd have never taken you to be one who worries so much about that," Irun said sarcastically.

"Just as I am absolutely certain that you are truly too much of a dumb fuck to comprehend why I actually *do* care," Batch retorted. "As much as I find the Synners to be little more than mercenaries with special abilities, it's the life I've decided to continue living. Not for gold, but *glory*, you goat-plowing turd," he said with a disgusted look on his face. "*Oi*, take that back!" Irun said. Edryd rolled his eyes after overhearing their belligerent conversation. "You two never know when to shut up, do you?" he spat.

Batch looked over at Edryd on his left and shrugged. "What? Don't look at me," Batch said, attempting to deflect Edryd's piercing gaze. "It's not my fault he has the brain of a field mouse and the mouth of one of them damned harpies," he said. Irun shot him a look of disbelief and scoffed. "I have no such thing," he began. "I happen to have the best grades in timed logical reasoning, mind you. Besides, mocking someone's intelligence often means you have very little, yourself," he continued as though comparing grades might have somehow helped his case.

"It's not that your grades don't mean anything," I began

saying with a grin on my face. "It's just that you really are an idiot who loves running his mouth." The three of us boys chuckled, however, Irun was white knuckling over the comment for the next few minutes, praying his beloved Isla wasn't listening.

She was.

I watched as Irun caught her gaze, blushed, and immediately began to fume over the our laughter. He had never really enjoyed being the ass-end of our jokes, but it's not like he didn't make any at our expense. Basically, he was a bit of a shithead who didn't know how to laugh at himself, though that didn't make him any less our friend.

"Don't worry about them," a female voice came from behind him. He turned to face the beautiful Isla, whom he had desired since he first laid eyes on. He felt warmth coming from her blue-eyed stare. He attempted to shift his gaze away from her, and yet failed as he locked onto her golden hair flowing in the breeze.

"I'll do my best," he said bashfully. "I pray that you do," she returned with a warm, friendly smile which he embedded in his memory like an engraving in stone. While I couldn't read his thoughts, the look on his face made me think he was taking everything into: his recent past mishaps and faults, as well as this most recent attempt at trying to fit in with the other Synners - of which none had succeeded - and must have felt at a loss.

He must be ridiculing us in his head. Poor bastard never learned that it's not that we don't like him, he's just a bit out of touch, I thought, watching him click his tongue and shake his head in our direction.

I knew he wouldn't stay angry forever, for the image of Isla seemed to nullify any feelings of anger or hatred the more he thought about her, or so he would always tell us.

After our banter, I looked around excitedly, for I had never left Codrean's walls before on an expedition since having become a Synner. Not to say that I hadn't left the fortress, but it wasn't as if we'd ever gone much further than a kilometer or two.

The only exception to this, however, was during my childhood, and those few, short years I spent outside the fortress itself. I was in awe to see so many kinds of trees lining the road. Cedar, oak, elm, redwood, pine, spruce, and hickory were just a few of the trees I recognized from the books I had read during my time within the walls.

To finally see these magnificent beings up close and personal is like nothing I've ever felt before, he thought. *It's almost as though I can feel them pulsating with the same mana we Synners draw from the Ethereal, though on a much more tangible level,* I thought as I gazed at my surroundings with my jaw just slightly agape.

The trees moved and swayed in the cold wind, as though they were some of the ancient Dericoed of Caegwen – giant trees that could move about of their own free will without posing a threat to anything or anyone unless threatened. The rain from the day before had washed away most of the fresher tracks along the road, though the deeper cart-wheel grooves could still be seen. Birds sang and flew overhead, aiming towards their nests in the canopy.

It's so peaceful out here, I thought.

I finally decided to look ahead, and saw a large fork in the road with a way-post standing between the two paths. "Take the right," Bernar shouted back to the company. The company pulled on the right side of their reins and everyone flowed down the path as one body. I rode by the worn down oak post, with deeply scratched markings in its planks pointing in the direction of other cities. The first board pointed to the North of their current position towards Elvsbyen – a town of tradesmen and fishermen who lived on the Elv Avliv River. The second pointed towards their current destination – Coltend Castle, where the king had summoned them for an, as of yet, unknown reason.

I can't help but wonder what Coltend looks like, after all, I've only heard stories and tales of its grandeur. Some of Coltend's greatest leaders have also come from there, from what I've read, and now that I'm finally on my way, I can't wait to see it for myself, I thought.

We continued down the well beaten path for a few more kilometers, when Garett spotted something a few hundred meters down the road.

"Master," he began. "What is it, Garett," the Master asked. "I count thirty or more glicks converging on a single wagon a short ways away. I believe it to be in our interest to investigate the matter, as they have never been seen this close to our home," he stated. The Master simply nodded. "Ill news, indeed. Take eight of the more experienced Synners with you, and four of the lesser experienced, for they have yet to feed their blades," he said. "Very well, Master," Garett replied. He nodded and looked back towards the small company.

"Edryd, Batch, Irun, and Thoma," Garett called out. The boys and I looked at each other with a fair amount of surprise on our faces. I began looking for my brother, praying he could give me some final advice about the dangers we were about to face. Bernar spun his horse around at hearing my name being called out and rode back towards me.

He curved around and rode up to my side. "This is your chance, little brother. Don't fuck this up by trying out your spell just yet," he said quietly. "Don't worry," I began, "I'm smart enough to know that *one should never use an untested spell in open combat*, unlike someone I've heard of," I finished his sentence with a grin.

Bernar chortled and grinned back, riding over to the Master's side. Edryd, Batch and Irun were already becoming nervous, and I think some of their nervousness began to bleed onto me, as well. Their palms and foreheads began to sweat, even in the cold of the early morn, and it was easy to see that things could go very wrong *very* quickly.

We looked at each other, each seeking reassurance, though there was not much to be found, for each and every one of us was just as scared as the other. Irun turned to take what he thought might be his last look at Isla, and she returned his frightened stare with a warm, encouraging smile.

"The rest of you lot back over there, with me," Garett pointed to the corner of the triangular formation. The eight of us who were there – four bow-casters and four sword-casters – nodded in agreement, and kicked our spurs into our horses' sides.

"Let's move," Garett ordered, and as soon as those words left his mouth, my heels found themselves in my horse's sides. The thirteen of us rode off towards the downed cart at a gallop. I looked back at my older brother who simply grinned and nodded as though he were encouraging me onward.

"We're in it now," Batch began, catching up with Edryd, Irun and I. "Let's not put our training to waste, now shall we?" he said, obviously trying to sound much braver than he was outwardly showing. "Did your training involve running your mouth? Or, maybe, you have some kind of *Master Plan* behind your words," Garett spat back towards him, to which Batch could only respond with silence.

"*Oh*, you don't? I thought not. Now, shut the fuck up, and *focus*!" Garett said, looking back at the rest of us, too. "Smooth," Irun said under his breath with a smug look on his face.

"Listen up," Garett began. "We've ourselves a small army of creepy-crawlies out there, so don't go getting too far ahead of yourselves," he began. "Sword-casters, do not expend yourselves by using mana. Use the sword techniques you should have drilled into your very souls by now and you will survive. Remember your training and do not panic no matter how bad things get," he said.

His words hit us like a bucket of cold water, as the realization set in. The four of us had never *been* in an actual fight, and our inexperience was evident enough in the way we were talking with each other.

Master Garett was right, of course. We *had to* focus. We *had to* follow our training. It was the only thing that was the likeliest to keep us alive, after all. I glanced at Ed and the others momentarily, each of them meeting my gaze with likely the same thoughts behind their eyes: this could be our first battle of many, or our last.

No one said a word.

"Archers," Garett called out to the ones behind the sword-casters. "Stay within bow-shot, and infuse if necessary. Otherwise, aim for the gaps between their scales around their shoulders. That should slow them down enough for one of the sword-casters to take it down fully," he said, giving the signal to fan out into formation.

The bow-casters pulled back and spread out – two on either side – while the sword-casters spread themselves to form their own miniature boar's head. Garett pulled back towards the rear center to get a better view of the battlefield, while one of the seniors took his place. The glicks were still approaching the downed cart, moving at an incredible speed. The four of us rode in formation behind the more experienced Synners.

As we got closer, I got my first look at one of those bastard glicks in person. There was something to be said about seeing something like that in a drawing in a book versus seeing one in real life. Nothing in a book could ever have prepared me for the smells, sounds, or anything about their existence.

It was a humanoid creature, with olive green scales that ran from the top of its head to the base of its feet, and down its back forming an external spinal cord that ran from its hip up to the base of its neck, fanning out towards its arms, and running down their lengths. Its mouth was mostly covered in needle-like teeth that dripped poison to aid digestion of its prey. Rows upon rows of these teeth lined the inner part of their mouths.

Is there even an antidote for that? I thought, trying to recall the lessons I'd had since I was a child.

Its strong leg and arm muscles underneath the scales made it a formidable enemy for an initiate Synner, I noted, and with those thoughts, I began feeling something I'd never truly felt before.

Fear.

It came over me like a blanket of ice being unrolled on my abdomen and flowed throughout my body. I could feel my hands shaking and heart beating faster, while my lungs were desperately trying to pump enough air to compensate for the thumping in my chest. As my palms began to sweat, I could feel my leather gauntlet beginning to be soaked through with sweat. My hair was blowing in the wind, but for a few, uncomfortable strands that were stuck to my face and forehead from perspiration.

The two swords had never been so comforting to have as Celer kept his galloping pace without missing a beat. I was still two-hundred meters away from the glicks when he heard Garett call out. "Draw your swords!" he shouted.

I drew my riding sword from over my shoulder with my

right hand, pulling it out of its leather-bound sheath as it gleamed in the morning sunlight. It was as sharp as I could get it, which meant it could shave the hair off a face if needed, and I gripped the blackwood and leather wrapped handle as tight as I could. The intricate criss-cross wrapping of the leather was so perfectly engineered, that even should one's hand be covered in blood, it wouldn't slip out of hand.

This was an advantage, because it was primarily used on horseback and was much lighter than the longsword Synners were known to use. The pommel - as was the custom of every Synner school - had the school's and Synner's name inscribed in runes wrapped around it. The guard had been forged square, then twisted - made to look like a daemon's horns - and curved upwards at the edges. It ended in two sharp points, curved inwards towards the blade to avoid having the guard itself stab into the wielder.

One hundred meters, I thought, gauging the distance.

I looked over at Edryd and saw he was already getting into a good striking position, leaning forward with his sword's hilt at the height of his chest with the point aimed forward, and decided to get into the same position. "Alright, boys, remember their weak spots: shoulder blades, armpits, backs of their legs, groin and under their chins," one of the older Synners said, as if he were sounding off items on a grocery list.

"Got it!" I replied. He looked over at the Synner who'd given the advice and instantly recognized him as Roburn of Helvir – one of the senior Synners, who'd been on numerous hunts. His charcoal black hair being shaved on the sides and the long, interwoven braid running down what hadn't been shaved had been his trademark for the past decade.

"Thank you for the advice," I said. "*Eh*, no need to thank me," Roburn replied. "I'm sure you'd do the same, if our places were swapped," he said. I nodded sincerely and looked ahead towards my approaching foes.

Twenty meters.

The boys riding on both his left and right side made choosing a target that might not be another's a difficult task, but he managed. He locked on to it and focused on striking it at the right moment.

Remember to lean into the cut to make sure the bastard doesn't get back up, I heard the Master's instructions in my head once more.

Ten meters.

The time to strike was close at hand, and I could already feel my muscles tensing up. I followed the muscle tension in my lower back and briefly shifted my weight back in the saddle for extra momentum. The sword in my right hand was beginning to rise up behind me, my arm now slightly bent and flexed, preparing itself for the impact to come.

Five meters.

My target had approached just as I'd calculated it would, and so I began my swing. I knew the added momentum from the Celer's speed would add much more force to the blow, in comparison to simply swinging on the ground, and I banked heavily on this fact given my lack of physical strength. I leaned my head forward, my chest almost pressed against Celer's nape at this point, and swung with all my might.

The sword cut through the air, finding its target. I gave a grunt of exertion as the sword bit into the scales on the glick's forehead, splitting them wide open and releasing their sickly, green ichor. My sword, slicing through the scales, bone, and the underlying fleshy material that was the monster's brain, gave a sound akin to an egg being crushed. My sword reemerged on the other side lathered in thick, green blood.

I breathed heavily, feeling the copious amounts of adrenaline flowing through my veins. The glick had been my first kill as a Synner, and I knew, right then and there, that the fire born inside after that first kill hungered for more. I continued riding forward, and another two targets came into sight, feeding the ravenous flames within.

I swung again at one target, then another, followed by a third, hearing the same egg-crushing sound coming because of the strikes, while a fourth was crushed under Celer's hooves.

Batch, Edryd and Irun were also feeding their swords, and in the first few minutes of battle, the three had already killed at least seven glicks between them. Roburn – not wanting to miss out on the killing – began his sword song. He jumped off his horse and began charging his first target. Just before he arrived, an arrow struck the marked one square between the eyes. The glick let out a ghastly squeal like a slaughtered pig, and Roburn glanced backwards to the general direction the arrow had come from. He couldn't find who'd fired the arrow, but he could guess who it was.

I kept riding forward, slaughtering at least two more glicks before I was taken by surprise. A glick jumped up from my left side and knocked me off my horse, taking me to the ground with it as it clawed at my armor.

Damn, that hurt! I thought as I landed on my right shoulder.

The glick scrambled to its feet after the fall and began to head towards me, regardless of whether I had fully recovered. The monster threw an overhead claw down to my right side, and I pirouetted out of the attack as gracefully as I could, given that I was still a little dazed from the fall. I gathered my wits for a moment, and another strike came towards my gut. I jumped back on the balls of my feet, and almost slipped due to the rain-soaked ground from the previous day. Even with the handicap, I'd just barely managed to curve my body to avoid getting hit.

My riding sword had fallen out of my hand with the fall, and with the barrage of attacks, all I could do was focus on not getting struck while trying to find a small opening to draw my sword from my hip. The monster attacked again, this time trying to slam my head to the ground, which I was forced to sidestep. With a bit of my momentum's help, I drew my longsword with a wire wrapped handle and twisted guard.

I managed to distance myself a little from the monster. My guard was poised, with my sword held up at head height, left hand gripping the pommel, and right hand choked up on the hilt by the guard. My left leg was more extended than my right which supported the bulk of my weight. I could feel abdominal muscles tightening to keep myself steady through the pain from the fall, making me wince.

The monster stared intensely at my sword, then darted its slit-like pupils over to me, widening its already large eyes even further, getting a grin out of me in response. "Come at me," I said as threateningly as I could. The creature seemingly understood my words. As the chaotic battle raged around us, it began to flick its scales together as if both to challenge me and let the others know not to interrupt our duel.

I furrowed my brow, and the glick showed its horrid teeth in response. It came forward, with the same squealing sound he'd heard before, only this time much more vicious and hateful. I stood my ground and awaited the perfect moment to strike. It came at me like a rabid dog to fresh meat, sprinting as quickly as its legs could carry it.

When it was just outside of a normal strike's range, I pushed hard from my right leg, turning on the ball of my left foot, and jumped. The movement sent him into a spin and the rest of my body followed suit. The sword, having lagged behind just a little, came down from my right side with the added force from the spin and struck the monster's collarbone, splitting its torso into two, uneven, bloodied chunks. Green blood sprayed across my face and covered my jerkin in a light sheen of its filth. "Damn, that stinks!" I exclaimed with a disgusted look on my face.

Garett had, apparently, seen the attack happen and I caught him grinning pridefully.

From where I now stood, I could see Roburn's sword singing a beautiful tune of slaughter and gore, while the archers kept back and provided cover fire for the lesser experienced Synners. Their broad-head arrows and ash shafts with alternating goose wing-feathers performed perfectly against the gaps in the glicks' hard scales. The wind made it a little more difficult to be as precise as they usually were, but they'd been trained for that over the course of years. Their arrows, shot from recurve riding bows, soared through the air and struck their marks with incredible precision, even with the morning breeze. Meanwhile, Edryd's sword and horse were covered in glick blood, as he swung to cut yet another one down.

Looks like he's doing alright, but... Oh, shit! I thought, as I noticed a glick preparing to launch itself.

"Edryd!" I tried to call out, but through the cacophony of battle, it fell on deaf ears. He was fighting voraciously when a glick knocked him off his horse in the same manner that I had been just a few minutes before. "Edryd!" I yelled again, much more desperately this time, and sprinted to help my best friend.

Edryd didn't have as bad a fall as mine, but he was still visibly hurt from it, wincing in pain as he pressed the hilt of his sword up to his shoulder. A few of the neighboring glicks turned and saw the young Synner desperately trying to get back on his feet and grab his sword at the same time, and began to charge him. I continued running towards Edryd with my sword in my right hand, flowing behind him in the air.

Ed managed to get into his guard position - with the sword low, and the point aimed behind him. This provided for an excellent uppercut position, and it was his favorite for groups of attackers during training. The four glicks who were charging him all came at different speeds, but he was ready for them.

He can't take them all at once, I have to do something, I thought.

As I watched them begin their charge, I decided to act. Regardless of whether I'd tested it, I knew only one spell I could cast in time that would deal damage to the glicks around him. My eyes turned into the obsidian ovals once more, as I *reached into the Ethereal, drawing mana from the world without time. I felt the warmth flow from my fingertips, rolling over my whole body and* condensed the mana to my left hand as I ran. I held the sphere for a few seconds, patiently waiting for the glicks to be in a closer bunch than how they were at the moment.

They continued to charge towards Ed, and in doing so, unconsciously converged into a tight group.

Ed, on the other hand, could only watch as his attackers approached, but the fire in his eyes told me he was calculating whether he could strike them all at once, even with his arm being in the state it was.

I kept sprinting, feeling my mud-caked boots getting heavier as I went, making it difficult to continue at the same pace I had been at only a few seconds prior. I saw the glicks approaching faster than I could get there, and knew I had no time left to get any closer. The jade sphere of mana had gotten so hot, my glove felt as though it was catching fire.

"I hope this works," I muttered as I drew my left hand back over my shoulder. "Duck!" I shouted, throwing my arm forward and extending my hand to release the spell.

The ball transformed into a whip-like tendril that moved

at an incredible speed towards my friend. Luckily, he saw I cast the spell out of the corner of his eye, after having looked for me when I told him to duck. Edryd, seeing the whip-like spell coming quickly, ducked and rolled to his left as fast as he could to get out of its way.

I flicked the whip, wrapping it around the oncoming glicks' torsos and groins. I followed it up with the same motion I had used on the Pyrus spell, flicking my index finger from the base of my thumb to the tip, and ignited my spell. The mana-flame traveled along the tendril and reached the intended targets, melting flesh and bone wherever the mana had been present.

Their limbs flew away from their bodies after having been viciously severed by the spell. All four glicks fell to the ground in chunks of molten flesh and bubbling blood. Roburn saw the spectacle, though he was too occupied with slaying the remaining glicks.

Shit, I used too much mana, I thought as my vision blurred. I noticed something was amiss with my core, the housing for what could essentially be my soul stuck inside my chest and beneath my heart, but was instantly occupied by another oncoming glick.

Garett, who had been watching the battle from a distance, decided it was time for the bow-casters to finish off the stragglers. "Infuse!" he called out, and each bow-caster's eyes turned into obsidian ovals. *They drew from the Ethereal,* however, instead of condensing it to their bodies, *they condensed their mana to the bows themselves.*

The mana coated the bow's curves and string, becoming denser at the grip and anchor point. Having nocked their arrows, the mana flowed into the arrow itself. With an index finger above, and the middle and ring fingers below the arrow's shaft, they were ready. "Aim!" he yelled, and all picked their targets, judging the distance. "Fire at will!," he called out. The arrows – now enhanced with mana – rapidly soared through the air without being tampered with by the wind.

The remaining glicks were few and far between, but the bow-casters' arrows found their marks. They rained down from above, and struck the glicks' heads, piercing their scales, bone, and flesh. The arrowheads came out on the other side, just between the bottom of their jaws and their necks. As soon as the arrows struck, each one fell limp as a boned fish, and dropped to the ground with a 'thud'.

Just as I was about to strike, my attacker crumbled onto the bloodied ground after the arrow had struck its scaly head. It skidded a short way on the slick ground, coming to a halt just before my feet.

That was close, I thought.

I looked around, watching the remaining monsters fall like haunches from a butcher's rack, slamming into the ground. Their green blood soaked their limp bodies and seeped into the ground beneath them. The stench of sour meat began to overwhelm and surround us. Most of us had kept our composure, except for Batch.

Poor bastard was the first of us to vomit up his breakfast in projectile form.

The bow-casters on the hill's slope began to laugh at us poor bastards below, wallowing in our enemies' reek. At that point, I was barely phased by the smell now, since I'd already had it in my nostrils for the past few minutes, and I knew how to control my body well enough to not puke.

I would be lying if I didn't say that I came close once or twice.

The taste of bile was enough for me to react by swallowing my morning oats back down from whence they came. I shook my head and immediately turned towards where Edryd was now motionless on the ground. "Edryd!" I shouted, desperate to find him unharmed after the spell had blown the creatures' limbs off into all directions. Irun had already reached him and was kneeling by his side.

"He's wounded!" Irun shouted back. I felt a chill go down my spine as I rushed to Irun's location and saw Edryd lying on the ground, unconscious. He had a large talon mark across his chest and shoulder that had been bleeding profusely for quite some time.

"We need some help over here!" I called out while Irun was trying to make sure the wound wasn't as severe as it looked. Garett himself rode over and dismounted from his black stallion. He rushed over to the us, kneeling at Edryd's side, and briefly looked between the flaps of the sliced jerkin. "He'll live, but I need to close this wound if he's going to continue to have that option," he said. "Give me some space, boys," his eyes glowed with an intense, amber color.

He was in the timeless world – the light shafts still spinning and colliding overhead. He rubbed both of his hands together in a circular manner, and began pulling the tendrils towards him, condensing the amber mana directly to his hands – each hand having its own sphere. His eyes returned to their normal state, and the mana remained in his hands. "Open the flaps of the jerkin for me, Thoma," he ordered in a calm voice. I moved as quickly as I could to open them, coating my hands in my best friend's blood and recalling the severed limbs as they flew through the air.

One of the claws must have hit him as it flew. Damn it, I thought, making sure I didn't avert my gaze from what was happening in front of me.

Garett placed both of his hands over the open, bloodied gash that was the young boy's chest and shoulder. He alternated his index and middle finger to slowly release the spell. The wound began to sew itself shut, using the tendrils of raw mana to both pull the separated skin together and seal it shut. The heat produced from the spell was enough to sear the skin, giving it an even tighter seal. The smell of burning flesh and blood filled the air near the downed boy, and I almost couldn't bear to see it.

"There," Garett said with a sigh of relief. "The bleeding has stopped, but he'll have to be careful for the next few days. Wouldn't want that opening back up, now, would we?" he asked. "No, Master Garett," I replied. "I'll see to it that he recovers properly," I said. "Good. Make sure he gets put in one of the wagons. He won't be riding on horseback for a few days by the looks of things," Garett said. "Yes, Master Garett," I replied.

The rest of the convoy came down the hill, and met up with us and the rest of the bloodied Synners. When the Master arrived, he gazed out over the small amount of havoc the young ones and the bow-casters had wreaked, and smiled.

"A pity Edryd isn't awake at the moment," he said. "I'd have loved to congratulate him for his bravado in combat. Holding his ground to face at least three of these bastards at a time is nothing to sneer at. See to it he gets a comfortable spot on one of the wagons to be able to recover," he said, looking at one of the nearest Synners, who responded with a slight nod. "But that's not even mentioning the spell that was cast as they were advancing," he said in a subtly praising tone, while looking at me.

I looked down at my muddied and blood-soaked boots, humbled by the compliment given by the Master, his second in two days, and tried to hide a grin. "Master," Garett began, "We best be on our way. We've at least twelve leagues ahead of us, and I for one would like to be there before nightfall," he said. "Very well," the Master said.

"Wait," someone cried out. An old farmer crawled out from

underneath a few sacks of potatoes. He had a long, unkempt beard with white hairs among black. He was mostly bald, and had probably seen at least 60 winters.

"Yer a' headin' out yonder-ways, ain't ye?" he pointed South-East. "Yes, my good sir," the Master replied, giving the elderly man a once-over glance. "One would imagine that you're not here only to be attacked by these foul beings," he continued. "Aye, that be true," said the elderly one. "I was on my way to me farmstead when me wheel got stuck in yon puddle o' mud. When I was a leapin' from me wagon, I saw the bastards a' comin' from about a league off to the East," he said, raising an index finger to point in the general direction of the morning sun light.

"I see," said the Master. "I hid meself from them foul beasts, so as to avoid gettin' in the way of progress, if ye get me meanin'," the farmer said with a rapid succession of head bobbing movements. "Yes, I get your 'meaning'," the Master replied. "What is your name?" the Master asked. "Jehn Boone, at yer service," the old man replied.

"Very well, Jehn Boone," the Master began. "Safest of travels, and gods' speed to you and your oxen," he nodded. "Thank ye, master, and thank the young-uns for savin' me wagon 'n' oxen," Jehn replied, smiling from ear to ear. I, Batch and Irun nodded to the elderly man, and began to mount their horses. Edryd was carried to the nearest wagon, and placed on top of a sack of bedding materials by two of the bow-casters.

Bernar rode up next to me, grinning as he always did. "I told you never to use an untested spell in combat," he said, adjusting his ass in the saddle. "*Oh*, and I imagine I was supposed to have allowed my best friend to die a death worse than I can imagine," I replied with remorse seeping through my tone as I fought back the emotions of nearly having killed my best friend. "No, not at all. But what's important here is that you pulled it off," Bernar began. "So, I suppose now would be as good a time as any to give you the apology I owe you for having doubted your capabilities," he said, widening his eyes and lifting his eyebrows.

I was puzzled to hear that, but nodded. "Thanks, I guess," I said solemnly. "*Bah*, don't thank me till we're at the castle and Edryd's awake," Bernar said. I nodded once again and mounted my horse.

We reformed their original formation, and waited for me to get into position. Once I was, the Master gave the signal to begin moving once more and they were off, heading South-East to Coltend Castle.

The place where everything I knew would begin to be put to the test.

CHAPTER 4

Coltend Castle

We kept a decent pace over the course of the afternoon until reaching the castle. As we went over the rolling hills, and beneath the tallest trees I'd ever seen, I rode alongside Edryd who lay in the back of one of the carts on top of a few sheets of now blood-soaked linen.

I honestly should have thought about the possibility of that happening, he thought. *I now know the reason why they always warn us never to use an untested spell in battle. You're a fool, Thoma Fayren. Just like your father,* I thought, mentally kicking myself.

Bernar pulled up next to me, eyeing us both carefully before speaking. "He'll be alright," he began to say after seeing the worried look on my face. "He's a strong boy. Well, stronger than you anyways, but then again that's not hard to be now, is it?" he said in an attempt to cheer me up in his usual way. I slightly raised my eyebrows and grinned from the corner of my mouth.

"You're an asshole," I said with the same expression. "Like I said, I wouldn't worry about him. He'll heal in about two days," Bernar said comfortingly. "It was my fault," I said curtly, my line of sight moving from my brother to Celer's nape as my eyes began to water.

"I know I should've tested the spell before today, and now my friend has paid the price for my stupidity," I managed with an ever-growing lump in my throat. "You managed to save him from being outnumbered and killed. Nothing more, nothing less," Bernar said as if stating the obvious. "I'd be focusing more on *that* fact, if I were in your shoes," he shrugged.

I looked back at my brother with bloodshot eyes, feeling the salty fluid greatly caressing the green of my irises.

"Thanks," I said with no small amount of difficulty. "*Bah*, no need to thank me. Just remember to always try to focus on the *positive* side of things," Bernar said. "Otherwise, you'll get lost whilst wallowing in your own self-pity, and nobody likes a whiner now, do they?" he said, expecting an answer. "No, they don't," I said, sniffling back a small string of snot and wiping the remainder on my sleeve.

"Good. Glad we got that cleared up," Bernar said, patting me on the shoulder. "Now, do your best to clear your eyes and get that slime out of your nostrils. We're almost at the castle," he finished and rode ahead to be at the Master's side once more.

I did what I could, but I knew the skin around my eyes would likely still be a bit red. We rode over the last hill, and at its peak, we saw it in the distance with its mountainous backdrop.

Coltend Castle.

I almost couldn't believe my eyes. Granted, they *were* still full of tears, making my vision a little blurry as a result, but from what I *could* see, it was *massive*. I forced myself to blink a few times in hopes of clearing up my eyesight.

Until this point in time, I'd never seen anything that large that wasn't a mountain. The walls were forty meters high, and made of solid granite slabs. On top of the walls stood guardposts made from the trees of the nearby forest, and were placed at regular intervals along the circumference of the wall.

The Western Gate stood tall and mighty at twenty meters tall, and made of steel and cedar. It was a formidable obstacle for any attempts of invasion or against almost any form of enemy, though I never really thought any army would've been dumb enough to try.

The palace, where the royal family resided, stood in the exact center of the circular wall. The towering structure rose far above the wall as it gleamed in the late afternoon sun, reflecting the last rays out towards the countryside.

It's like a lighthouse. Although, instead of water, there is a vast expanse of land, I thought.

"We're almost there," the Master called out. "Now pick your jaws up off the ground, and let's get a move on," he shouted back. Everyone put their heels to their horse's sides, and trotted down the hillside.

Irun and Batch rode up next to me, whose eyes were only now clear enough that I could lift my head up and look around without being embarrassed, and trotted alongside me. "Have you ever seen anything like that? 'Cause I sure as shit haven't," Batch began. "I have once or twice before being inducted into the Synners," Irun replied.

"My father was a trader. He and I would often travel together to deliver our village's goods as a form of taxes to the king. My mother was a Synner, and after a few trips with my father, she decided that being a trader wasn't a life I should want or have. She was a very strong-willed woman, and so I was induced into the Synners. If I had to go back and choose between a trader's life and a Synner's, I'd choose the Synners any day," he finished.

Batch glanced over at him with a look of surprise. "Your mother was a Synner? I'd always thought your father was," he said with no small amount of surprise in his voice. "Aye, she *was*," Irun said, his tone falling with the last word. "Oh, I'm sorry. I didn't know she'd..." Batch said. "It's alright," Irun interrupted. "The only other person who knew about that was the Master. So, you don't have to say sorry. You had no way of knowing, after all," Irun replied brushing off the emotional wave that tugged at his vocal cords.

I looked over at Irun and then towards the ground as though I had felt some sort of mirrored connection with his own story. "I can understand what you must feel whenever you talk about it," I muttered, not sure he could hear me, and even less if I'd wanted him to. "I'm sure you do," Irun replied with an empathetic nod. I returned a chagrined smile, but decided it was probably better to face forward and not focus on mine and Bernar's past. "Well, at least now we don't only get to hear tales of the Castle. We're going to be able to live the details of those stories as soon as we enter those walls," I said, trying my best to change the subject.

As lame as it sounded, it worked.

Batch and Irun looked at each other and then back at me who held an obvious and almost boastful grin on my face. "Be honest, I, do you really think the Master, Master Garett and your brother will simply allow us to meander about, spending our small quantities of pocket money on taverns and women?" Batch asked, already knowing the answer to his question.

It was a rhetorical question, however, Irun simply shrugged in lieu of an immediate response.

"I think after what we pulled off this morning, we should be allowed a little time off the leash they keep us on," he said after a few moment's pause and with no small amount of sarcasm in his voice. "I agree. While I've never had a woman, nor ale to go along with one for that matter, I think it's about time boys of our ages learn about that, no?" I asked, my mind running rampant with what that might actually be like, and whether

I'd be able to do anything about it in the castle.

I, of course, was wrong.

"Best not get too far ahead of yourself, young one," Master Garett said, forcing a ghostly expression on our collective faces. Master Garett had overheard the entire conversation and now knew what our late-night activities would be, should they be able to leave their rooms. He looked at the three, and pushed his bottom lip out a little.

"I'm merely disappointed, though not surprised. I suppose that's what I'd do, were I in your boots," he said with the face of someone who'd just thought of a good memory. "Just pray your asses are actually going to be allowed out at night," he said, turning his head back towards the castle. We looked at each other, probably all wondering whether going out at night was even a possibility.

I can't put my finger on it, but I can feel there's more to him saying that than we think, I thought as I looked over at the trio of riders ahead of me.

I wonder just how much they really know about the happenings of the world, and what our roles were within them, I thought, sighing heavily in the process.

We were approaching the castle's walls. It became evident just how *massive* the flags in the castle were. From where we were, I gathered it was almost a kilometer at that point, I could finally begin to see the details on the flags that flew above the massive gate.

The square flag of Coltend Castle had sewn on it the image of a griffin devouring the sun, while crushing the moon with its talons above an unfurled scroll with indecipherable words on it. To be honest, I had no idea what they meant, if anything at all, as they were still far too blurry for me to read them. As the sun was just about to set on the distant horizon behind the hills they had ridden over earlier in the day, the entirety of the castle's face was illuminated by the golden rays.

"The size of these walls is starting to make my neck hurt from looking up at them," Irun said, rubbing his nape. Batch and I agreed with his statement, catching ourselves also rubbing their napes. About fifty meters from the gate, the guardsmen's faces were becoming increasingly detailed, but then again, so were ours. "Keep your mouths shut unless you want flies getting in," Bernar said, trying to be as levelheaded as possible. Batch and Irun chuckled, but understood what he meant. When we were about fifty meters from the gate, a voice called out from behind the large cedar and steel bar gate.

On the gate itself, there was a smaller doorway that appeared to be heavily reinforced so that it wasn't the weakest point of the gate. On the doorway, there was a small steel hatch, just big enough to fit a man's face. When we got close enough, the hatch opened quickly with a sharp *crack*. "Hallo, there!" the voice called out. It was a man's voice, and only judging by the sound, I knew the man to be a large one.

I thought guardsmen were meant to ask the age-old question of who we are, but it's odd how he didn't ask what our names were. Not to mention he's got the oddest way of saying Hello *I think I've ever heard,* I thought.

"Hello, there! I am the Master Synner of Codrean, and as you can see, I have a small party with me. "*Ja*, I can see them, Master," the man on the other side replied. "Then I presume you know why we're here," The Master said. "*Ja*, I know why, and I already knew who you were even before I opened the hatch, Master," the man said. "I'd seen you from the top of the wall, and recognized your armor shortly after. Took me a while to pinpoint where it was from, but I got it right. You simply confirmed it," he said cheerfully, closing the hatch.

I could hear orders being barked from behind the gate as its chains became taut, lifting the massive gate. The chains creaked and strained to lift the mighty gate, wrapping around a large drum winch tightly. Batch, Irun, and I tried peering under the gate to see who could get the first glimpse, but Bernar whistled softly to get our attention. He subtly shook his head to prevent us from doing so. With no small amount of dejection, we settled back into our saddles.

Once the gate was fully raised, the man stepped out from behind the nearby pillar of the guardhouse. He was a very large man indeed, as I had guessed from the sound of his voice.

Well, I'll be damned. He must be one of the descendants of the giant tribes in the North, I thought.

The man stood at least a head taller than anyone present, had long fair hair, deep blue eyes, and a thick well-kept beard that grew all the way down to his medallion. His armor was plate metal, not leather like the Synners' uniforms, since his was made for being able to withstand blows that could crush a man without it. It was polished bright, and his red cape split in two lengths just above knee height. His left pauldron had the Griffin of Coltend's insignia.

That must mean he's left-hand dominant. It's difficult to fight against that, since their guards are all mirrored, he thought, as I noticed his great sword hung from the right side of his hip.

The Master rode up to him and nodded, gauging his size. "Gods above," the Master said. "It's easy to forget how large members of your race are, though, in all my years, you're the first I've met who is *this* tall," he said astonishedly. The man stood almost as tall as the Master on top of his horse and stared at him cheerfully, his flat face showing a large smile. "What is your name, guardsman?" the Master asked. "Sir Magnar Thorsen, Master," the giant replied, handing him an apple.

Thorsen? Sounds like someone descended from the gods themselves, I thought, taking note of the name.

"Well, Sir Thorsen, I thank you for the welcome, but must bid you farewell, grateful for the hospitality as I am," the Master said with an air of respect as he flipped the apple in the air. Thorsen gave a slight bow in response. "I take it you know your way to the palace, Master?" Thorsen sensed, his eyes darting across the Master's features and confident posture. "I do, indeed. Thank you for your concern," the Master replied.

As we moved through the massive gate, we passed by the giant, nearly a half-head taller than we were, even on horseback. He looked at us briefly, noting our equipment and any accolades we might have had, greeting us with a smile and a firm nod. We immediately felt we had no other option but to automatically respond by doing the same, though our smile was more of a nervous one than anything else.

Bernar saw the exchange and chuckled. "Never seen such unruly boys put in their place so quickly by anyone other than the Master or Garett," he said cheerfully. I knew I felt the need to say something witty in retort, but failed to think of anything in the moment.

As soon as the last few of our group went under the gate, the large gate came down and was quickly locked into place. Batch, Irun and I began to look around at the nearby houses, where a few doorways began to allow inquisitive eyes through the cracks.

Coltend Castle had a social system where the common folk and the upper class were drastically separated. The common folk had to plough and till the land surrounding the castle to make ends meet, whilst the rich simply sat back and paid next to nothing for the commoners' hard work. The housing differential was so great that the small wooden shacks, or the poorly built brick and straw houses were but a stone's throw away from each other, and that upset many of the rich.

They would often complain about the filthiness of the poor, who could be seen throwing their buckets of piss and shit out of the window in the early mornings. The younger children would attempt to see if they could hit a 'Big Belly', their term for a tax collector, with a clump of shit as they made their rounds.

They rarely missed.

Along the main street, countless beggars leaned on the walls of the houses, begging for alms and donations to feed their empty bellies. Their cups and cracked wooden bowls were empty. "Even with all of the riches of Coltend, nothing means more to them than a person stooping down to place a single coin in their cups," Bernar said, noting my expression. My dour expression, apparently, could somehow show that I sensed their desperation and sadness as though I were in their position.

"Don't think too hard about it," Bernar began. "Feeling sorry for them won't do you much good in the long run," his brother said. "But I can't help it," I retorted. "I feel as though one day I'll be able to help them, and the fact that I can't do anything about it at the moment makes me angry," I said, furrowing my brow.

"You've always had a good heart and attitude," Bernard said. "Hold on to it while you still can. Seeing enough of the world how it really is might change you," he began with a heavy sigh. "However, if you can hold on to that level of empathy, then you'll be the strongest of us all," he finished his sentence and noticed it was taken to heart.

"So, you're telling me you don't care about other people. Is that it?" I asked after a brief pause. "I still care about *a few* people. You and the Master are two I can name off the top of my head, at least," Bernar said sarcastically. "*Ah*, I see. A little cold-hearted, but I think I get it," I nodded.

I began to look around and observe the filth and grime on their faces - the days of accumulated dirt under their fingernails during their days plowing and tilling fields could be seen from a few meters away. Their whispers couldn't be heard through the cacophony of the street, but I could guess that they were commenting on our armor and general appearance.

The sound of our hooves resonated down the small alleys that ran perpendicular to the main street, and small children ran to the roadside to see what all the commotion was about. Pointing and staring were amongst the most common actions, while whispers and giggles were a close second from some of the older girls. Irun and Batch noted a few who seemed to be their own age. "Don't even think about it..." Garett said quietly toward the pair, destroying their hopes.

Bernar and I stifled a laugh when we saw their faces.

We continued down the street without speaking for the most part, but when we reached the general marketplace, it was teeming with busy shopkeepers, angry shoppers, and show animals being kept in place by their trainers. There was so much to look at that I finally decided to ride up to his brother's side, knowing my idiot self would get sidetracked and, consequently, lost.

"Do you think we'll be allowed to leave our quarters?" I asked, pushing Celer up to my brother's side. "Not sure about you, but I'm definitely getting out of there," Bernar replied with a shit-eating grin.

The moment the last word had left his mouth, I noticed a red-haired prostitute, wearing little more than a corset and stockings, was standing on the balcony of a two-story house which had been laced with red ribbons. "And that's likely the place I'll be all night," he said with his head nodding in the building's general direction.

"You're sure you'll have the coin for an all-night expedition with every woman in that... *establishment*?" I asked, knowing my brother's nearly insatiable lust for women. "Believe me, little brother," he began. "Soon as I'm done with the first, the rest will give me a discount after they hear what I've done," he said confidently.

I heard Isla groan in disgust as soon as she understood what he meant, but I could only give her a tight-lipped, awkward smile.

"Are you sure about that?" Roburn chimed in from my right side. "I've heard stories about the ones here," he said as if he had more knowledge than he cared to share. "I suppose you'd know all about them. You might even be the cause of a few of those stories," Bernard said with a wry smile. Roburn chuckled and turned to me with a sly smile on his face. "You know, I would take you along with me, so I could show you the ones to avoid, at least. They've been known to not be clear of the... *illnesses*," he said with a hush on the last word.

"You mean they've got some kind of plague?" I asked with genuine concern in his voice. "More like a sort of *rot*, but sure, we'll go with that," both Roburn and Bernar simply laughed, refusing to elaborate any further.

We neared the main palace and were shocked at the sight of the gate. Two golden griffins facing each other loomed over the main gate. The scarlet cloth hung from the top of the ivory imbued gate; the intricate designs portraying the beasts crushing the moons on each door.

The Master raised his hand, a signal to the gatekeeper, who looked out over the edge, and called out to open the doorway. Two guardsmen pulled on massive levers which, through ingenious mechanisms, made opening the gate easier than one would think. The giant doors swung open with fluency and grace, without making much of a noise.

The others and I were in awe at the sight now before us as well. Tall pine trees lined the sides of the road. Beneath the trees, a fence of interwoven roots had been formed, as though the trees themselves were connected to each other. The street was made of smooth granite slabs, each carved and covered in resin to keep it smooth. Seen from above, the pattern formed the Griffin of Coltend with its wings spread.

All of us, except for the Master, Garett, Roburn, and Bernar, of course, looked about in awe. Behind the fence we saw fountains and a large open garden with fair maidens picking strawberries from the bushes. Their long, red dresses had their hems trimmed just enough to not drag along the floor.

Down the road a little way, the doors to the main palace could be seen, with a score of guardsmen on either side. Their gear looked a little less garnished than Thorsen's had been, but they were all equally well-equipped. Each man stood on a single step of the stairway that led into the main Palace. I looked over at Batch, who shot me a look as if to say *I want their armor, too.*

"Do you know what those two large flags are, Thoma?" Roburn asked. I shook my head. Even with the lessons I'd had growing up, there was limited information on such boring stuff like flags. "Those are the flags of the Church of Mideia, and the Warrior's Guild," he began. "The Church is a nasty bunch to deal with, but the Guild, if I'm being honest, isn't anywhere near as rough. They can at least hold a civil conversation without feeling the need to spout some insults about us," he continued, catching himself from spitting on the ground.

The stairway had a long carpet running all the way down in a strip to the base, while the flags Roburn had mentioned earlier hung overhead. The Church showed its colors of green and the image of a person reaching out for help to a serpent that hung between a sword and a staff in the shape of a cross. The Warlords Guild - also well known as the *Barracks* - hung their standard of an ox and a blade linked together by a chain on a blue background.

The remaining flags were of those of the neighboring cities and villages which the castle would attend to, and each proudly showed their colors and markings. Some were rather obscure, others entirely offensive. Nevertheless, the castle had always wanted to prove that they were unified no matter what, so even the offensive flags were shown.

As we neared the main stairway, we finally got a closer look at the guards in their armor. "Magnificent work, isn't it?" Bernar asked, looking back at the three of us who nodded vigorously. "It really is extraordinary," I said with my eyes as wide as they could be. "For them to be standing there like that for hours and hours on end like that is impressive. Either they're extremely well disciplined, or their armor must be lighter than it looks," I suggested.

"You have a point there, Thoma," Master Garett began. "Their armor is forged under the supervision of a master smith, who just so happens to be an elf," he said matter-of-factly. "An elf?" Batch asked, as though he hadn't quite heard it correctly.

"Yes," Master Garett said. "You see, they have special techniques for making armor light and strong. Not only that, but a single piece of armor might last you a lifetime, if you take care of it properly," he continued. "They're certainly not cheap. I'd wager a breastplate alone is about two-thousand crescents," he said with a bit of uncertainty. Our collective jaws dropped. "T-two thousand?" Irun chimed in with eyes as wide as mine.

"It's an investment Coltend is willing to make. After all, it is *the* central trading hub for all four countries," Master Garett said. "But we haven't seen anything that would suggest as much," Batch said curiously. "Not yet," Master Garett replied. We didn't really understand what he meant by that, so we simply looked at each other and shrugged.

"Halt!" Garett shouted after he had seen the Master raise his hand. The whole party came to a complete stop and began to dismount. Our legs hurt from riding for the better part of the day, so it was quite a relief to be able to stand on our own two feet again.

"All of you, listen up! Master's got a few words for you," Garett shouted again and everyone looked at the Master who was stepping forward. "I want you all to listen closely, as I will only say this once," he began with an air of caution as he looked at all of us.

"This is mainly directed to the juniors of the party, so I will be curt. Where we're about to enter is full of influential people and politicians from all four countries. They will be scattered around the palace, so mind who you talk to and how you talk to them. As tempted as you may be to try and do something out of league simply because you think I won't be watching or hearing about it later, *don't*," he said with his intonation falling heavily on the last word.

The three of us gulped dryly and tried to keep a straight face to the best of our abilities.

"Not that I expect you to, but you've been warned," he said. Bernar grinned, trying to hide it from the others. "Don't forget that just because we're amidst other people, and important ones at that, never be caught off your guard. Do you understand?" he said sternly. "Yes, Master," everyone said in unison. He nodded and turned on his toes - like he had the night before - and proceeded towards the stairway.

"You heard what he said?" Batch asked. "Yeah, though I find it rather odd how they would simply all be here at once without something bigger going on," Irun replied.

I wonder what he's not telling us, I thought.

At the top of the stairway, they were met by a short man with graying slicked back hair and a large stomach. He was clean shaven, and wore Coltend's colors on his doublet. "Welcome, Masters," he said bowing low. "My name's Fulco, and I am honored to be the one tending to your needs on behalf of King Truls," he said cheerily as the wrinkles around his eyes scrunched up. "We're honored to have been invited," the Master replied. "Tell me, good man, where might our accommodations be?" he asked plaintively.

"Follow me, good sirs," Fulco replied with a motion, and they walked through the doorway. Once inside, I couldn't help but notice the tall, granite pillars that supported the great roof lathered in carvings of grandeur and battles from times past. There were, also, six stained-glass windows that had depictions of the gods, one for each window.

The floor had the red strip of carpet leading all the way down the hallway to the end of the large room. Benches were placed in rows facing the back of the room, where the king and queen would sit. The hall was far quieter than I had expected it to be, at least for the time being, though I would be lying if I said I'd noticed it from the start. I, like the others, was *way* too busy looking at all the details carved into the pillars and such.

If only Edryd were awake to see this, I thought.

"This way, please," Fulco called out and turned to the left wing of the room where there was yet another stairway. We followed him up the stairs, and on the walls, we saw paintings of the old captains of the Guard, depicted in fine oil paintings.

"I'm just going to assume he's taking us to the barracks

portion of the palace," Irun said. He had been hoping to sleep on a comfortable bed for once. "Seems like that's where we'll *all* be sleeping," Batch replied. I was in too much awe to come up with any intelligible response. "You will have all of the necessary items to take care of yourselves and your equipment, so shut up for now," Bernar whispered back. "Yeah, but sharing a room with the Master was *not* on my bucket list of things to do before I eat dirt," Batch muttered under his breath.

My brother merely chuckled and shook his head.

"We've arrived," Fulco said promptly, pushing open a door to a large room with numerous beds lined up beside the walls. Batch spotted a hallway that looked like it led to a bathing area, and nudged Irun excitedly.

"I shall summon the servants to take your..." he paused, getting a glance at my armor that still had a few bloodstains from the battle earlier in the day. His eyes opened wide at the sight of me, and quickly put his hand to his mouth.

This poor fucker hadn't noticed it before.

"My goodness is that...?" he began. "Yes, it is, good sir," the Master cut him off. "We'd very much appreciate it if the servants could assist us in getting their garments all cleaned up by tomorrow," the Master said politely. "I-I-I assure you they'll be cleaned by then," Fulco said with a slight bit of disgust in his voice. "Thank you for your troubles," the Master said, smiling warmly as Fulco scurried off to find the servants.

The Master turned around and smiled. "He turned about as green as the blood on your armor, boys," he said. It was the first time anyone aside from Bernar or Master Garett had heard him say something with a hint of humor.

We weren't entirely sure it had been meant as a joke, so we just grinned as a result. "Let's get cleaned up and get some food in our bellies," Bernar suggested to everyone, noticing the awkward exchange. "Yes, I'm aching to try their apple cobbler. I hear it's superb," the Master said.

"Never would have taken you for having a sweet tooth, Master," a voice came from behind us. We all turned towards it, only to find that it was a servant girl. Her hair was covered by a red head wrap, except for a single lock of black hair that hung from the brim down to her pale cheek. Her deep, green eyes flicking from one person to the next indicated that she felt as though she had done something wrong.

Gods above, she's gorgeous! I thought.

"I didn't even hear you approaching, young one," the Master said, genuinely surprised.

This was true. In fact, *no one* had heard or seen her coming, which came as a surprise to us all, especially the Master.

"I'm sorry," she said quickly. "I had no intention to startle you. Especially not all dressed up like that in fancy armor," she said. "Not at all! It's alright," the Master said warmly. I still hadn't taken my eyes off her when she caught me staring at her. I briefly blinked and shook myself out of my daze, trying to wake up from the trance her beauty had put me in.

I noticed Bernar grinning at me out of the corner of my eye, as well.

"What is your name, child?" the Master asked calmly. "My name is Meliss, Master," she said timidly. "Well, Meliss, would you do us all a favor and take our garments to have them cleaned? I'm sure Fulco has probably already instructed you to do so," the Master said. "Yes, of course, Master," she replied quickly. "But they need to be off your bodies for me to wash them, Master," she said quietly.

The Master smiled and turned. "You heard the young lady. *Strip*," he said both playfully and with an air of command that no one *dared* to defy. Irun, Batch and I looked at each other seeking counsel, though there was none to be had.

None of us youngsters had been in our undergarments in front of a lady before, let alone entirely naked, so most were apprehensive to be in that state. That's not to say that we didn't have female Synners. We were merely separated when it came down to bathing, changing clothes, and sleeping. Aside from those things, we did everything else together as equals.

"Except for the females who will change in the bathing area," the Master began, gesturing for the women to go. "The rest of you can get started," he said. When we hesitated a little, his eyes flared with a bit of mana, adding to the intensity of his next word. "*Now*," the Master said sternly with a slight tilt in his head.

We each felt a jolt of fear run through us, and reluctantly began removing our jerkins while our cheeks flushed with blood. I tried my best to avoid eye contact with Meliss to *not* make the situation more awkward than it already was.

Meliss, on the other hand, was entirely unphased, as if she felt almost nothing seeing us strip. It was, apparently, a common thing for maids and servants to wait on other people to undress so they could take their clothes. To her it was nothing more than a few bloodstained people changing their attire.

To me on the other hand, it was the most embarrassing experience I had ever had in my life.

First impressions are everything, right? How can she be so beautiful yet so unphased by everyone being naked in front of her? It seems cruel that someone would have to see so many different people in their birthday suits enough times to become numb like that. Especially at her age, I thought while mentally admiring her beauty.

I quickly finished undressing, and I felt something I hadn't really felt in years: *exposed*. Thankfully, it wasn't just me, as some of the others did as well. The tell-tale sign of this was the awkward manner in which they placed their jerkins, undershirts, and undergarments into the small trolley she brought.

When it was my turn to put my stuff in the trolley, she smiled at me. I froze on the inside as butterflies did somersaults in my stomach, but I tried to keep my arms and legs moving, making it look like this was *actually* my normal state of being. I caught her gaze as I let go of my blood-soaked jerkin, and she smiled at me, giving me a knowing nod.

Fuck, I thought.

I stepped away from the trolley without turning around, but she just kept staring at me. She couldn't have been much older than I was, and yet we'd had this strange connection; one I'd never heard of before.

At least, that's what I *thought*.

"Well, then," the Master said, clearing his throat after noticing the connection between the two. "*Oh*," Meliss said, breaking whatever line of thinking ran through her mind. "Right away, Master," she said, grabbing the handles of the trolley and scurrying out of the room. She almost ran into the frame of the door on her way out, and it was clear her mind was somewhere else entirely.

Bernar laughed at me just as she turned the corner. "For someone as quiet as she was when she arrived, she was a bit clumsy on her way out," he began. "Although, she didn't even have to say a fuckin' word, and she's got your prick all tied up in a knot," he said in jest. "What, I can't think someone's beautiful?" I asked defiantly.

"Of course you can. I'm just doing you a favor by telling you not to get hung up on her after only seeing her once, you twerp," Bernar said. I raised an eyebrow questioningly, mostly because I couldn't tell if he was joking, or if it was just my lack of experience getting the better of me. "Just take my word for it," he cautioned. "Alright, *alright*! I get it," I retorted somewhat reluctantly.

"Gentlemen," Fulco called out, relieved to not see bloodstained clothing everywhere, as we all turned to face him. He was walking through the doorway with two servants just then, each carrying a bundle of clean, red, linen undergarments. "These are for you after you bathe and, if you so wish, you may keep them when you leave. We are as generous as we can be with our guests," he said with an air of pride.

"Thank you," the Master said, grabbing one from the pile. The two servants began handing them out according to size. Comments on the softness and smoothness of the undergarments came *en masse*, and others could simply not fathom the quality of the material. "I will leave a servant for you just outside the door should you need any food or drink," Fulco said.

"Thank you, dear Fulco," The Master said. "We've had a long journey, so for now, we shall all retire. Tomorrow is a big day from what I hear," he continued. "*Oh,* very much so, Master," Fulco said, with some excitement.

There it is again, I thought.

"I'll leave you to it," Fulco said as he bowed and walked out the door. "Let's get cleaned up and rest, shall we, lads?" Master Garett said, turning to face us. Everyone nodded at his command and headed off to the bathing area Batch had spotted previously. "But, what of Edryd, Master Garett?" I asked. "He's being taken care of. Quite possibly by that young maiden who was just here, I might add," Garett said.

Lucky bastard, I thought, relieved to hear my friend was in *very* good hands.

The air outside might not have been as cold as it was at Codrean, but the stone walls made for excellent insulators from the sun's heat. Bernar took the bed next to mine and plopped himself down, locking his fingers behind his head as he let out a heavy sigh. "Not going to try and light this bed on fire, too, are you?" he asked mockingly. "I'm pretty sure I've learned my lesson already. Thanks," I replied with a sarcastic grin. Bernar gave me a thin-lipped smile, nodded, and turned onto his side.

First the Master told us that important figures were in the area, and then Fulco made it seem more grandiose than I originally thought. What's really going on? I guess I'll cross that bridge when I come to it, I thought.

I closed my eyes and imagined myself back on the grassy plain, with the Ethereal's majestic light show looming overhead.

The next morning, I woke to the sound of a rooster off in the distance. I looked out from the window beside my bed and saw a large muster of people gathering around the doorway by which we had entered the castle the previous evening.

The sun was just coming up over the side of the high wall, and a few beams were entering the room, gently caressing some of the beds and stone tiles in their paths. I rubbed my eyes, trying to clear the need for sleep from them, and noticed a few around me were doing the same.

Master Garett walked in just as I was mentally preparing myself to get out of bed. "Rise and shine, daisies," he yelled, stirring some of the Synners who were still asleep. He was already in full harness, his jerkin smelled of lavender and looked almost as good as new. I scurried out of bed in a rush, only to find my jerkin cleaned and hanging at my bedside.

So clean. Almost as if there was never any blood on it to begin with, I thought as I caught the lavender scent on my jerkin as well.

As I was putting my gear on I kicked my brother, who had apparently slept through Master Garett's booming shout, to get out of bed. "I'm up, you daft little..." he didn't finish his sentence, instead, he threw a pillow at my face, hitting me square in the nose. I caught the pillow mid-fall, and swung back down at him, aiming for his head. "Then get out of bed already, you lazy fuck-nugget," I said jokingly. He stuck his tongue out at me, and for a moment I wondered whether *I* was actually the older brother.

Batch and Irun were having some trouble getting into their attire, but that was quickly remedied when Garett used a bit of his mana to pull down the top part of their jerkins that had shrunk a little due to the cleaning.

After a few minutes of hustle and bustle, brushing and tying hair up, getting jerkins, boots and hose on, everyone was ready and formed up. Batch, Irun, Roburn, and I all stood at attention in the front row. The Master looked out over everyone, and did a quick check to ensure none had weapons on them. "We're not allowed any weapons inside where we're about to go, so I'm just making sure no one was dumb enough to forget that," he said, almost as if reading all of our thoughts.

"We must go, gentlemen," Fulco said as he stopped in the doorway. "Right this way," he gestured, directing us out of the room and down the hall to the right. The Master went first, then Bernar, Master Garett, followed by the others and I.

Fulco led us back down the same hallways and halls as we had come through the previous evening, and I still couldn't shake the awe. Every time we walked down a hall, I'd notice something different about it. A new painting, carving, or something of the like. It was all so new to me that it took me longer than expected to take it all in.

"What do you think all the commotion is about?" Batch asked with a bit of nervousness. "I wish I knew, but my guess is that it's going to be important. Otherwise, we might not have needed to be here, let alone have so many important figures walking about," I replied. I had already been thinking about that since looking out of my window earlier that morning. Nevertheless, I had been unsuccessful in getting the answers I wanted. Batch took note of the worried look on my face, sighing quietly as he shook his head.

After a few short minutes walking, Fulco stopped and turned on his heel. We weren't expecting a man of his stature to move so eloquently or quickly, so we ended up paying close attention to him without being instructed to. "Through this doorway, you will be in the presence of various leaders from all around the Continent," he said with a grandiose air. I almost froze solid at that last word.

I've never seen anyone from outside our country besides Mom, and I barely remember her as it is, I thought, feeling a sense of nervousness come over me.

Fulco turned his attention to the Master. "I'm certain your Synners will know how to behave themselves in the Council Room, Master," he said, looking for reassurance. "Of course, my good Fulco," the Master replied with confidence. "*Ah*! All is well, then," Fulco said with relief. "In that case, we may enter," he said.

Fulco moved to the door and pulled on the lever that kept it locked. The lever clacked and thudded, and the door swung open, as my eyes opened wide. Fulco stepped aside to the left, and showed us into the Council Room. As we walked through the doorway, we saw leaders from all regions sitting around the largest meeting table on the Continent.

The four Lords - King Truls Wishert of Coltend, King Mads Oden of Hjalfar, King Bashaa Ibn'Escea of Harut, and King Elhael Phrys of Caegwen - observed our entry as they stood near their respective seats. The table's details could be seen from afar, and portrayed carvings of past battles of between monsters and men. The gold ring that lined the edge of the table was covered in runes – ancient spells for calming and harmony, good judgment and understanding, respect and industriousness. The table's frame had been carved from a solid oak tree that had once been touched by the gods, and had grown taller and broader than any other of its species.

On the walls, there were countless monster heads – some with horns, some with ghastly mouths agape – hanging from wooden frames with their mouths spread wide in a menacing manner. The stained-glass windows were also present, with details of rivers and forests, instead of battles, to remind those present of what they were gathering for.

I walked cautiously behind my older brother. My friends, consequently, walked closely behind me. Everyone was wondering just what was going to happen at this apparent council meeting. Some guessed it was to talk about trade routes, while others thought it would be about farming goods.

None were so close, yet so far from the truth.

"Ladies and gentlemen, please be seated," Fulco called out. The four kings sat down first at the apex of each quadrant of the table. The others sat between them, mixed as they were. Harutians with Coltenders, Hjalfarians with Caegweni.

Well, that's unusual, I thought.

"I know what you're thinking, but it helps maintain a sense of equality during the council," Master Garett whispered, after noticing my raised eyebrow. Once the Lords had been seated, the rest of the warriors and councilors sat down. I sat next to my brother, while Master Garett sat next to the Master. Batch and Irun were split between a Harutian warrior and both tried to avoid cross communication as a result.

Truls had his wife, Queen Leona of Maeredia, sit at his right side. Her beauty was angelic, to say the least. She was wearing a red dress with her black hair tied up in a fanciful bun. Her pale, blue eyes, and a perfect complexion, in some instances, had led her to be mistaken for an elf of Caegwen, though it was always quickly proven otherwise due to the lack of pointed ears.

"Your majesties, ladies, and gentlemen," Fulco began. "Please take note of everything that will be said here today, for it may change the course of our history in this world. Feel free to ask questions, so long as they are relevant to what is being discussed, otherwise they will be ignored by the council," he concluded. "As the primary host of this council, King Truls Wishert of Coltend will be the one to commence," Fulco finished, bowed, and stepped back.

Truls pushed back his chair and stood. His long, graying hair floated softly on his shoulders, while his beard was neatly trimmed for the occasion. He was not a small man, by any means, for his eating habits had caused him to be overweight. His red doublet was stretched tightly across his body, making breathing difficult.

His eyes were dark blue, and the bags under his eyes from countless drunken nights showed their weight. His aquiline nose had a large bump in the middle, while the crown he wore had the pattern of the Griffin carved into it. He also wore a gold-plated necklace that had depictions of his accolades and feats as a younger man.

"My lords and ladies present," he began with a voice of rolling thunder. "I am certain most of us here know the reason why I've summoned this council," he said. I looked over to Batch and Irun, each of us raising an eyebrow and shrugging in quick succession.

"These monsters have recently increased their assaults, emboldened by something we do not yet understand. Their numbers are also rapidly approaching undefendable levels, and we simply cannot sit on our hands any longer. This matter must be resolved before it wipes out our supply lines and mercantile routes. The Synners of the Continent have been doing their best to suppress their numbers in each respective country. However, no matter how many of those ugly bastards they slay, the bastards keep coming back," he said, and raised his voice a little at the last word.

"Our leading experts on the monster incursions, as well as the Synners of Codrean, believe we have found the answer to rid ourselves of these bastards once and for all," he said with an air of finality.

Ah, so that's what the secrecy was for, I thought.

"The Underworld has found a way to leak their monsters through portals that begin in their worlds, and end in ours. Now, I know how that sounds, however, I beg you to let King Elhael Phrys of Caegwen explain it in greater detail, for he is far more intelligent than I," Truls said. He sat back down in his chair, while Elhael was pushing his chair back.

He stood at least a head taller than anyone in the room, and his fair silver hair, straight as an arrow hung down to his middle back. His nearly perfect complexion, lack of beard and bright green eyes made him stand out amidst the others. His pointed ears were sharp, but had a certain elegance to them that matched his other features perfectly.

"I thank you, King Truls, for the compliment," Elhael began, his voice sounding like a river flowing softly through the air. Much less brutish than the one who had spoken before him. "Indeed, what King Truls has said is true. Unlike their original entry to this world - the cause of which we have yet to understand how or why it happened - my scouts have found such a portal in the forests of Caegwen. After having observed it for three months, they noted that once every full moon, the portals open and these foul beasts pour out until the morning sun closes the portal," he continued.

"This is not exclusive to Caegwen, however, as there are portals in every country, we just found ours first. We are still unsure why this is happening on such a consistent basis. We currently lack the manpower to make any attempts at closing them. The only foreseeable way to close such breaches in our realm is through extraordinarily strong spells, though other suggestions are more than welcome," he said, glancing around the room.

"My mages are tirelessly working on ways to close the aforementioned, however, any recent attempt at closing it has failed drastically, resulting in the deaths of more than a few of my warriors," he said, with a drop of tone towards the end of his sentence. "Regrettable as their downfalls are, we must move on. I propose that my mages work in conjunction with the others scattered around the Continent, so that we can put an end to these incursions," he said with conviction.

"I agree, your majesty," the Master said, raising a hand. "The more people we have working on how to close them, the sooner results will come. However, I must ask the following: How do the portals open, and are they two-way or one-way portals?" he asked. "We believe them to be two-way," Elhael replied. "However, none of my men thus far have had the courage to attempt to go into one," he said dejectedly.

"I believe we should mount a party of the bravest men and women, volunteers of course, to go in and at the very minimum see if it is in fact a two-way portal," Bashir said, raising his hand. Leona instantly turned her head towards him. He was the son of King Bashaa, and a good-looking man overall; tanned, dark haired, with pale green eyes. His close-cut hair and beard showed he cared much for his appearance. His warrior past had given him a strong and able body to match, so it was no small wonder why she'd be interested in him.

"I don't entirely disagree with you, Prince Bashir," Elhael said. "However, I must ask you where you may find such valiant folk to pull that off," he said with curiosity. "We could always let Mideia do it," said someone not seated at the table.

My brother and I winced at the exact same time.

An old, hooded man stepped out from behind Truls' guardsmen, and began making his way towards the table. He was hooded, with the sign of the Church's sword and staff sewn into his robes. The hems were dirty, and the areas around his knees were well worn out from kneeling often. His face was wrinkled as unfolded clothes, and his beard looked like a gray cloud. His eyes were pale and gray, yet saw more than most.

"Mideia will save us," the old man began saying. "He has always been there for us in our times of need, and he will be with us now," he said with conviction. "Father Mourtis. How nice of you to join us," Truls said courteously. "Who is this man and what is he doing in a war council if he is a priest?" King Bashaa asked angrily. "This is the high priest of the Church of Mideia," the Master said.

"That's all well and good, but what is he doing in a war council?" Bashaa asked once more, more angrily than before. "Essentially, my Lords, they want the eradication of all things deemed evil by their god," the Master said. "Unfortunately for the followers of Mideia, smiting evil hasn't exactly been on his *to-do list* of late," the Master said with a grin.

Mourtis was white with rage. "How *dare* you blaspheme against the one true god who stands above the rest, you non-believer?" he began, screaming at the top of his lungs. "*Non-believer?*" the Master asked calmly. "I *know* that there are many gods, I simply don't believe yours is the most powerful," he continued calmly. Mourtis furrowed his brow. "Mark my words: He will smite you down with bolts from the sky, and brimstone from the deepest corners of the Underworld," he bellowed threateningly.

"Have you ever been to the Underworld before, priest?" the Master asked calmly. Mourtis was surprised by the question. "N-no, I have not! Of course not! What a ridiculous notion!" he retorted. "Well, if you had, you would have known there is no brimstone there, and that it is also not geometric in shape, I might add," the Master began. "I don't know for sure how powerful Mideia is, or what *bullshit* you spue to your followers, but if you think he could strike me down, I'd love to see him try," said the Master threateningly.

Mourtis was taken aback, while the rest of us, Bernar and Roburn included, stifled our laughter at the prospect of the Master verbally demolishing this priest. Mourtis' eyes burned with a fire no one had seen or even guessed the old man had.

"Calm down, you two," Elhael interjected, his voice raised just enough to get their attention. "Bickering over such menial things is pointless right now. Let us focus on what we must do to rid ourselves of these beasts," he concluded.

"He's right. It may be entertaining to the rest of us to watch the High Priest squirm, but King Elhael has a point, nevertheless," Bernar chimed in, giving the elven king a knowing nod which was returned in kind. Everyone calmed back down, and the sound of light laughter faded. Mourtis was glaring at the Master who kept a straight face the whole time.

Just then, I felt an urge of mana flowing through the room, but I couldn't pinpoint it due to all of the other casters in the room. I tapped Bernar's shoulder, "I think we've got a problem here," I whispered. "I felt it too," Bernar began, leaning in a little closer. "But this is a war council, and there's not a single turtle shit I can do about it without starting an all-out war over breaking tradition," he said while looking around the room.

I'd best keep an eye out for anything that seems suspicious. I didn't like the feel of that. Not one bit, I thought, scanning the room for anything out of the ordinary.

"Well, then," King Mads began in a grunty voice after clearing his throat. "We need options, and fighting like dogs over meat about what to do won't solve our problem. I agree with sending a party as King Bashaa had suggested before, however as to how we will acquire such brave people might be more complicated than we think," he said, looking at everyone in the room inquisitively.

"Advertising a certain amount of gold per person willing to go might do the trick," Leona said, forcing everyone to turn their attention towards her. Bashir's eyes opened wide as he blatantly stared at her.

If his facial features could write words, they would have something regarding how beautiful she is strewn across them, I thought, noticing the man's obvious lack of lustful disguise.

"I agree with Queen Leona, though it will take no small amount to convince young men and women to take up a task that they might not return from," Elhael said. "The proper amount for each willing person will be decided in accordance with whether they have family and before the actual test takes place," Truls said.

"So, we are all in agreement on this happening, I take it?" Bashaa asked, gazing around the room briefly. "I believe so," Elhael replied. "All in favor say *aye*," Leona called out. A unanimous *aye* resounded from every man and woman present, and all looked towards Truls.

"Then, my dear gentlemen and ladies present, I believe our council here is finished for the moment. We will reconvene after lunch," Truls declared. "Kings Elhael, Bashaa, Mads and I shall meet once again to discuss the economic viability for each country," Truls said. The four nodded to each other and began to move away from the table. "All are now excused," Fulco called out, and showed the leaders to the door.

As we were leaving the room, Mourtis stopped the Master, and began speaking to him privately. I took note of the expression the High Priest had on his face during their conversation.

Damn it, I can't hear what they're saying. Although, judging by how intense the High Priest seems, it almost looks like he's threatening the Master, I thought.

Just then, a servant came up to me and interrupted my thoughts. "Young master," the servant said. "Your friend is awake and is asking to see you and the others," he said with excitement. My eyes opened wide at the news, and I curtly nodded my head. "Thank you for the news! It's much appreciated," I said briefly, running off taking Bernar, Irun and Batch along with me.

Just before I left the council room, I saw Leona staring at Bashir, who tried to avoid staring back, but had a hard time keeping his eyes off her. "Come, my sweet," Truls said, putting his hand on her shoulder. She shuddered in what looked like disgust, but began to walk alongside the king.

That was weird, I thought, but quickly dismissed that line of thinking, as I had a new focus in mind.

I ran into the nursery, and almost knocked over a healer or two on the way in. I found my friend, though only one eye was open. "Thoma," he said weakly. "Edryd! You're...you're...," I didn't want to finish. "No, I'm not *blind in one eye* if that's what you were going to say. It's just a bit hard to open it with all the clotted blood around it," he said. "I'm relieved to hear that," I said. "Well, it could have been much worse," Batch began. "You could have lost your prick," he said with a chuckle. Edryd wheezed heavily from the pain that was laughing, but he still had a smile on his face.

"So, tell me," Edryd began. "What happened?" he asked with genuine curiosity. The other boys and I began telling of the battle and council, while in the meantime Bernar was warming up to a nearby nurse.

She rejected him shortly after he began speaking.

After a few hours of talking about their experiences the previous day and on that day, we bid farewell and a speedy recovery to Edryd, and went to our dormitory. I sat down on a bench in the bathing area and went over the information and all of the things I had seen that day.

What the hell was that mana burst? I thought.

CHAPTER 5

Valdis

Far in the northern region of Hjalfar, where travelers are seldom seen, a citadel lay deep in the mountains. A man dressed in a long, black robe meandered the vast halls of the long-forgotten citadel, Valdis. He eventually seated himself in a throne located in a large hall, and made use of the arm rests that had been built into it.

His long, black robe draped over the edges, while the holes and tears near the hem gently kissed the floor. Around his neck hung a necklace with an eye carved into a small, round crystal.

As he sat, he stared straight ahead of him from under his hood, through the eye-slits in his mask, as a deep, purple glow shone through. He pondered about the world outside his fortress, as it had been years since he had been in a town or castle.

He sighed at the memories that returned, and his breath that seeped through the mask formed a small vapor cloud in front of him.

His eyes glowed more intensely, and he lifted his hand, transforming the small cloud into what resembled a talon. He spun it around in midair for a short time, gazing at its complexity and perfection, whilst boosting his own self-esteem. He soon became bored of it, and dismantled the vaporous claw - making it disappear into thin air.

I grow tired of waiting for that idiot to return, he thought. *Perhaps I should remind him why he's still alive,* he grinned maliciously, pleased with the thought.

He looked about him once more, the thin layer of mist on the stone floor indicating it must have been a colder day than usual, though he never felt cold of any kind at all. He looked upward and saw the high-arched hallways that lead to chambers only he knew of.

The citadel had its highest peak above his throne, and the deep, violet hue scattered throughout the hall. It lit up the walls of bent horns made from an unknown metal, which hung the heads of various types of formidable creatures. Wyrms, ochelons, glicks, and many other types of such beast trophies were present.

These creatures were once heralded as the greatest in the Continent. Now, look at them. Reduced to nothing but trophies, staring into the abyss of an unforgiving world, praying nothing stares back at them; but I am, he thought.

He formed the claw once again, and this time struck one of the trophies off its hook with a rapid strike, shaking the entire hall to include the skeleton of a wyrm that was poised behind the throne. The hall grew dark once more, soaked in its violet hue. Suddenly, he heard footsteps coming from the end of the hall.

Ah, the prodigal idiot, he thought.

The young man came up to the foot of the steps that led to the throne, ignoring the destroyed trophy nearby, and kneeled. "My lord, I bring news from Coltend," the young man said, visibly exhausted.

"Catch your breath and be out with it, boy," the Masked One

said, his voice sounding like thunder rolling across the sky. Athar, the young man, breathed heavily for a few beats, his long dark hair rising and falling along with his broad shoulders.

"My lord, the kings of the Continent have decided to join forces to find a way to close the portals," he said nervously. "Ah, so that's why the council had been called," the Masked One realized. "Fools. They should have tried that centuries ago, when monsters first entered the realm and the gods still gave a damn about them," he said ironically.

The young man shuddered.

"But tell me, boy," the Masked One began, "King Truls still rules in Coltend, does he not?" "He does, my lord," the young man replied. "*Ah*, I'm surprised that the arrogant narcissist has decided to take action for once," the Masked One said. "Not only you," the young man said under his breath. The Masked One didn't hear the comment, and if he did, he simply didn't care much for it.

"You have done well, for once," the Masked One said. "Come with me, I'd like to show you something," he continued. "Might I ask what it is you would like to show me, my lord?" the young man said. "No," the Masked One replied, almost cutting the young man off. "Simply follow me, and you will see," he said impatiently.

The Masked One got up from his throne and began to walk down the steps, going past the young man who was still kneeling. His dark robe dragged across the floor, following his every step. The young man rose to his feet and followed closely behind. "You know, you're the first non-beast I've ever shown this part of my tower," the Masked One said to the young man.

"I'm honored, my lord," Athar replied. The Masked One undid the mana ward placed on it, causing it to open. The open path before them could only be described as a spiraling path to the Underworld itself. Down at the bottom of the stairway, a blood-red light flickered.

Athar gazed downwards to the bottom, and could only hope to think that whatever was there wasn't meant for him, for the sounds he could hear resonating through the unlit hallway were gut wrenching. "Come," the Masked One said and began down the stairway. Athar was reluctant to follow.

I don't have much of a choice here. We all die someday, I suppose, he thought and followed behind his master.

About halfway down, the light at the bottom went from a deep crimson to violet as the Masked One approached the entrance.

The entrance had a marking in runes above it that served as another mana ward to keep anything from trying to get out. The Masked One passed through it as though it were only a filament of water, but Athar had a hard time working through it, until the Masked One lowered his ward for a moment. "I had forgotten you are not as strong as I am," he said with an air of displeasure.

It's your mana, after all, Athar muttered in his thoughts.

Athar looked around him and noticed the walls of the spiral soon became cages.

These go from smallest to largest - the smallest of these is about as large as a small cabin, he gathered.

Inside the cages, were beasts - both magnificent and terrifying ones. Some of the monsters tried to break the bars to their cages whenever they walked past one. Growls, snorts, sneers, and maniacal cackles were the order of the day between the beasts.

"They can't reach you from there, but I'd keep an eye on the addia over there," the Masked One said, pointing at a large, empty cage. The young man looked over at it, but failed to see anything. He decided to move a step closer to see if his eyes had betrayed him.

Suddenly, the monster seemed to appear out of thin air, and reached out with one of its two long tentacles. Its brown, leathery skin was coated in a nearly transparent gelatin, and its lidless eyes glowed a bright green with rounded pupils

It smacked the ground between it and its would-be prey. Athar jumped back in fright, managing to dodge the attack. "You are an idiot indeed," the Masked One said with disappointment. "If I say *don't go anywhere near something*, I damn well mean it, now move along," he said angrily.

I can't believe something like that exists! I just barely saw the tentacle coming, and almost fucking died! The Synners must be incredible to fight something like that, Athar exclaimed in his mind.

He scurried up to his master, and tried to not disobey him again.

They made their way down the spiral to the final cage, passing all kinds of beasts and creatures that he had only ever heard of in legends. When they reached the final cage, he began to realize why the creature inside the cage was all the way at the bottom. Within it lay a royal ochelon. Majestic, yet threatening. All he could do was stare in awe.

"Beautiful, isn't it?" the Masked One said. "Very much so, my lord," Athar said whilst admiring the beast. It stood about sixty meters tall, with pale, white fur and a horn on its forehead.

Like a cross between a unicorn and an ogre, but more threatening, he thought.

"You may be wondering why I've brought you here to see the horde beneath this place," the Masked One said, glancing over toward his servant. Athar could only nod his head. "I've come to show you what true power *really* looks like," he said. "My lord, this is an incredible beast, to be sure, though why you keep them in cages is beyond me," the young man began. "I have always assumed - being as powerful as you are - that you could control them, regardless of whether they're in a cage," he concluded.

"I *can*," his master replied. "Although, the expenditure of mana is quite high. I'd rather keep them where I won't have to use it perpetually until I find another way of controlling them," the Masked One explained. "But that is beside the point," he began, shaking his head. "I've brought you here to see how well you would handle yourself amidst such creatures. Showing any signs of weakness is probably the quickest way to being eaten by them," he said.

Athar swallowed dryly.

"It seems as though you are comfortable enough around them. Although, your lack of experience is... telling," the Masked One said. "I've had my fair share of experiences with beasts, although I should mention that an *addia* was not on that list, my lord," Athar explained. "Ah. Well, you won't make the same mistake twice, will you?" the Masked One asked ironically. "Of course, my lord," the man replied. "Good. That is the very least I expect from a bastard like you," his master said with disgust. He could feel the sting of those words, but said nothing.

"My lord," he began after a short break in their conversation. "What is it?" his master asked. "I'm assuming you have some sort of plan to disrupt Truls' plans to destroy the portals," Athar said matter-of-factly. "I do indeed," the Masked One replied. "However, there is one final thing I need to be sure of before I show you what that will be," he said and turned to stare his 'idiot slave' in the eyes.

With his master's hand placed on his chest, he closed his eyes in fear. "Look me in the eyes," the Masked One said. Athar reluctantly gazed into the glowing of his master's eyes through the small slits in the mask, and felt an unease he had never felt before.

I can feel him digging into my soul, like a parasite writhing to make its way out of the body, he thought.

His thoughts began to race, though it was not by his command. Rather, it was the work of his master. Worrying that he might have suppressed a memory his master wouldn't like, he tried to follow his own thoughts; going over every memory, every emotion, every heart-breaking moment.

The Masked One found what he was looking for, and pulled his hand away from his chest.

After what felt like an eternity, he released Athar from his grasp, and the *idiot* nearly fell to the floor, gasping for air. "H-how?" he asked shakily. The Masked One held up a dark blue orb of pure mana he had retrieved from Athar's chest. The young man's palms began to sweat, and with his knees buckling at the sheer pressure of having his soul dug into, he strained to stay on his feet. The Masked One glared at the sphere for a moment, as if confirming he had everything he needed. He looked at his servant, and smiled wickedly beneath his mask.

He was right.

"I hope you're ready for what I'm about to show you, Athar. Your cooperation just now will be one of the keys to our success," the Masked One said, condensing the small sphere of mana into the palm of his hand.

That's the first time he's called me by my name. Then again, I don't think he ever asked for it. Did he only find out after digging through my soul? Athar thought.

"What do you want to show me, my lord?" he asked with an air of caution, still shaking from the spell. The Masked One didn't reply, but proceeded to undo the ward on the royal ochelon's cage. Just as the ward was dispelled, a rune made of mana appeared on the creature's head to control it. "Follow me," the Masked One commanded. The creature exited the cage in a zombie-like state. "That means you too, Athar," he continued.

I should be astonished at his abilities, but after having felt him dig through my soul, I can only imagine what this creature is going through, he thought.

Just behind the cage was a door that led to an incredibly large summoning circle. Through the slits of his mask, his eyes glowed an even deeper violet, as the tendrils that once flowed from them were drawn into his eyes as he *reached into the Underworld. Though its use was not as widespread as that of the Ethereal realm, it still held its own power. A dark and devastating power, one granted to him from the Undergod, Volzuk.*

He looked about him and saw the exact inverse of the Ethereal's spiral above him. The streaks of power were dark and nearly lifeless, except for bolts of lightning that sewed their ways though the streaks. They moved about in a monochromatic dance, one streak weaving into the other, all heading towards a dark circle in the middle of the sky far above him. Around him lay a dead forest.

Trees lay fallen about him, while bones and oozy smells stung his nostrils. With every step he took, a burst of ash-like powder engulfed his feet and ankles. To his right lay a river of blood, where carcasses of fallen beasts were strewn upon the sides. Off in the distance, he heard the desperate screams of a glick being devoured by another, but paid it no heed.

It was a wonder in and of itself that anything could survive there at all.

He looked up at the dark circle in the sky, and reached. Dark tendrils of mana voraciously swarmed down and engulfed him faster than the ones in the Ethereal had gone to Thoma, however, he had many more decades of experience and excellent control. When he had drawn enough, he cut his link to the underworld, and his eyes brightened once more.

He condensed the dark cloud to his left hand, where he formed a large, scarlet claw and drew it back. "What do you plan to do with that, my lord?" Athar asked nervously. "This," the Masked one said, grinning beneath his mask. The claw rapidly struck the royal ochelon's chest, but the creature didn't react. After a few seconds of astonishment, the man noticed the blood that had spilled onto the floor moving into the air where it became stationary.

Just then, a mist of mana began to seep from the creature's body, eventually bursting it into chunks of meat. The blood, sinew, and entrails were flung around the room by the explosion, as well as Athar's face.

He let out a yell of disgust, and vomited his breakfast from earlier that morning. "What the actual fuck?" he asked, desperate for an answer other than 'just for fun'. "Stop being so weak and look," the Masked One said, visibly disturbed by his servant's attitude. He was also covered in entrails and blood, but he had to maintain his focus on the task at hand.

Athar looked over at the claw that had impaled the beast and noticed a glowing, red orb in its grasp. "What... is that?" he asked, astounded at the sight in front of him. "This is a core," the Masked One said. "A core?" the man asked incredulously.

"Yes, though it is more commonly referred to as a soul. You see, the core - or soul - and the body are not one and the same. It is made of pure mana, and bodies - like ours - are not. It can be altered, broken, repaired, or even transformed into something else entirely," the Masked one began.

Why does he sound... sad? Athar thought.

"The core is often considered the heart of any living plant or creature, though the core resides within the heart and is not the heart itself. Some creatures have more than one core and heart, making actions like this a bit more challenging. By removing the core, the rest of the body becomes practically useless unless its core is returned. If you destroy the body *while* removing its core, then it has nothing to command, thereby allowing one full control over it provided you have the skill," the Masked One explained.

Athar was stunned. "So, what you're saying is that the core is what controls the body? Is it not the brain of the creature that does that?" he asked. "In essence, the brain performs the bodily functions needed for things like eating, speech, and movement. The core is what commands the brain to perform those actions. A body cannot function without its core, but the core has its own properties that allow it to exist autonomously," the Masked One answered.

"I think I'm beginning to understand, my lord," Athar said, still trying to wrap his head around the concept. "But what purpose does a core have without a body to make use of its commands?" he asked.

His master chuckled malevolently.

"Observe," he stated as he outstretched the hand holding what he had taken from his slave, and began to meld it into the ochelon's core. The two spheres collided, exchanging mana in a beautifully colorized dance. The result produced a purple aura around the core.

I can't believe my eyes. What is this feeling? I... his train of thought was interrupted by his master.

"What do you feel?" the Masked One asked. "I-I wish I could explain it, my lord. I can feel a *part* of me is present, like a familiar doppelganger of sorts, but one that does not *belong* to me anymore," Athar attempted to explain.

"That is because it doesn't. Not anymore, at least. Remember, the core and the body are separate from each other. What I have done is taken a piece of your core - a few of your memories, to be exact - and infused it with the creature's," the Masked One began. "You see, there are various forms of magic and mana in this world, many of which I do not have the time nor patience to explain right now. Those fools in their castles think there is only the kind that the Synners have. However, I am going to show them what true power is as the herald of *my* master's second coming," he said.

His master? A second coming? When was the first? Athar thought.

"You look confused," the Masked One said, tilting his head slightly. "I am, indeed, my lord," he replied. "This is precisely why I needed you to see this. You're going to help me, as you are one of the catalysts needed for it to happen," he said with a dark tone. Athar swallowed hard, and nodded his head. "That's why you took a piece of my core - *my memories,*" the young man said, finally understanding.

"Originally, I did not think you would have much more involvement in this matter, but your past is going to play a vital role. I was commanded, and now so are you. You don't have a choice anymore, Athar," the Masked One said, looking him dead in the eye. "If you did, I'm certain you wouldn't remain here in the north, serving someone you loathe," he continued.

Athar could say nothing in return.

"I own you, as I have since the day you arrived here in Valdis. But now, we both serve a much higher purpose, and an even darker power," the Masked one said in an unusual tone. Athar felt a chill go up his spine, and it made the hairs on the back of his neck stand up.

The Masked One turned away from the young man, facing the claw that still held the purple orb. He brought the claw close, and after taking a deep breath, plunged the claw into his own chest. The orb was absorbed into his body, and the effect was immediate.

Mana began to flow throughout his body, as he spread his arms wide, allowing it to envelop him entirely. His old robes and scratched mask were rejuvenated, and he grew about a palm taller.

Athar stepped back with eyes opened wide, watching his master contort while his physical structure changed in front of him. The Masked One's fingers began to turn a light shade of gray, and his nails began to look more like the beast's claws. The young man could barely believe his eyes.

How is this possible? he wondered.

A few seconds later, the Masked One regained his composure, and admired his newfound look. He noticed Athar had stepped a little further away, and rightfully so, as the sight he had just beheld was terrifying to say the least. An elongated and satisfied sigh resounded throughout the massive room. The Masked One looked at his hands, now modified from the ochelon's core.

He stretched his arms, and grew accustomed to their new weight and overall appearance. He moved his fingers about, feeling their newfound strength, and nodded with satisfaction. "Whatever core you decide to internalize, you gain some of the original host's attributes," he explained, his voice a little deeper than it was before. "The attributes received are generally randomized, but all in all contain the essence of the creature. This..." he paused, turning his hand into a fist.

This is how it begins, he thought, as Athar recoiled a little further from him.

He was already terrifying before, but now, just being in his presence is something else entirely, the young man noted, still moving away.

"What is our next step, my lord?" he asked, still growing accustomed to his master's new visage. The Masked One turned to face his subordinate. "Many of these creatures are territorial by nature, and often get into brawls if left unchecked. However, that is not to say they cannot be controlled, as you saw with the ochelon," he began. "I'm sure that, by now, you've noticed the summoning circle beneath our feet," he stated.

"I have. Although I'm not entirely sure what you're going to do with it, my lord." Athar replied shakily. "Stand back," his master ordered him.

The Masked One *gathered dark mana once more,* and snapped his finger. A deep rumbling shook the ground, as the circle began to glow with the same violet color as his eyes. Large, diamond-shaped crystals began to sprout from within the circle. He began to channel his mana into these crystals. "This circle's purpose is to bring these from the Underworld, as they hold special properties unique to that place," he began to explain.

"As I've said before, controlling these creatures one by one is difficult, and so I have devised a way to cut out my need for direct control. The royal ochelon's core, now infused with my own, will leave its mark on the mana I imbue. It takes some time to fully charge them, but it can be done passively - another benefit of using the circle with my mana signature. All creatures must bow to something more powerful than they are. It is embedded in their instincts. By using the mana within these crystals to power the spell I cast on the horde, they will answer to me, and only me. Do you understand?" the Masked One explained.

"Yes, my lord," Athar replied, nodding his head. "Good. I have one last thing I need to show you. Come with me," he told his subordinate.

They exited the large room, and proceeded down a hall to their left. A doorway at the end of the hall led to yet another large room that appeared to be filled with nests and eggs from the creatures held within the citadel. Athar could hardly make out what he was seeing, given the dim lighting of the room. His master noticed his strenuous attempt to see all that was before him, and infused him with a bit of mana, allowing him to see more clearly in the dark.

Athar's eyes opened wide with astonishment. The nests not only hit the ceiling, but they extended to the end of a hall that turned out to be nearly as large as a small farm. "By the gods both light and dark, what is this?" Athar asked. He could barely speak the words, as his thoughts began to run rampant. "This, Athar, is a breeding ground," the Masked One said. "A *what*, my lord?" Athar asked.

"The Undergod and I have been working in tandem for many a century now, and he has given me new ways of bringing hordes of beasts into this realm," he explained. "So, you mean to breed hordes of the beasts and unleash them on the countries?" Athar asked. "Precisely. Throwing those idiots in their castles for a loop when they realize the portals aren't the only way these creatures emerge," the Masked One said mockingly.

They ventured deeper into the hall, and Athar soon found himself wandering around, observing all the different kinds of nests and eggs that were present. Eventually, he stumbled upon one of the eggs that had fallen to the floor beside one of the larger nests.

What are you doing down here, little one? He thought as he reached for it.

"Step back," the Masked One commanded Athar who instinctively did just that. His eyes glowed once more as he outstretched his left hand. Mana could be seen gathering in the palm of his hand, as he said a few words. Slowly and carefully, he encased the egg in mana, putting it back where it belonged. Suddenly, the egg burst with mana-flame, blinding Athar, and scorched the nest in which it lay.

Out of the smoke and burst of heat, they heard a grunt and a snort. Athar uncovered his now stinging eyes to see a small fire golem, covered in ash and flame staring up into their eyes.

"Magnificent creatures aren't they?" the Masked One asked. "Once they are old enough, they have been known to breathe fire, although only a few recorded cases exist," he said with some disappointment. "I thought only wyrms were capable of that, my lord," Athar said while staring at the golem's features. Its eyes were pure amber, and its body was a mixture of volcanic stone and flame. Within its mouth, burned a white flame hot enough to melt anything the golem would bite into.

Athar couldn't tear his eyes from it.

"Wyrms are the most common creatures to have that talent, but there are other beasts which just so happen to have that same gift," the Masked One explained. The golem lay down in its nest of ash and stone, and fell asleep during his explanation. "Come, we must let him grow to at least half his size before he is ready for battle," the Masked One said. He led his slave over to the next oversized nests across the way, and cast once more, only this time, a frigid wind flowed from the center, and nearly froze Athar's boots solid.

Within the thatch, there lay a small ice golem. White and light blue crystals formed its general complexion, while its eyes were as black as night. Athar looked at each of the golems with awe.

He had never seen one before, much less two different types in the same day.

"They will hold their own, and spawn new ones of their own ilk every eight weeks, for they do not need sustenance other than mana," the Masked One said. Athar looked at the two and shook his head to make sure he wasn't dreaming.

He wasn't.

After feeding the pair of golems some of his own mana, the Masked One turned towards his servant. "The time has come at last," he said ominously, interrupting Athar's focus on the pair of small creatures. His confused expression gave him away. "We must speak with him," the Masked One said. "Him?" Athar asked, stepping away from the pair. "The Undergod," his master replied with an air of severity.

Athar felt his stomach do a somersault.

CHAPTER 6

The Return to Codrean

A week had passed since the first day of the council, and most of us were fairly satisfied with our stay. Many went to the main market where all sorts of items, trinkets, and elixirs could be purchased at reasonable prices.

Edryd, who had finally recovered from his wounds and was able to walk, went with Batch and I to the market the morning we were meant to leave. Irun and a few others had gone back to Codrean a day prior to scout the roads ahead in case of another incident.

We roamed the market early in the morning while the stalls were still being set up, buying trinkets and other mementos we could bring with us on our journey home. In the meantime, the Master and the other Synners were gathering their gear and packing their newly acquired items. There wasn't a lot of time left before we would have to ride back to our fortress, so most of the others were grabbing their gear and packing their horses.

After about an hour or two of scouring the marketplace, we were making our way back from the main marketplace, when we noticed everyone was nearly finished packing. "Shit, we took too long. We should hurry," I said, urging my friends to pick up the pace. We rushed to gather our belongings to avoid being left behind. Batch, after having gathered his own small amount of gear, helped Edryd with his.

"*Ah*, I was beginning to wonder when you bastards would show face. Have a fun night out on the town?" Bernar asked sarcastically, having noticed us scurrying about. "How much longer before we set off?" I asked, ignoring the shit-eating grin on my older brother's face. "Not much longer than you think, so hurry up," Bernar responded. "It's not as if we knew we'd have to leave today," Edryd shot back. "Yeah. Normally we have at least a twelve-hour warning before we go anywhere," Batch chimed in. "We *did* have one, we just fucked up and should have kept a better track of the time we spent outside," I said regretfully.

"Well, the Master has declared that we should leave as soon as possible, so I gave out orders for everyone to pack their shit up and get going immediately," Bernar said with a shrug. "We weren't informed of that," Edryd began, as we all looked to each other for confirmation. "I'm sure that's because we weren't even here in the first place," I said, not having any other answer.

"Where the hell were you guys, anyway?" Bernar asked. "We were at the market," I replied matter-of-factly. "Uh-huh. Pray tell, doing what, exactly?" my brother asked, completely unconvinced of my response. "I'm serious, we were! We bought trinkets and such for ourselves," I replied quickly, producing a small sackcloth bag and waving it in front of him. "Shouldn't you have done that yesterday?" Bernar asked, swatting the bag aside.

"Ed's shoulder has only just gotten better, and we were not going there without him," I replied. "Now, if you'll excuse us, big brother, we've got to finish *packing up our shit and get going* 'before the Master verbally and morally destroys us," I continued. "Alright, alright. On your way, *young ones,*" Bernar said through a small burst of laughter.

We made our flight down the hallways and up the stairways that led to our chambers. We quickly gathered our gear, which, once again, was hanging on their bedsides, cleaned and dried; just like the first morning they had been there. I found a note pinned to my jerkin, and unfolded it to read the contents.

Remember me, please. Yours, M. I read, scratching my head to try to figure out who the hell this *M* was.

The words had been messily scribbled on the small parchment. I looked around to see if I could find whoever wrote it, but to no avail. I figured it must have been the servant girl from the first night, as it was the only person who made any sense in my head for it to be.

Damn it, what was her name again? Melanie? Marissa? I struggled to recall her name, scratching the back of my head in brief contemplation.

I haven't seen her since that night, and I doubt I'll be returning here anytime soon, I sighed. *By that time, she'll probably have found someone who will want to take her hand in marriage or whatever it is people do these days. It saddens me to think that I'll probably never get to see her again, but her beauty has left its mark in my memories. Don't think I could ever forget her, even without the note asking me not to,* I thought, chuckling lightly to myself.

I scribbled my own note, folded it, and left it on my pillow, praying she would find it. I placed her note in my riding bag in a pocket where I was sure it wouldn't be wrinkled or torn. The others finished gathering their things and I noticed no one else had gotten a note. I chuckled and grinned from ear to ear, thinking I, momentarily, was privileged.

We rushed downstairs to our horses and tied our bags to our

saddles. We looked about for the Master, but he was nowhere to be seen. Garett was already mounted and called for attention. "Listen up, you lot," he began as everyone turned to face him. "We're heading back to Codrean, and the Master has given both myself and Bernar explicit instructions to go ahead without him. He will catch up to us soon enough," he said. We all looked at one another, as this was both unprecedented and unusual behavior for the Master.

Something's not right, I thought, trying to piece together any semblance of reason I could.

"Let's move!" Garett called out. We spurred our horses, and began to follow him out of the large gate before us. Just as we were about to cross the threshold, I thought it might be a good idea to get one last look at the palace itself. It was beautiful in its design, to be sure, but I quickly noticed something even more beautiful stood in one of the lower windows.

That's her! I thought, barely able to see her through the reflection of the glass.

She was, apparently, looking for me as well, as she held up the note I'd left her and waved it from side to side. Her hair was tied up in a strip of cloth that wrapped around her forehead and covered her ears, tying itself together at the back. She found me amid the other riders and our eyes met.

I humbly nodded to the figure in the window. My eyesight was good, but I only noticed the tear running down the left side of her face a little too late. I felt I had no choice but to continue on ahead, not looking back another time lest my heart drop further. I couldn't figure out why she was crying, after all she had only known me for about a week, but I was sure I wasn't going to get an answer any time soon.

After riding for the better part of an hour, I could feel the sun's early rays begin to warm my back. The air was still a little chilly, and I was certainly more than happy to feel those rays welcoming me into their embrace.

Just as I was about to get lost in a daydream of my muse, I heard hooves thumping in the distance, ones that didn't quite match the pace we were at. I glanced over my shoulder to see what it was, and sure enough I saw a familiar person coming towards us at nearly a full gallop.

The Master had finally caught up to our group.

"Well, well. I'd say it's about half past the time you were supposed to catch up to us," Garett was saying while the Master rode up to his side. "My apologies, I had some rather unpleasant business to attend to back at the palace," the Master said, his eyes glowing like they would whenever he was angry. Bernar noticed, and shot a nod back to me, even though I had already guessed as much.

"Well, aren't you glad that's over and done with," Garett said cheerfully. "I suppose I am, indeed. Although I doubt that that was the end of it," the Master said. Garett raised an eyebrow, and shrugged soon after. "*Bah*. With all due respect, Master, *fuck them sideways*," Garett said. "Tell me, for I'm certain you must know more than I regarding them, what *respect* are they due?" the Master said angrily.

"I meant with respect to *you*," Garett said calmly. "But to answer your question: Not even the amount a beetle can shit," he said. "Glad to hear we're on the same page," the Master said, finally calming down a little. Garett, who had known the master since he was a boy, knew his personality well enough to be the only one able to calm him down in times like these.

I wonder what happened back there, I thought after their brief exchange.

We rode on for a few more hours, eventually stopping for lunch beneath the shade of a few pine trees that lined the path.

After washing down the dried meats and bread with a bit of ale Fulco gracefully sent us off with. After our meal was finished, we tidied up, and kept on toward the fortress. When we were about a league away from the main fortress, I felt something I'd never felt before; like a pebble scratching at my core. Shortly after, I spotted a silhouette against the nearly setting sun.

What's a raven doing out here? I wondered, calculating its trajectory, trying and failing to properly shield my eyes.

It wasn't that ravens were rare, by any means, but since they were normally used as rapid forms of written communication, they often required special permissions to leave their homes. Those, however, were usually easily identifiable with the leather pouches they carried.

I can't see if it was a messenger raven with the sun making my eyes water. It did come from the direction of the fortress, but it might just be nothing, I thought, shrugging it off as I rubbed my stinging eyes after staring almost straight into the sun.

About a kilometer outside of Codrean, Bernar and I both spotted a second raven flying overhead in the same direction as the last.

"Brother," I whispered, leaning forward in hopes that he could hear me. "I saw it. Was there one before it?" Bernar asked, turning in his saddle to face me. "There was, but I had assumed it to be nothing more than a lone raven since I couldn't see it well enough with the sun beaming into my eyes," I replied. "Shit," my brother muttered.

I didn't quite understand my brother's preoccupation at the moment, so I leaned in to see if I could hear what Bernar was telling the Master. The Master quickly snapped his head towards him and then back towards me.

What the fuck is happening right now? I thought, confused at the odd exchange.

I was taken aback by the intensity of the glare. I also had no idea what was going on, making everything that much worse, thinking I had done something wrong. An unsettling feeling began to brew in my stomach, as I watched the Master whisper back to Bernar, who nodded in agreement and slowed his horse who shook its head from the pull on the reins.

"Little brother, I need to tell you a few things once we arrive. *Do not* let anyone else know where you are going after I do so, do you understand?" Bernar asked with a seriousness that was not like him at all. "I do," I replied, still uncertain of the reason behind the request. "Good," Bernar said and rode back up to the Master's side, continuing an inaudible discussion.

"I'm not entirely sure of what just happened, but I'm going to assume it was nothing good," Edryd said, having kept an eye on the whole exchange. He had been riding next to me the whole way, after all.

During our return to Codrean, he and I talked about my adventures in the castle and the run-in with the servant girl. It put Edryd's mind at ease to know that even though he had missed many things, he was still knowledgeable of them.

However, this was clearly something different altogether.

"Damn right about that, Ed," I replied. "I'm guessing you can't tell me much, if anything at all," Edryd said, almost rhetorically. "I don't even know enough to say anything about it. I'm just as confused as you are, if I'm being honest," I replied, upturning my lower lip and giving him a shrug.

Edryd simply nodded his head, and looked onward. Batch was close behind, and ended up overhearing most of our conversation. He looked at me for an answer, but when he received nothing but a confused shrug as a response, he merely shook his head and sighed.

We entered the main courtyard to Codrean, where the Master,

Bernar and Garett were clearly in a rush. "Feed and water our horses," the Master called out to one of the nearby servants, who rushed to get his job done as quickly as possible. The Master motioned to me subtly, prompting me to dismount and walk quickly after unlacing my pack from the saddle.

"Sorry about this, Ed, but would you mind taking Celer for me?" I asked. "You're gonna have to tell me what that was all about later," he said with a sly grin, taking my horse by the reins.

I caught up to the Master and the others just before entering the fortress. Down the cold stone corridors and, up the stairs, the four of us went to the Master's office. I rued over the memories of the first time I'd been in the dimly lit room full of books, scrolls, and other strange objects.

The Master seated himself in the carved, wooden chair, and folded his hands together, steepling his fingers together on his chin. Bernar closed the door behind us, and peered out of the eyehole to ensure they didn't have any eavesdroppers.

"How much do we know about this raven, and where did it come from?" he asked bluntly. "I'm afraid there isn't much to tell, Master," Bernar replied, walking from the door. "Thoma told me there had been a second one before the one I saw about half a league out from here," he continued. "Is that so?" the Master asked.

I quickly nodded in agreement, receiving a sigh from the Master in response. "Well, this isn't good news. There *is* one thing I would like to check on, and I think now would be as good a time as any," he said, pushing his fingers away from his chin and giving me a look I couldn't quite put my finger on.

"Thoma, you have not yet atoned for your mishap the other night, so I will have you take this task on yourself. Obviously, Bernar will instruct you on what you'll need to take with you on your investigation, but for the most part, you will do it alone," he said.

Shouldn't something this important be a job for someone more experienced? I thought, recalling the punishment I'd chosen and realizing now that the two were somehow connected.

"Hold on, I'm doing this alone? If it's that important, shouldn't Bernar be coming with me?" I asked, genuinely concerned at both the amount of trust the Master had in me, and whether I'd be able to pull this off.

"Well, yes," the Master replied. "I know of your skills, young as you may be, and so I entrust this task to you. The three of us have other matters to attend to, and you're the only other one we can trust right now," he said calmly. I looked at my brother, who simply nodded reassuringly.

"As you command, Master," I said, looking back at the Master. "Good. Bernar, take him to the armory. Move as soft and quick as shadows, for this is of utmost importance and time is *not* on our side," the Master said.

"I'm sure there's more to you sending him off alone than you're telling us," Master Garett said to the Master. "Of course there is," the Master admitted. "However, there are some things about him that need to be brought out, and this is a good opportunity to do so," he explained, glancing over at me with a wry smile on his face.

"As far as I can tell, there's nothing particularly wrong with the boy," Garett said nonchalantly as if I weren't standing right in front of him. "I'm not saying I can *read minds*, but I *have* seen his progress," the Master began. "Given that he's Bernar's brother, I also know I can trust him to *nearly* the same degree," he continued, giving me a knowing nod.

I would be lying if I didn't feel a bit of pride surge within me.

"As you wish, Master," Garett shrugged, walking over to

the door to let us out. "Don't forget to stay on your toes, lad," Garett called out just before closing the door behind us. I simply raised my hand in acknowledgement.

"Okay. Run that by me again," I said as we were walking down the corridors that led to the gear room. "Run *what* by you again?" Bernar asked. "You know what I mean," I said, beginning to feel that ice-cold fear again.

"I'm supposed to explore the rumored cave on my own, and the only thing I have to go off is that those rumors are true about there being a massive creature inside. Not to mention the fact that I've only been in a real fight once. Is that right?" I asked, not knowing what to think or feel at that moment.

"If you remembered everything I said, why ask me to tell you again?" my brother asked. "*Oh*, I don't know. Maybe because I'm about ready to shit my pants, and then waddle about like some dwarf whose pants are too big for him? Also, what does any of this have to do with the ravens we saw earlier?" I asked.

"Don't worry, and speak less," my brother said comfortingly. "As small of a turd as you are, I'm sure you'll be just fine down there. Besides, it's not like you've never swung a sword before. Simply remember your training, and all will go well," he said, putting his hand on my shoulder.

Bastard ignored my other question, I thought, gulping dryly.

As soon as we arrived at the armory, I was astonished at the number of options before me.

Generally speaking, junior Synners were not allowed inside under normal circumstances. The main reason being that juniors seldom fought in battles, so all we had to do was learn to keep our training gear in proper order and hone our sword-casting; the basics for any Synner. Only when we became seniors would we choose our specialty and actually use it on expeditions.

My eyes sparkled as I glazed over the various sword choices presented before me. There were bows, swords, shields, axes, and spears hanging on all four walls of the room.

I don't think I'd do well to choose a piece of equipment that I'm not familiar with, I thought, moving away from the walls without swords on them.

Most were too long or heavy for me, but the choices I had of long swords, bastard swords, and broadswords was palpable. I picked up a long sword, and began swinging it around, testing its weight. Its black, wire-wrapped hilt fit nicely in my hand as I gripped it tightly.

The sword had a pommel shaped like a bear's head, and a slightly upturned guard perfectly balancing it. It was a stunning piece of work, to say the least, and I knew it would last me a lifetime if properly taken care of. My eyes gleamed with joy and awe, nearly forgetting the reason we were there in the first place.

"Here, let me see that," Bernar said, stretching out his hand. I handed it to him and he looked it over, testing its weight and balance. "It's a good sword and, since I don't believe you'll be growing much taller, I think this is a good choice of weapon," he said. He handed the sword back to me just as I was finishing the last loop of the sheath's strap around my belt. I slid the sword in smoothly, and a satisfying *click* halted the blade.

I smiled like a toddler in a bakery full of sweets.

Bernar walked over to one of the racks, where different sized wooden masks that only covered the top half of one's face were hanging. "Here, you'll need this," Bernar said, putting the tied leather loop around my neck. "What am I supposed to do with this?" I asked, curious about the eyeless mask. "Just put it on," Bernar said almost tiredly. I looked at the oddly shaped mask, and covered my eyes with them, pulling the knot-bead at the back a little tighter to get a snugger fit.

"This is fine. I can't see a fucking thing out of this," I said, rather annoyed. "Give me a second, shit-bird," my brother shot back mercilessly. I sighed and shrugged, accepting my fate.

Bernar's eyes solidified in their golden color as he *reached into the Ethereal to draw mana. His gathered tendrils were* redirected to the palm of his hand, where he shared the cloud with his other hand. He rubbed his hands together, and cast with his first three fingers joined together, moving across the strange-looking mask, engulfing them in mana.

He condensed his cloud into the mask, and suddenly, I felt my jaw drop.

Within the dimly lit gear room, his visual senses were enhanced ten times over. The room itself was no longer a darkened cellar full of weapons beneath the fortress, but a glowing, living one. I could see my own breath move freely through the air, as though it had been lit aflame. The room appeared to be lit by the sun itself, and I could see even the smallest creature from across the room as though it were placed in front of me.

"*Aha!*" I said aloud through a bit of excited laughter. "See? I fucking told you to wait," Bernar said with a grin, flicking my forehead. "You're right, you're right. I should have listened to you. I won't ever doubt you again," I said bashfully.

"It's alright," Bernar said. "Just remember that once they're taken off, the spell will no longer be active, and you'll have to re-cast, do you understand?" he asked. "Yep, got it! Wait, what was the spell again?" I asked through the smile on his face.

Obviously, I wasn't really paying attention.

"We'd better be on our way," Bernar said, ignoring my question. "The darker it gets, the more violent they become," he continued.

They? I wondered.

After leaving the fortress, and about a twenty-minute walk later, we reached a gate at the back of the main fortress that was covered in moss and other flora. Bernar pulled the lever on the door that led outside the wall, and we started down the overgrown path.

Every step I take feels as though my heart will jump out of my mouth and beat upon the floor, I thought nervously, as the reality of my situation was finally kicking in.

I held back the urge to hurl after the first few hundred meters. After about two kilometers, and a few more urges to puke later, we came to a cave in the rocky formation at the base of the nearby mountains. The sun was setting behind the mountains and the air was becoming colder as we stopped at the entrance of the cave.

"Put your *eyes* on. It's gonna be dark in there," Bernar said. I nodded and put them on promptly as I waited for him to activate the mask once more. A smile instantly grew on my face as the vision enhancement was drastically expounded upon now that we were outside.

"I don't think that will ever get old for me," I said through a slight chuckle. "I've been using it for years and it hasn't for me, yet," Bernar said. "But enough talking. It's time to find out what that raven might have sent out, and I need to return to the Master quickly," he continued.

"But why *here* of all places? I mean, it could have come from anywhere in the castle, right?" I asked. Bernar sighed and shook his head. "There are... *items* in there that you will find to be of great value," he began, choosing his words carefully. "Can't you *at least* tell me what they are? Or even what they look like?" I asked, still just as confused as before. "You'll find out once you've slain the *bastards*," Bernar replied. "Now get in there and get some," he said, giving me a slight, encouraging shove.

I nodded in response, but I couldn't help but wonder what was in there. Regardless, I drew my sword, and passed beneath the entrance to the cave.

This is it. I don't fully understand why I'm supposed to do this on my own, much less why anyone hasn't slain whatever is in here already, but I've got to survive this. Survive. That's the key. Yeah, I should focus on that, I thought, trying my best to quell the unease in my stomach.

My footfall was silent on the soft moss that grew within the cave which stunk like a thousand dead bodies. Nevertheless, I knew I had to press on.

Ugh, I don't know how I'll be able to draw a breath with this gods-forsaken stench driving itself up my nostrils. Push through, get it over with, and take a bath, I thought, shaking the smell out of my nose.

The *eyes* I was wearing made the cave look as bright as day, every little detail stood out in the pitch-black cave. I walked as cautiously as I could, with my new favorite sword grasped tightly in my gloved hands. The air was thick and humid, while absolutely silent save for a sudden, deep rumbling ahead of me, trembling the ground beneath my feet.

Sounds like that came from behind those rocks over there, I thought.

I strafed around the corner of the rock formation that lay in front of me, and sure enough, there it was.

An ochelon? By the gods both light and dark, this thing is fucking massive, I exclaimed in the realm of my own thoughts.

The beast lay in a ditch with a pile of bones surrounding it. Its short, brown fur coated the majority of its body except for its massive claws, face, and lower half of its stomach. Its large, strong maw could bite a man in half with no effort at all, and two tusks protruded from its lower jaw. The large eyes, capable of seeing well in the dark, were covered by a gray, leathery skin that was much thicker than the average hide.

I breathed heavily, trying my best not to make any further noise. My adrenaline had already been coursing through my veins for some time, but now, it seemed like my heart was about to burst through my chest. I took a step back and felt a crunch under my foot. I quickly looked down to see what it was, and instantly regretted doing so.

I had crushed something's remains.

A chill went up my spine, and my heartbeat even faster. The beast began to stir soon after the sound had reached its ears. I felt a wave of icy fear pass over me. The beast lazily began to wake up, grunting while its large muscles began to lift its body. I was frozen in a mixture of fear and adrenaline.

Fuck my life, I thought.

The beast sniffed the air, and snapped directly towards me. Its eyes were burning bright with anger and hatred. It let off a grunt as it rose to its full height, towering at least four meters above me.

I swallowed dryly.

The beast roared loudly, almost piercing my eardrums, and swung its massive claw in my direction. My eyes opened wide, staring at the incoming blow, and I rolled backwards, just dodging the deadly swipe.

Remember your training. Always keep your eyes on the beast's center of mass, that way you can see where the blows are coming from, I recalled.

I got to my feet, and bared my teeth. The beast recovered from its failed attempt to squish its newfound enemy. Its saliva dripped down to the ground, which made a splashing sound as it hit. I, looking up at it in despair, began to strafe around the beast, to at least make myself a little bit harder to hit. It swiped again, and I rolled back once more feeling the wind of the blow rush by me.

How am I supposed to get in to hit this thing? I thought, pushing air through my teeth.

The ochelon was beginning to get frustrated, and so it raised both hands and smashed the ground in front of it, trying to crush me as I adeptly stepped out of the way. The shockwave, however, could not be avoided and sent the ground I was stepping on up into the air, taking me along with it.

I rose up to about the same height as the monster and I swung at the beast's face, making a gash in its cheek. The beast staggered back a few titanic steps and spread its arms to swat me out of the air. I narrowly escaped the blow, and absorbed the fall by rolling.

The beast recovered from the blow, and became enraged at the smell of its own blood. It curled over and got on all four claws, and began to charge. I rolled out of the way to the right, leaving my sword out perpendicular to me, cutting deeply into the beast's leg. It stumbled and I attacked its now wounded leg once more, cutting deep into flesh and sinew this time.

The beast stumbled briefly, and tried to sweep me off my feet as it fell, but I jumped over the long arm that wanted me. I cut a few more times, only to further invoke the beast's rage. Within a split second, it turned and struck me with the opposite arm I had been expecting, digging deeply into my jerkin and back muscles. The hit sent me flying across the cave, and I screamed in pain when I hit the cave's wall. I began to recover from the monstrous blow, and I felt a sogginess that wasn't there before.

I was quickly losing blood.

Damn it, that doesn't make things any easier, I winced.

I recovered from the attack as best I could, blood streaming from my back and forehead. Just as I was turning to face my enemy, the beast was already sending another blow my way. I managed to leap out of the way, and narrowly escaped a second just like it, not even a second after the first.

The beast spun around as quick as lightning with its claw extended, and just missed my gut. I cut down with my sword, and severed the beast's wrist at the joint. Blood sprayed all over me, and the beast roared with the pain of having lost a claw. I was surprised it had done so much damage with so little effort, and smiled through the pain for the first time since I arrived.

I love this sword, but I need a damage boost to kill this bastard. Just cutting off a claw won't be enough to disable it, but I know what will, I thought.

My eyes went black *as I went into the world without time to gather mana. I drew from the sky, wrapping the tendrils around my sword and* condensed the mana into it.

The beast, still in agonizing pain after the loss of its claw, roared uncontrollably. While the beast was distracted, I flicked my finger, and ignited the condensed mana. The white flame lit up the cave naturally, making it harder for me to see with the *eyes* still doing their job.

Finally, an opening! I rushed in, escaping the incoming blow by the width of a hair.

I screamed and cut upwards into its gut with my flaming sword. The cut was deep enough to partially disembowel it, and the smell of seared flesh filled the air. The beast fell to its knees, leaning on the one remaining claw it had. I cut at the joint, severing it from the body.

I breathed heavily, feeling the pain from the gash in my back, furrowing my brow and looking the beast in the eyes. "Your claws belong to me now, and so does your life. Thank you for the fight," I said aloud, my voice filled with a power I hadn't felt before. The beast leaned on the bloodied stumps that replaced its claws and stared into my eyes, while its innards fled its body.

I looked it straight in the eyes and let out a war cry, driving the sword up under its gaping mouth. The flaming sword pierced the other side of its skull, and its eyes rolled back into its head. As I pulled the sword out, the beast fell to the ground, laying in a pool of its own blood.

"I did it! By the gods' shit, I did it!" I exclaimed, chuckling weakly as I did. I stepped away from the steaming body. My chuckle turned into a full-blown laugh, but was quickly interrupted by the sharp pain in my back from the blow I had received earlier. I was drenched in blood, and could smell the iron in it that was soaking into my jerkin.

I didn't care as much as I should have, since the adrenaline was still heavily influencing my pain receptors.

I felt another sharp pain in my back, and *I drew from the Ethereal once more,* condensing the mana to the opened wound. I flicked my finger once more, and the mana was lit, searing and sealing the wound. I fell to my knees, screaming from the immense pain that was the result of charring my own flesh.

That's gonna leave one hell of a scar, I thought.

After I stopped the bleeding, I began to get a better look at the cave, noticing details I hadn't come across during my battle.

There are so many bones on the ground, it's a wonder how this creature even finds this much food to eat. Wait, Bernar said the word bastards *not* bastard, I thought, feeling a cold stone sink in my gut.

The harsh reality set in, as I observed the body of the ochelon I had just slain. "It's a female..." I said more loudly than I had hoped to. The moment those words left my mouth, I noticed a pair of glowing, red eyes surrounded by fur of the same color glaring at me from the depth of one of the many outlets in the cave.

The male ochelon had arrived, and it made the female look like it was but a toddler in comparison. Its bright red fur stood out in the vision of my mask, giving a much more menacing feeling than the female ever could. Its claws and tusks were much, *much* larger than that of the female's, and I knew immediately that this would be a challenge.

"You've got to be shitting me…" I said, readying my sword once more. The enormous male towered over the lifeless body of his mate, and nudged it with the back of its massive claw. It glared at me so intensely; I thought I would collapse.

I can hardly stand as it is with the gash in my back, and now this guy shows up? He's at least twice her size, and I've just killed his wife. Damn it! No other choice but to use that spell at the start of the battle. This can't be a drawn-out fight or I won't survive it. I thought as I began to consider my options.

I drew yet again *from the Ethereal, gathering as much mana as I knew I could handle* and condensed it into my sword, desperately trying to control the sphere through the pain. I hoped to land a similar blow as I had to the female, as the mana-flame's intensity grew exponentially. I lifted the flaming sword and pointed it at the creature as I stared into its glowing eyes.

"Hey, you oversized abomination! Your life or mine. Let's do this," I challenged, knowing my odds of success were slim.

The ochelon charged as though it understood the words, immediately launching an attack aimed at my head. I barely ducked under the blow, with the pain of my wound nearly rendering me unconscious. I struck upwards, aiming for the elbow joint, but the only thing my sword sliced was air.

An attack came from overhead with the intent to squash me, but with an adept pirouette, I dodged the attack and sliced again. I found my target, but even with the mana-imbued sword, it did little damage.

"*Oh*, come on!" I shouted, meeting the monster's eyes after realizing the lack of damage. The creature roared as it flicked me into the wall like an insect. My back slammed into it, the pain riddling my body as I gasped for air. I could hardly stand, and noticed the creature looking at the wound curiously.

"So, it *does* hurt," I said aloud. The creature snarled, realizing that the mana-flame wasn't dissipating. I thought back on my very first battle, and what my own spell had done to those glicks.

If I can use that on this bastard, I might just stand a chance. Mana-based attacks seem to work on him, even if my sword skill doesn't deal a lot of damage, I thought as I watched it scream.

After observing the ochelon for a moment, I sheathed my blade, and did my best to focus on what I was about to do. Although, it was something I'd never even dreamed of attempting before now.

Driven by necessity I took one deep breath, as *I drew once more from the Ethereal, gathering as much as I could in both hands.* The creature, now moving towards me a little more cautiously, noticed what I was doing. "I don't know if this will work, but you're going to kill me if it doesn't, anyway," I said, spitting out a wad of blood that had pooled in my cheek.

"Come and get me, you angry son of a bitch," I seethed.

The creature, showing more intelligence than I had anticipated, charged at me, moving much more quickly this time. I dove under the creature's hind legs, avoiding the blow from both claws, and was now behind it. My eyes began to glow like my older brother's, though less refined, as mana could still be seen seeping from them.

I whipped both of my arms, releasing the mana I held in my hands and wrapping each of the beast's limbs in it. "Hold this for me," I said with that same power from before in my voice. I screamed as I pulled the tendrils away from the creature's body. The ochelon roared, and tried to fight against it, but as this was a battle against mana, there was little it could do but feel its limbs being torn from its body.

"Tell your wife I said *hello*!" I shouted in response.

A squelching sound could be heard beneath the loud roar that resonated throughout the cave, as the massive limbs were flung in opposing directions. The ochelon's massive body flopped to the ground, as its blood meshed with the previously formed pool. my eyes stopped glowing, as reality set back in.

"Fuck!" I shouted, realizing that for a few moments, the pain had subsided while I was casting the spell. I panted heavily, feeling the pain from every bruise, scratch, and cut growing more intensely by the minute.

I fell onto my knees, reveling in the silence after my victory. Even through the immense amount of pain, I chuckled. "Master sure knew what he was talking about. *Keep your sword sharp and wits about you*," I said with my best imitation of the Master's voice. Through the quiet of the cave, I began to hear footsteps rapidly approaching.

Please don't be another creature. Please don't be another creature, I thought.

Bernar sprinted into view, stopping a few paces away from the entrance of the main cave. "I heard the roar come to an abrupt stop, and thought you had been squished," he said, seeing me on my knees. Since I was still losing blood, I could only weakly smile at my older sibling.

"*Oh*, shit! Are you okay?" Bernar asked, realizing I wasn't my usual self. "Do I look okay?" I replied weakly, but still maintained my smile. "With that attitude, I guess you're better than you look," my brother said warmly. "*Heh,* you should see the other guy," I pointed towards the pair of carcasses and multiple body parts strewn about the cave.

"Gods above and below!" Bernar exclaimed. "I knew they were ochelons, but I didn't think they had gotten this large yet. How the hell did you...?" I lost consciousness, falling flat on my face.

A few minutes later, my eyes reopened, and I could feel a calming warmth over me.

Did I die? I thought as I began to regain my focus.

"How do you feel?" my brother asked, helping me sit upright. "A little better, but my back still feels like it's on fire," I said, moving my shoulder around. "Well, you did *sear* the wound shut. Good thinking, by the way," Bernar said. I grunted and groaned, barely able to get to my feet.

Looking around, I realized how much darker the cave was without the *eyes* to help me. "Here," my brother handed me the mask which I donned with a little difficulty. Shortly after, the cave became bright once more with the infusion of Bernar's mana.

Observing our surroundings for a few moments, I walked over to a curious object near where I had encountered the first ochelon. I moved in to get a closer look. "A torch? It seems to have been freshly lit, too. Maybe not even a month old," I told my brother. "That's odd. No one other than the Master should have come through here recently," Bernar stated.

I wonder who the hell would have gotten past not one, but two *of these titans,* I thought.

I stepped over the dead ochelon's torn limb, and moved towards where I had seen the female sleeping. Its lair was covered in old, gnawed bones from many meals.

I felt a small gust reach my sweaty cheek.

A breeze? Better check that out, I thought.

I moved into the deepened ground where the beasts had lain, and noticed a small crack in the rocks. "How good are you with earth manipulation?" Bernar asked, seeing what I had found. "I'm not as good as you, that's for sure. Care to do the honors?" I asked weakly.

Bernar snorted, but seemed glad to see me in better shape than when he first arrived. He gathered *mana from the Ethereal, and condensed it* to his left hand. He pushed his hand forward, seeping the mana into the rock. It pulled the crack open like a curtain, scattering dust and gravel as it moved. After the dust had cleared, we walked through the hole Bernar had made, looking around the revealed room.

Books? Scrolls? What in the world are they doing here in a place like this? I thought.

Shelves as high as the ceiling were completely filled with books, and lined the walls of the inner chamber I had just stepped into. There was a desk in the corner of the room, which had various notes strewn across it. "Someone obviously left in a hurry. Either that, or this person is more disorganized than Batch," I told my brother.

The two of us looked over the notes, analyzing the titles and what secrets they held in the ink. "These are probably the oddest names I think I've ever seen," I began.

"*Dissection* by a certain Nexis Pelantyr. I wonder who that is. Here it talks about uses for the plant the Master mentioned. Look, there's an incomplete copy of it. It's not the same handwriting. Someone else was obviously in here, but what they copied is hard to tell. Judging by the handwriting itself, whoever did this must have been in a rush," I continued. "I agree," Bernar said, reviewing the handwriting. I took a glance at the other notes, but found nothing of importance.

I moved over to the shelves to read over the selection of books. '*The Effects of the Ethereal*', '*Habits Of Trolls And Other Beasts*', '*A Voyage To The Underworld*', '*Wards And Other Defenses*

Against Dark Magic', 'How To Make Alcohol By Using Citrus And Mana', I read to myself.

The last one *definitely* caught me off guard.

Not even gonna look at it. Think I'm still too young for that, I thought.

I shot another glance over at the first book I had seen, and noticed something was different about it than the others present.

Must be a good read. It doesn't have much dust on it. I can tell it's been frequently read, and possibly more recently used than the others, I thought.

I picked up the book, and began sifting through the pages. I turned a few pages, and realized a small number of them had been torn out.

Damn, just when it was getting good, I thought.

"Bernar, come look at this," I beckoned. My brother immediately recognized the book and noticed the torn-out pages. "This is bad," he began, his eyes widening. "This book... We need to inform the Master quickly," he said urgently. I took the book with me, and left the cave through the main entrance.

There was still so much more to be seen there, but it's too dark to tarry any longer. I'll have to come back another day, I thought.

We set off at a slow trot rather than a walk as we made our way back to the fortress.

CHAPTER 7

Queen Leona

A few days after the Synners had left, Meliss carried a tray to the queen's bedroom which had the morning light seeping through the curtains in front of the vast windows. She set it on the bedside table to the right of the sleeping beauty. She did so carefully to avoid awakening the person who was still sound asleep in the oversized bed. Under the thick, red covers to her left lay Leona, the queen. She slept on her back, and her fair black hair strewn across the goose-feather pillows made her face look like it had been swallowed by the night sky.

Meliss double checked the tray to ensure it was filled with the best breakfast treats before stepping away from it. Fresh bread from the bakery - toasted with a small cube of butter on the side - scrambled eggs, and a green apple were the order of the day. She walked back to the small basket she had brought, and picked up the small pot of tea.

I hope she wakes up before it cools. It'd be a pity to have her drink it cold, she thought.

Just as she completed her thought, Fulco stepped through the door with a look of disappointment on his face. "Come now, Meliss. This is not an hour at which a queen should be sleeping," he said in a loud voice. Meliss felt embarrassed that she had done something wrong, and looked down at the ground in silence.

"My queen, you must rise," he said aloud, drawing the massive curtains aside, tying them respectively. Light beamed more brightly into the room, and struck Leona in the face. Her eyes squinted and squished as she turned her head away from the source of her distress. "Wake up, milady," he continued after opening the second curtain wall.

The room was fully lit, and she knew now that there was nowhere for her left to turn. Not even her small painting station was safe from the beams. Her eyes opened but a little, and her pupils shrunk from the intensity of the sun. "It pains me to be woken in this manner," Leona said with a raspy grunt. Had she not been so beautiful, one might have assumed it was the voice of some disgruntled dwarf.

"Be swift, milady," Fulco said. "It's almost midday, and yet here you are hibernating like a bear in winter. It is not the most gracious thing for a queen to be doing," he said. Leona rubbed her eyes, and removed the covers to get out of bed. Her feet landed on rabbit pelt slippers, which were soft and warm.

She sat on the edge of the bed for a few moments, staring at the food Meliss had brought her. She grabbed a slice of the toast, and took a few bites out of it, but shortly put the remnants of the now violated bread back on the tray. She picked up the cup of tea, and used it to wash the dry toast down her throat. "Milady, where are your manners?" Fulco asked, appalled at her demeanor. "Where are the lords and ladies?" Leona just as abruptly.

Fulco merely shook his head.

"Oh, you don't see any here among us? So then tell me why I ought to act like a queen if I am in the confines of my bedroom, for I simply do not know," she said with an air of arrogance. Fulco scratched the back of his head and looked down at the floor. Leona smiled, knowing she had won the small argument, and proceeded to finish eating her breakfast.

When she was finished, she turned to face her servant, whose expression of defeat still owned his face. "My dear Fulco," she began to say while smiling genuinely, "do me a favor and summon Clare so that I may dress," she said. "Right away, milady," he replied, bowing out of the room. Meliss remained in the same position she had been in since Fulco had called her out on her benevolence towards the queen's sleeping habits.

"Has anyone ever told you that you would have beautiful children?" Leona asked after looking at Meliss' body for a few moments. "My lady?" Meliss asked, startled by the question. Her complexion went from a pale white to a bright red in an instant. "Good graces, Meliss, there's no need to be so bashful," Leona said playfully. "It was a simple question from one woman to another," she said.

"Now, do be a good sport and answer my question," she pleaded. "I do not believe so, my lady," Meliss replied. "Come now, you do not need to reply so formally," the queen said with a warm smile. "Imagine as though I were a regular human being, instead of a queen. As I have said before, there are no other lords or ladies present," Leona said to make her feel more comfortable.

Meliss pondered over the reason for this new form of treatment for a few moments, but found none. She looked back at her queen. "I don't think anyone has had the guts to tell me so, except for you," Meliss finally replied in an extremely thick accent. "I beg your pardon. I barely understood what you said," Leona said, taken aback. "Your accent is most definitely not one from the Continent. If I were to guess, I would say that it is from the Gramm islands," she concluded.

"And you'd be right," Meliss replied smiling. "My folks are from there, and they brought me here to the Continent as a wee babe. Pa died when I was about six winters old. Ever since I can remember, I've helped my Ma tidy up other people's houses. Work had been regularly scheduled for us, and one day, we found ourselves cleaning Father Mourtis' house. That was the day Fulco found us. He admired our work, and offered us positions here at the palace," Meliss explained.

"And an excellent job you have done thus far," Leona said without sarcasm in her voice. "Thank you," Meliss replied. "You said your 'Pa' died when you were only six, which makes you how old, now?" Leona asked. "I have eighteen winters behind me," Meliss replied. "Good graces! You don't look your age at all," Leona said in shock. "You're much more of a woman than I was at your age," Leona said through a curt giggle.

The sound of footsteps resounded from the bottom of the stairway, and Leona heard them clear as a whistle. "That must be Clare, the heavy old goat that she is," she said, pursing her lips. "Listen, Meliss, it was really nice to get to know you a little, and I look forward to learning more about you," Leona said. "Thank you, my lady," Meliss replied with a curt bow. Just as she was getting back up, Clare walked through the door with the queen's robes for the day.

"Forgive me for taking so long, my lady," Clare said with her chest rising and falling. She was at least twice Meliss' height and weight, and had her light brown hair tied up in a bun. "I was having a discussion with Fulco as to what you should wear today, but we did not come to a conclusion. So, I brought a few of my personal choices, much to his disapproval," she explained. The sweat dripped down from her brow and rolled over her round cheeks.

The whites of her hazel eyes and her nose were red, suggesting she had been drinking, as opposed to doing her job. She was anything but a healthy person. "I see," Leona said, taking note of Clare's composure. "Well, it doesn't matter. Let's get this over with," she said. "Yes, of course, my lady," Clare replied.

"Ah! An excellent choice, my lady," Clare said, staring at the blue dress that took a few minutes for Leona to choose. "Here, let me help you into it," she said while walking over to Leona, who was observing her gait.

That's not the straightest of lines she's drawing on the floor with her feet, she thought.

When Clare got closer, Leona could clearly smell the alcohol in her breath, and soon found herself gasping for a drag of clean air. "My lady, I need you to turn so I can unlace your gown," Clare said. "Certainly," Leona said, trying to expend as little of her reservations of air as possible. "Is everything alright, my lady?" Clare asked after clearing her throat. Her breath went straight into Leona's face.

Her breath is making my eyes water, Leona thought.

"Yes, yes," she briefly replied, and turned around, with her eyes all teared up. Meliss was now standing opposite of her queen, who tried to read the desperate gestures for relief, however, she was unable to make out what Leona was trying to say.

She drank eel vodka, Leona tried to mouth to Meliss.

She did what? Shrank a sealed froth cat? Meliss mouthed back, giggling as quietly as she could.

No, no, no, Leona mouthed. *She. Drank. Eel. Vodka,* Leona said, pausing every word to try and make herself more understood.

Ah, eel vodka, Meliss mouthed back while nodding her head.

Leona grinned, and was desperately trying not to burst into tears of what before would have been disgust, but now were of laughter. Clare stood up once more with a grunt. "There, all done, my lady," she said, and the waft of eel essence and vodka went back into Leona's eyes which teared up once more as a result.

"Get that off of you while I get the dress, milady," Clare said. Leona shrugged off the gown she had worn all night long. Her slim, proportionate body in combination with silky, smooth skin made it no surprise that she was lusted after by nearly everyone in the kingdom. She did not bother hiding her breasts, after all, there was no one else in the room besides her, and her two servants. The windows were too high for anyone to see into the room from the outside, so there was no risk of her nudity being exposed.

Clare came up behind her, swathed her in the blue dress, and tied up the laces. "Come, see how you look in the mirror, milady," Clare said, pushing the mirror towards her. Leona faced the mirror and smiled brightly. The dress followed the curves of her body as though it were a second skin she was wearing. The dip in the fabric near her breasts was a little more promiscuous than what she usually wore, but due to the warming weather, it seemed appropriate enough. "You were right, Clare. This is a beautiful dress indeed," Leona said, turning and twisting, watching how the dress flowed. "Why thank you, milady," Clare replied, smiling from ear to ear.

The queen was now fully awake, especially after the magic the eel vodka had worked on her eyes. "I'm sure my husband wouldn't want me to tarry any longer than I already have," she said. "Of course not, my lady," Clare agreed. Leona gave her dress one final twirl in the mirror, and began to walk towards the door. Her two servants followed closely behind.

A few moments later, she was in the throne room, where Truls was having a small debate with Elhael, Mads, and Bashir who was there with his son Bashaa. "Ah, and there she is!" Truls said loudly. The lords turned about to see who he was talking about. Their eyes were so glued to her slim figure that they practically devoured her with them.

"Come, come! We were just talking about having a feast later on this evening, and we were wondering what sort of theme it should have," Truls said, reaching out for his wife's hand. She didn't allow her hesitation to show, but took the king's hand and stood at his side. "Well, I don't know about any sort of theme, although I do know what I want to have for supper," Leona said. "And what might that be, my sweet?" Truls asked. She felt disgusted by the name he had called her.

She looked at the other lords for a moment, but had slight difficulty taking her eyes off Bashaa. "Zebura," she said with eyes still fixed on Bashir's son. He had bright green eyes, a gift from his deceased mother, which made them look as though they glowed in the morning light that beamed through the upper windows.

"I'm not one to question the queen's choice, however, I was expecting something along the lines of a boar or perhaps something less exotic that we can't get anywhere else," Mads said. "I could always change my mind, King Mads," she replied, smiling gracefully. "Zeburas are known to be eaten as a sign of peace between kingdoms. With this being the first time in nearly a century that our countries have been in unison over a common cause, I see no reason why we shouldn't indulge in it," she explained.

Mads let out a hearty laugh for a moment, and the other lords joined in. "A very astute observation, my lady. Does anyone disagree with the queen?" Mads asked cheerfully. "No complaints here, my lord," Bashir answered. Leona almost lost control over herself as he looked at her, smiling. She caught herself at last, and gave a brief chuckle.

"I suggest we begin the preparations," Truls interjected, noticing the exchange. "Each of you has a long journey ahead come tomorrow." "Indeed," Elhael agreed. "Although most of us may travel the same distance in opposite directions, the Rhydian Pass is a narrow one, and a harrowing experience at that," he continued. "I can only imagine the perils that may lie along the way," Leona added. "I will send a prayer to the gods for your safekeeping on your journeys home," she added. "Thank you, my lady," Bashaa said, the tone of his voice shaking her very core. She gracefully smiled and nodded in reply.

It's difficult to be around him with my husband present, she thought.

"Very well, then. I will have Fulco see to the preparations for the feast, while these fine gentlemen and I discuss a few final things before they all depart," Truls said. "I will be with you in a few moments, my lord," Bashir said. "I would like to speak to the queen for a brief moment," he continued. Truls shrugged, as though he had not a care in the world about what they discussed. "We shall head towards the market. Join us when you can, my lord," Truls said. Bashaa bowed, as he watched the others head off, already deep in conversation.

"I have a favor I'd like to ask of you, my lady," Bashaa began. Leona held a surprised look on her face. "And what might that be, my lord?" she asked. "You see, my son was only able to arrive on the morning of the council, and, unfortunately, missed the tour we received of the castle given us by Fulco. He has always wanted to come to Coltend to visit the magnificence of the great castle." Bashir began. "If there is a possibility of you, my lady, giving him the tour yourself, I would consider it a great honor," Bashir said.

I've been caught. He saw right through me, she thought to

herself, and swallowed.

"I would be delighted to give him a tour, my lord," she said, trying to maintain her composure.

This sly dog is trying to get me alone with his son, after all. Oh, be still my heart, she thought.

"Most excellent! Allow me to give you my thanks for such an honor," Bashir said excitedly. "There is no need for thanks," she said and smiled at him nervously. "Oh, but there *is*, my lady!" Bashaa said stubbornly. Leona chuckled nervously, allowing her inner lack of composure to show a little. "If you insist, my lord," she said, regaining her composure. Bashir bowed out, leaving the queen and Bashaa alone.

"Shall we, then, milady?" Bashaa said in his enticing voice, as extended his arm. She said nothing, but took his arm and they were off. "Enjoy yourselves!" Truls called out with a brighter than usual smile on his face. The two of them returned warm smiles toward the group, and continued walking.

"So, milady," Bashir said, his voice had a very strong resonance and a thick, eastern accent. They had only walked for about a minute before either of them had said anything at all. "So, prince," Leona replied. She was as red as a beet, and had a hard time hiding it. "Walking in silence when in such good company would be an absolute waste," he began. "It would, indeed," she replied, charmingly.

"To be brutally blunt, and bluntly brutal, I simply have to ask: Why were you staring at me so fervently just now?" he asked. "By the Graces! You don't waste a second, do you?" she asked. "Frankly, I'm astonished as to why you'd want to know at all," she said, feeling her composure whittling away. "It is painfully obvious that I am the wife of the *great* King Truls. That fact *alone* should have steered your gaze away from me," she stated with little confidence in her own words.

Bashaa tilted his head. "The *'great'* King Truls..." he said inwardly, wondering why she had used that tone. "Well, my lady," he began, "in my culture, it is common for one to not wait around to speak one's mind. It helps to avoid... *confusion*. Therefore, I am doing only what my culture and people have taught me. I apologize if that was inappropriate," he said apologetically.

I didn't know their culture was like that, she thought.

"In that case, it helps make your question make a little more sense," she said. "However, to answer your question just as brutally blunt, and bluntly brutal: I am very interested in you. You're a very handsome man," she said sheepishly. "I knew from the start that this 'tour' of the castle was a farce," she continued.

"Ah!" he exclaimed, showing off his bright smile. "You see, I had figured as much, though I wasn't sure. I thought it would be better to ask you as soon as I had the opportunity, given the fact that I will be leaving in a few days," he said. "So, you knew. The whole time?" she asked. "Yes, that is correct," he replied.

"And did you and your father plan for us to be alone like this?" she asked, with a bit of indignation in her voice. "Not exactly," he retorted shyly. "I simply assumed there would be some form of tour for me, though I didn't account for the possibility of it being with the most beautiful woman I have ever seen," he replied.

She blushed.

"If you keep this up, I feel as though my head will explode from compliments," she said with her eyes wide and her left hand to her chest. "I'd rather it didn't," he said, looking deeply into her eyes. "For the world would suffer such a loss, that I do not honestly believe that it would ever recover," he said. "What makes you think that? You barely even know me," she retorted.

Keep your composure, woman! she shouted internally.

"I know a strong woman like a hound knows its prey," he replied with a sly grin.

And it's gone. My composure has abandoned me. Perhaps I should wave at it as it passes by, she thought.

"Now that *is* interesting," she said, taking note of the things he said. "How did you learn that?" she asked. "When your father has a whole harem of women at his disposal, and you are but a small child who does not know much about the opposite sex, you tend to learn a few things by either observation or actually listening," he replied. "Something few men are capable of," she said in compliance with his last phrase.

"A man must know how to do a few things if he is to succeed in life: how to do battle, how to hunt, how to manage his property and money. And, of course, how to treat a woman," he said matter-of-factly. She could feel the butterflies in her stomach beating their wings. "These are all, with exception of the last, things that require only a small degree of skill. People can be trained to do those things. However, knowing how to treat a woman not as an object, like most do in my culture, but as a person requires an entire shift in perspective. Respect and privacy, rights, and confidence; these things are vital to give, as they are due, to an equal," he concluded.

"I am truly impressed to hear that coming from someone who - as you stated before - grew up with a harem of women at his disposal," Leona said in disbelief. Her thoughts began to run freely about him, and she hadn't once stopped herself thinking about what kind of man he really was. "I aim to impress, my lady," he said slyly. "Particularly when my opponent is the 'great' King Truls," he said with emphasis.

Leona felt something click in her mind, and she immediately looked to her left and found the large wooden doorway that led downstairs to the cellar. She smiled. "Follow me," she said. "Where are you ta...?" he began to say. "*Shhh*," she said, cutting him off and putting a finger on his mouth. She grabbed his hand, and dragged him down into the cellar.

It was lit by two torches near the doorway. On each pillar that supported the racks of enormous barrels of wine and other spirits, there was an unlit torch for each one. Meads, wines, vodkas and ciders were neatly organized, and labeled accordingly with stamps of ink, or brands charred into the wood. They stepped through the door, their eyes taking a short time to adapt to the torchlight of the room.

"This way," she said, leading him between racks and shelves that held the countless wooden barrels. The sound of their footsteps was dampened by the barrels in the dark, chilled room.

She stopped herself by leaning up against one of the nearby barrels, staring at Bashaa. Her inviting eyes were straining to be able to see him properly, but she managed. He said nothing, as he could feel her intent, and moved in to kiss her by putting one hand on her waist and the other on the lower half of her face. While they were kissing, he undid the laces to her dress, and it fell to the ground. In the meantime, she undid the sashes that held up his pants, and she heard the cloth hitting the floor. She turned around, leaning against the barrel, and no sooner was his pelvis meeting her backside with his hands on her hips.

They had only just begun to make love, when they were interrupted by a noise. "What was that?" she whispered. "I'm not sure," Bashir replied, pausing his thrusting movement for a few heartbeats. "It's probably something small, judging by the sound of it," he said, unconvinced. "If you say so," she said, and they continued what they had started a few moments ago.

About half an hour later, they finished and had to put their clothes back on in the dim light. Bashaa fumbled with the laces, attempting to replicate the knots Clare had done earlier that day. "That will have to suffice," he said, tying a knot he often used on his horse's reins. "Pray no one notices the knot," he said. "That's comforting," she replied sarcastically. Leona peeked out of the cellar through the crack between the frame and the door, seeing not a single soul about them. "We're clear," she whispered back to Bashaa, who followed her out, taking her arm as if nothing had happened.

After a few minutes of walking and awkward conversation later, they were back in the main throne room. The tables were already being set up for the feast later that evening, but did not find the other lords. "Truls must be showing them the garden, or perhaps the market," she concluded, breaking the silence.

"We'd better hurry to them. Otherwise, suspicions might arise," Bashaa said, intensifying the pace of his gait. "I'm certain they already suspect enough," Leona retorted. She was only a little shorter than Bashaa, but felt a degree of difficulty keeping up with him, especially in the clothes she was wearing.

They went to the garden first, but found only empty hedge-lined trails to the large garden maze that lay at the back of the palace. "They must be at the market, if they're not here," she deduced. "I really hope you have a plan to explain our elongated absence. After all, a tour of the castle couldn't have taken that long" Bashaa said nervously. Leona felt a twinge of displeasure at his lack of faith in her.

"Yes, I do. We go to the market, find them, and tell them that we had no idea where they were, and that we spent the entire time looking for them. A half-truth, if you will," she said matter-of-factly. Bashir nodded. "Lead the way, milady," he said. "We both know where I'd lead you if I had a choice," she said quietly through a thin-lipped grin. He smiled, and continued walking.

They made their way down a few flights of steps that eventually led to the main market. They looked out over the hundreds of small tents and booths that were the organs of the market itself. The racket produced from countless shopkeepers and clients yelling at each other to haggle for better prices resounded across the enormous courtyard. The market itself had a wide variety of supplies such as meats, hides, fauna, flora, precious stones, and jewelry.

"I think I might know where he may be," Leona said, looking out over the hoard of people under the midday sun. She took him by the hand, and walked into the crowd of people. Without guards to pave the way for her, she finally felt what it was like to be a regular person in her own skin. Rubbing up against countless sweaty and grimy people, as well as breathing in the same air as maybe a hundred others took a toll on her psychological health, but she pressed on.

"Through here," she called back to her companion, and they turned down the main street of the market, where, at long last, there was a little room to breathe a drag of fresh air. "I pray I never have to cozy up to a hide seller to get by again. The stench on that man," she said, still feeling the man's sweat dripping down her cheek. "That is because you only just missed the butcher himself. I swear he smelled worse than a thousand carcasses," Bashaa added as though it were a contest to see who had suffered more. Leona laughed, and it made him smile.

"We'd better keep moving," she said, regaining her composure. "I agree. Let's go before someone notices the queen herself without guards in their midst. They might cause a rabble, or worse..." he said cautiously. They walked for about fifty more meters, before they finally found the king himself, surrounded by the other lords, and a few animals they had chosen for the feast. They quickened their pace, and one of the guardsmen noticed them.

"Make way for the queen!" Thorsen called out. In an instant, everyone formed a line to the side, making a clear path for her to walk down. "Aha, my queen! Thank you, Thorsen," Truls said. "I am here, my lords," Leona said with a brief curtsy. "We have concluded our tour, and went looking for you. Our small journey led us here, though we were hard pressed to find you" she said.

"You could have simply asked one of the servants," he replied, with a little distrust in his voice. "I could have, but where would the adventure be? I have never been in such a crowd as this one, nor do I think I shall ever be again," she said with a chuckle in her voice.

"*Adventure*?" he asked. "It was foolish and dangerous to do so. Doubly so in the company of one who does not know his way around," Truls said with a darkened tone. "However, I am glad you are both here with us." "Thank you, my lord. I apologize for our tardiness, as the queen's knowledge of the castle was enthralling," Bashaa returned with a low bow. Truls subtly sneered at the man.

"Well, my lords, the sun grows hotter by the minute, and the feast this afternoon approaches quickly," Truls stated. "Indeed, we should return. I don't want to show up to the feast smelling like I have just come off a battlefield," Elhael agreed. Truls whistled, and a young servant boy came running out of the nearby group of guardsmen. "Boy, take these animals up to the butchers, and if you tarry for a moment, you will pay for it dearly," he whispered. The poor servant boy quickly nodded, and took the animals by their mouthpieces, tugging firmly until they began to follow him.

"That will probably take at least four hours to be prepared," Mads said while watching the young boy lead the animals down the street. "Chances are very good. Fancy a wager?" Elhael asked Mads. "Now, now," Leona interrupted. "Just be sure to know that we have some of the best butchers and chefs on the Continent here," she said boastingly.

"Indeed you might, and as such, I wager three hours before the beasts are prepared," Elhael said. He was a very intelligent elf, and was often thought to be the brightest on the Continent itself. "If you insist," Mads said with a shrug of his broad shoulders. "What shall we wager?" he asked. Elhael grinned. "Money, of course," he said slyly.

"It's settled, then," Mads said smiling. The two shook on it, and turned back to the small group. "Well, then," Truls began, eyeing the handsome prince once more. "I believe it best we all head off to rest and ready ourselves for tonight's festivities. Everyone agreed, and they began to walk through the marketplace, through crowds and gazes back to the main palace. Bashaa accompanied his father, while keeping an eye on Leona's figure swaying a few feet in front of him.

"Magnificent, isn't she?" his father whispered, breaking the scene of them down in the cellar that was being replayed behind his eyes. "Hush, father. Truls might hear you. You know he can speak our language," Bashaa cautioned. "Like all the other ruling kings, we all must know each other's languages as though they were our own. However, his guards don't speak it, so we're free to comment on whatever we like as long as we keep it down," Bashir said.

His son shook his head. "It is unwise to risk it, anyway," Bashaa said. "Oh! Undo the calamity that is thine mammary, Bashaa," his father said. "You know as well as I do that she is a goddess amongst men and women of this world. Are you so dense that even mana would bend around you to not acknowledge her beauty?" he asked. The sting of the insult clearly shook

Bashaa to his core.

He doesn't know about what we did, which probably means no one else does. Good, he thought.

"I understand, father. I just do not wish to do so whilst in the presence of the king himself," Bashaa said in return. "Fearing things that may not come to be reality is folly, my son," his father said. "Take a gander at her while we're still here, and when we have departed, no one will know you have," he said. "I'll take it into consideration," Bashaa replied cautiously, but with a grin on his face. His father smiled back and nodded, returning his posture to its regular state. He looked over at Elhael - who seemed not to have been paying attention - and was content at the fact.

They made their way through the streets, guards clearing them of any forms of threats, and making way for the royal party. People who watched them go by went down on one knee, kneeling for them.

"Your people love you, it seems," Elhael said, now walking beside Truls, noting upon the kneeling citizens. "I couldn't give a turtle shit about them," Truls replied. "They kneel for you and the others, not for me," he said. Elhael was shocked to hear him speak in such a way about the people he ruled.

"I am saddened to hear that. Truly, I am. May I ask why it is so?" Elhael asked, hoping to catch a glimpse of the humanity a king was supposed to have. Truls shook his head. "I'm not certain you would understand, King Elhael," he said. "In my tongue, my name means 'wise one'," Elhael said, raising a thin eyebrow. "Very well," Truls said, yielding.

"It began long ago, a few short days after my coronation. My father's passing was taken as a heavy blow by the society you see today. He was a just, fair king who was loyal to his subjects. He did everything in his power to ensure that his people would want for nothing, ensuring that nobody would want to leave the perfect city he had turned Coltend into. Unfortunately, and after many years of doing so, he fell ill to some dark sickness. Some say it was a curse, others say he was being poisoned," he said, with a dead stare aimed at the ground beneath a wicker basket near the side of the road.

"I'm assuming that you have theories of your own," Elhael said, attempting to capture the king's divided attention. His mind was wandering, receiving flashes of his father on his deathbed. He snapped back to attention, and was visibly shook at the memory.

"Forgive me," Truls said. Elhael nodded. He knew what Truls had seen. "Indeed, I do have a theory of my own, although I am not at leave to share it with one other than myself. I pray you understand," he said. "I do, curious as I am as to what it is, however, I must respect your privacy," Elhael said. Truls nodded.

"At any rate, his lavish and revered lifestyle came to an end when his bookkeeper came to him with an account of all he had spent over the last 70 years of rule. He had spent so much that there simply wasn't enough gold in the kingdom to pay it off. It seemed odd to him, being that Coltend had been the main trading hub over the last few centuries, but he accepted his fate after asking for an investigation of exactly what had happened. Before his end, he told me that he loathed himself for being foolish enough not to have been more attentive to such matters. After all, he had now tainted his reputation as being careless, leaving the fate of his kingdom in the hands of my seventeen-year-old self. I did what I had to do to keep this country afloat," Truls explained.

"They hate me for what I've done. Gods, even my own wife hates me. Fuck them. I would do it all over again to save this country, if that's what it took."

"I had no idea it had gone to such an extent," Elhael said, astonished at the gravity of the kingdom's past. "I had heard tales of both joyous and woeful moments during his rule. Nevertheless, I could never have imagined it being that harrowing of an experience," he continued. "Well, now you know why I don't give a shit about them anymore," Truls replied. "I do, indeed," Elhael replied, solemnly nodding his head.

They continued walking onward in silence, until they had reached the palace - which, after the king's monologue, was a stone's throw away. They went their separate ways to prepare for the banquet. Leona glanced once more at Bashaa, who nodded, and turned to follow his father - who, unfortunately for him, was going in the opposite direction.

A few hours later, everyone reconvened at the vast banquet hall for the feast. The tables were set out in the form of a large 'T' - a custom handed down from generation to generation. At every feast, the tables were laid out in the form of the first letter of whatever the king's name was. The tablecloths had the insignia of the castle sewn into each one - a daunting task, it seemed, but the seamstresses around the castle were glad to have done the work.

They had been well remunerated, after all. The large plates with their silverware were set out atop the tables, and the food was laid out down the center. Pheasant, venison, pork and lamb were served at the tables, coupled with potatoes and other vegetables. Large soup bowls were on small carts loaded with bowls and spoons to meet the needs of the guests. The guests had their cups filled with wine and mead from the cellars.

The tone of the feast was a joyous one, with a small band of troubadours using lively notes to rile the guests into a glad mood. The servants of the palace sat separate from the royalty, though mixed and coupled with the guardsmen. Jokes were made, food was thrown and stuck in beard hairs, grease, wine, ale and mead ran down chins, laughs were loud and occasionally maniacal, resounding throughout the hall. All in all, the feast was in full swing, and all seemed to be going smoothly.

"This is a grand feast, if ever I've seen one, King Truls," Mads had to bellow his sentence over the uproar that was the feast. "And this venison is incredible! You must tell me what the secret is!" he exclaimed. "Thank you for your kind words, King Mads, however, I regret to inform you that my chef is a magician when it comes to food. As everyone knows, a true magician never reveals his secrets. Sadly, not even to his own king," Truls said with a smile.

Mads simply shrugged and raised his glass in the general direction of what he thought was the kitchen, when in truth, it was the men's lavatory. One of the male servants walking out of there saw the horn raised in his direction, and he winked at the king in response. Mads' eyes opened wide, and his face paled. He quickly proceeded to drown himself in the remaining alcohol in his drinking horn. Elhael had seen it happen, and burst into an almost uncontrollable fit of laughter.

"Axes, arrows, spears, bears, and monsters," Elhael said each word between laughing spurts. "You have encountered all of these, and yet one wink from a man who does not share your sexual preference and you go white as a sheet of clean linen." Mads became mildly infuriated that someone other than he and the noble had noticed, especially the fact that it was the overly observant elf. "Now, now," Elhael said, raising a hand to try and calm Mads down. "We are never going to speak of this again," Mads said coldly. Elhael nodded quickly and both began laughing at the situation.

The male servant returned to the table designated for close

servants of the palace. "Oh, hey! What's that on the f-floor?" Clare said, looking down at the stone floor. "Behold! It's a f-fuck to give. I think you've lost it, Leland," she said cheerfully. Leland looked at her in confusion. "He won't kill you over something so s-simple as that. It's a feast and people have been - *hic* - drinking for a while," she continued, slurring her words.

"Fine," Leland said, "but if my body is found with a slit throat tomorrow morning, at least we'll know why." "Calm yourself before you burst a vessel," Meliss threw in her two cents in a vain attempt to calm Leland down. He was visibly distraught. She passed him a full mug of ale. "Chug, you nervous wreck, chug!" she said with a smile. He looked at her, then at the mug which seemed to magically have appeared in his hand. He threw the contents of the mug down the back of his throat as fast as he could and shook his head. "There. Now do that a few more times and' you're good to go," she said, still smiling.

"I don't blame you f-for doing what you did, *Leeeland-uh*," Clare said with a heavy hand on his not-so-muscular shoulder. "Hell, I'd have done the same if it were Prince Bashaa doing that to me," she said. "You fancy him?" Meliss asked. "Of course! Have you s-seen his eyes, and the way he looks at you with them?" she asked playfully. "They are marvelous, indeed. It's no wonder the lady he was with earlier couldn't resist him in the cellar," Leland said in agreement. "And that's supposed to mean something to me?" Meliss asked. "Wait a minute," Clare said, reaching for a moment of clarity. "He was with the queen for the better half of the afternoon. You don't think...?" she said, stopping herself halfway through.

Fulco was walking right behind her as she said it, and his eyes opened wide. He glared at them viciously. After a moment's pause, he realized that he already knew the answers to the ones he would have asked. He sighed heavily and continued walking towards the royal end of the table.

"Holy cock-sneeze. I think he heard us," Clare said, trying to sober herself up. "We'd best be out of here," Leland said. "No. We can't leave now," Meliss said sternly. "If we did that, we'd only paint bigger targets on our backs," she continued. "Ok, then, mastermind: What the actual fuck are we supposed to do now?" Leland asked. He began shaking out of fear. "Nothing we can do besides acting as naturally as possible. Keep drinking," she replied.

At the royal table, the Zebura was brought out, and Truls rose from his chair. He flipped a wooden mug and smacked the lid on the table, making a loud knocking sound to get everyone's attention. "I'd like to propose a toast," he began, slurring his words a little and rocking back and forth. All eyes were on him. The three servants swallowed hard, concerned about their knowledge having leaked out to the last person it shouldn't have. "On this most auspicious of evenings, I would like to have it known that I am glad to have such good and loyal company to share this with," he said. Everyone clapped and cheered unanimously. He raised his hand to calm them.

"Tonight, we - the rulers of the countries of the Continent - have gathered here to celebrate peace amongst ourselves. That is not to say that we don't have the very real threat of the monsters lurking just outside our castles and citadels. However, we are celebrating something that has not happened since before my father's father was king. We are gathered here as friends, and brothers in arms to rid ourselves of those ugly bastards who take our husbands, our wives, and our children." There was another cheer. He raised his hand again.

"Tonight, we will partake in this glorious feast to truly show that no matter how different we may be culturally or physically, that we are of one mind and of one common goal: peace," he concluded. Thunderous applause resounded throughout the hall. He smiled, looking at the companions who sat at his table, and slumped back into his chair.

Elhael pulled the servant who had brought the meal to them aside. "How long did it take to prepare the Zebura?" he asked quietly. "According to the master chef, it was four hours exactly," the servant replied. Elhael burst into laughter and pointed a finger at Mads, who was flushed. "Told you, you drunken bastard! Now, pay up!" he exclaimed cheerfully. Mads sighed deeply, and removed the coin purse from his side. "Take it," he mumbled. Elhael took the purse and tossed it in his hand with a light chuckle, and placed it into his lap.

Truls cut the first slice of the dark, steaming flesh, then handed it over to his queen, who sat immediately next to him. She nodded slowly and deeply. The next slice went to Bashir, who also nodded, and gave thanks in his native tongue. Leona looked at him, wondering if he knew about what she and his son had done just a few short hours before meeting them in the market.

He caught her eye, smiled, and nodded to her as well. She nodded back, and immediately saw Bashaa, who sat just beyond him. He followed his father's example, and she felt a nervous stir in her belly.

"*Fuuuuuck*," Clare whispered after seeing the short exchange. Meliss glared at her to shut her up. Clare noticed, immediately taking her eyes off the two and promptly gazed into her emptying mug. In the meantime, Truls continued cutting the steaming meat before him, passing the slices down to both Mads and Elhael, who nodded and gave thanks.

"To peace!" Truls called out, raising a slice of the flesh in one hand and a mug of ale in the other. "To peace!" the others in the hall returned, and the kings proceeded to bite into the Zebura's meat. Everyone cheered except for Leland, whom Fulco noted.

After the feast, the three left the hall, and went their separate ways towards their dormitories. Meliss went into her room, only to find a folded nightgown on her bed with a note on it. "Thanks for being the best 'lass' I've had the pleasure of meeting in a long time," the note said, and was signed with only the letter 'L' at its base. She smiled, briefly forgetting about the possibility of her and her friends dying after having been overheard.

This fits as if she had it made for me, she thought.

She gave it a quick twirl and giggled at the flayed movement it gave. She bent over to look over it once more, and then slid under the covers of her bed.

The following morning, Fulco was doing his habitual rounds about the castle, ensuring everything was in order. After completing his checks on most of the areas in the castle, he found himself in the kitchen where a brunch was being prepared.

Smelling the fresh pastries and fruits being prepared and sliced, he smiled at the scent of it all. Washing the fruit to be prepared was none other than Leland, who could think of nearly nothing else other than last night's happenings.

Between the hangover and anxiety I feel, I don't know which one is worse, he thought.

"A late start today for all of us, I imagine," Fulco said, stopping beside him. The dark circles around Leland's eyes grew wide, and his heart began to race. "Lucky to have survived after last night's festivities, wouldn't you say?" Fulco asked. Leland simply nodded and dared not to look at his potential interrogator. Fulco noticed that he was nearly unresponsive, save the nodding. "Might I have a word with you in private, Leland?" he asked quietly. Leland felt his heart stop for a moment, and broke into a cold sweat. He nodded again, and followed Fulco to the large, nearly emptied pantry.

"I'm not going to mince my words and just be done with it," Fulco began. Leland managed to raise his head to look at Fulco, but could barely withstand his gaze. "Do you, or do you not confirm that our queen had some form of physical... *interaction* with Bashaa during their little expedition yesterday afternoon?" Fulco asked sternly. Leland's face paled even further than it already was. "Answer me," Fulco said calmly, but in a voice that chilled the very air around them. Leland looked for some form of escape around him, but found nothing. "Answer me," Fulco said again.

This is it; this is why I'm going to die, Leland thought. *He knows.*

"If I have to ask you once more, Leland, I promise you that I will not be as amiable as I am trying to be here," Fulco said sternly. Leland's lips fluttered, and he mumbled words indistinctly. "Could you repeat that, please?" Fulco asked. "Alright, alright!" Leland finally broke down. He was in tears. "I hadn't any clue he was with the queen before last night when the ladies and I were talking about the kings. I saw him entering the cellar yesterday, but I didn't see whom he was with," Leland said through bubbling spit. "Once I saw him enter the cellar, I figured he had gotten lost somehow. I went to investigate whether he was lost, and I heard... *noises.*"

"What noises?" Fulco inquired. "Like he was having his way with someone. At first, I thought it was some servant girl he might have coerced into doing that. Clare was the one who informed me about his *expedition* with the queen." Leland replied. "We stumbled upon the conclusion that they had done something in the cellar," he said quietly, hoping that no one else would hear. "I see," Fulco said. "Clare and Meliss, correct?" he asked. Leland nodded quickly, desperately trying to keep his knees from buckling out from under him. "Clean yourself. You're making a mess," Fulco said, handing him a handkerchief from his left pocket.

"So, with the information from Clare and your knowledge of him having his way with someone, how does the young one fit into all of this?" Fulco asked. "She had nothing to do with it! She was just at the wrong place at the wrong time. Again, I swear, she had nothing to do with it," he replied after blowing his nose. "*Oh?*" Fulco asked surprised. "She tried to shut us up before we had gone too far, but it was too late for that. We figured you had overheard it since you walked right past us," Leland explained.

"I see," Fulco replied, nodding gravely. "Who else knows about this?" he asked. "No one except for the thr-... four of us, now," Leland replied. "And the other two will keep their traps shut?" Fulco asked. Leland nodded, and sniffed a wad of snot back up his nostrils. Fulco was disgusted by the sight, and looked away.

"Alright, so here's what you're going to do," he began. "You're not going to tell another living soul about this, and if I catch wind that you did... well, let's just say I don't know what they *won't* do to make you suffer for it, understand?" he said with a tone Leland hadn't expected to come from him. Leland nodded quickly, wanting only to be free of his living nightmare.

"Good. Now get the fuck out of here, get back to work. Keep your mouth shut, you hear me?" Fulco asked, stepping out of his path to the pantry doorway. Leland shot out of the pantry and immediately went straight back to washing the fruit, not even looking about him to see if anyone had noticed his physical state or not.

Little did he or Fulco know that just outside the pantry door, someone had eavesdropped on their entire conversation. The rumor spread like wildfire around the palace, and within two days, the entire kingdom had heard what had happened. On the third day, yelling could be heard throughout the palace.

"Tell me the rumors aren't true, Fulco," Truls begged his servant. They were in his private study, surrounded by notes, books, scrolls and lit candles. Though dawn was on the rise, it was still dark enough outside to know that it was still a few hours away.

"I'm afraid so, your majesty," Fulco solemnly replied. "Leland, the manservant, had seen them walking about the palace without any guards present, and Clare had heard people making love in the cellars," he continued. Truls' eyes were bloodshot and had dark circles around them. He paused, staring off into one of the dark corners of his study with dead eyes. "I will have his head on a spike. I will make his ancestors weep once they see how he enters the afterlife. In pieces," he said, his voice rumbled like a rockslide. "But what of the peace you so loudly proclaimed the other night, your majesty?" his servant asked, visibly shaken at his king's reaction.

"Imagine you were in my place, if you will, Fulco," Truls began. "You hold a council of peace, and yet there goes one of your so-called 'allies' behind your back to plough your wife," he said, raising his voice at the last segment and glaring at the person standing before him. "I wish you would tell me exactly what the fuck that is supposed to do to a man," he said. Fulco remained silent, casting his gaze towards the ground around his feet. "Tell me!" Truls bellowed.

"I don't know, your majesty. Really, I don't," Fulco finally spat out. "What I do know is that if you kill Bashaa, the peace treaty will be broken, and you will be fighting a war on two fronts, which has never worked for anyone in the past, your majesty," he said.

"Then what the actual fuck am I supposed to do, since I am not allowed to gut the little weasel-shit?" he asked. "Talk to his father and have him punish his son, your majesty," Fulco said, leaning in and lowering his voice. "We both know of their customs regarding such matters, your majesty," he continued, insinuating that whatever came as a result would not be a lovely sight to behold.

"You're a fool if you think a man like Bashir would punish his own son in such a way, Fulco," Truls said. "I believe he would, in fact, congratulate his son for having his way with my wife. After all, she has been and still is desired by all men who cross her path," he continued. "*Almost all*, your majesty," Fulco said. "Ah, yes," Truls nodded, realizing what his servant meant. "In any case, they have laws that are imposed that would not allow him any other way to avoid such a thing, your majesty," Fulco replied.

Truls toyed with the idea of Bashir suffering at the hands of their laws, however, his imagination began drifting to the satisfaction it would give him to wring the life out of the 'weasel-shit' himself. He looked back at Fulco, and nodded in agreement. "Very well, arrange a meeting with Bashir and his son in the main hall when daylight comes. Oh, and Fulco," Truls said. "Yes, your majesty?" Fulco inquired. "Tell no one what we've discussed," Truls said gravely. Fulco nodded, bowed and turned to walk out of the study, leaving Truls in his seat in the candlelit room.

Dawn came, and Truls sat atop his throne, while Leona still slept. The morning light shone through the stained-glass windows, lighting the main hall's walls with all sorts of different colors. His eyes burned due to sleep deprivation, and was leaning heavily on his right arm.

Fulco swung open the mighty doors and passed through

them, not even glancing at the guards who stood watch in full harness and in silence. "King Bashir, and Prince Bashaa of Harut, your Majesty," Fulco announced. Truls' eyes regained their burning hatred at Bashaa's name. Fulco took his leave, and proceeded down one of the halls.

"King Truls," Bashir said in a loud and firm voice. "King Bashir," Truls said, trying to hide the hatred in his voice. "I do not fully understand why only we two have been summoned, whereas my advisors and other members of the party remain asleep," Bashaa said, with uncertainty ruling his tone. "That, my lord, is simply because I decided I didn't want them here," Truls answered. "You see, this matter is between the three of us. *Oh*, excuse me, the four of us. Although only two of us know who the fourth one is," Truls said, glaring at Bashaa who noticed his gaze was directed at him.

"My lord, you are speaking in riddles, and it is too early in the morning to try to decipher them," Bashaa said, rubbing his eyes. "Then, if your feeble little mind cannot solve them, why don't you ask your son?" Truls said sarcastically. Bashaa's eyes opened wide, and he immediately looked about him for some kind of support. He had forgotten for a moment that it was only he and his father who had been summoned. "Tell him, boy," Truls said, impatience ruling his voice. "Tell me what?" Bashir looked at his son who began to shake his head.

Truls rose from his throne. "He. Fucked. My. Wife," he said, accentuating his words with the sound of his heavy foot fall. "My son would never do such a thing, my lord," Bashir said in disbelief. "Tell him, tell him how it is all a lie," he said nervously. Bashaa couldn't move, he simply stood there looking like a paralyzed half-wit. "Tell him!" Bashir continued to try and coax him to speak.

"You've been had," Truls said, moving towards the pair. "I

know the dirty little secret you and my wife have together," he said with his voice low. "My lord," Bashaa began. "Don't you dare call me *lord,* you oozing prick-sore," Truls yelled in the young man's face.

"This is a conversation where, apparently, status does not matter. You come in here, drink my wine, gorge yourself on my food, and have the nerve to plough my wife? You are not a prince. You are not a man. You are nothing but a worthless cur, and I would not be surprised if you had a shriveled worm for a prick. You have defiled my wife, shamed my kingdom, and both under my very nose. I would have you dragged through the streets by your balls for all that you've done, and I will ensure that you make it to the Underworld myself," he bawled in rage.

Truls reached back under his tunic to draw a large dagger, and thrust it at lightning speed into Bashaa's neck, spewing blood onto his wrist and forearm. Bashir screamed in terror as his bleeding son fell to the ground. Truls began to step over his writhing legs, and kneeled down on top of his chest. His eyes glared with hatred, and his knuckles were white due to his grip on the dagger. He began to sever the dying man's head off, while Bashir turned and ran out of the door as quickly as he could, calling his men out to flee the castle. Truls separated head from body, and danced in the man's blood for a short while, holding the head by the hair.

Fulco re-entered the hall after hearing the scream, and fainted at the sight of Truls dancing in blood, holding the head in one hand, with the dagger in the other. Truls looked about him and noticed his servant on the ground. He cared nothing for him since he had just slain his newest enemy. His guards hadn't moved an inch, after all, there was nothing they could have done to stop it from happening. He chuckled to himself, and it increased to a fit of maniacal laughter.

Leona rushed down the stairs to see what the scream was about, and found her husband in the pool of blood, and screamed. Truls turned to look at her, his face was spattered with blood, and the rest of him was now covered in it.

She held back bile as best as she could, and bolted back up the flight of stairs she had just come down. She ran through the hallways and finally found what she thought to be a sanctuary in the confines of her room. She entered it, and slammed the door behind her, bolting it in fear of her husband.

By the graces, that was Bashaa's head in his hand, she thought, nearly vomiting once more. *Shit, that means he knows about what happened, and I'll probably be next by the looks of things.*

Bile had returned to greet her mouth once more. The fear of her husband coming to kill her had almost overwhelmed her, so she went to the corner of her room, and burst into tears.

Meanwhile, the king was dismembering the man he had just killed in the main hall. Thorsen and Gorm - the captain of the guard who dressed similarly to Thorsen - walked in, shocked at the scene. "Your majesty," Gorm began in a low voice. "Shut up and listen to me, Gorm," Truls growled. "Gather the men, and chase down Bashaa and his party if they follow him. Otherwise, kill them here," he said.

Thorsen and Gorm looked down upon the parts of the man, and decided it would be best not to question the king's decision. "It will be done, your majesty," Gorm said, disgust clearly showing on his face. The guardsmen left, and Truls grinned as he severed the second leg from the torso, placing it into the pile of body parts he had now created.

He bundled up the pieces into the dead man's robe, and dragged the chunks outside. He ordered the guards to give him their spears and they did so without question, save for the ones about what was left of the Harutian prince. When he arrived at the front gate of the main palace, he unraveled the pieces, planted the spears in the ground, and skewered the body parts. The head faced outward with its lifeless, gaping expression portraying a silent scream. A few of the guards who had been posted just outside that gate had their breakfast coming out of the wrong hole in a flash.

Truls finished what he believed to be his masterpiece, and spat on the lifeless head. He began to make his way back towards the main palace, where he found Gorm riding out with his war party to hunt down Bashaa and, possibly, his men. He grinned, and continued his way towards Leona's quarters. He made his way up the stairs with a spattering sound due to the blood-soaked shoes he was still wearing, and began calling out his wife's name like one would if they were calling their pet.

"Leona! I know you're in there, Leona. Don't hide from me, my sweet. I'm not going to hurt you, I simply want to speak to you," his massive voice called out in an eerie tone - the likes he had never emitted before.

She was still in the corner of her room, her eyes swollen from weeping when she heard her name being called. A chill went down her spine, and she stood up. The sound of her husband calling her drew closer to her door, and she began to desperately look for something to defend herself with. There was nothing she could see that she would reach before he came in. She heard the click-flack of the bolt being undone by the key he possessed, and her stomach felt like it was turning inside out.

"Ah, there you are, my dove," he said in a disturbing tone. She could barely breathe at the sight of him. "You murdered him!" she exclaimed. "Yes, I did; ridding the world of yet another vermin," he replied. "How could you do this after saying what you said at the feast?" she asked.

He paused for a moment, appearing to be deep in thought.

"Because I wanted to," he replied. "You see, my dove, a man does not defile another man's wife without paying for it one day or another," he began. "He defiled you, the rumor spread like wildfire, and now the whole kingdom thinks that I'm a fool, and that you are a worthless whore!" he shouted the last five words.

Leona was shocked, and her eyes watered as her disgust for the man she had once married grew exponentially. "Prove me wrong," he said, noticing her countenance. "Tell me that you didn't let him have his way with you, and that I made one of the largest mistakes of my life," he said.

Leona paused. She knew that he might kill her if she told him the truth, but she stood her ground. "I won't prove you wrong," she said. "What?" he asked, darkening his tone. "I won't prove you wrong, because it wasn't he who had his way with me. In fact, it was the other way around," she said. "He tried to charm me with his worthless wit, but deep down all I wanted was a good fuck because you can't even keep it up. Not even when you force yourself on me as you have so many times in the past, you prickless pig," she said.

"You bitch!" he said, smacking her to the ground with a backhand strike across her face. "I have given you everything in my kingdom, everything you have ever wanted, and this is how you repay me? By shoving some wart-laden prick up your snatch? I will see you pay for what you've done as well," he said with fiery eyes, walking towards her. She was quickly on her feet, and attempted to circle around him without paying too much attention to her surroundings.

She rammed into her easel, and had to lean on it for a brief moment to regain her balance. He smacked her across the face once more. The blow forced her to turn around, and he began to lift her dress.

Tears streamed down her cheeks.

"Help!" she cried out in despair. Truls covered her mouth, muffling her voice. "No one is going to save you now. Not Bashaa, nor anyone else in this fucking place. You're in my kingdom. My rules are the only thing that apply here, and currently, my only rule is that I don't have any rules. I don't have to be careful of what I do to you" he said in her ear through bared teeth.

She glanced down, and through her tears saw a thick paintbrush lying on the easel before her. She bit into Truls' finger, and he reeled with the pain. She had drawn blood. "You fucking whore!" he yelled. He stepped towards her, and she rammed a paintbrush upwardly under his jaw, piercing his brain. Blood ran down her hand and wrist as his eyes rolled into his head. Leona pulled her impromptu weapon out of his jaw, and watched his body fall to the ground, where it wriggled and writhed like a beheaded serpent.

The king was dead, and she breathed heavily.

Her body felt as though it had been lit aflame from the adrenaline flowing through it. She still held her weapon in her hand. It was covered in blood and other tissue. She could hear the bubbling sounds of her attacker's blood leaving its body and leaking out onto the floor. She wiped her forehead clean of the sweat, and cleared her eyes of the tears that still welled up in her eyes. She shook her head, and dropped the weapon. She walked over to the fresh body, and looked at it for a few moments.

I feel calmer than I ever have in my entire life, she thought as she wiped the remaining tears from her cheeks.

She had to figure out what she was supposed to do with the body. She sat on the side of her bed, staring at it for a few moments, recovering from it all.

I killed the king. He probably would have killed me, and I know people will believe me if I said he would have, she thought.

She stood up from her bedside, and grabbed hold of his beard. She tugged so hard his head almost came off, skin tearing at the base of the neck. She continued until the body began to move in the same direction she was. She dragged him down the stairs, hearing the blood smear across the steps, while his hands and feet flopped about like boned fish. She could hear a commotion of people and servants gathered in the main hall.

They must have heard about Bashir, she thought.

She continued to drag the king's body down the stairs, only to find that Bashir's body was no longer present, and that only a puddle of dried blood remained.

Everyone in the hall looked at her. She was covered in blood, dragging the king's body by the beard. She looked at the servants who had gathered around. Nobody said a word. She continued to drag the body across the floor over to the throne's steps, where she paused for a moment.

She was panting heavily, and decided she needed to sit down. She looked up at the thrones, both hers and her now deceased husband's. She walked up the steps, dragging the body behind her, laying it on top of the carpet between the thrones, and seated herself on the larger of the two. The others in the room simply stood still and watched. She placed her arms on the armrests provided by the throne itself, and looked out over the people. A few of the servants tended to Fulco, who had hit his head hard when he fainted.

"The king is dead. He killed Prince Bashaa of Harut, tried to rape and kill me. He failed the latter, and now I am your ruler. If anyone objects to this, speak up now," she said. Everyone stood quietly, glancing back and forth at each other to see if any one of them would say something. "No objections? Good," she said. "Let this be a new beginning. A new age for Coltend.

A new age, for the people," she called out. The people, who were still processing the information, clapped slowly at first, but picked up speed after a little while.

Cheers began to be called out, and Fulco - now awake - smiled at her from a distance.

This will be a new beginning indeed, he thought and proceeded to make his way next to the queen.

He reached the steps, and was careful not to look at the body that lay at his queen's feet. He swallowed his breakfast. "I was the king's advisor, and now I will serve you just as I have served him, my queen," he said. "I *know* you told him, Fulco, but I thank you for giving me a final reason to kill him," she replied. "Think nothing of it, your majesty," he said, smiling nervously.

The people continued to cheer as more came in to discover what all the commotion was about, and those who did joined in with the crowd. Leona looked out over the amassing servants and smiled.

My turn, she thought.

CHAPTER 8

The Undergod

The Masked One led his apprentice down the gloaming halls, where the meeting with the Undergod was to take place. "May I ask you a question, my lord?" Athar began. "It would seem you already have, but yes," the Masked One retorted. "How is it that you first came into contact with the Undergod?" the young man asked skittishly. "As you will come to know over time, Athar, there are many things that happen to us that may drive us to some... *extreme measures*," the Masked One began.

"Some men choose easier paths, by simply making a deal with him or fate itself. Others, not unlike myself, choose to try and work together with him to achieve a greater goal. He is very impatient, capricious, and unforgiving, so you must mind your manners," he continued.

"You didn't answer my question, master," Athar said shyly after a moment's pause. "And you noticed like anyone with half a brain would, might I add. Perhaps you're not an absolute waste of a core," the Masked One replied. "I will not answer that question for one of two reasons: the first is because it is sensitive information that I am not about to disclose. The second is simply because I don't want to, so shut your trap, and follow me without saying a word until we reach our meeting point, understood?" he said, clearly irritated. Athar felt a chill go down his spine.

Shit. I can't do anything or say anything without the cheese falling off his bread. There's something about him that feels familiar from my life before coming here, and I can sense that it is just under my very nose, Athar thought. *I knew I should have paid more attention to those books my father always tried to make me read.*

"Yes, my lord," Athar replied, trying to hide the sigh he wanted to let out so badly. They continued walking down the dimly lit halls, passing countless other staircases that led to, as of yet unknown places to the young man. After a few minutes of walking, the Masked One finally reached the doorway to his private study, where he unlocked and swung the door open with a wisp of mana. The two of them walked in, and Athar noted the details within the room to memory.

A large pentagram of salt in the center of the floor, candles on every point, a large crystal in the very center of the drawing itself, and a desk at the base of it. It looks like another summoning circle, but this time it's more complex, Athar thought.

"And you would be right," the Masked One said, answering his slave's thoughts. "How the...?" Athar said, astonished. The Masked One, uncharacteristically, chuckled. "I have always been able to read your thoughts, even the ones never meant for me," he said, interrupting what Athar was about to say.

He froze.

"Oh, come now. Did you really think I would take you in without being able to keep tabs on what goes through your puny, little mind?" The Masked One asked. "Until I extracted your deepest memories that lay within your core, I could only hear immediate thoughts. But now? Now I know everything. There is nothing that you will ever be able to hide from me," he said. Athar stood in silence both in his mind, and in his mouth, while his head hung low.

"Calm down, Athar," he began. "The reason I am revealing this is simply that if you think *I* am horrible for doing so, the Undergod can and *will* do much worse to you," he continued, leaving Athar shaking more deeply than ever. The Masked One grinned maliciously, and turned about to face the pentagram drawn on the floor. Athar's eyes remained wide open, remembering everything he had thought in the presence of his master.

The Masked One's eyes darkened as he began drawing power from the Underworld. Once he had enough encapsulating him, he broke his connection, and raised his hands. A ball of dark mana began to grow between his hands. "I request an audience," he said aloud, and cast the sphere down into the crystal placed into the center of the pentagram, shattering it.

The entire room began to shake and vibrate with a ferocity Athar had never seen before, and he was genuinely concerned that everything would begin to crash and fall. There was a voluminous puff of smoke from where the crystal once was, and a mixture of horrid smells like rotting flesh and sulfur filled the air. Athar could barely breathe, whereas the Masked One was accustomed to such smells.

A disgruntled voice like thunder rolled out through the smoke and across the room, shaking all of the books on the nearby shelves off of their supports. "Who dares disturb me?" the Undergod asked. "Oh great and mighty Volzuk, I have summoned thee to council," the Masked One replied. The Undergod looked down upon the one who had summoned him. "Have I not done enough for you thus far?" asked. "You have done more than enough, my lord, however, I have yet another question to ask you," the Masked One replied. Volzuk tipped his nose. "This had better be worth my time here, worm," he said. "It is, my lord," the Masked One replied.

Athar nearly puddled himself once his senses realized who stood before him.

I wasn't aware of the actual size of the Undergod until now, and had only ever seen inaccurate depictions of him in books back home, he thought.

His lengthy horns nearly scraped the ceiling, talons grew down nearly past his knees, and his overall figure was that of a mountain of rotting, twitching flesh. The skinless figure loomed over the two humans, like a troll to ants, gazing down upon these inferior beings. His eyes burning bright with a blood-red fire, flames licking the base of his horns.

His sharp features would strike fear into any who looked upon him, Athar thought.

Before the Masked One could answer his master's order, Volzuk's gaze pierced Athar's core. The long, fleshy tentacle-like goatee hung heavily from his chin, swaying with the movements of his head. "Who are *you* to judge my appearance?" he asked the young man who could have been easily confused for a marble statue. His jaw pushed forward so that an underbite showed. "My lord, please forgive my servant's ineptitude to keep his thoughts to himself," the Masked One replied, stepping in front of Athar. "Speak then," the Undergod said after weighing his servant's words.

"According to our agreement, I am to overthrow the powers that rule this continent by using the creatures you have gifted me, and bring you what you requested. The outcast Synners, among other traitors to the Continent, will come to aid us in our quest once the time is right. All of this has, so far, gone according to plan. However, a promising endeavor has been drawn to my attention," the Masked One said.

Volzuk's brow furrowed. "Careful, mage," the Undergod

began. "You know the origins of what you speak of, and I am not inclined to toy with your idea of using what I need on your little experiments. You already have powers far beyond most of your kind. Adding fuel to your fire thinking it will aid my own is folly. I know what the plant can do, and, if you use it how you are planning to, you might find that things will not go your way." he continued. Athar could feel the mana being used to pull the thoughts out of his master's head.

"I have to try, my lord," the Masked One began. "The Synners have become increasingly capable of cutting down our minions, and we need a way to bridge the gap in power if we are to succeed in our plans," he explained. "*My* minions, you mean," Volzuk said threateningly. "I am thoroughly disappointed in you, *Masked One*," he said the name with a hint of sarcasm. "I had hoped that you would differ from the other humans of your world, and show true strength and wisdom unlike the ones before you. Yet here you are, acting as foolish as you consider your servant to be," the Undergod said. His tone was about as grim as his features were.

"I have not come to grovel and beg at your feet, Lord of the Underworld," the Masked One began with an air of irritation. "I have simply come seeking your advice. We both know that even with dwindling numbers, the Synners still pose a threat," he spread his arms, and paused for a moment. His eyes were now little more than slits after a brief, pensive pause.

"A *threat*? To whom? To you, perhaps, but not to me. Their fortresses, armies, weapons, and spells mean nothing to me," Volzuk said angrily.

"If they truly pose no threat, then why do you need my help?" the Masked One asked, knowing the risk of doing so. Athar, who had been trying to maintain his composure, nearly gagged at the Undergod's swelling power. "Silence!" Volzuk shouted, losing his composure. "You dare to use that tone with me, you insolent worm?" he shouted in fury. "I can just as easily strip your power from you, leaving you to rot like the flesh upon my body," he said, his voice vibrating both the mage and servant's bones. The young man swallowed hard, thinking that his master had just invoked the rage of this dark god.

"You should already know what the gods of the Ethereal have done to me. There is not a moment more that I will waste discussing this. Uphold your end of the bargain, and bring me what I asked for. If you fail me, you will suffer," Volzuk said frustratedly. The Masked One sighed. "You seem to have forgotten who *I* am, my lord. It is true that you are powerful, but not all-powerful yet," he said in a dark tone. "You could strip me of the power you have given me, but may I remind you that I had no small amount of power before pledging my allegiance. Now that I know the ins and outs of the dark power you gave me so long ago, it would only be a matter of time before I could return to my former state," the Masked One replied.

The Undergod grunted deeply. "If I had my way, I would have rid you of existence all those years ago," he said. "Except you didn't. You, no matter how frustrated you may be with me, need me alive," The Masked One began. "You are not yet strong enough to maintain yourself in *both* worlds," he continued with confidence. "That is the *only* reason you are still alive," the Undergod threatened.

"That doesn't frighten me as much as you think it would, my lord," the mage replied. "You're bolder than before," Volzuk said in a curious tone. "I have to be, if I am to do your bidding, my lord," the Masked One replied with a grin. The skinless figure sighed in disgust at his servant. "Do what you must. Just give me what I require," he said.

"Then, I will continue as planned, my lord," the Masked

One replied. "Although, the Kings of the Continent have just made it a little more difficult to continue our original plan," he continued. "Fear not, for their time, too, is coming to a close," Volzuk began. "I see that their demise has already begun," he concluded. "What do you mean, Great One?" Athar, who had finally mustered the courage to speak, asked shakily.

The massive figure drew closer and stared into his core. Athar began to tremble even more, as he felt a similar sensation to what his master had done to his core earlier. "Ah. I *do* know who you are," Volzuk said, the flames of his eyes nearly consuming the young man.

Damn, of course he knows, the young man thought. *I can hardly withstand the pressure of his presence.*

"As for your question, I will not ruin the fun for you, but you will see," Volzuk said mysteriously, returning to his original position. Athar shuddered, but the Masked One did and said nothing. He was too focused on maintaining the connection between himself and the Underworld.

"Your servant is more interesting than I originally thought," Volzuk began with a curious tone. "If he betrays you, what will you do?" he asked. "I will gut him and feed him to the beasts I have locked up here," the Masked One replied.

I know you can hear me, and I knew you wouldn't hesitate if I did something of the sort, Athar's thoughts directed themselves to the Masked One.

So, what else do you want from me? his thoughts traveled, but were met with no response.

"I can also hear you, boy," Volzuk said, sending a chill down Athar's spine. "However, if you are even half the man you should be, then say it with your voice, not your thoughts," he continued.

The young man stepped forward, gazing upward into the

Undergod's eyes. "Great One, you know who I am and where I am from," he began. "With all of the topics covered in this conversation, I want to know what role I supposedly play," Athar said, barely able to hold his ground against the massive figure before him. The Masked One sneered at his audacity to move towards the Undergod.

"I will not tell you, for you must see that for yourself, Athar," Volzuk began. "If I were to tell you about your future, as I currently see it, you might begin to think too highly of yourself. The future is always changing, and you knowing yours would be jeopardizing the fate your master and I have waited so long to weave into motion," he continued. Athar was taken aback, absorbing the words that had just been spoken to him. "I understand, Great One," Athar conceded with a bow.

Volzuk nodded. "Do not forget what I have said here," he said, pointing at the pair. "We will not, my lord," the Masked One replied. "Speak with your contacts around the Continent, and do not fail me," the Undergod replied, quickly lowering his hand, twisting the smoky floor and drawing it towards the floor. The large figure vanished into the cracks of the stone floor beneath his two servants, and whatever remained formed a thin layer of fog at their feet and ankles.

Impressive, Athar thought.

"I thought I told you to keep your mouth shut," the Masked One began, turning towards his apprentice. "You said I was to keep my 'trap' shut until we had reached our meeting point, my lord," Athar replied. "You were supposed to have remained silent the whole meeting," the Masked One retorted. "You never said anything of the sort," his apprentice replied.

The little shithead is already taking after my example, The Masked One sighed.

"Follow me," his voice rumbled, and he began to walk briskly.

"Where are we going, master?" Athar asked. "You shall see," his master replied. Athar had a hard time keeping up with his master, whose stride was considerably much longer than his. After what seemed to be an eternity of winding, dark halls, they had finally made it to the entrance of the great library.

"Whoa," Athar said, his excitement showing clearly on his face. The bookshelves lined the twenty-meter-high walls, packed so tightly a knife's blade could barely fit between them on some shelves. "Your limited mana abilities should be augmented, even if only a little through these books. Many of these I have acquired from the black market, banned by mages and Synners alike," the Masked One began.

Athar's jaw dropped, and he began to smile. "You want me to learn from these forbidden books, master?" he asked, recognizing a few of the titles. "Forbidden for who? There is no such thing as 'forbidden' if one has enough power. Prove yourself worthy of them," his master said.

They reached the grand hall of the library, where books of all kinds, shapes and sizes lay, with no ladders to be seen. "Master, how am I to reach the ones I cannot grasp with my arms?" Athar asked. "Find a way," his master replied. Athar turned and looked around him, wondering where to begin.

'History of the Continent', 'A Voyage To The Underworld', 'Dissection, by Nexis Pelantyr', 'The Undergod And What We Know', 'Spells For Those With Baseline Mana Manipulation Skills, by Feranger Efer', he read the few titles to himself and instantly reached for the last one.

"My lord, what is this?" He removed it from the shelf it was on, covered in dust and other particles he couldn't identify. He brushed off the dust and showed it to his master. The Masked One closely observed the book his servant presented to him. "Hmm, this one might be a good place for you to start. After all, you have much to learn," he said. "That was... uncharacteristically supportive of you, my lord," Athar said, knowing that whether he said his thoughts aloud didn't matter anymore.

"*Uncharacteristic*, you say?" the Masked One asked. "Normally, you have some demeaning remarks to make, but I think this is the first time you have shown a side that is far more... *human* than I am used to, my lord," Athar explained. His master stood in silence for a moment as if pondering how to respond to the comment.

"Athar, I have always sought power," the Masked One began. Athar's ears perked up like a dog hearing the word 'treat'. "And throughout my many, *many* years procuring it, I have often found that those who do not seek power, or get excited by the prospect of it are useless to me. Until I had pulled those memories from your core, I had assumed you to be weak-willed, skittish, and an idiot in my eyes. That perspective has now changed," he continued.

"However, given your history, I can see much more potential in you than before, and so, I will help you gain what you seek. That which you hid deep in your core from the world," he said in a much warmer voice than Athar had ever heard before. "Y-you're going to mentor me, my lord?" he asked. "*Mentor* is a strong word. Think of it as more of a *push in the right direction* than anything else. There is only so much I can do for you, since you will eventually walk your own path," the Masked One concluded.

"*Walk my own path*," Athar repeated the words. "What do you mean by that, my lord?" he asked. "I have already said too much," his master replied. "Use this hall as you see fit. I will be expecting you to be here more often than not, as I will have a few glicks to bring some of your things down from your room that you will need." Athar blinked.

I can't believe what I'm hearing. It's like he's turned into someone else entirely in the span of a day, he thought.

"You really should remember that I can hear what you're thinking," his master said calmly. Athar sunk his head into his chest. "Forgive me, my lord. I will take my leave and study at your behest," he said sheepishly. "Good," the Masked One said, leaving the hall.

Athar traced his finger along the spine of the book his master had suggested, and opened it.

This is the author's signature. How long has this book been around? he thought as his eyes finally met the preface.

"This book, incomplete as all good magic books should be, serves as a guideline to the one who desires to acquire a higher knowledge than those of his or her colleagues, or as a review for those who already have. All spells and incantations do not require a basic knowledge of mana to learn, as I aim to instruct those how to properly draw from both Realms. Though many believe that one must be a direct descendant of one who has imbibed the famed plant's formula, this is not so, as I will demonstrate in the first chapter," he read.

Did I read that correctly? Holy shit, this changes everything for me! he thought, proceeding to read over the sentence once more.

He flipped through the next few pages, some intentionally left blank for note taking, and found himself reading over the first chapter.

"With that being so, it is important to acknowledge that the plant simply makes mana manipulation easier, more effective, and poses much less risk. But with enough concentration, and paying close attention to my instructions, one should be able to perform to a close level as one who has. Perhaps, one day, even surpassing them. The process, which I will now describe, is crucial in its order: First comes the Silence. Not of the world around you, but the silence of one's thoughts. One must not think of anything other than the task at hand

to prevent those thoughts from interfering with one's ultimate goal. Second comes the Immolation of Consciousness. The most difficult part of connecting to the other Realms lies here, for an untrained and unsilenced mind will cause one to lose grip of reality, driving one mad."

That's not very comforting. I can see why this is one of the forbidden books, Athar thought.

"The Immolation of Consciousness requires one to disconnect one's consciousness from one's body. The reason for it being called Immolation is that once you have disconnected, you become vulnerable to the happenings of the Real. There are, of course, multiple stages one can reach of attunement, allowing them to maintain their Immolation of Consciousness and continuously draw mana while performing tasks. Those who are capable, however, are few and far between, as oftentimes the requirements needed to achieve that are true life and death situations that can unlock the core's potential."

"Although this may sound daunting and considerably harrowing, fear not, for time in the Real is slowed to a halt, granting you time to do what you need. However, one false move in the realm from which you draw, and only half of your consciousness will return to your body, while the other roams the vast near emptiness of the realm from which you are drawing. Time in the Real will return to its normal pace, although one will be about as conscious as a potato is of its own existence, making one truly vulnerable."

"This is where the formula comes in handy, for the one who drinks it, does not run that risk. Seeing as how you, dear reader, are either unable to perform the ritual properly, or simply cannot get your hands on the formula and plant themselves is why I am writing this. The third step is the Draw. This requires one to reach out, as though to grab something in thin air, and coax the mana to do your bidding. Directing it where it needs to be for usage. A word of caution: Condensed mana can get very hot, very quickly, so it is customary *to have a ward-ring or something of the sort to protect one's skin and clothes from being charred. I have provided one such ring with the copy of the book, just in case one hasn't got one on their person."*

Athar turned the book over, and found a leather pouch sewn into the back of the book. He pulled out the ring and wondered at it. It was a pure silver ring, and yet instead of feeling cool to his touch, it felt warm, as though it had been placed in a bath of warm water. He put it on, and the ring shrunk itself to fit his ring finger perfectly.

"Heh," he chuckled.

"One must remember that after one has drawn from their realm of choice, one must condense it to the location of the origin of the cast. Spells are used to activate the condensed mana, and can only be released by using one of the innumerous variations. Assuming that one knows nothing, practice the following: Opening the palm of one's hand, and scrunching the fingers without making a fist will leave one in the starting position for the Exar spell.

"To cast, one needs simply to reopen the fingers, pointing in the direction one wants the mana to go. This will create a powerful blast of power. The more mana one can channel, the more powerful the spell. This can be done in reverse as well, to pull objects towards oneself. That is the Inar spell."

"Now, one must find a quiet spot, preferably with plenty of room about oneself. Ensure that there is no way in which one may be disturbed. Every living thing should be removed from the vicinity, on the off chance one's consciousness does not return to the body, of course."

"This is mad," Athar said aloud, nervously smiling.

"Candles and such are not required, though they are useful should one try and perform this during the late hours of the night. For one's first attempt, it is required to either sit or kneel with the toes bent and touching the ground for extra stability, as the return of consciousness

tends to knock one off one's feet the first time."

Athar walked to the center of the large, circular library, and kneeled with the book still in hand.

"Deep, timed breaths with eyes closed are advised, to achieve maximum relaxation. During this time, one must clear one's mind of all other thoughts, as they tend to get in the way of things. Once one has completed that task, and the full amount of available concentration has been achieved, one must choose between the Ethereal and the Underworld. Good emotions will drive one's consciousness towards the Ethereal, whilst ones such as anger and hatred will take the path less traveled to the Underworld. One must be mindful of the choice one is to make."

"All that to say it is time for you, dear reader, to attempt it for yourself. Remember: Silence, Immolation of Consciousness, Draw, Condense, and Cast. Good luck," the end of the first chapter had written near the bottom of the page.

"Alright," Athar said aloud as though it would boost his courage. He closed his eyes and breathed in and out in a calm and concise manner. Thoughts of his life before coming here to serve the Masked One returned. Partying, drinking, whoring and gambling where the days never seemed to end were thrown into his mind's eye all at once. He concentrated on removing them from his mind, though it took longer than expected.

Damn this is difficult, he thought.

He continued battling his memories for the Silence for hours on end. He had lit hour-candles to try and keep track of just how long it would take him, should he succeed.

His mind finally cleared after a few hours, and there was the *Silence. He dared not acknowledge that by thinking of any words, but he had found it. Silence. It had come at last, and he felt a peace ruling him. He maintained his breathing pattern almost subconsciously, and began to focus on what he had to do next: choose an emotion to rule.*

He hadn't thought about it before, but he was unsure of which one to pick. He felt both good and bad in him, however he was unable to decide which to veer towards.

In his newfound form gazing into the formless world, he could see a pair of spheres forming in front of him, one was bursting with color, while the other appeared dire and gray. He remained there, he could see himself from outside of his physical body, kneeling in the center of the library that began to spawn in around him. He looked down upon himself, taking note of the candles whose flames were stopped in time. He knew he had been there for a long time, and hadn't expected it to have taken such an eternity. He looked back at the two spheres in front of him.

If I am to do my master's bidding to reach my goals, I must choose the dark, though I shudder at the thought of what is through it, the words crept in his mind, and he battled to get them out.

He regained his control, and furrowed his brow, walking towards the grim looking sphere. Tendrils flew from the dark sphere, and pulled him in rapidly.

He was in the Underworld.

The dark, vast wasteland with the body-ridden bloodstream and dead trees lie about him. He breathed in the air, though he didn't need to, and the stench ran up his nostrils, almost knocking him off his feet that weren't yet firmly planted. He could hear the Underworld and looked about him quickly to ensure nothing was coming his way. He was shaken to his core, but maintained his focus.

He looked up at the dark sphere in the sky, enveloped in the dark streams of mana and thought back to the information from the book. "Draw," came into his mind, and he did so smoothly and calmly. It took a few seconds for his will to pull from the sphere, but when it came, it came down with a force he wasn't expecting, aggressively enshrouding his body. "Condense," the word showed up in his head, and he forced his will to move the mana towards his hand. It wavered a moment, and flowed slowly. He had to focus as much as he could to move it even an inch along his body.

Finally, the dark sphere was formed in his hand, and he could feel the warmth resonating from it on his face and upper forearm. He formed his hand according to the text, and returned his consciousness back through the same way he had come, both spheres growing more distant as he moved back into the Real.

The force of the return was so great that it knocked him backwards, and he had to use his free hand to support his weight. The candles had gone out, as there was a burst of air coming from the mana in his hand. "I've done it," he said with a laugh, glaring at the mutating sphere in his hand. "*Haha!*" he chuckled nervously. He didn't want to accidentally lose control of what had taken him so long to accomplish.

He recomposed himself back to his original position, keeping his eyes fixed on the sphere.

Cast, the word entered his mind.

He had maintained the shape of his hand, and thought about a direction to cast. "I'd better do it upwards so I don't knock anything over," he said aloud. He raised his arm upwards, never tearing his glance from the sphere. He breathed deeply once his arm had reached its full extent. "Here it goes," he said with a nod of his head.

He quickly opened his fingers to their maximum, and the sphere spread out from them, releasing a dark gray burst of mana that let off a deep *boom*, contorting the air around it.

"Holy shit," he said, exhaling in astonishment, and breathed heavily. "Holy shit," he said aloud again, and began to laugh. It was the first time he had laughed that hard in what seemed an age. He laughed so hard his stomach muscles began to cramp up. He controlled himself and tried to regain his composure, keeping his stomach muscles from locking up once and for all.

He looked for the book, and found it a little ways away. He scrambled over to it, realizing how physically taxing it had been on his body. He fell over on his belly, and crawled towards it. "More," he said in an exhausted voice. "I think you've had enough for one evening, Athar," a voice came from behind him. The Masked One had been watching him the whole time from the doorway.

"It feels good, doesn't it? All of that power in the palm of your hand," his master said with a slight touch of pride cutting through his voice. "I can't believe it," Athar said. "You should. I didn't expect you to get it on your first try, let alone cast such a powerful *Exar* as that. Now that I am certain you not only seek power, but embrace it, your status has certainly moved up with me," the Masked One said.

"I feel so weak, I don't even think I can stand," Athar said, panting heavily. "Drawing from the Underworld has its perks, but also its disadvantages," the Masked One began. "You see, drawing from the Ethereal is easy as it's not as taxing, but it's not as powerful as the Underworld," he said.

Athar grunted as he drew the book closer to him. "Keep it and study it," the Masked One said, walking over to his servant. "Here, drink this," he threw a small flask. "What is it, my lord?" Athar asked. "Since you have only just begun, you will need something to keep your vitality up until you learn to absorb souls, like me," the Masked One replied.

"Is that another reason for absorbing a core? Like why you did what you did to that ochelon, my lord?" the young man asked. "Precisely. For now, however, it's best if you get some rest. We have more work to do tomorrow, and you have more studying to do while I'm unavailable," the Masked One said.

Athar opened the flask, and smelled the contents. "Ugh, it reeks of deathmold," he said through coughs. "It is. Well, a diluted version of it, anyway," his master replied. "Now that you have drawn from the world of the dead, you must maintain that connection at the ready at all times," he explained.

    Athar looked up at his master and nodded. He put the flask to his lips, and shot back the contents, holding his breath. He squinted and squirmed at the taste, coughing heavily when he had finished. "Welcome to true power, Athar," the Masked One said, grinning under his mask.

CHAPTER 9

The Master

Following the battle with the pair of ochelons, Bernar and I made our way to the Master's study. The skin around my new scar was taut and still felt a little odd under my shirt, but I decided to ignore it as best I could.

Well, this will take some getting used to, but it's fine. I've got something the others, aside from Edryd, don't have: The first of many battle scars, I thought, wincing as I tried to move my shoulder, but the pain riddling my entire body was still too fresh for me to walk comfortably.

"How are you feeling?" Bernar asked. "I should be okay to have this conversation with the Master, but I might not wake up in time for training tomorrow," I said sarcastically.

"I'm not expecting you to show up tomorrow, but we have to tell the Master what we found before either of us can get any rest," my brother said regretfully. "*Fuuuuck.* Well, don't mind me if I pass out during the meeting," I said as playfully as I could muster. They walked through the doorway that led to the study, but quickly realized the Master was not present.

I wonder if he has a copy, I thought as I glazed over the books on the shelves.

We were both looking over the other books, hoping to find a copy of the one they had found in the study in the beast's lair. *"Dissection,"* I said to myself repeatedly, running my fingers along the spines of a score of books. Just as I was doing so, there was a knock on the door. "May I enter my own study?" the Master asked. I was startled at the knock, but Bernar had seen him coming and pulled away from the shelf. "I'm sorry, Master. I was only looking for…" I trailed off, noticing something in his hands.

"For this?" the Master held up a green book. I looked back at the shelf and noticed it was missing from right where I was about to look. "Y-yes, Master, but how did you…" I began. "I know why you've come, young Thoma," the Master cut me off with a smirk. "I know a lot of things, like what you found down there in the cave," he continued.

"We both have a lot of questions, Master. Though he probably has more than I do," Bernar said, trying to take the load off me, noticing I was visibly nervous about the whole situation.

We can't stop now. If we do, we'll lose all our momentum and the freshness of the information, I thought.

"I hope I have some of the answers you're looking for. However, you must ask the right questions," the Master said, motioning to the chair. Bernar helped me sit back in the chair with the carvings, as the Master sat with perfect posture in his chair, with his hands folded on his lap.

"So, tell me about what you found," the Master began. "With all due respect, Master, you already know what I found," I replied. "I do, but I want to hear it from you," the Master replied. I blinked and tried to collect my memories about the place.

"It was well hidden, behind where the beast had made its lair. There was a wall of rocks that could not have been formed naturally, so Bernar and I investigated. Mana induction seemed to be the only way to open the way to whatever was behind it. We found a study that seemed like no one had been there for many years, and everything was covered in dust. All except for the main desk, where there were some hand-written papers strewn across the top of it," I explained, hoping I had remembered everything correctly.

"And what exactly was written on the pages?" the Master asked me. I was fiddling with my fingers as I tried to find the right words to say. "Whoever was in there was trying to copy something from a book by a certain Nexis Pelantyr called *Dissection,* Master," I replied.

"*Ah*, yes. This one I have here," the Master replied, tapping the book on his desk. "The one I saw was old, and there were a few pages that had been torn out, Master. Almost as if they were trying to solve a riddle with the book as their guide," I said.

The Master didn't look as surprised as I thought he might, and Bernar showed concern about the reaction. "*A riddle*, you say. I was wondering how long it would take, after all, it is only a matter of time before it begins," the Master said ominously. I looked at my brother in utter confusion. "What do you mean *begins*, master?" I asked.

"You're a smart boy, Thoma," the Master began, unfolding his hands. "I'm sure you've conjured up some form of hypothesis as to why that book in particular was out of place with its pages torn out," he continued.

I thought about what the Master was trying to get at, but felt I didn't have enough information yet, so I decided to push my luck.

"From what I saw, the book contained information about the plant that the gods had given our kind centuries ago," I began.

"What do you suppose they tore out?" the Master asked. "I

believe there is someone who is trying to uncover its secrets; ones that weren't meant to see the light of day again, Master," I finally replied after a long pause.

The Master smiled grimly. "*That* is what I meant by *begins*, Thoma. Can you guess what was on those pages?" he asked, though I could only shake my head in response. "Do you believe they got what they came for?" the Master asked. "No, Master. At least, I'm not sure," I replied.

The Master raised an eyebrow and tilted his head. "Why do you think that is?" he asked. "I don't know, Master," I replied. The Master looked at Bernar, and Bernar nodded in agreement as if they had spoken telepathically. "Thoma, I think it's about time I shared something with you," the Master said.

Does Bernar already know this, then? He didn't mention his name, I thought.

"There are... *forces* in this world," the Master began. "These forces were once great powers that helped rule this world. Elven scholars were the first to discover them and have researched their existence for a long time. There is, however, some disagreement among the scholars as to what happened to a lot of the information we once had," he continued with a solemn tone.

"Some say that these powers are where the gods themselves draw their power from, while others claim that they are what commands mana and the natural world," he explained. "I'm confused, Master. What does this have to do with what was in the book?" I asked.

"There was a time where we had the answers as well, but some few-hundred years ago, all that vital knowledge was stripped from us. Every book, every scroll, and every memory regarding much of what happened during that time," the Master began, opening his own copy of the book. "Even my own book has had those pages torn from it. Look," he said, turning the book towards me.

"But why would anyone, or *anything* want that knowledge gone? Wouldn't the progress we'd made back then have benefitted this world?" I asked, genuinely confused as I stared at the remnants of the pages left behind, but the Master shook his head.

"Whatever the contents of those pages were, they have been lost to time. However, one of the elven scholars had a divination. A gift from the gods themselves, warning him that a war would be waged, and the weavings of fate would determine the fate of not just our world, but of *all* realms. Unfortunately, much of the information on the *source* of that prophecy was lost," he explained.

I could feel a weight on my chest, the words hitting me like a ballista.

"I see," I said, maintaining my composure.

There's something else behind all of this, but I don't have the knowledge or the resources to figure out what that is. If not even the Master has full knowledge of that time period, then who would? I thought.

"Those ravens we saw earlier on our way home; what was that all about?" I asked, deciding to shift the focus on the conversation. "The only times ravens leave from the direction of this fortress is when something is being sent somewhere. The approving authority for any transmittal of information *has* to go through me, and me alone," the Master said gravely.

"So, whatever it was that raven was carrying, then…" I began, but didn't finish. I knew the answer already. "Precisely," the Master said, as if reading my trailing thoughts. "While the contents of the torn pages themselves have been lost to time, there is still much information there that has been safeguarded for generations," he explained.

"And the beasts? Why did you have me slay them if they were safeguarding this information? Was that all for nothing, master?" I asked, feeling the pain swell once more. "Not exactly," the Master began.

"You see, when an ochelon is charmed, it should, technically, only answer to one master as long as the charm is maintained. However, breaking that charm and replacing it with another is an extremely difficult spell to use, not to mention dangerous. Those ochelons you slayed were no longer under my command, and would have transmitted information through mana to their new master at the next opportunity," the Master explained.

I guess that explains why they were so hasty to try and kill me, I thought, recalling how swift the female ochelon was to attack me.

"I had also not forgotten about your punishment for setting a mana-flame loose in your dorm, and figured this was a prime opportunity to make use of your skills. Well, that, and I wanted to see whether you could unlock the second stage of mana manipulation," the Master said with a sly grin.

Is that *what that feeling was? No, no, that can't be right,* I thought.

"You gambled on whether I could do that mid-fight?" I asked, incredulous to what I had just heard. "You're still alive, so I take it you fared well enough against such foes," he said, glancing at Bernar who nodded in agreement.

"Well, aside from the scar on my back, my head feeling like it was crushed, and my shoulders burning like hot iron, yes, Master," I replied with a squint as I tested the skin on my back. "The first of many, Thoma," the Master said with a shallow smile.

I looked about the room pensively, digesting the information

I just received. It wasn't often that I got a chance like this to ask such existential questions, and after having heard his real reason for sending me to that sanguine menagerie, I knew I had to keep seeking answers.

"Something troubles you?" the Master asked, noting my composure. "Indeed, Master. I can't help but wonder why all of this is happening now. Why couldn't this have begun when I was at least a little older, or more capable of handling whatever is coming our way," I replied.

Bernar raised his hand to the master, as if stopping him from answering that statement. "Little brother, I know you better than anyone," he began. I was surprised to hear his voice and looked at him intently.

"Within the cave, there is only one way in, and one way out. Many things in life have different ways of being achieved, but when it comes to challenges or difficult times, it is much like that cave - one way in, and one way out. Sometimes, the only way out is *through*," he said, his voice laced with a severity I'd rarely seen in him.

"The Master and I have both seen our fair share of difficult times, many of which neither of us would like to relive. You are just now facing your own challenges, and we will be here to help guide you *through* those times. When you're ready, you will find yourself to be much stronger, as painful as those experiences may be," he concluded, lightly flicking my brand-new scar.

"I know you're trying to help, but it still hurts, brother," I said, responding to the flick. "Of course it does, shit-bird," Bernar said playfully. The Master observed the two of us and smiled lightly. "You two remind me of a story from a long time ago," the Master said, his voice carrying a much lighter tone than usual.

We both looked at him, confused at the light-heartedness of his voice.

"It was a long time ago, before even my predecessor became the master of Codrean," he continued. "Would you like to hear it?" he asked us. "Of course, Master," Bernar spoke out.

"A long time ago, there were twins named Taegin and Ardrin, and they had a good relationship with one another. Both of them were inducted into the Synners at a very young age, but Ardrin was more unruly than his sibling. So unruly, in fact, that the master at the time had a hard time keeping him under control," the Master began as the two of us listened attentively.

"On their fourteenth birthdays, Taegin wanted to throw a surprise birthday party for their birthday, even while knowing his brother hated surprises. It wasn't much, nothing more than a few stolen cakes from the pantry and a few mugs of ale. Not everything went as planned, however, and Ardrin was nowhere to be found. Taegin, worrying about his surprise being ruined, went out to search for his brother," he continued, nearly losing himself in thought for a moment.

"His brother, however, was being bullied somewhere by some of the other Synners who were just a few years older. They began pushing Ardrin around, toying with him. He cast a flame cloak around him to try to fend them off, but lost control of his mana. As a result, the bullies' bodies were quickly engulfed in flame. They died then and there, and Ardrin was outcast from the Synners. Taegin wasn't aware of what had happened, nor that his brother was outcast. Even after years of searching for the cause of his brother's sudden disappearance, there was no answer. No amount of distractions or training could satiate his desire to see his brother again," the Master said.

"Well, that got dark," Bernar said abruptly.

The Master chuckled softly. "What I'm trying to say is that

you two have a fantastic bond," he said, a warm smile growing on his face. "Don't ever let that go," he said, the warm smile turning chagrined and pained.

We pondered his words for a few moments, recognizing the value of them. "I don't suppose Ardrin was ever found, was he, Master?" I asked. "It's been a long enough time to where I think he would have died of old age, or something of the sort. As far as I know, he was never found," the Master replied, his face expressing indifference with a lower lip rising over his top lip.

"I see, Master," I said pensively. "If you don't mind me asking, but how is it that you know the story in such detail, Master?" I asked. "That's because I knew them both quite well. We were good friends, back then," the Master replied solemnly.

Nothing could've really prepared me for the shock I felt, but Bernar, for whatever reason, seemed unfazed.

How old is this geezer anyway? I thought.

"His brother told me the story countless times. He longed for redemption for not escaping the school and going after his brother when it happened, but found none as he took his own life about six months later. Our old master told us the full story a few times after his death to set an example on how Synners should conduct themselves," the Master said.

"Damn," I said solemnly. The Master looked at my face, and knew what I was thinking. "You thought I was Taegin, didn't you?" he asked. After a moment of trying to find words to say, I decided that a single nod would suffice. "Sorry to disappoint you, but he's been dead for a long time now," the Master said. I said nothing.

I'm trying to piece it together, but I feel something has been left out, I thought.

"Either way, I thank you for coming to me with your findings," the Master said. "I won't bother you any longer. It's getting late, and you had quite the eventful day," he said with a smile. "If you find any more information as to who invaded the study, come to either Bernar or myself directly. Is that understood?" he asked. "Yes, Master," I replied with a nod. I struggled to rise from my seat, but Bernar came to my aid.

"I think it best if you check in with Garett tomorrow, Thoma," the Master said, noting my struggle. "I'll have him tending to you these next few days, and I'm sure he'd like to know about how you got that scar," the Master said. I nodded once more, and walked out of the room. The Master remained seated in his chair, staring off towards the out-of-place book on the shelf across the room.

The following day after lunch had been eaten, the dull clang of training swords could be heard clashing throughout the halls. I, who had just finished Garett's healing session, decided to follow the sounds to their point of origin.

"*Ouch*! That hurts," Edryd shouted, rubbing the shoulder that had just been struck. "Calm down, you little wuss," Bernar said with a laugh. "It could have been much worse," I said while walking into the training yard. "Thoma! I'm glad to see you're alright," Edryd exclaimed.

"Do me a favor, and tell your brother he's an asshole for me, will you?" he said, pointing to Bernar. "I already know I'm an asshole, shitwit," Bernar said, smacking Edryd upside the head. "Hey!" Edryd exclaimed, trying to give back the blow. Bernar dodged it easily, and chuckled lightly.

"You missed," I said with a laugh. "I know I wouldn't want to be in the way of one of those," I continued. "Yes, but the turd you have for a brother keeps testing it as though it had never been damaged in the first place. He even challenged me to an arm-wrestling match, if you can believe it," Edryd said. I raised an eyebrow towards my brother.

"What?" Bernar asked. "Gotta test it and make sure it's not still fucked," he said. "There are better ways to test that," I said, shaking my head. "Like what?" Edryd asked.

I could've sworn I saw my brother's eyes twinkle like a star in the night sky for a brief moment.

"You, versus Bernar and I," I said maliciously. "*Oh*, no. *Fuck* that with the might of a wyrm," Edryd said, crossing his arms in front of him. "I think it's a great idea! Never really had the chance to see you in a two-versus-one," Bernar jeered. "You two are gonna gang up on me, now?" Edryd asked, panic showing clearly on his face.

"We'll be nice, don't worry," I said with a grin towards my brother. Edryd sighed and shook his head. "I hate you both," he said, to which Bernar and I chuckled.

"*Oh*, come on! It'll be fun!" Bernar said. Edryd wasn't happy about the way he had said that at all. "This is gonna hurt, isn't it?" Edryd asked. "Probably. If you don't fuck up, it won't," I replied as if I were a professor coming to a simplistic conclusion. Bernar chuckled and readied himself.

"Begin!" Bernar called out, immediately starting a charge towards Edryd. Bernar struck from above, but Ed parried it by sliding the incoming sword off his and away from his body. I attacked from the left side, and Edryd danced out of the way of the blow, only to block another from Bernar who was waiting for him.

I struck again from above, but Edryd blocked it, throwing his weight against me as I pirouetted out of the way. Bernar stuck again, this time aiming for his legs. He blocked most of it, but the tip struck the base of his calf, throwing him off balance.

Edryd regained his stance, recovering from the blow with a grunt of pain. "It didn't draw blood, so don't be a turd about it," Bernar said. Edryd grinned, and lunged at Bernar, who deflected the blow. I attacked immediately afterwards from behind, and Edryd twisted his sword behind his back with the force from the deflection to stop the other incoming blow.

I feinted an attack, and twisted out of the way of Bernar's next one that I knew was coming in behind me, aimed directly at Edryd's hurt shoulder. Ed grunted with the blow, but kneed Bernar in the stomach, and spun around, attacking me with a twisting leap. "That's my move, fucker!" Bernar shouted playfully. "I'm borrowing it," Edryd replied through a wry smile.

Bernar grinned, and moved in for what would be a blow to end the fight, but I got there first, repeatedly attacking Edryd in a quick succession of blows. He had a hard time keeping up with them, but managed to find a gap amidst the barrage, and swirled to trip me.

I hit the ground hard and was immediately winded, feeling the sting of the fresh scar racing across my back muscles, while Bernar was coming in for his turn. Edryd blocked the blows and tried to counterattack, but Bernar saw it coming.

He *had* baited him into it, after all.

He grabbed Edryd's sword arm, and kicked his legs, throwing him to the floor. Edryd sputtered, losing his breath from the impact.

"*Eh*, you're okay," Bernar said looking down at the coughing boy. "Not bad for someone who's just come out of the ward," I said as I got to my feet. "Could've been better. I still feel the injury is limiting my movement a little. On that note, I'm surprised you moved as well as you did with your own wounds being so fresh, Thoma," Edryd replied, extending his hand for help from Bernar.

"*Oh*, I was in pain the whole time, but I couldn't allow you to show me up so easily," I replied with a pained chuckle. "In the future, keep an eye out for open spaces like that one I had to trip you," Bernar said, dusting Edryd's backside off. "I will," Edryd replied with a nod.

"Well, guys, it's been fun, but I must go," Bernar said. "Kick your ass some other day," Edryd said. "You wish! Cocky shithead," Bernar said with a laugh. I smiled as I walked over to Edryd and put a hand on his good shoulder. "I'm sorry about that, by the way," I said, gesturing to the other. "Don't worry about it," Edryd replied. "Better that than being mauled to death by those fucking bugs," he continued. Flashes of the scene rushed into my mind like a white-water river.

Nope, I thought, quickly dismissing the memory of the glick challenging me with its scales.

"I suppose you're right," I said, my head sinking. "In any case, I'm sorry. I had never actually tested my spell before using it back then," I said solemnly. "*Ah,* so that's what that was," Edryd said surprised. "Yeah. I know we're never supposed to use untested spells in battle, but it was all I could do from where I was at the time," I replied.

"Well," Edryd began, putting his hand on my shoulder. "If it's of any consolation, I'm still alive. Thanks to you," he said warmly.

I smiled, truly relieved to hear that.

"Good to have you back, bud," I said and gave Edryd a hug. "Don't go all soft on me," Edryd said with a chuckle. We laughed for a short while, and began walking back to the main fortress.

"You know you're going to have to teach me that, right?" Edryd said. "I don't know if I can do it well enough to teach, but I'll try," I replied. "How long did it take you to come up with something like that?" Edryd asked. "Three months," I replied, scratching the back of my head.

"*Three months*? Holy shit," Edryd said with wide eyes. "Haven't given it a name, yet. As one who has lived to tell the tale, why don't you give it a name," I suggested. "How about *Whip of Doom*, or *Chaos Bind*?" Edryd asked, almost before I could finish my sentence.

I laughed, genuinely surprised at the speed with which he answered.

"*Whip of Doom* sounds a little foreboding, don't you think?" I asked. "Nope. Sounds about right to me," Edryd replied with a grin. "Seen it work firsthand. I'd say it's pretty *dooming* to anyone or anything that gets in its way," he said. "*Whip of Doom* it is, then," I said with a laugh.

We continued walking for a short time, when Edryd heard something. "*Ah*, it's just a raven," Edryd said. I looked for it, and saw it flying towards the South-East. "Shit," I muttered, my eyes opening widely as the realization hit me.

Please, let me be wrong, I thought, seeing the pouch on the fowl's chest.

"What? It's just a raven, Thoma," Edryd said dismissively, not understanding the look on my face. "Not just any raven. A *carrier* raven. Follow me," I said, sprinting towards the fortress. "What the..." Edryd said, and rushed after me.

We went through the doors of the fortress, and straight up to the Master's study, where Bernar, Garett and the Master had just begun holding council. I burst into the door, and saw all six pairs of eyes staring at me curiously.

"Master, forgive my intrusion, but was it you?" I asked between breaths. "Calm down and tell me what the matter is. Was *what* me?" the Master replied. There was no surprise written on his features, but his tone suggested he knew I was about to say something that didn't bode well for anyone.

"Another raven. Headed South-East," I said, catching my breath. The Master's eyes opened. "I thought we'd found him already," Garett said, incredulously.

"Apparently not," Bernar replied. The Master remained still, looking straight into my eyes. He broke my gaze, and walked about the study. "Come in and shut the door. You too, Edryd," the Master said. Edryd looked over at me, though all I could respond with was a terse nod as I shut the door behind us.

"What I say here, stays here, understood, boys?" the Master said. We both nodded quickly, but remained silent. The Master cast a spell on the door, blocking all sound from potentially leaking through the wood and spaces in the door frame.

"To make sure we're all on the same page, here: It seems we might have a traitor in our midst," he began. Edryd looked at me with questioning eyes. "I know the hearts and minds of everyone in this room, but I must ask you, Thoma: do you trust Edryd?" he asked.

I nodded my head. "He was the one who spotted it first, Master. It couldn't have been him," he replied. The Master showed understanding of my words, and continued his own.

"Edryd, you might not be aware of this, but the fact remains that someone has been sending out unreviewed messages to someone outside the fortress," he continued, the air of severity hanging heavily in his tone. "Who would do that?" Edryd replied, immediately understanding the gravity of the Master's words as his face paled.

"It could always be someone sending a love letter," Garett said. "Not likely. The day of our return, Thoma saw two ravens flying that way, one just before we had crossed into our land, and the other before entering the fortress. Which most likely means that someone was trying to keep track of our location, and judging by the frequency, someone not too far away from here," the Master said.

Ed and I glanced at each other briefly. "There are only farmers and their families living near enough for something like that. Even if it were one of them, what business would they have in knowing our position?" Bernar chimed in. "Farmers sell their goods at the marketplace in Coltend at least once a week," Garett began.

"Precisely," the Master agreed. "The problem is the following: three ravens. The chances of the first two being a farmer are pretty high, but this one just now is too close to be anything of the sort. Thoma, where did you see it come from?" the Master asked. "I didn't see it initially, Master. Edryd had pointed it out for me only after I heard its call," I replied, gesturing to a nervous Ed standing right beside me. "But which direction was it coming from?" he asked.

If I give the wrong location, it might spell death for a simple farmer. I have to watch my words, I thought.

"I saw it come from the North-West corner of the fortress, Master," I replied. The Master was visibly shaken. "Our fears have been confirmed, then," the Master said grimly. "The study?" Bernar asked. The Master nodded, and looked at the four of us in the room with him with a piercing gaze.

"It's one of our own," he said gravely.

"The North-West corner of this fortress is where the study lies. Now that Thoma has killed the beasts and cleared the way for the traitor, it only confirms what I have been thinking these last few months. However, that's not to say I've merely been sitting idly by and not taken any precautions," he continued, giving me a knowing nod.

I finally understood.

He sent me there because he trusted me not to give away the secrets he was trying to keep inside, I thought.

"But Master, those pages on the table held nothing of value. At the very least, none that I could see. What else was hidden away in there?" I asked, both concerned and confused.

"The location of the Gwynnleaf plant. The one the gods themselves gave us," the Master replied seriously. Bernar and Garett knew what this meant. "How could we have been so careless?" Garett asked aloud.

"We weren't entirely careless," the Master began. "They could have been after just about any other piece of knowledge in there. However, the precautions I took were to charm the ochelons and cast a spell that jumbled the words in all the books except the one you found, Thoma," he concluded.

Why the hell would he leave the most important information unscrambled? I thought.

"But why those pages, Master?" Edryd asked, feeling just as confused as I was. "Because the only way for us to confirm it was one of our own was to make sure that the information being sought after was the only thing left of value. This puts us in a better position to defend it, as we now know exactly *what* they're after. As to *why* they're after it, I do not know," the Master replied.

"So, you decided to bait them by having me slay the monsters, and leave the information within reach to confirm your suspicion?" I asked, trying to make sure he understood it correctly. "Yes. It was a gamble on multiple fronts," the Master replied. "I knew you were capable of it, and it was a true test of trust, the sort I have with everyone in this room. Including you, Edryd," he continued. "Me, Master? But what have I done to deserve that level of trust?" Edryd asked, genuinely unaware of why that was so.

"You're Thoma's best friend, and if he trusts you, then I am inclined to trust you too," the Master replied. Edryd blushed hard, and shuffled his feet. "Thank you, Master," he said with a hand on his chest, leaning into a grateful bow.

"I know your parents to be great Synners, and I know that

you have the same fire in your heart as your mother did when I trained her all those years ago," the Master said with a slight smile. Edryd had never heard the Master say anything of the sort, and nearly burst into tears.

"Back to the matter at hand, however, this new development has confirmed my reasoning. Now it is up to us to find out who it is," the Master said. "I'm guessing you have some sort of plan," Bernar said. "I do. The five of us present will begin to look for irregularities about our comrades. It could be anyone here, so we must keep a close eye out for anything that seems abnormal about them. Garett," the Master said, commanding the attention of the old archer.

"Yes, Master?" Garett asked. "You are to keep a close watch on the bow-casters. Even equipment irregularities should be noted upon," the Master said. "Will do, Master," Garett replied. "Bernar, you are to keep a watch on the sword-casters the same way Garett will," the Master said. "As you command," Bernar replied.

The Master turned to the two of us who nearly buckled under the weight of his stare.

"You two have the most vital roles, so pay close attention to what I'm going to say. Bernar, Garett and I are the Masters during training, which means that it is highly unlikely that the traitor would say anything or do anything revealing around us. Seeing as how no one else knows you are in on our little plan, you are to be our eyes and ears within the barracks, understand?" the Master asked, looking us keenly in the eyes.

"Yes, Master," we both said at the same time. "Keep an eye out for unusual things, like the others and myself will do from here on out. However, pay even closer attention to your circle of friends," the Master cautioned.

"Master, why must we focus on our friends so much?" Edryd

asked as his mind began to race. "I am going to tell you why, but I want you to try to figure it out before I finish," the Master replied.

"You are very closely knit in your friendships, Edryd, and I know you care a great deal for them. However, as it currently stands, the likelihood of someone outside your circle accidentally spilling something that may or may not be revealing is extremely low. Before we left for Coltend, I had made a comment about Thoma's use of the Kyr spell, do you remember?" the Master asked.

"I do, Master, though what relevance it has escapes me," Edryd replied. "Everyone there *knew* I was talking about him. He is Bernar's brother, who is my right-hand man before even Master Garett himself. Not to mention his frequent visits to my study..." the Master said, letting his words hang a little in hopes that Ed would begin to piece it together.

"So, that means: the traitor, or *traitors*, will think that Thoma knows more than he should," Edryd began. "Therefore, they will try to get the information from either him, or those closest to him," he continued, finishing off the Master's train of thought.

"Excellent. You really are a bright one, Edryd," the Master said, smiling. Edryd looked at the Master's scar, which didn't seem as threatening as it used to. "Thank you, Master," he replied with a smile.

"So, it's settled, then," Garett began, allowing himself a mild stretch as if readying for a training session. "Everyone knows their job, and it is vital that none of what has been said here ever gets out to the others. If it does, our plans are foiled, and we will have to start from scratch," he continued.

"Exactly. Now, let's get to it, gentlemen. We've got a long road ahead of us," the Master replied. All of us, except for the

Master, proceeded out of the room, and down the stairs.

At the base of the stairway, we all went our separate ways, and proceeded to the day's training schedules. Swords, bows, and hand-to-hand combat drills were being conducted across the training grounds.

Ed and I were nervous, desperately trying to pay attention to our surroundings and not getting hit by a stray training sword in the process. Bernar took over for the senior that was overseeing their training, and began teaching them new move sets and combinations to test out on each other. Grappling, disarming, tripping, and guard weaknesses were all addressed during our four-and-a-half-hour long exercise.

Near the end of our training session, we heard a call from atop the fortress walls. "There's someone coming," the bow-caster who stood guard called out. "Hold," Bernar called out to his trainees, and headed towards the main gate. When he arrived, he opened the hatch through the main doorway to find a hooded figure on a white horse.

"I bring news of Coltend, and of Caegwen," the hooded figure said in a near angelic voice. Bernar instantly recognized the accent, and was taken aback. "Open the gates," he called out. The mighty wooden gate was opened, drawing everyone's attention as the rider came into the fortress. He rode a short way while the door was being shut, with Bernar following closely behind.

The hooded figure dismounted his large horse, and stood nearly a head taller than everyone present, including Bernar. He drew back his hood to show a perfectly carved face, with bright yellow eyes. His face was bereft of any facial hair, and his jawline was perfectly symmetrical to the rest of his features. Small, hooped earrings of gold and silver intertwined hung from his pointed ears. Bernar looked at the figure, desperately trying to put a name to a face.

"Don't you recognize me, Bernar?" the elf asked, grinning brightly. "Anwill *Taffy*, you old bastard!" Bernar exclaimed and proceeded to give the elf a hug. It was not customary for an elf to greet or be greeted with little more than a handshake. "*Taaff*, actually, but I do recall you always having issues with elven names," the elf said with an uncomfortable smirk.

How the hell does he know an elf to that extent? Did I miss something? I thought as I walked up next to my brother.

Anwill noticed my look of confusion, and offered a slight bow. "I am Anwill Taaff, Synner and emissary of King Elhael Phrys of Caegwen," he stated. "I thank you for your… *hospitality*, Bernar. I am glad to see you, as well," Anwill said, happily retreating into his comfort zone of a meter. "But I am afraid that I am not here on friendly matters, you see. I must speak with the Master," he said.

"*Ah*, yes. Well, if you will follow me," Bernar said, leading the way. Anwill looked around him, taking note of everyone's faces and their functions. Elves had, by trait, an excellent memory. A true gift for ones who lived as long as they did.

"A thousand years, and yet this place remains very much the same as it did all those years ago," he said, taking in a deep breath. "The first of us were trained here, until we built our own schools to train in," he continued. "Welcome home, then," Bernar said with a chuckle. The elf smiled, not something he did very often. "It's good to be back," Anwill said, following Bernar to the main fortress. I and Edryd looked at each other in sheer confusion.

Making it through the Rhydian Pass alone is a feat in and of itself, so why is he here? Unfriendly matters, was it? I thought, but no answers came to mind.

CHAPTER 10

The Rhydian Pass

After the murder of his son, King Bashir rode his horse to near-absolute exhaustion as it foamed at the bit, and snorted heavily.

I've just spent the last two days at a gallop, and I don't think my ass or the horse can take much more, he thought.

He observed the path behind him, desperately searching for anyone who might be following him. The sun had begun to set, and he could just barely see a glint of the Coltend's tower reflecting the setting sun's rays. He had ridden as fast as he could from Coltend Castle, over the Lucent River, to reach the base of the Rhydian Mountains.

I know this horse well, but its hooves are covered in dried blood from riding over countless twigs and rocks in the road. I don't know how much longer it will survive without food and rest, he thought.

He promptly decided to make his small camp near a stream that ran down the mountains. The small fire he made did little to shun the cold air that came down the mountains, and the sheep-hide bed only just maintained its warmth on the cold floor. The horse lay next to him, taking the blunt force of the wind. Bashir nibbled on a field mouse he had killed and tried to roast over his small flame. It was still partially raw, and he struggled with every bite.

"You've done well," he said to his horse, patting it on the neck after taking another bite of his questionable meal. He had stolen it from one of the men who had gone with him to the council, who had been waiting for him outside of the palace walls.

"I know you cannot speak, and yet I feel as though I must know your name," he said, still stroking its massive nape. The horse shook his head slightly. He was pensive for a few moments. "I shall call you *Hatal*. Do you want to know what it means?" he asked, breaking his silence.

The horse didn't reply, obviously.

"*Ah*. Right. Well, I shall tell you anyway. It means *hero* in my language. Your strength saved me from what could have been a most horrible death. I thank you," he said with another pat. Hatal leaned his head over his rider's shoulder. "We make a great pair, you and I. Once we arrive in Harut, I will ensure that you are fed an entire bowl of lush red apples. How does that sound, huh?" he said, stroking Hatal's long hair.

The horse snorted heavily, and rubbed the side of his face up against Bashir's. "Heh, you're a good horse," he said with a smile. "Let us rest now. We have only one final stretch before we're home. You're very strong, Hatal, and I know you and I will make it," he said comfortingly. He leaned back on the horse, and curled up to keep himself warm.

I wonder what Bashaa would say if he could see me now, he thought.

Thoughts about the journey ahead began to flood his mind, but he pushed them aside, as memories of his son began to flood his consciousness. Bashaa had been his pride and joy, the brightest of his sons. The others had died from an unknown disease after eating too much pork one feast. Bashaa and his son had been absent that fateful evening, and when he returned, he found three of his sons in the morgue, covered in white linen.

"Do you know the pain of loss, Hatal?" he asked. The horse, once more verbally unresponsive, perked his ears up. "I don't suppose horses feel remorse or heartbreak, do you? Not that I would know what goes through your minds. But as it currently stands, I have no more sons. No heirs to continue my line. No joys left in this world. I witnessed that *monster* slash my last remaining son's neck, and defile his corpse," Bashir said angrily.

"As for my other sons, I just wish I could go back in time and be, at the very least, present for their final moments. I..." he choked, tears welling up in his eyes. "I have failed, Hatal," he began, struggling through his tears. "I have failed as a King, as a husband, and as a father. Just look at me, now," he gestured his arms at his own body.

"I am nothing. An empty shell of my former self. A shadow and a thought of what once contained joy, laughter, and pride in myself and my sons. Now, I am here pouring my soul out to a fucking *horse*, all while fleeing for my life." Hatal, not understanding exactly what was said, but feeling the emotion behind his words, gently leaned his massive head on Bashir's shoulder. The man, touched by the gesture, burst into tears.

My dearest Bashaa, how I miss you. I feel as if a part of my soul has been torn from me. You were the last heir to the Ibn'Escea line, and even if I do have another child, I doubt they could live up to your reputation. You have joined the spirits of your brothers and forefathers, but your memory will live on with me. I will make Truls suffer greatly for what he has done to you, my son, he thought.

Hatal quivered, feeling the anger, frustration, and hatred growing. Bashir, considering numerous ways to potentially torture Truls, emitted a dark energy around him. The horse, being sensitive to such things, gently nudged his master as if to break the train of horrific thoughts.

Bashir snapped out of his attitude, and noticed Hatal's face had come awfully close to his own. "Wh-what? I can't want revenge for what that piece of shit did to my son?" he asked. Hatal, without budging so much as a hair's width, snorted. The man seemed to understand what the horse meant and sighed. "Even without words, you amaze me with your insight. Yes, yes, I will set that aside for now. We do have a long day ahead of us tomorrow, and the Pass will be no easy trip," he stated. He gave Hatal another pat, and turned over to try to get some rest.

Morning came, and the tip of Coltend Castle could still be seen off in the distance, shining brightly with the morning sun beaming off its highest peak. Hatal was already awake, and prodded his master with his nostrils flaring in his face. Bashir wriggled, responding to the nudge.

"I'm awake, I'm awake," he said, petting the horse's nostrils and chin. He put out his fire with his piss, and scattered the soaked ashes as best he could to not leave any trail to be followed. He rolled his small bed back up, and mounted it to the side of the saddle, looking over his shoulder to see if anyone had caught up to him.

"We must go, Hatal," he said, getting his foot in the stirrup and throwing his leg over to the other side. He clicked his tongue, and they were off. The Rhydian pass was about two kilometers up a steep, winding trail. It was primarily used by merchants who sought to sell their goods in the markets of Coltend, though not all made it through without trouble.

About halfway up the trail, he heard a sound coming from behind him. He stopped his horse, and looked back to try and see what it was. Captain Gorm rode up the steep slope and had - as far as Bashir could tell - about forty or more men following closely behind. Gorm's eyes opened wide. "There he is! After him!" he shouted. "Shit," Bashir said, and dug his heels into Hatal's sides.

Neither he nor the party of men behind him could go very quickly up the steep slope, and the other, fresher horses were beginning to catch up to him. His heart raced and his first thoughts were that he was going to die, without telling his people what had happened. He had assumed that his men - whom he had left behind in his flight - were already dead.

He pressed on.

Hatal was breathing more and more heavily, desperately trying to keep up his pace. His eyes were wide, and Bashir knew he wasn't going to last much longer at this pace. The riders got closer and closer to him, and they were within bowshot of him now. "Hurry, Hatal! We must make it over this ridge," he yelled, digging his heels in once more.

The ridge he saw was that of the peak of the pass - which if one were to stop, had quite an amazing view of Caegwen to the North-East and Harut to the south. "Come on!" he yelled once more. Hatal gave it everything he had, and finally made it over the ridge. The riders weren't too far behind. "Hyah!" Bashir shouted, urging his horse to pick up the pace on the flat ground. "I think we made it, Hatal. Keep going," he said, patting his horse's nape.

The Rhydian Pass was known for being confusing, for those who did not know the way. The harsh weather of the mountains had destroyed all the wooden signposts that had ever been placed there, so traders resorted to carving signs into the rocks themselves. Bashir knew this, and looked for the carvings that lay at the beginning of every road.

"There!" he said aloud, and turned his horse in the right direction, just managing to turn the corner in time to avoid being seen by Gorm and his riders.

The party made it over the ridge, only a few short moments after Bashir had already disappeared. "Damn it. Where the fuck did he go?" Gorm yelled aloud, hoping one of his men had seen a trace of him. They looked about them for any signs of tracks, but found none in the well-used pathway's solid dirt. "Find him!" he shouted. The men dismounted to get a closer look at the ground. The merchant's tracks were embedded deep into the ground, and most were still fresh from the last caravan that had passed through there the previous day.

"Nothing here, Captain," one of the guardsmen shouted. "Nor here, Captain," another chimed in. Gorm looked about him, hoping to find even a horseshoe mark out of place. He heard a rustling in the bushes nearby, and turned to find out what it was. He dismounted and walked over to the origin of the sound, drawing his sword.

I have you now, you piece of shit, he thought.

He stepped as quietly as he could, and when he was close enough to where he thought nothing could escape, he saw the tip of an arrow sticking out from behind one of the bushes. "Ambush!" he called out, backing away. All the men heard his cry, and drew their swords immediately. They formed a circle with their backs to one another's, and watched as the figures began to sprout out of the bush.

The figures were none other than elven raiders, clad in dark green. Their tunics and boots were mud stained and most had holes in them. Each one had a curved blade, and a knife lashed to their leather belts by a dark brown sash. Hardened by the elements, their hands and forearms had scars that could be seen through the holes in their gear.

"Raiders," Gorm said aloud. "Some may call us that, whereas I would rather call my people and I *opportunists*," one of the elves replied to the remark. He was standing on a tall rock that lay at the side of the pass. "*Thieves. Bandits. Good-for-nothing degenerates*: All of these are quite derogatory terms for free folk who have been cast out of their homes, and seek a living elsewhere," he continued. "You mean making a living off of other people's hard work," Gorm said.

"Indeed. For most, they have plenty more than they need. Their greed is their downfall," the elf replied. "However, we do not take from all who come through here. Those who are visibly inferior to the other merchants we tend to leave alone, after all, we know what it is like to be in their shoes," he continued.

"A thief with morals. Never thought I would see the day," Gorm said, shaking his head. "Live as long as I have, and you will come to find that stranger things have happened. There is nothing wrong with having morals, as the dichotomy of good and evil is all but a matter of perspective," the elf said, taking a closer look at the man.

"What is your name?" the elf asked. "I am the captain of the guard of Coltend Castle," Gorm replied. "And I am not as dumb as you presume me to be. Now, answer my question: what is your name?" the elf retorted, his patience beginning to run thin.

"Gorm," the captain replied. "Are you sure it's just *Gorm*?" the elf asked. "Just *Gorm*," he replied. "Well then, Captain Gorm. My name is Gwili Gwynn, and it would seem we have at least one thing in common," Gwili said. "Let me guess: both of our names begin with the letter *G*? How adorable," Grom said with as much sarcasm as he could muster at the moment. Gwili chuckled. "Indeed, but my troops and I are wondering what it is you and your party are doing so far from home, Gorm?" he asked.

"We seek a lone rider who passed this way a few moments before you interrupted us," Gorm answered. "We interrupted you? It was you who could not find the rider's tracks speedily enough," Gwili replied with a laugh. "You dare mock the captain?" one of the guardsmen shouted. "Oh, but I *do* dare. I have you and your bed warmers surrounded, although you are only able to see myself and the few who stand beneath me," Gwili replied.

"Shut the fuck up, Carl," Gorm said quietly.

"I'm certain there's a way we can be reasonable about this whole situation, Gwili," he said. "Is there, really?" the elf replied. "Yes, I believe so. You see, we have no business with you and your troops. All we seek is the rider who came through here," Gorm replied. "Forty-some-odd men after one man? Sounds a little unreasonable if you don't mind me saying so," Gwili replied, raising a thin, dark eyebrow. "I know how it looks, but the man we are after has done something terrible against my king, you see," Gorm said. "Well, indeed he must have, if there are to be so many of you after him. I would have liked to have gained that sort of recognition," Gwili said with a chuckle.

Gorm was becoming increasingly frustrated with the words being said to him. "Can't we simply go on our way, and be done with this?" he asked. Gwili digested the question carefully. "I'm afraid not," he replied. Gorm furrowed his brow. "You see, I know who the lone rider was, and I know where he was headed off to. There was a reason I didn't stop him," Gwili answered. "And what reason might that be?" Gorm asked, clearly irritated.

"You see, Gorm, the Rhydian Pass is used by merchants from all four countries. Every one of them knows we reside here, and if they refuse to leave us tribute - be it money or food - we will take it by force. However, if a lone rider passes through here, then he is not to be touched by myself nor any of my men. Seeing as how you are no mere merchants and have excellent gear that my men and I would rather take for ourselves, it is only logical that we exert our rights here. We, of course, won't kill you, provided you don't resist. Leaving you naked, but alive," Gwili replied.

"You pompous bastard!" Carl shouted back angrily. "Don't do it!" Gorm called out, but Carl wasn't listening. He had been looking for the nearest elf to take down since the beginning of the conversation, and decided to pounce on his prey. Some of the others had done the same, and they went in for the kill. Gwili raised his hand, and arrows were fired, one for each soldier, striking them between their eyes. Their limp bodies slammed the ground beneath them, blood spewing from the wounds.

"Damn it, Carl," Gorm cursed.

"Why does no one ever listen to me? What do I have to do to show that I am a man of my word?" Gwili sighed. "Alright, I concede, Gwili. We will give you our..." he stopped. He felt a rumble in the ground beneath his feet, and knew it couldn't be an earthquake. "By the gods both light and dark," Gwili said, his eyes opening wide. He saw the large figure that approached them. "Ice troll!" he shouted. Gorm turned to the direction he saw the elf facing, only to see it.

The troll was at least five meters tall, with white ice crystals embedded in its tough hide. Its teeth were massive, with two tusks sticking out - each about as thick as a man's thigh - from the base of its large jaw. Its hands and feet were both stocky, and could easily turn a full-grown horse into jelly with a single blow.

"Formation!" Gorm yelled. The rest of his men saw the creature approaching them at a run, bellowing what seemed to be a war cry as it did. It shook Gorm to his core, for in all of his years of experience, he had never actually seen one before. "Steady! Don't shit through your teeth, men!" he called out to his men.

Fifty meters.

"Focus! Aim for his eyes and ankles!" Gorm said. The troll was headed straight for them. "Fire!" Gwili called out, and the arrows soared. The elven arrows were mostly aimed at its large head, though most were deflected by the crystals. Some of Gorm's men had struck the soft parts of the thick hide on its lower thighs, while most simply were also deflected by the crystals. It grunted from the pain of the arrows that found the spaces between its spotty armor, but kept its pace.

Fifteen meters.

"Ready your swords!" Gorm called out.

Five meters.

The monster had arrived, and with it came death. It swung its strong arms down from behind, as it smashed through the thin line of soldiers. Gorm, luckily, was between its legs, and cut at its left ankle while ducking beneath them, catching a small glance at the waste the beast lay to his men.

Tough fucker aren't you? he thought.

He recovered from his strike, only to find a blooded, limb-ridden fist swiping backwards to get him. He rolled out of the way, and watched a few of his men, trying to stab at the beast's now exposed gut. It swatted the few men away like little blood-filled mosquitoes.

Gwili was still on his rock, watching what would have been a large amount of good armor going to waste due to the troll. He nocked an arrow in his bow, and didn't pull until the beast had turned around. He saw his target, which was surprisingly small for such a large beast. He drew an arrow to his cheek, and released.

Unfortunately, the troll had seen him preparing for it, and breathed out a cloud of freezing air, stopping the arrow in its flight. "Damn it," he said aloud. He moved to another rock and tried again, this time trying to avoid being seen. He drew an arrow to his cheek once again, and this time the arrow met its mark, puncturing the dark sphere that was the troll's eye.

It reeled in pain, frantically trying to remove the arrow from its eye socket. The removal wasn't going to happen any time soon, and the remaining soldiers - Gorm included - hacked away at the beast's ankles, forcing it to kneel. It swatted away a few more men with its free hand, and the remaining men cut deep into the beast's stomach, eviscerating it. The blue-blooded entrails leaked out on top of the men, covering them like a pig in a mud puddle. The large, emptied corpse of the ice troll fell, making the ground tremble.

Gorm was panting hard, and looked about him at the havoc it had wreaked on his party. The morning sun reflected off the armor and blood strewn across the pass. More than half were dead, and the remainder of them were either puking off in the distance, or covered in the blue entrails. He had gotten some of it on his arm, and proceeded to wipe it off with his red cape.

"That went well," Gwili said from atop his new rock. "*Well*? What the fuck do you mean that it went *well*? Half of my men are dead, while the others are scarred for life!" Gorm shouted. "Look on the bright side: at least only half of them are dead," Gwili replied cheerfully.

Gorm spat in response. "If you and the rest of your pox-ridden bastards hadn't held us up for so long, none of this would have happened," he said angrily. "You say that as if all elves are omniscient. I had no idea such an incredible beast was to come this way. If I had, I would have hidden you, and stripped you naked only after the creature had passed," Gwili replied, raising his palms in a shrugging motion.

"That's comforting," Gorm said sarcastically. He looked about him once more at the devastation before him. "Men," he called out. His remaining men looked at him, hoping things wouldn't escalate further. "Grab the ranks off your fallen comrades' armor. We must take them back to their families," he commanded stoically. Gwili, impressed at his resolve, commanded his men to keep watch along the other pathways. The remaining soldiers began looking for recognizable pieces of their friends. Some of them had lost their best friends, while others, perhaps, had lost a brother. Tears welled in their eyes as they picked up the shreds of blood-soaked armor.

Meanwhile, Bashir had ridden down the other side of the pass, and reached the small town that resided at its base. It wasn't very large, but he was more than certain that they had what he needed. "We made it, my friend! We're safe," he said to Hatal, who neighed in response as though he were happy to see a town. He rode towards the small town, and a few of the townsfolk had seen him from a way off.

He dismounted when he got close enough to the nearest stable, and felt his inner thighs burn after having ridden for so long. He drew a cloth across his face to avoid being recognized, and grabbed the horse by the bit, walking it over to the nearest stable.

The small houses were well thatched, and it seemed to be a prosperous place. Located at the foot of the mountain, where most of the trade from Harut had to pass through, it was no small wonder as to why this little town had been so prosperous.

"I must speak with the owner," Bashir said, handing the stable boy the reins. "He's right over there, sir. Give me a moment and I will lead you to him," the boy said, tying the reins to the nearest post, which was already equipped with food and water. "Follow me, sir," he said, and walked briskly towards the main doors of the stable.

The stable boy led him straight to the owner's house which

lay a little way down the cobblestone street. "Thank you, boy," Bashir said, handing him a few small coins that were worth at least double what the boy had earned all month. "Thank you kindly, sir!" the boy exclaimed with joy-filled eyes. The boy ran off, to get back to his work, and Bashir proceeded to knock on the wooden door.

"Who might you be?" a voice called out from behind a steel latch. "I wish to speak to the owner of the stables, where I have had my horse tended to," Bashir replied.

I can't let them know who I am. If those men on the hill find my tracks and trace me here, at least these people won't know who I am, he thought.

"He's busy at the moment," the voice replied. "Tell him it's urgent," Bashir said impatiently. The voice sighed behind the door, and there was the sound of a latch being drawn back. The door opened, and there stood a large man, with a full beard with scraps of food still stuck in it from breakfast. The man was at least a head taller than Bashir himself, and possibly weighed twice as much. His light-colored tunic had a few stains on it, and it was clear to see that this man cared little for his own appearance.

"What is it, then?" the large man asked, irritated that someone had interrupted his peaceful morning. "I know you have a raven cage here, and I would like to send a message. In addition, I would like to pay to stable my horse in one of your stalls," Bashir said.

"If I'm supposed to let a masked stranger who smells like a dead horse and who has not given me his name use anything of mine without payment, then you are mistaken," the man replied. Bashir was taken aback by the way he was being treated for he had never been treated with such discourtesy.

"Fine," he sighed and removed the cloth from his face. "My

lord," the man bowed immediately, his face as white as a cloud. "Shut up," Bashir said quietly, lifting the man upright. "No one knows I've come this way; do you understand?" he said. The man quickly shook his head.

"In any other situation, I might have had your head for such disrespect," Bashir said threateningly. "I'm sorry, my lord," the man said, Bashir stopping him from bowing again. "Stop calling me that and fetch me some parchment, a feather, and ink," he said. "I always leave a stack of parchment there by the cage, but I'll fetch the feather," the man said, and ran off to get it before he made his visitor even more disgruntled.

He returned a few moments later with a stained goose feather and a small inkwell, and handed the contents to Bashir. "Here you are," the man said. "Finally," Bashir said, quickly grabbing the items out of the man's hands, and began to write.

Prepare to march on Coltend Castle. King Truls has murdered my son, and I will have revenge. King Bashir Ibn'Escea, he wrote on the parchment.

He signed the message with wax, and used his ring to imprint his signet. He folded it up and stuck it into the small, leather pouch that would latch on to the raven's chest. He took a raven from the cage, and lashed the contents on to the animal. "The Harutian Palace," he said, and the raven cawed in response to the command. He threw it up into the air and watched it as it headed in the direction of his home.

"What was that for, if I may ask," the man said. "War," Bashir replied with an evil smirk on his face. The man's eyes opened wide. "I thought the council taking place was to be of peace," the man said. "What is your name?" Bashir asked. "Akmed Al'Talik," the man replied.

"Well, Akmed, if you allow me to hide here in your home - not that you have much else of a choice - I will tell you why I will have war, instead of peace." Bashir stated. "You can have my room. I'll take the guest room," Akmed replied, nodding his head. Bashir grinned and followed the man up the flight of stairs to his quarters for the remainder of the day.

The large room was a complete disaster. Bottles, plates, bowls and other such items lay strewn across the floor. They looked as if they had been there for the past few days, and the whole room reeked of spilled wine and rotting food. The once-beautiful, handmade carpets that lay on the floor had intricate geometric designs on them. They would have been a wonder to look upon, had they not been covered in filth. Bashir looked around him in disgust.

This is the best he has to offer? It might be better than the guest room if the man was offering to take it. "It will have to do," he said with a sigh.

"Forgive me, my lord," Akmed replied. "I have not quite been myself these past few months," he said gloomily. Bashir turned to face the man, and saw that something was troubling him. "What would drive a man, such as yourself, to live in these conditions?" he asked, noting the man's solemn expression.

Akmed's eyes began to well with tears.

"It's my wife, my lord," he said with a choke in his voice. "She became increasingly ill, and no physician could figure out the problem. That started about six months back, and she died of a fever about a week ago. I... I have not yet recovered from her loss. She was everything to me. She fed me, clothed me when I needed it, helped me set up everything I presently own. She was my lover and my best friend all in one. There wasn't a circumstance in the whole world that would tear us apart, in her eyes. I-I wasn't always a rich man, but I married into her family for more than just that. She was nothing short of an *angel*, and now with her loss..." he couldn't finish his sentence.

Bashir put a hand on Akmed's shoulder. "I am truly sorry for the way I treated you," he said. "Had I known, I am certain I would have acted differently," he continued. Akmed burst into an uncontrollable fit of tears, and fell to the ground weeping as he went. "I will see to it that your establishment lacks for nothing once I return to the palace," he said comfortingly. "Y-you would do that for me?" Akmed asked, tears streaming down his large cheeks and into his thick beard. Bashir nodded, and consoled the crying man for a while.

A few moments later, Akmed's crying had come to a halt, and he picked himself up off the floor. "I'll get this cleaned up for you. It's the very least I could do," he said, beginning to stack a few of the bowls. Bashir began to grab a few of the bottles off the floor. "Wh-what are you doing? This is my mess, and my responsibility, my lord," Akmed said, trying to stop him.

"And as your king, it is my duty to help my people, so I will help you clean up, anyway," Bashir said in return. The man smiled, and they began picking up the old bowls of food and empty bottles off the floor.

Meanwhile, the raven flew as fast as its wings would carry it towards the palace, and it made it to its destination by nightfall. One of the guardsmen who stood watch at the palace's raven cages room heard the incoming bird cawing a short way away. He turned to watch the carrier land, and pant heavily on the roost that was provided for it. He walked over to the perch and saw the pouch on its chest, unlacing its bindings.

The bird flew over to where food and water had been placed, and ate its fill, while the guardsmen unpacked the contents. He withdrew the parchment, and noticed the king's signet stamped in wax on the front. His eyes opened wide, and hurried towards his captain.

The palace was a beautiful place with intricate tapestries

and carvings so beautiful, they could easily be identified as the works of a master artisan. The nearly seamless stone floor of the palace was beige and cool to touch, and each one had a pattern that was painted on it. The perfectly aligned pillars and walls supporting the palace made for excellent ventilation in the summer, and insulation in the winter.

The guardsman sprinted down the staircase from the raven tower, through the vast halls to his destination, arriving there without being short of breath. "Captain," he said. "Yes?" the Harutian captain replied.

He was covered in a two-layer tunic that was slightly open at the neck. It provided protection against slashing, but very little against stabbing movements, but lightweight armor came at that cost. His beige and brown sashes were wrapped around his waist, tying the large scimitar to the right side of his body. He had one red sash tied around his right arm, showing his rank.

"Captain, we've received a message from our king," the guardsman said. "Let me see it," the captain replied. The guardsman handed the small parchment to him, and he read its contents. His eyes opened wide with a fiery anger. "Our king wants a war. Ready the men, we ride at dawn for Coltend and honor," he said looking at the other two men he had been holding council with before being interrupted.

"But, captain," one of the other men began, "King Bashir has ridden there for a peace council. I don't understand why we would ride there in full gear ready for war." "The reason for that is that Prince Bashaa has been murdered by the king of Coltend," the captain snapped back.

"It's written here, and in the unmistakable hand of King Bashir. Read it yourself, and if you don't believe in our king, then you have no place in our ranks. Would you want to stay put and suffer the consequences once he arrives, or would you rather obey the orders as you have been taught to do?" the captain said angrily.

The man knew the consequences of disobeying a direct order, especially one coming from the highest command. "Of course, captain," the man said with a nod.

"We ride for the Rhydian Pass, and Coltend at dawn. For our king, his deceased son, our country, and for our honor as warriors," the captain said sternly. He pulled a scroll from the shelf behind him, and read it over to ensure that it was the correct one. He put the ring that lay on the desk in front of him onto his right hand, and dipped it into a small container of hot, blue wax.

He stamped the paper with it, and his insignia clearly showed in the imprint it left. He waited for it to dry completely, and handed it over to one of the other men in the room. "You know what to do," he said. The man saluted, and proceeded out of the room.

The order was given out, and all the men were assembled by dawn. Horses had been fed, and swords sharpened. Three-thousand men left the Harutian capital of Sardamin, riding for honor.

And to war.

CHAPTER 11

Athar

"I feel... strange," Athar said, looking at his hands. He was still in the library, where had just discovered his newfound powers. "You will feel like that for a while. At least until you gain mastery over yourself," the Masked One replied. Athar rubbed his temples. "I feel like I've been hit by a carriage. Does it always feel like this, or does it get better with time, my lord?" he asked.

I remember feeling like that, too. How long has it been since? his master thought.

"It will get better with time. After all, that was your first time having your consciousness truly separated from your body. It's only natural that you would feel a whiplash effect the first few times," he explained. Athar noted his master's composure, but decided to not say anything and glanced around the room.

"The books that are here, my lord," Athar began. "What about them?" his master asked. "There are so many of them, but I think I am beginning to see, or feel - I still don't know which - tendrils of mana coming from more than a few of them, my lord," the young man said, finally being able to stand without shaking. "I would much rather you figure out why they are like that on your own, for I have important matters to attend to," the Masked One said dismissively.

"Right now, I cannot and will not give you all the answers, as that would only stunt your growth as a mage. I prefer a more *practical* approach to teaching, after all, and a little challenge does well for one's development. Besides, it wouldn't be anywhere near as entertaining," the Masked One replied. "Is that why you came here, my lord? To see me struggle?" Athar asked.

"In truth, I knew you wouldn't struggle as much as one who didn't have your... *heritage*," his master said, pronouncing the last word slowly. "I understand, my lord," the young man replied, bowing his head. "Make sure you don't destroy anything," his master began. "I won't even begin to explain what I will do to you if you do." Athar felt a chill go down his spine once more, and swallowed to clear his throat. He nodded, and his master went out of the library.

The Masked One left the library and headed straight for the spawning chamber. The countless nests and tall shelves there were teeming with newborn monsters of all sorts. Above them was a high, transparent walkway that was suspended in the air by mana-infused crystals. There stood a dark figure whose silhouette could only be described as grotesque and misshapen. The Masked One's eyes glowed as he channeled mana towards his feet. He began to levitate up to the walkway, and landed on it like a feather having fallen to the ground.

"I assume all goes well with the spawn," he said to the figure. "Indeed, my lord, it does," it replied. The figure's voice was more of a gurgle than a normal voice, and the sharp, protruding teeth made him difficult to understand. "Do you remember your first day here in the Real, Karak?" the Masked One asked. Karak nodded, and turned to face his lord. His crimson eyes and grotesque features could barely be seen in the gloom of the chamber.

"I do, my lord. I remember first casting my eyes upon my new reality, after having been drawn out from my home in the Underworld," Karak began. "This world is much less *dead* than the one I come from, but you already know that. Plenty of fresh bones to gnaw," the creature gurgled.

"Tell me, Karak, do you know why I have left you in charge of the ones who lie below us?" the Masked One asked him. "No, my lord. I always assumed it's because you knew I could kill anything that tried to go against your wishes," Karak replied. "While that is partially true, it is not the whole truth. The reality of why I chose you is a bit different," the Masked One began, walking along the pathway. "It is because I know that if there is one I can trust within my small circle of allies, it is you," his lord replied. "I am honored to be called your ally and not your slave, my lord," the creature bowed, its figure distorting the darkness around it.

"As you know, Athar has only just begun to tap into his powers, and yet I feel something is amiss. I have peered into his past, and while I found what I was looking for, there was something even *my* power couldn't break through," the Masked One began, scratching beneath his mask. "Do you worry that his heritage might sway his allegiance?" Karak asked. "I'm already certain that it will. It is merely a matter of time before he tries to make his move," the Masked One grimaced beneath his mask. "However, if the legends are to be believed and he becomes what I think he might, I must ask you to put an end to him by whatever means necessary. For now, at least, I want you to keep an eye on him as often as you can spare it," the Masked One said.

"Requiring the services of a daemon such as myself, my lord...

It is an honor," Karak asked in disbelief. "I'm sure that it is. Since he has already begun his training, you must begin whenever you have finished your duties here. Report your findings back to me the moment after every training session he conducts, understand?" the Masked One asked. "Yes, my lord," Karak replied.

The Masked One's eyes glowed once more, and he let himself down from the walkway.

He will not fail me; of this I am certain. However, Athar's newfound powers will grow exponentially, for I have now seen that he is not as much of an idiot as I had originally thought. He might prove to be a formidable ally, or end up complicating and disrupting my plans, he thought on his way back to his study.

The violet gloom that lined the dark hallways and walls fluctuated as he passed. He arrived at his study, and looked about him, ensuring nothing had changed since he was last there. Everything appeared to be in order and in its proper place.

Excellent, he thought.

As he began to *draw mana from the Underworld*, writing feathers and scrolls began to float about the room, aligning themselves in preparation to receive dictation. "Begin," he said aloud, and the feathers began scribbling the words that entered his mind. He *drew even more power*, and condensed it to his right hand. The black, swirling sphere in his hand was then cast upon the floor that spawned featherless, winged beasts with sharp talons, and pale eyes. "End," he said aloud, and the writing utensils floated back to their original places, while the scrolls folded themselves, and went into their respective pouches.

He lifted them up, and strapped them onto his winged creatures. "Fly now, to the outcast, the hated, the disdained, and most vile of Synners. We have work to do," he commanded. The creatures squawked in reply, their sharp beaks opening wide to let out a deafening cry. Their featherless wings spread wide, and they flew out of the opened window before them.

There was only one left after the flock of creatures had left.

"This one is for the Castle. Take extra care to not make yourself seen by anyone other than him," the Masked One said. The creature flew off through the window, and turned in the opposite direction of the others. "So it begins," he said, watching the creatures soar into the moonlit night.

Meanwhile, Athar was still in the library, practicing his control over the Inar and Exar spells he had learned. Through every spell cast, he sought to remove the books from their proper places, draw them to him, and place them back in their original locations.

I've been at this for hours, and I still don't know how much I'm progressing. At least, I can't tell, he thought.

There were more than a dozen books strewn across the floor around him. He sighed deeply, recovering some of his fatigue.

The headache has lessened a little bit, but my master said that it would take time to get used to it. Time that I do not have, he thought. *If I can absorb myself in this newfound world of mana manipulation, I know that my goals will grow closer the more I practice.*

He practiced a few more times before nearly reaching his current limit.

This is more taxing than I thought it would be. I might not like him as a person, but gods above and below, the master is strong. Also, this deathmold solution is still just as unbearable as it was the first time, he thought as he sipped from the vial once more.

I've read through Farengir's book at least twice, but something is missing. Either that, or I haven't figured out what using this dark power truly requires, he thought. He observed the book in his hand, and flipped through the pages, hoping to find an answer.

What's this Kyr spell? I've never noticed it before, he thought.

He observed the diagrams that described the correct motions and quantities of mana required to perform it.

Alright, one more time, and I think that's all I'll be able to handle for tonight. Or is it already today? I don't even know anymore, he thought. *How long has it been since my master was here?*

He noticed his hour-candles had gone out, and saw the colors of the early dawn cast through one of the openings far above him.

Dawning already, eh? I'd better give this everything I've got. A final hurrah! He closed his eyes, and focused, remembering the order of operations given to him by the book.

Silence, Immolation, Draw, Return, he reviewed the words over in his mind, just before halting his thoughts.

He reopened his eyes, and they were the obsidian ovals once more. *As he focused, he sent his consciousness towards the dark sphere, but he heard an indistinguishable voice coming from the sphere of light now behind him. His eyes glanced at the bright one briefly, and it flared up like a flash of sunlight through the window of a dark room, causing him to lose focus.* His consciousness returned to his physical body, and he sighed.

"Fuck," he said aloud.

Just as he did, he heard a dripping sound coming from behind him. He could barely move; much less be able to turn and catch whatever it was that had made that sound.

I've never heard this place drip before. It's not even raining outside as far as I can tell, he thought. He reached for the flask, and took another swig of the disgusting solution.

"Ugh," he said, his face contorting itself. After a few seconds, his vitality returned, and he proceeded to stand.

Shit, I forgot to put away the books, he thought. He stacked them up, and placed them on the ground next to where he had taken the first one.

I'll come back tomorrow. For sure.

He remembered the dripping sound, and tried to relocate where it had come from. He observed the ground nearest to the main entrance, but found nothing. *Wasn't here,* he thought. He continued to scour the library for any signs of liquid, but found none.

That couldn't have simply been my imagination. Someone, or something was watching me, he concluded.

He decided his investigation would have to wait for some other time, as he knew he needed to rest for his attempts the following day. He left the library, casting one last glance upon it and grinned. He turned about, and proceeded down the gloomy halls that eventually led him to his chambers.

He opened his shutters, only to find himself blinded by the morning sun. His eyes shut almost immediately, shielding themselves from the blinding light.

It's just like the sphere of light in the Between, with the exception of that weird voice, he thought. *I was in the library for a really long time, indeed,* he thought.

He closed his shutters with his eyes reduced to small slits on his face, and relaxed once the light had been removed from the room. He recovered from his short-lived ordeal, and took the flask out of his pocket, placing it on his bedside table. He sat down on his bed, staring at the flask for a few moments, eventually tucking himself in under his blanket.

He lay awake for little more than a few minutes, reviewing all that he had learned. He tried to contain his excitement for what the next day might hold in store. He closed his eyes, thoughts running wild, and decided to quiet them with the techniques he had learned earlier to be able to sleep.

Meanwhile, the featherless creatures made their ways to their destinations, avoiding being seen at all costs. They hid themselves from prying eyes during the daylight hours, using terrain features to do so as they moved to their destinations. The first of them arrived just after midnight in northern Hjalfar, where a group of outcast Synners resided. They had created their own little society of thieves, marauders, and murderers - living under no man's rule. It was a cold night for this time of year, and most remained indoors, except for one.

A hooded figure left his house, after having noticed the silhouette of a winged creature blocking his view of the full moon. He followed in its general direction, leading him a short distance outside the main town. He found the creature up on a low lying branch of an oak tree, with its wings folded like a large bird of prey. The hooded figure was startled at the sight of the creature, once he had gotten close enough to see it under the moonlight. Its dark skin shone under the light of the moon, and its pale eyes reflected the moonlight, making it look like something straight out of his worst nightmares.

"What are you?" he asked quietly. The creature responded with a quiet snort, and turned itself, showing the pouch on its back. The man cautiously stepped forward, after all, he had been trained to trust no beast he would ever encounter. After realizing the creature meant him no harm, he reached out and opened the pouch, removing its contents.

The time has come for those of you who read this message to take back what was once taken from you. Your positions of power. Your dignity. Your families. Your loved ones. Join me, and take it all back, cutting down all those who oppose you. Slay the leaders without mercy, and bring their reigns to an end. Only after doing so will you answer to no man and be free to rule your country as you see fit. Take back what is rightfully yours. Take back your homes. Revive your stagnant and wasted lives, and give yourselves the opportunity to be great once more.

Join me, and I will help you regain that which you have lost. I am the Masked One, and I have spoken.

"What is the meaning of this?" the man asked, taking another gander at the moonlit creature.

Why is he acting now? Something must have changed, he thought.

"I will answer the call," he said, and the creature snorted once more, and flew off from whence it came. *I must tell the others.* He ran back to the small town, and began calling out the names of his friends and allies. They opened their doors to see him, standing in the middle of the housing district, with a scroll in his hand and arms spread wide.

"By the gods both light and dark, why must you call us out at this time of night?" one of the women asked. "Anders, you'd better have a good reason for waking us up at this hour," the woman called out. "I have received something that might aid us in our fight," Anders said aloud. "And I suppose it's that pamphlet you've got in your hand," the woman said.

"Unni, I know you've always doubted me," Anders began. "However, this time I ask you to trust me." Unni spat in retort to the comment. "Why should we?" she asked. "I mean, every raid you have ever led us on has gotten us shit for progress," she continued.

"I know, but the banishment has not been kind to any of us, regardless of what part of the continent we're from. We need hope," Anders replied. "I ask all of you who are listening to hear me now," he shouted. "I have received a message from the Masked One," he shouted. More faces began peering out of the cracks of their now opened doors. "Let's take back what's ours! Our homes, our lives! Let's join him, and take it all back!" he continued shouting.

More doors opened, and people began to come closer to hear what he had to say. "He's promised to help us get it back, and we've all heard tell he is immensely powerful," he began lowering his voice, realizing he didn't need to shout any longer. "And you got all that from a scroll? You expect us to believe that the Masked One himself would aid us?" Unni asked. "Read it yourself," Anders replied, handing her the scroll.

She read the contents of the scroll, and her eyes opened wide when she recognized the handwriting, as each person had their own style of using mana to write. "Everyone listen up," she called out. The gathering crowd cast their eyes upon her. "What Anders said is true. I have verified the information myself, and I will best anyone who dares to call me a liar," she began.

Nobody said a word.

"After reading this message, we now have a choice before us: act on it, or die a boring death of old age and sickness," she called out. "Fuck dying of old age!" one of the men in the crowd called out. "Let's take back our home!" another chimed in. "I want to *live*, not *survive*!" a third rang out. More and more comments began to pour in, and Unni and Anders smiled at each other. Anders raised his hand, motioning for silence amidst the people. "It's decided, then. We will ride for Odensby at first light!" Unni shouted so that everyone could hear her clearly.

"Get your gear together, and let's get our lives back!" she shouted. There was a cheer as soon as she finished her sentence. She gave Anders a look of approval, and he smiled back at her. They went back into their houses for the night.

The other creatures had made it to their destinations, and each of the message's recipients answered the call. Harutians, Caegweni, Coltenders; all of these gave their replies to the creatures, and watched them fly back towards their master.

The lone creature that had departed last from Valdis finally made it to its destination, but since Coltend was such a populated country, it only traveled under the cover of night. The difficulty thereof only increased when it arrived at the well-guarded Coltend Castle. A hooded figure was there in the aviary that night, awaiting a response from his master, when finally, the creature arrived through the main window. He went to the creature, and removed the parchment from the pouch.

It has been set in motion. Do. Not. Disappoint. Me.

The figure understood what it had meant. "I will not, my lord," the voice said from under the hood. The creature snorted, and flew off to deliver the response. The figure watched the flapping of its wings, and felt a sense of accomplishment. The figure knew the time had come to begin paving the way for his master.

Over the course of the days that passed, Athar spent most of his time in the library, practicing his newly acquired skills. In just two days' time, he had learned over half of the basic spells, and could cast them with less difficulty than before. He realized he was becoming stronger at an alarming rate, but at the end of every session, he heard the dripping sound.

He feigned ignorance of its existence, to see what would come of doing so, and yet, during that time, not much had changed.

I've got to figure out what or who the actual fuck is stalking me. This is absurd, he thought one night in the comfort of his bed.

He desperately tried to shun the thought from his mind, quieting it. After many hours of trying to do so, he finally gave up, and got out of bed. He put on his clothes, and grabbed a candle from his bedside table aimlessly walking down the halls to see if the dripping would come after him.

What if it's a monster on the loose? I'm not skilled enough to take one down just yet, I don't think, he thought.

His palms began to sweat, and adrenaline coursed through

his veins. His heart rate rapidly increased, immediately becoming more aware of his surroundings. He continued to walk, without a distinct direction to follow, and after a few minutes, he heard it.

Drip.

Fuck me, there it is, he thought. *Alright, calm down and keep moving forward. Don't look back right now. Wait for an opportunity.* He continued walking, pretending not to notice the sound that had reached his ears.

The library. That's where I'll face it, he thought. He turned down the halls he had come to know over the past few years and began making his way towards his now-favorite room in the whole citadel.

Drip.

He made it to the library, his candle had almost gone out from all the walking, but its little flame persevered.

I've finally made it, and I know it's close behind me, he thought.

He walked into the library, and kneeled in the center, as though he were about to practice - even though he had already spent most of the day doing so. He pulled out the flask of deathmold solution, and set it at his left side with the cork pulled out.

Drip.

He heard it, and tried to locate its origin without turning around. *It's here.* He closed his eyes, and focused once again to silence his mind. This time, though, he had little or no difficulty in doing so. His eyes went dark, and *he sent his consciousness to the Underworld. He stretched out his hand - drawing the dark tendrils of mana towards him from the dark sphere in the sky. The mana enveloped him, and he condensed it to his hand with the ring. He pulled himself out of the Underworld, and* returned his consciousness.

He instantly reached down for the flask, and took a large

swig, giving himself a small buffer for the backlash he knew would come later. He managed to maintain the sphere of mana in his hand, and knew what he had to do.

Drip.

Alright, here we go, he thought. *Three, two, one.* He fell backwards, landing on his back, and aimed his Exar spell at a dark figure that was on top of the bookshelf above the door. He released the mana and the blast reached its target, knocking it off of its perch.

As it was falling, he rolled onto his belly and quickly got to his feet. He sent another blast behind him to boost his speed, and sprinted towards the lanky, misshapen figure. With increased speed, he jumped on top of it to pin it down with his weight.

The creature squirmed and wriggled, like an earthworm being baited to a hook, but he held its arms firmly. "I've got you now, you piece of shit!" he shouted in its face. The slimy, protruding teeth tried to bite his arm, but Athar had bent his arm just enough to avoid it. "What the fuck do you want from me?" he shouted. The creature gurgled and continued squirming.

Athar headbutted it, breaking one of its horrid teeth and accidentally cut into his eyebrow. Blood dripped from both of their wounds. "Answer me!" he shouted again. This time, the creature didn't wriggle, but simply began to cackle. "Our master said you were gaining power quickly, but I didn't expect this much," Karak said, his gurgling voice sending a small chill down Athar's spine.

"He sent you to spy on me, didn't he, you slimy fuck?" Athar said threateningly. "He did," Karak said with what was meant to be a chuckle. "Why?" Athar asked. "He is just being cautious as to your allegiance, given your heritage," the creature replied. "Why the fuck would he be concerned about that? I hate my father, and I would kill him myself if I ever got the chance," Athar said. Karak gurgled the black blood from his missing tooth.

"He knows that there is a part of you that won't be entirely willing to do his bidding," Karak replied. "He knows everything there is to know about you, Athar," he continued. "Only I know myself better than anyone. He cannot possibly think that I would betray him," Athar said, disturbed at the news. "No, you don't. Not yet," Karak replied.

Athar was angry. Angrier than he had ever been in his life. "After all of these years, he still doubts me? So be it. Take me to him," he said. "He's not to be disturbed. His orders, not mine," Karak replied. "Do I look like I give even the smallest, runniest, turtle shit?" Athar asked, growing increasingly angry.

"Take me to him, right now. Otherwise, I'll headbutt you again and again until your teeth are coming out of your asshole," he threatened. "Alright! Fine! I'll take you to him, but don't expect a warm welcome," Karak replied maliciously. Athar released him, and both got to their feet. Athar recorked his flask, and stuck it in his pocket.

Karak led him down the halls, to find the Masked One in the room where he had first had his encounter with the addia and the ochelon. "My lord," Athar called out. The Masked One was standing in front of yet another ochelon's cage, much smaller than the royal ochelon whose soul he had absorbed before. He appeared to be talking to it, in its own language of grunts and snorts. What he said, Athar would never find out, but he knew it couldn't be anything good.

"Athar, come closer," the Masked One said without turning around. "I know why you're here, and I hope you will understand why I think the way I do," he said as his servant drew closer. "After all these years, you still doubt my allegiance to you? How could you? I've given you everything I had to give. My service, time, life. All of it! Even though you know I hate you, I still haven't betrayed you, and I won't, either!" Athar shouted. "Not yet," the Masked One said curtly, his eyes flaring mildly. "I have given you access to mana in return for your service, although there is much that you can do for me, still," he replied in a sinister tone. Athar's heart raced once again.

"I have taken you in. Fed you. Clothed you. Shown you things you would not have been able to even get close to otherwise, and still you are displeased with me for sending one of my allies to observe your progress? You have no idea the trouble it has been to rid the world of knowledge of your existence. I even had to influence a young prince's mind, contorting it to my will to lead your father to his long-overdue death. I gave him knowledge he would not have found if it hadn't been for me," he continued.

"What are you talking about?" Athar asked. He was confused as to why his master was saying what he was. "Come now. Did you really think I would let the world know that Athar Wishert still lived? The bastard son of King Truls, and the heritage your bloodline carries? If you did, then you truly are the imbecile I believed you to be," the Masked One said. "What heritage? What the hell do you even mean by that? You've said it before, and yet I still have no idea what you mean, my lord!" Athar said, taken aback.

"I didn't either when you first arrived all those years ago," the Masked One said angrily. "I might now know a much fuller extent of your past, but there are still things even I cannot manage if they come to fruition. For that reason, you had to be placed under a careful eye. One that was, apparently, not careful enough," he continued, glaring at Karak.

"There is no use in fighting back now, Athar," the Masked

One began. "There is still much for you to learn, and I do not have the time to argue with an insolent child who needs careful observation," he continued. Athar clenched his fist tightly. "I cannot and will not do anything against you, my lord. I might hate you for how you treated me for all those years, but you have given me knowledge, and opened my eyes to mana. For that debt, I can't betray you, even if I wanted to," he replied.

"I'm glad you recognize that, Athar," the Masked One said, calming down a little. "Believe me, the situation is much different than you think it is. If anything, I put you under observation to protect you," he continued. Athar was stunned. "Protect me from what?" he asked.

"The very thing I couldn't, and wouldn't want to unlock when I looked into your core," the Masked One said.

CHAPTER 12

The Elven Emissary

Edryd looked at me with wide eyes. "I don't suppose you know how your brother knows the elf?" Edryd asked, still staring at the friendly exchange between Bernar and Anwill. I could only shake my head. "I'm just as confused as you are, to be honest. When did they even meet? How long have they known each other?" I asked, trying to piece together details.

"Your brother is a fifth stage, right?" Edryd asked. "What's that got to do with anything?" I asked. "Well, maybe he had some training over in Caegwen. It's the only logical assumption I can make right now, anyway," Edryd said, scratching the back of his head.

I observed the friendly nature with which my brother and the elf spoke with each other.

"What's all that about? Wait, who even *is* that?" Batch interrupted from a short distance away, gesturing toward the emissary. "I had just finished my training when I saw the rider come in. I figured I'd come and see what's going on for myself," he continued.

"Don't know, yet," I replied with a shrug. "He's only just arrived, and so far, the two, now three, of us have more questions than answers," I continued. "Well, there is an elf of Caegwen here in Codrean, so I dare say that something smells, and it's *not* the smell of roses," Batch said.

Batch, Ed, and I watched Bernar and Anwill walk towards the main fortress, conversing over something I couldn't overhear. The two went fully out of earshot, and I turned over to my friends, who were also just as puzzled as I was.

"I'm sorry I've been absent these last couple of days. Bernar has me training some new moves with Irun, and it's been quite... *uh*, painful," Batch said, scratching the back of his head.

"It's alright," Edryd began. "Hell, if I had to be put through Bernar's training, I think my arms would be jelly. *Oh*! Wait, they are," Edryd said with a chuckle. Batch looked at Edryd's previously wounded shoulder. "On the bright side, at least you'd have emergency food readily available," he said with a sarcastic smile. "I sometimes wonder if not a few marbles short of a full bag," Edryd replied with a disgusted look on his face.

"Disregarding *that* fucked up mental image, I've actually been able to get back to training," Edryd replied. "That's true, and we still kicked your sorry ass. No mercy for arms made of jelly," I said with a shrug. "See? I knew I should've kicked you in the balls when I had the chance," Edryd shot back immediately. The three of us laughed at each other, recognizing the ridiculousness of the situation.

"It's good to be with you two, again," Batch began. "As much as I hate to admit it, I've missed you guys. A few more days and I would have begged you two to swing by and watch me kick Irun's ass," he said with a grin.

"I've always thought Irun was the better of you two," Edryd said with as much sarcasm as he could muster. "*Oh*, don't get me wrong, he's still a damned-good swordsman; but with a little help from Bernar, I've finally managed to best him more than once," Batch said with pride.

"Well, well," I said, raising my eyebrows. "I think the four of us should have a sparring session to see who's the best of us. Jelly arms and all. Speaking of *shit-for-brains,* where is he?" I asked.

I looked around to see if I could find the fourth member of our little fellowship. "I've only just noticed something," Edryd began, leaving us with a confused look on our faces. "Well, I mean, he could be off training, but Irun hasn't been seen in some time by anyone other than you, Batch," Edryd said.

"He tends to run off to study his mistakes after each training session, or so he says," Batch replied with a shrug. "He hasn't really done much else other than that," he continued.

I looked at Edryd with a raised eyebrow. Batch noticed the exchange. "I'm not even going to ask what that was about, but let's get back to the matter of the elf," he said nonchalantly.

"Well, let's examine what we know," I began. "He rode all the way from Caegwen to speak to the Master. Bernar has known him for a long time. We've only been back about a week or so since leaving the palace where King Elhael was with members of his council. I didn't see him, but he must have been somewhere near the castle, as it would have taken a much longer time to get here. Am I missing anything?" I asked.

"Well, there was that situation with the ravens, where the Master freaked out for some reason. Maybe they were meant for him?" Batch added. "True, which was rather odd, I mean, it's just a raven or two," Edryd chimed in.

He feigned his ignorance quite well, and I released a breath I didn't know I was holding.

"Well, a raven could mean a number of things," Batch began. "It could've been someone from the nearby farm, or something similar to that, at least," he said.

I was surprised, to say the least, and shot Ed a quick glance. *That's the same conclusion we had reached before the Master told us of the possibility of a traitor,* I thought.

"True," I said with a nod. "For all we know, it could have just been that. However, it still doesn't explain how quickly he arrived, nor what the actual fuck that elf is doing here, though," Batch said. "Well, we won't figure out much if we're just standing around," Edryd said.

Batch looked at him in surprise. "You're saying we should eavesdrop on their conversation? You know the Master can practically see through walls, right?" Batch asked. "I know he can, but there's gotta be another way we can find out why he's here," Edryd replied.

"So what do you propose?" I asked. Edryd grinned with obvious malicious intent. "Well, he likes drinking, doesn't he? Maybe we could bribe him with extra rations or something," he replied suggestively.

"Do you really think he's going to accept that as a worthy trade?" I asked, though I already knew the answer as Edryd's face sank. "I just want him to spill the beans on what they talked about," he said, finally understanding what I meant.

"Well, well, well. There goes Ed's innocence. Never thought I'd hear that bribery was on the table coming from you," Batch said with genuine surprise. "I'm not saying he would accept the bribe, but if he *did*..." Edryd trailed off.

I looked at him and nodded. "It would be very helpful to understand the situation," I began. "However, all we can do now is wait for them to be done," I concluded, patting Edryd's non-injured shoulder twice.

Just as Bernar was shutting the door behind him, he subtly gestured for me to follow him. It took me a second to understand what it was he wanted from me, but after he repeated the gesture, I finally understood.

"Ed, I have to go," I whispered out of the corner of my mouth as I subtly flicked my head in the direction of the door. "Go on, I'll catch up with you later," he shot back quickly. "Hey, Batch, I've got a question," he said, trying to distract our mutual friend.

I followed my brother's direction and made my way to the Master's study. As I cracked the door open, I saw that he was leaning on his desk, looking over a few scrolls with the others. He heard my footsteps coming up the stairs, and looked in my direction before any other of the visitors had even noticed I was there.

"Greetings, Thoma. Nice of you to join us," the Master said, glancing up from the unraveled map before him. "Greetings, Master," I said shyly as I closed the door behind me. "Please, sit. We're about to start," he said, gesturing toward a small, wooden stool in the corner of the room.

Time for the adults to talk, right? I thought as I gingerly made my way to the stool.

"It's good to see you again, Anwill. I'd be lying if I said I was expecting you to visit us," he said, extending a hand toward the elf who clasped it firmly. "Indeed. I came as quickly as I could, when I heard the news," Anwill replied.

"You couldn't have come all the way from Caegwen simply to give me news," the Master said. "No, truly I have not. However, I must attend to the matter at hand with haste, as time is of the essence," Anwill replied. "Please, take a seat," the Master motioned to the chair with the carvings.

I think it's best if I shut up. Gods above, I'm not even supposed to be here, I thought, sitting quietly.

"Master, I bring news of Coltend and something that will be of great interest to you. However, I must speak of Coltend first. A few days ago, Truls brutally murdered the young Harutian prince Bashaa over the accusation of having intercourse with his wife, Queen Leona," he began.

"*Oh*, shit," Bernar and I said in unison from the back of the room. "Indeed. However, after the murder, Bashir fled, and Truls sent a small party out to hunt him down. The very same day, Truls died at the hands of the very person whose honor he was trying to protect - or so his servants say," Anwill said.

"Queen Leona," the Master said with a nod. "Precisely. Now she is the one ruling over her subjects at Coltend Castle. While Bashir's state and location are currently unknown, we know he made his way towards the Rhydian pass, which would be the logical choice. After all, it's the shortest and most direct road to take back to his home," Anwill said.

"He's always been a good rider, so I'm sure he made it," the Master said, digesting the new information. "However, I must now speak of my home, Caegwen, where situations have arisen that may prove to be worth your while," Anwill said. "Another queen murder her husband?" Bernar asked jokingly.

"If only it were that simple," the elf shook his head. "Master, as you well know, the monsters only come out of their portals from the Underworld every full moon. However, three days ago, a portal opened during the daytime; an unprecedented event in and of itself," the elf said, leaning forward.

"During the day? This does not bode well, indeed," the Master said with a slight frown. "Truly. The Commander of the Myrdinian Synners, whom you know *quite* well, has managed to organize enough troops to hold shifts over the locations and slay the few that passed through the portal. Although, the last one that opened was far too close to our capital for comfort," Anwill said with his head aimed at the floor.

"They are growing bolder by the day, or so it seems," he began once more after a brief pause. "King Elhael and Queen Aurae, as well as myself and others of the elven council, believe the Undergod to be attempting to make a move of some sort. As things currently stand, we still do not know what he's after," he said with a hint of anger in his voice.

"Your Synners," the Master began, rubbing his scar lightly. "What about them?" Anwill asked. "They didn't notice anything strange about the portal, did they? The Commander didn't put anything out regarding its composition?" the Master asked.

"The reports said it was emitting dark tendrils of power that faced towards the North, but I fail to see how that is relevant," Anwill said. The Master looked at his visitor with questioning eyes. "If you don't mind me asking, but how old are you exactly?" he asked. "Eight-hundred and eighty," Anwill replied with a curious look on his face. "*Ah*, so it was just before your time, then," the Master said.

Just before his *time? How old* is *the Master anyway?* I thought, caught entirely off-guard by the strange reveal.

"Excuse me, but what does this have to do with the portal?" Anwill asked, genuinely confused. "About fifty years before you were born, a citadel was discovered in the far northern regions of Hjalfar. They called it *Valdis*, which is derived from their language meaning *the dead goddess*," the Master began to explain.

Valdis? That's not a Hjalfarian name, is it? I thought, genuinely confused.

"The citadel was named as such, given the fact that all who attempted to explore it in the years that followed never returned. The fact that the tendrils were facing in its general direction, could have something to do with the reason why it appeared in the first place," the Master continued calmly.

"You're suggesting that the Undergod is somehow connected to this *Valdis* place, Master?" Bernar asked. "Exactly," the Master replied with a slight nod. "I believe something stirs there, and it is anything but friendly," he continued.

"I know what lies there, and *he* is growing more powerful every day. It would stand to reason if there were a connection to that place with the Underworld," Anwill said ominously.

"You do?" the Master asked with genuine curiosity. "Indeed, Master. It's..." Anwill was about to answer when a window was broken by a rock thrown from outside. All of us turned to look at Bernar as he picked up the stone.

Portal. Monsters, I managed to read, my eyes opening widely as I snagged a glance at the scratchings on the stone.

Bernar quickly looked out of the window, to see Edryd and Batch pointing towards the south. Bernar glanced over the low, grassy hills, his eyes opening wide. "What is it?" the Master asked. "You couldn't have come at a better time, Anwill, as it's been a while since we fought side by side. Guess what just showed up at our doorstep?" Bernar said incredulously.

The Master's eyes opened wide, as did everyone else's.

"Sound the alarm and ready for battle," he said, getting out of his seat. "Have you got a sword with you?" the Master asked the elf. "What kind of Synner would I be if I didn't?" Anwill replied with a grin. "Good. Be ready to use it. Thoma, with us, now!" the Master commanded, to which Anwill and I replied with a unified nod.

"Sound the alarm!" Bernar shouted out of the broken window to Ed. He was startled by my brother's mana-enhanced command and quickly sprinted over to the bell, signaling the alarm. There were still Synners honing their skill in the training ground who heard the call as we raced down the stairs to the courtyard.

"What's this all about?" a senior Synner asked his training partner, running toward the sound of the commotion. "Sounds like we've got trouble," I heard Roburn reply. "Gear up, boys!"

he shouted to the others. "We've got a real fight coming our way! Time to put all that training to some good fucking use! Now, move!" he shouted, and everyone scrambled to switch out training swords for real ones.

"Hurry the fuck up!" Roburn shouted again. "Pray to the gods that you're not about to become a glick suppository!" he shouted.

After a few precious minutes, each one had our battle-ready equipment secured to our jerkins. We quickly mounted our respective horses, when I noticed Irun running up, still fumble-fucking his gear as he moved towards us.

"I heard the alarm ringing, but what's the situation?" Irun asked. "We're under attack," I said. "A portal not too far south of here is spewing glicks out faster than I can piss. Where the hell were you?" I asked.

"I was studying and didn't hear the bell until about a minute after it had begun ringing," Irun replied. "Well, get a move on. Things are about to get ugly," Batch said. Irun nodded, mounting his horse that Batch had had the stable hand fetch before.

The Master turned his horse to face us as the gate opened behind him. "Our enemies are at our gates, and we must not let them breach our defenses. All of you have trained your entire lives for moments such as this one, and I expect all of you to know exactly what you're doing out there. Protect this fortress, no matter the cost. Is that clear?" he shouted.

There was a roar in response. "We ride!" he shouted, and the large gates swung open, allowing everyone to leave as quickly as possible. We galloped out from the fortress, and immediately turned south, riding directly towards the growing horde of monsters. The monsters were considerably disorganized, and always used their numbers to overpower an enemy.

Not today, I thought, taking the portals into consideration.

Within the next few minutes, we were getting close enough to our new targets. "Formation!" Garett shouted. We formed three boar's heads and maintained our speed. The formation was triangular, hollow in the middle, and served as a wedge whenever there was a line that needed to be broken.

Three-hundred meters.

The southern wind began to blow, and the stench of the oncoming horde of glicks and daemons became palpable, prompting some of us lesser experienced Synners to almost greet our late lunches. "Gods above and below, they smell awful," Irun said to Batch who rode by his side in our boar's head. Batch took a deep breath through his nose.

"Like a thousand pieces of rotten bacon put under the sun," Batch noted. "Or an ochelon's ass," Irun said, trying to take his mind off the stench. "Not helping. There might be one there for all we know. So, focus!" I replied curtly.

Two-hundred meters.

The portal could be seen clearly. A violet swirl of mana, with dark tendrils of power facing the north-east poured out the horrid creatures. The monsters screamed and gurgled their war-cries, and could be heard from nearly a kilometer away.

It was the first time I'd ever laid eyes on a daemon outside of a textbook. Its disfigured body and blackened, rotting skin almost made the glicks look like something straight out of a child's bed-time story.

"Swords," the Master shouted from the center of the second formation, a short command which we all followed promptly. "Bow-casters," Garett called out, and the rear part of the formation pulled back, drawing their bows and nocking their arrows to pick off any stragglers.

Their eyes went dark as they infused their bows with large amounts of raw mana. Their bows began to glow different colors, according to the effect they wanted. Garett raised his hand to signal the archers. "Loose!" he called out. They freed their arrows just in front of the three formations, weakening the enemy's line.

Fifty meters.

Here we go again. Just like last time, lean in and... I thought as I swung down from my right side, hearing the familiar sound of a crushed skull as thick, green blood sprayed my cheek.

I kept moving forward, hacking away at anything that was within striking range, hitting more than a few targets as I did so. The boar's head was successful, wreaking havoc on all that got in its way. Heads flew and blood sprayed up in the air as our swords sang the song of war.

My sword-hand was now covered in obnoxious green blood, but I pressed on, slaying more than a dozen on my first pass. Edryd, too, was having his blade sink into the screeching monsters. "Take that, you ugly fucks!" he shouted, giving himself courage to face whatever came next.

The boar's heads finally broke with the swarming creatures, and it soon became every man for himself. Roburn was riding into one of the thicker clusters of daemons, when suddenly, one of the horrid creatures jumped up, knocking off his horse. He fell to the ground with a thud, and was soon swarmed by the very ones whose blood he had already spilled so much of. "Roburn!" Edryd called out, and hacked his way over toward him.

Shit, did I just watch him die? I thought, watching them pile on top of where he landed as my stomach turned.

Just as I was thinking that a large explosion of mana was released from the newly formed mound of daemons and glicks, setting all of them alight. They squealed and attempted to swat out the mana-flames.

Roburn, whose braided hair was now coated in his own blood, as well as the monsters', stood up and cast the Pyrus spell. The flame cloak surrounded him, keeping the unburned monsters at bay for a short while he seared his wounds shut.

Edryd rode towards him, and dismounted his horse quickly when he arrived. "I've got your back," he said, cutting down a few daemons in the process. "Just don't get yourself killed," Roburn replied, glaring behind him with glowing eyes. Both stood side by side, severing limbs and removing heads from shoulders.

I was still on my horse, but I too was nearly knocked off the same way I had been in my first battle. I leaped off the back of my horse, who proceeded to crush a few creatures to make its escape, and rolled to my feet. In the same moment, I severed my attacker's head at the jaw, sending a spray of blood into the air.

A few more glicks came rushing towards me, and I got into my guard once more. Chaos reigned about him, but in that moment, it seemed as though the whole world was shut out, leaving him and the monsters.

Three daemons on the right, two glicks on the left, I thought.

I calculated who would come first in a split second. The first glick jumped at me, aiming a sharp claw for my head. I ducked under the blow, and struck its gut, spilling entrails on the ground beneath it. Two daemons came from opposite directions, sprinting towards me.

Shit, they're quick, I thought.

I saw the first claw being raised, and knew that would be the first one to strike. I glazed the blow off my sword and took off its head with a spin. The other one was now within striking range, and its claw found its target, cutting into the flesh on my left arm. I barely even felt it through my armor and adrenaline, and severed the claw the next claw that came for me. I swept its legs, causing the creature to fall on its back. With my eyes darkened, I *drew mana from the Ethereal* and sent an Exar blast downward, crushing the daemon's skull.

"Three down," I said, glaring at the remaining creatures in front of me. The glick fluttered its scales, and the daemon produced a horrifying, knocking sound by smashing its teeth together in protest of my bravado.

"You're dying first," I muttered toward the daemon. I pushed off my left leg, dashing quickly towards it. I brought my sword down, making a diagonal cut that split the creature in two, spilling more blood and entrails onto the ground.

I twisted my body quickly, jabbing my mana-infused sword into the final monster's eye socket, causing its head to burst into flames. I watched as it hit the ground with a wet *thud*. I took a moment to survey my surroundings, and get a better sense of what was going on.

We're winning, I thought as a flash of bright green sent glicks and daemons flying into the air.

That's a powerful spell if ever I've seen one. I rushed over to the origin of the flash, hacking down four more on my way there.

Anwill was busy exploding glick after glick, while the Master and Bernar had infused their swords with mana. Their swords glowed a vibrant red, and cut through the oncoming creatures like a hot knife to butter. Anwill continued casting in conjunction with the cuts made by his sword, obliterating any beast that met him.

I watched them for a moment, ensuring that no other creatures were around me first. Suddenly, loud roars came from the direction of the portal. "Ochelons!" Irun called out over the screeches and screams of battle. Bernar, Anwill, the Master and I cut down the remaining enemies around us, and cast our eyes upon the lumbering beasts. Four of them could be seen exiting the portal that closed behind them, their eyes glowing red, and claws spread wide, ready to strike.

"Finally, a challenge. Ready for *round two,* shit-bird?" Bernar asked me. Anwill turned toward us, listening intently to our conversation, as if something had peaked his interest. "More like *round three,* fuck-ass. Lead me to the slaughter and purging of this filth from our doorstep," I said, nodding with determination, not wanting to show my absolute exhaustion at this point.

Anwill scoffed and chuckled in amusement, but didn't voice his thoughts.

The Master knew I was already tired from fighting, but he knew that if I stopped right then and there, that it would be no different than giving my neck to an executioner. "Go, now!" he commanded after a curt nod of acknowledgement of my resolve.

The four of us ran towards Irun and the ochelons. Edryd and Roburn had bested the creatures around them, and they converged on the ochelons as well. The roars were deafening, and sent chills down everyone's spines, save the Master and Anwill, who had many more years' experience in fighting them. "Thoma, Edryd, Roburn, Irun. You four take the male on the right. Bernar, Anwill and I will take the other three on the left," the Master ordered. "Yes, Master," we replied.

We spread themselves out, not caring about the chaos that continued behind them as it was being taken care of by the other Synners. We had a new task now: to take the bastards down. The ochelons bellowed their challenges to us, rumbling the ground and air alike.

The Master's eyes glowed even more brightly as he cast a fireball to draw the attention of the largest male in the middle. Anwill did the same, drawing the one on the far left to him as he shot a spell at it, searing its fur.

"*Ah*, it's been a long time," the Master said with a smile, watching the annoyed beast come towards him. He got in his guard, the Vom Tach, and held his longsword with both hands just above his forehead.

He waited.

The others and I circled around our own challenger, closing in around it. The ochelon swung its muscular arms, though each blow was dodged adeptly.

Why is he waiting? I asked myself after glancing at the Master standing still in his guard.

I turned my head just in time to see a large claw coming straight for me. I stepped out of the way and cut off one of its fingers.

Meanwhile, the Master was still standing his ground. Anwill and Bernar were already engaging their enemies, combining spells and sword strikes to weaken the ochelon's tough hides. The Master focused on his enemy, who now came at a charge ready to strike. He watched the large claw as it rose into the air with his peripheral vision, keeping his eyes fixated on its center of mass.

The beast swung down from its right side, and the Master simply stepped out of the way, removing its wrist from its arm in the process with one, swift cut. The ochelon roared in pain, and swung again at about waist height. The Master rolled out of the way, and was quickly on his feet, keeping his eyes fixed on the beast.

It tried to slam the ground beneath him, and he stepped out of the way of the large paw that was now where he had been just a moment ago. He dashed forward, cutting the tendon at the ankle, forcing the beast to stumble in front of him.

He rushed forward once more, stabbing a vital organ. The

beast roared, and swung again with its claw in an attempt to swat him like a fly. The Master leapt over the attack, severing its wrist in the process. "Two bloodied stumps and a strong bite are all you've got left," he said, already back on his feet.

The beast roared and tried to squash him with both of its stumps. The Master dodged the blows, and jabbed his sword into its face, piercing an eye. The beast roared once more, and swung blindly, desperate to find its target. He dodged the attacks, and went around the beast to strike at the remaining tendon above its heel.

It fell with a roar to the ground, unable to get back up, swinging one last time to reach its mark of empty air. The Master had rolled out of the way, and was now in front of it. He raised his sword, and turned it on its point.

He struck downward, pinning the beast's head to the earth below. It gurgled blood, as the Master's eyes glowed more intensely. His sword pushed the mana into the creature's head with such force that it caused it to explode, leaving naught but a puddle of blood where its head once was.

The Master pulled his sword out from its head, and looked over at the others. Anwill was finishing off his enemy with a stab to the gut and a burst of mana, leaving a hole the diameter of a wine barrel in its chest.

Bernar, on the other hand, had managed to get on top of his ochelon and sliced into its nape. It fell to the ground with a resounding *thud*, twitching for a few moments as Bernar stepped down from the creature.

The Master cast his eyes over towards me and the others, who were only now getting a foothold against the ochelon. Anwill walked over to him, looking for any straggling creatures. "Anwill, that was amazing! When were you going to teach me that move?" Bernar asked, walking over to the pair and wiping the blood off his sword.

"Whenever you come back to Caegwen, I will," Anwill replied with a warm smile. I turned to see the gaping hole in the creature, and met Anwill's eye before dodging yet another blow.

"Should we help them?" I heard him ask, preparing to draw his sword. "No. Don't help them. They seem to be doing alright in terms of damaging it, but I want to see them work as a team," the Master said, halting Anwill from approaching us.

Edryd and the wounded Roburn were dodging swats from the large claws aimed for them, while Irun and I tried to get close enough to cut its legs at the same time. The beast saw a flicker of sunlight off Irun's sword, and swung its claw which met its mark. Irun couldn't get out of the way in time, and was sent into the air for a few moments.

"Irun!" I called out. Irun's landing was anything but a smooth one, as it nearly knocked him out.

Shit. That could've been me. It's too tall to try and strike its chest. I've got to bring it down to our level and make it an even fight, I thought, remembering my own battle just a few days prior.

I dodged another swat aimed at me with a roll, and got in close enough to hack at the flesh behind its knee. It roared in pain, and kneeled on the ground. "Aim for his eyes!" I yelled at Edryd, feeling a slight sting of pain from the scar on my back after the roll.

Edryd's eyes went dark, and he cast a fireball aimed at the beast's face, doing little to no damage. "Mana flames won't work on their hide! Use your sword!" Roburn shouted. Edryd understood the command, and through the plume of smoke, he thrust his sword, just barely reaching its target.

Roburn, sliding under the hunched over creature, sliced into its gut. "Damn it, too shallow," he grunted. As the beast reared from the attack, it slammed the ground just beside me, sending me flying high into the air.

As I reached the apex of my impromptu avian mimicry above the beast, I saw its bare nape and aimed for it.

I have to land this strike. If I can just cut its nape, that will be enough, but how can I deal that much *damage to it?* I thought.

I brought my sword up just above my forehead, my sclera blackening for a moment as I did so. However, I could feel a familiar warmth streaming from my eyes toward my temples as my eyes began to glow intensely, leaking a mana trail behind me as I fell.

I gathered all my might, infused my sword with mana, and struck its nape as I fell, using whatever momentum from my weight and rotational velocity I could muster. My sword, severing the head from the large body, continued into the ground, leaving an explosion of blood, dirt, and mana in its wake.

The headless mass of flesh swayed, and blood bubbled as the air left its lungs. After a moment of idle rocking, it began to fall towards me, forcing me to get out of the way in the nick of time to avoid the crushing weight of the massive body. As I recovered from my roll, I breathed a sigh of relief as the blood from the creature created a small puddle around me.

"Holy leather-donut of the Kingdom of Assecheeks, that was amazing!" Edryd exclaimed, helping me to my feet. The Master and his group were smiling from where they stood, visibly impressed by what they had just witnessed.

"We've got to help Irun," I said, catching my breath. The three of us rushed over to where Irun had landed, but he was nowhere to be seen. "Where the hell did he go?" Edryd asked. "I saw him land right here," I said with no small amount of confusion in my voice.

"I'm over here," a voice came from a pile of dead creatures. "Irun," I said, rushing over to him. "I'm fine, thanks for asking,"

Irun said with sarcasm. I grimaced. "I thought he had crushed your ribcage," I said, looking him up and down. "He did, which is why I didn't return to help you," Irun answered.

"I stayed here casting what spells I could to patch them up, while you three took it down," he continued. "Well, at least you're not dead," Roburn said, slowly walking over to the three of us. Irun chuckled lightly, but instantly regretted it. "Right now, I kind of wish I were," he groaned.

"You've all done well," the Master said, after looking around and noticing the battle was nearly over. "Not as well as you, Master," I replied, hearing the bow-casters strike down stragglers as they attempted to flee. "Well, what were you expecting me to do? Let it have at me and then take it down all beaten and broken?" the Master asked with a grin.

Was that a joke about my fight in the cave? I thought briefly.

"Of course not, Master. It's just I've never seen anyone fight like that," I replied. "Of course you haven't," the Master began. "If you had, I wouldn't be the master at Codrean, would I be, Thoma? Although I did see you do something quite impressive yourself, did I not?" he asked, tilting his head a little.

I blushed hard, and nodded my head. The Master smiled, and turned to Irun. "Can you walk?" he asked. "I can, Master, though it feels like I've been run through by a tree trunk," Irun replied. "And you, Roburn? You seem pretty tattered and torn," the Master continued. "I can still walk, though this gash in my forehead will leave a handsome scar," Roburn replied, gesturing at the wound he was searing shut with mana.

"Very well, then. Irun, Roburn. Get yourselves on horses and ride back to the fortress with the other wounded," The Master said. The pair nodded, and walked past him, whistling for their horses. Irun mounted with a little bit of my help and was off with Roburn following close behind.

"He's a strong boy. Well, stronger than he *looks*, anyway," Anwill said, gesturing towards me. "He is strong, indeed," the Master returned. "A little odd, no doubt, but definitely a strong boy," he said as he watched Irun and Roburn ride off. The Master turned to face the two of us again.

I could hardly contain my embarrassment, but tried my best anyway.

"As I've said before, you've all done well. You and the others worked as a team without having pulled an *every man for himself* situation. Well, at least until you pulled that little aerial stunt of yours," he said lightly. "I didn't feel like I had a choice, Master," I said, defending myself.

"Choice or not, that was extremely dangerous, Thoma. You could have been turned into little more than a bloodied chunk, if you had missed. Still, it got the job done, and I must congratulate you for your courage, *and* for effectively using the second stage of mana in mid-combat," he continued.

"Thank you, Master, but that was not the first time I've managed to use it," I replied sheepishly. "*Oh?* When was the first?" The Master asked, genuine curiosity reigned over his, Anwill's, and my brother's faces. "During my fight with the pair of ochelons, Master," I began. "Like this battle, I felt I was out of options and somehow... *unlocked* it? I'm not sure how else to describe it," I explained, unsure of my own words.

The Master looked at Anwill with the same look he gave my brother whenever they seemed to communicate wordlessly. The elf gave him a nod and took a step forward. "That's because the second stage is normally unlocked through extenuating circumstances, but it *can also* be controlled through one's intent," Anwill explained.

I looked at him, even more confused than before. "If you ever find yourself in Caegwen, I would love to teach you more about the various stages, young one, or at least point you in the right direction until *someone else* decides to take over," Anwill said cheerfully.

He knows how to unlock the other stages? Is that how Bernar knows him? Who is this someone else *he's talking about?* I felt the thoughts rush through my mind, but quickly realized I was still mid conversation.

"I would love to receive your instruction, Anwill," I said with a bow. "That's *Master* Anwill to you, shit-bird," Bernar retorted.

"Wait, what the fu...?" I began, more confused than ever.

"*Oh*, Bernar, he's your brother!" Anwill cut me off. "He can address me as he pleases. Besides, he already has one *master*, so he doesn't need to address me so formally. In addition, I am no longer the master of Caegwen's Sionaer Synners. I gave that up just after you left, mind you," he said playfully. "Neither of those two reasons make much sense to me, but as you wish, Anwill," Bernar said, spreading his arms.

The Master observed Garett and his archers removing life from the bodies of the remaining creatures. He saw all was going well with them, and turned to Anwill. "That finishing blow you did," he began. "What about it, Master?" Anwill asked. "I assume they didn't teach you that at Sionaer," the Master said. "They did not, Master," Anwill replied. "That I learned from a young Synner a few centuries ago," he continued.

The Master raised an eyebrow.

"A *young Synner*? You must remember his or her name, at least," he said. "He never told me his name, I don't think. Only that I was to call him *Pelantyr*, Master," Anwill said pensively.

The Master's eyes flared.

"*Pelantyr*? You're certain of this?" he asked. "Yes, Master. I thought it was an odd name to call someone, as well, given its history" Anwill replied. "He was a young boy, possibly no older than seventeen at the time. He appeared to be well trained, and carried himself well," he continued.

The Master was taken aback, but tried to hide it as best he could, while I was listening intently.

There's something Anwill knows that the Master doesn't? I wonder why the name Pelantyr *had such an effect on him. He showed no sign of anything the time I asked him about it,* I thought.

"You must tell me more once we reach the fortress, Anwill," the Master said. "Certainly," Anwill replied. "We have much yet to discuss," he continued. Bernar was making his way over to our small group on his horse, bringing Celer along with his own horse.

"That was one hell of a flashy kill, shitstain," Bernar said, dismounting his horse, handing me the reins to my own. "So was yours, but I had help," I said, gesturing to Edryd. "All I really did was blind him," Edryd replied. "Thoma did all the dicing and slicing, not to mention the damage Roburn and Irun inflicted," he continued. "Well, you helped nevertheless," Bernar said with a smile. Edryd grinned. "It was the least I could do," Edryd said.

"Master," Bernar began. "The monsters have been slain, and we'd best be off to the fortress," he continued. The Master nodded, and signaled for everyone to retreat to the fortress. Edryd whistled for his horse, hoping it hadn't met some horrible fate.

Luckily for him, it hadn't, as it promptly showed up.

However, some of the other Synners or their horses had fallen in battle, and as a result, most had to walk home after having given their horses to aid the wounded. The sun was already setting as we began our short trip back to the fortress.

"Anwill," the Master began. "You would like me to continue

telling you about the young Synner, wouldn't you?" the elf asked. "If it's not too much trouble," the Master replied. "It is not, for that is yet another reason why I've come all this way to Codrean. A reason I did not wish to disclose with the others present," Anwill said. "You will have my undivided attention," the Master said.

I later heard from Bernar that they spoke through the night until the early hours of the morning, going through a few bottles of ale, as well as a few kettles of tea.

I lay awake in bed, going over the information presented throughout the day. There was almost too much to process, and I decided that while sacrificing sleep was never a good thing, it *was* necessary after everything.

This isn't going to end well, is it? I thought as my mind began to race.

CHAPTER 13

Of Kings and Outcasts

The Harutian army marched toward the Rhydian Pass, on their way to begin their war with Coltend. The raven they received from their king was enough to set them on the warpath. Their dedication to him was absolute, and knowing that their king was potentially in danger only fed their anger and hatred into even further depths. It drove them over the harsh terrain of Harut, and with every step, they knew that their fates were drawing nearer.

The commander of Bashir's guard, General Ari Vest, rode at the vanguard of the three-thousand-strong army, gazing out upon the landscape in search of potential threats. His armor, decorated with a bright, yellow sash, not only stated his position, but also the degree of his accomplishments in service to the king.

These vast, barren wastelands of sand and small shrubberies make up more than half of the Harutian landscape, and though we have learned to survive in such harsh conditions over the generations, it always poses a very real threat, he thought.

The dust clouds formed by the thousands of hooves and soldiers' feet further validated his thoughts. "General Vest,"

Colonel Khaleed Messir, Ari's second in command, said, trotting up beside him.

Ari turned his head to look at the man. He, too, was clad in the same light armor with a red sash, riding a large brown stallion. "How much do we know about our king's predicament?" the man asked. "Unfortunately, not much, Khaleed," Ari replied. "All the information about his current status is that which he wrote in his message," he continued. Khaleed grimaced. "For all we know, he could be dead by now. Pray to the gods that he isn't," Ari said grimly.

"I do not believe him to be dead," Khaleed began. "He might have made it to the town at the foot of the mountain pass. I've brought his armor just in case we meet him there," he gestured to the tightly packed satchel on the side of his horse. "I pray that you are correct in your beliefs, Khaleed," Ari said.

"If the worst-case scenario is to be our new reality, what shall we do?" Khaleed asked his captain. "We have only our duty that needs to be done: Honor our king and his fallen son as best we can," Ari replied. "That will be no small task. It might very well mean our deaths," Khaleed said gravely. "True," Ari began. "However, the fact remains that our duty calls us to do what we have sworn so many years ago. We must fight with honor and courage, and bring down the ones responsible in any way we can," he said. Khaleed nodded his agreement, and held a distant stare, digesting his commander's words.

They continued riding for the remainder of the day, reaching the town at the base of the pass by nightfall. The moonlit town was as quiet as a graveyard. Everyone was fast asleep by the time they arrived, readying themselves for the following day's work. Ari, Khaleed, and twenty others rode into the small town, while most of the army set up camp on the outskirts. Ari looked about him for the stables, and hoped that there would be at least one person awake to tend to his and the others' horses.

He rode up to the quiet, dimly lit stables, and a horse was frightfully awoken from its sleep by the sound of his horse's hooves. He quickly dismounted his horse, and ran over to calm the horse. He brought his hand up to its nape, patting it, to which the horse responded by lowering its head into Ari's chest. "There, there, my beauty," he said softly, holding its head.

"You are a fine horse, indeed, but you are not a horse of Coltend nor Caegwen," he said. He opened the stall door, and checked its hind leg to find the Harutian's brand scarred on its skin. "You're one of ours," he said softly, squatting to get a closer look. "Khaleed, come here, quickly!" he said as loud as current conditions would allow him.

Khaleed dismounted his horse, and walked over to his captain. "What is it, sir?" he asked. "Look," Ari said, gesturing towards the brand. "It's one of ours," Khaleed said, surprised. "It is. My guess is that our king managed to escape, and is somewhere here in this town," Ari concluded. "We must find him immediately," he urged.

He rose from his squatting position, and looked for the stable-hand. He found him a few moments later, fast asleep in a bale of hay. "Boy, wake up," he said quietly, shaking the boy. The boy jumped at being woken up in such a manner. "Who are you?" he asked, rubbing his eyes. "I am General Ari Vast of King Bashir of Harut's personal guard," Ari replied. "Bashir," the boy said quietly, recognizing the name had overheard in a conversation with his master.

"Yes, that's his name. Do you know where he is?" Ari asked. "He's here, sir?" the boy asked. "He must be. Otherwise, there wouldn't be a horse with the brand of the Palace Guard on its hind leg," Ari said, pointing to the horse he had just examined. The boy rose up, and walked over to examine the horse himself.

"The one who rode him wore a sash that covered his face and didn't give me a name, sir, but I have heard it before," the boy said, recollecting his thoughts about what had happened a few days ago. "Where did he go?" Ari asked the boy. "He said that he wanted to speak with the owner of the stables, so I led him to my master, sir," the boy replied. "Can you take me there?" Ari asked with an air of urgency. "My master will be sleeping, and he doesn't appreciate being woken in the middle of the evening," the boy replied. "Well, he might not like it, but he's going to have to answer me, regardless," Ari said. "Very well, sir, but don't say I didn't warn you," the stable-hand said begrudgingly.

He led Ari and Khaleed down the same roads he had taken Bashir just a few days before, and came to the same wooden door. "Thank you," Ari said, handing the boy a few coins for his troubles. The boy nodded with a smile, and went back to the stables to tend to the new batch of horses.

Ari knocked on the door, but there was no response. He tried again, and still, no response. "Shit," he said quietly. "Perhaps a stone to the window might help," Khaleed said maliciously, picking up a small stone from the ground. "I'm not here to destroy anyone's property," Ari said, disappointed in Khaleed. "I'm just saying we could... It's an option," Khaleed retorted with a shrug. "Fine, but pick a smaller one, at least. That one could take out a wild boar," Ari caved. "Probably wouldn't do shit to your mother, though," Khaleed said playfully.

You cheeky bastard, Ari thought.

Khaleed took a few steps back to get a better angle on his target window. He threw the stone, and it ricocheted off the window, falling back into his hands. Still, there was no response. He threw it again, with the same lack of response. "We're getting nowhere with this. Let me try," Ari said, picking up a rock a little larger than his Khaleed's. Just as the stone left his hand at a reasonable velocity, the shutters opened, and the stone hit the figure that replaced them. A grunt of pain resounded from the shadows in the window. "I think you hit him," Khaleed said. "Like I knew the shutters would open at that exact moment," Ari said with a shrug.

"Who's the belligerent *fuck* who keeps throwing rocks at my window and disturbing my sleep?" a voice said from the shadows of the moonlight. "General Ari Vest of Bashir's personal guard," Ari replied. "Ari?" the voice asked excitedly. "My lord? Is that you?" Ari asked with equal excitement. "By the gods, it *is* Ari! Haha! I will be right with you," Bashir's figure vanished, and the shutters closed as quickly as they opened.

A few moments later, the wooden door opened, showing a bloodied figure lit by torchlight. "King Bashir, I humbly apologize for striking you with a stone," Ari said with a low bow, realizing it had hit him square in the nose. "That was one way to wake one up without strong tea, for sure. Nevertheless, I have never been so happy to see a familiar face," Bashir said, rubbing the small amount of blood still dripping from the base of his curved nose. "Forgive me, my king," Ari said humbly.

"It's quite alright," Bashir replied. "Better a stone to the nose than a sword to the back like those bastards up on the Pass," he said, patting Ari on the shoulder. "It's good to see you, my friend," he said with a smile. He proceeded to give Ari a hug, and Ari returned it. "I thought we might have arrived too late," Ari said with a worried smile. "I'm a hard man to kill, apparently," Bashir said, returning the smile.

"My lord, if I may ask you what happened that would cause you to flee in such a manner," Ari began. "Well, as you know from my message, my son was brutally murdered by King Truls of Coltend," Bashir said sadly. "I witnessed the murder, as he cut my son's throat in front of my eyes. I managed to escape the king's wrath by stealing one of my men's horses, and riding alone over the Rhydian Pass. I was chased down by some of the king's men, whom I managed to escape by the skin of my teeth. My horse, Hatal, valiantly carried me to safety here in this town. I soon met the stableboy who led me here, where I was met by the owner of the stables. He graciously allowed me to stay in his room," Bashir explained.

"I mourn the loss of Prince Bashaa, my lord. He was always good to us, and carried himself well amongst the soldiers," Ari said solemnly. "You have had quite the adventure, my lord. How is your physical state?" he asked. "Aside from the recent encounter with Mother Earth's emissary, I am well. It truly was a harrowing adventure, one that I do not wish to repeat anytime soon," Bashir said. "We have brought your armor, my lord," Khaleed said, pointing to the stables where his horse was. "You have? Well that is good indeed," Bashir replied.

"What became of the men who chased you, my lord?" Ari asked. "I imagine they were stopped by the elven rebels who reside there," Bashir replied. "Ah, I see those pointy-eared bastards are good for something after all," Ari said with a sigh of relief. "Well, tomorrow we shall see what became of them, my lord," he continued.

"Yes, you have ridden hard and far, you must get some rest for tomorrow," Bashir said, patting his General's shoulder once more. "I will wake the owner of the stables, and tell him you have come to my aid. He will allow you to stay there as long as you need," he continued.

"Thank you, my lord," Ari replied. Akmed was woken up by Bashir, who explained the situation. Akmed agreed to having them stay in the stables, and told them so personally. The rest of the army, on the other hand, made camps just outside the town, huddling up next to their horses in hopes of gaining some warmth from them on that cold night.

Meanwhile in Hjalfar, Anders, Unni and the others had ridden for nearly two days with little food, and even less rest. When they were a few kilometers from their destination, they dismounted and gathered the gear they required for their mission.

"Take only what you'll need, as this should be quick," Anders stated. They tied the horses to nearby trees, leaving a few guards to make sure they were safe. They moved through the trees, making sure to move from cover to cover. They did their best to avoid being seen or heard by anyone save the moon, stars, and other creatures who ruled the night.

They arrived at Odensby with a few hours to spare before dawn, and details of the world around them could begin to be seen. The massive castle stood proudly at the edge of a short cliff within the city's walls, making a forced entry much more difficult with its limited avenues of approach. "This is it," Unni said to Anders who stood next to her. They were hidden in the tree line that surrounded the walls of the city.

"Archers, listen up," Anders said quietly. "Take out the guards who stand watch on the Eastern wall. You five over there," Anders pointed to a group of swordsmen, clad in furs and swords. "You will follow me up the wall to ensure the alarm doesn't get rung. We're going to take out anyone who stands in our way, understand?" he asked. "Yes, sir," the men replied in unison.

Unni watched as Anders gave the commands and smiled proudly.

Generally speaking, the outcasts and bandits don't need a leader in their day to day lives, but when it comes to a fight, they will always choose the one with the most battle experience to be the leader. Tonight is Anders' turn, she thought.

"Unni, you and your team will follow us and go North along the wall while we continue to clear the ramparts. Only climb up once the *all clear* signal is given. The rest of you will follow behind them, got it?" he asked again. "Yes, sir," Unni replied in unison with the others. "Let's do this," Anders said.

The archers strung their bows and nocked the first arrows to them. Anders looked about him to make sure everyone was ready, and under the light of the moon, he gave the signal to attack. The archers crept quietly through the tall grass that lay between them and the high walls. They hid behind trees, finding the best angles for their respective targets. There were only a few guardsmen on the ramparts, so their kills would be quick and quiet.

The archers' eyes went dark, as they *began to draw in unison from the Ethereal, each one pulling just enough mana that would be used to infuse their arrows.* They condensed the mana to their bowstrings and arrows with a Stil spell. They each picked their target according to their positions, drawing their bowstrings all the way to their cheeks.

They let their arrows fly, and the spells did their work of completely silencing their bowstrings *hum*, and arrows' flights. They struck their targets as one, and each man fell with an arrow in their necks, choking on their own blood and removing their abilities to call for help.

"Move in!" Anders said quietly to the men around him. They ran through the trees, and over the tall, grassy field, and strung their grappling hooks. They, too, used the Stil spell to silence their hooks' landing on the stone walls. They shot them up quickly, and made sure that the anchors were secured. "Climb!" Anders commanded quietly.

Using the ropes that hung from the hooks to scale the walls, Unni and her troupe followed close behind, remaining at the base of the wall. Anders and his men crept over the wall, heading straight for the guardhouse. They drew their daggers, and approached silently.

Time to silence these bastards, Anders thought.

He nodded to the men around him, and each one quickly silenced their targets with a swift blade to the throat. Anders signaled to remove the bell to keep it from being rung at a later time. He ran over to the side of the wall, and signaled for Unni and her troupe to scale the walls.

They reached Anders without making a sound, while the others were still scaling the walls. "How far North do you want us to go?" Unni asked quietly. "We will continue to clear out the western side of the walls. Take your team and head along the walls until you reach the rooftops closest to Mads' tower. Once you arrive, drop your hooks down to help us scale up to you," Anders said. "You're going to use the windows to your advantage, aren't you?" Unni asked slyly. Anders nodded.

"I will go in through the window to his quarters, and I'll gut him in his sleep. In the meantime, the others will follow Unni and clear the level below us. Keep watch for any of the other guardsmen who might get curious and silence them as needed," he said quietly. "Sounds like a plan," Unni replied. "Let's go," Anders said. They removed the hooks from their places after all had finished climbing.

Each team ran along the walls, taking care to avoid being seen by any who may lurk below. Anders and his men continued to clear out the Western ramparts, as Unni and her troupe reached their target destination with little resistance. "We can cut across the rooftops over here. Follow me," he whispered to his men, noticing Unni's signal to move in. No sooner were they off, jumping from rooftop to rooftop.

Luckily for them, the roofs were not made of thatch, but

from the main source of income for Hjalfar - granite. The nearby mines made it possible for all of the houses within the city to be made almost entirely of stone. The narrow, cobblestone streets below were bereft of any living thing aside from a few rats here and there.

This is going too smoothly. Something's off, Anders thought.

They made it to the secondary wall, which guarded the main tower of the palace. It wasn't as large as Coltend's, however, it was strong and could withstand nearly any attack from any form of siege weaponry. Anders noted upon the guards who stood watch on the inner wall.

Shit, she should have already cleared the guardsmen here, too, he thought.

Unni crept onto the rooftop above the guards, and signaled her team to take them out in unison. The poor bastards, drinking ale around an impromptu fire they had made to keep warm, never saw the blades that struck them down. Unni dropped the hooks off the side of the wall, aiding Anders and his team as they scaled them.

"We can't have any more surprises like that," he said, helping the last man behind him. "That wasn't my fault," Unni said quietly. "You're the one who spent all those years here, you should have been the one to remember that," she sneered. "This must have been built after I left," Anders retorted.

"Well, let's hope the only surprise left will be for Mads when he shits himself seeing you," Unni replied. "The question is, how the fuck do we get in there? The windows are barred shut," she continued, analyzing the situation. "Do you still have those hooks?" he asked. "Do you have shit for brains? Yes, of course I still have them," Unni said, still a little angered.

"If we can make it to the outside portion of the tower that faces the edge of the cliff, we should be able to get in just fine,"

Anders whispered to her, showing her an unguarded section of the tower. "You're saying they didn't fortify the windows over there?" Unni asked. "Never have. That's the last place any normal person would suspect an attack to come from," he said, patting her on the shoulder. She blushed, but Anders didn't notice in the shadows.

"Ladies first," he said with a barely visible smile. She nodded, and had one of the women with her infuse her bow and fire a grappling hook. It landed quietly, and they began to scale the tower, noticing which windows were the stealthiest entry points, and the positions of the guardsmen that roamed the floors.

Luckily for us, the dipshit left his window open, Anders thought.

"This is gonna be tougher than we thought with all those guards around," Unni whispered after reaching the top. "Can't turn back now. Remember, we'll go directly into Mads' room, while your team breach the floor below and clear the guards as quietly as you can," Anders returned.

"You should go to Mads alone," Unni said, turning to face her leader. "I know how much he has taken from you. Your position. Your home. Your family," she said, shaking her head. "How much do you actually know about me, Unni?" Anders inquired. "Now's not the time to discuss that," she whispered. "Right now, you must exact your revenge on everything he has done to you. You have the only right to do so," she said, putting a hand on his shoulder.

Anders let the words sink in. He looked back at her with tearing eyes barely visible under the moonlight and nodded. They silently made their descent to their respective entry points, and waited for everyone to be in position.

Three, two, one, Anders mouthed.

At the count of *one*, they pushed off the wall, and swung into the tower through the open windows, landing silently inside. Anders, who had gone directly into Mads' room, steadied himself and observed his surroundings. He noticed paintings of the old queen of Hjalfar, as well as the king's sons hung up on the walls. Furs were strewn across the floor, one of which he had landed on, and hunting trophies also hung upon the walls. The small desk in the corner - seldom used as it was uncommon for any member of the royal family to write anything in their own hand - had a few bits of parchment with indiscernible scribblings on them. The large bed that lay at the back of the room held but one, snoring - and extremely dangerous - person.

Meanwhile, Unni and three others had entered the floor just below where Mads' lay, quickly and quietly dispatching the guards that roamed the floor. "Let's go, we have more guards to kill," she said quietly, signaling to the small group. Anders crept up on the sleeping king, his blade gleaming in the light of the single candle that dimly lit the room.

My heart feels like it's about to leap out of my throat, he thought.

He took two more steps forward, but halted quickly when Mads shifted under the covers. After a moment's pause of carefully watching his target, he assumed Mads was still asleep.

I can hardly hear his breathing pattern. I need to slow my heartbeat, he thought. He took a slow, controlled breath, never taking his eyes off his target.

There are two things a person feels when they are going to kill. The first is a strong kick in the gut of adrenaline, making one's pupils enlarge and muscles twitch rapidly. The second is the realization that one is sending another's soul - be it an animal, monster, or another human - into the afterlife. The problem is that, sometimes, the second part doesn't come until long after the deed is done. That is the window where most mistakes are made, he thought, remembering his training with their old leader.

He continued to quietly creep across the room, his grip tightening around his blade that nearly hummed with hunger for its next kill. Unni, still downstairs, removed her blade from the last guardsman whose blood now made the floor slick and shiny, watching the stairs for any unwelcome guests.

She motioned for the others to cross the hall and get into position in case of an attack, as she proceeded upstairs to the front door to Mads' room. She silently opened the door, seeing the murderous, hateful look on Anders' face, and the blissful ignorance of the sleeping king.

Anders, Unni mouthed, waving her hand to catch his attention. Anders snapped out of his small trance, and recollected his thoughts. He nodded to Uni in response.

It's time to finish this, he thought as he crept up next to the frame of the bed.

Mads stirred a little under his covers, and Anders nearly became one with the bear-fur carpet beneath him. A few moments later, Anders stood at the side of the bed, and watched for a moment, observing every detail of Mads' face.

He looks just as he did all those long years ago, he thought.

He was shaking with anger and hatred.

He put his blade to Mads' throat, and covered his mouth with his free hand. Mads was startled, and tried to call for help in vain. Anders' hand muffled the cries enough to not be heard. "Shh," Anders hushed the man, his eyes downcast as if looking at an insect. "*No one is coming to save you now.* Isn't that what you told my wife and child all those years ago?" he asked, cocking his head to the side. Mads' eyes opened wide, as he recognized the one with the cold blade to his bare throat.

"*Ah*, so you *do* remember me. I can see it in your eyes, but do you remember what you did? Do you remember the things that not even the most loving of the gods could ever forgive you for? Because *I* do, and I *also* do not forgive," Anders whispered.

"You took everything from me. You murdered my wife, my child, and the one unborn. You stomped on her stomach while she lay with a knife in her throat, and our child's head in her hands on the ground in front of you. Your guards held me as I watched it all happen. You laughed as you spat in her face and pissed into her gaping mouth, calling her a *whore* as you did so. You chained me up, beat me to little more than a bloody mound of living flesh, and cut off two of the fingers of the hand that now holds a blade to your throat," Anders said, recalling the traumatic event.

Tears welled in his eyes, and ran down his cheeks into his beard. "You deserve a much more painful punishment than death, but unfortunately, fate has decided otherwise," he said. Mads squirmed and Anders struggled to keep his hand over his enemy's mouth. "You will not see the light of day, and you will become the plaything of the Undergod. There, you shall suffer for all eternity, and I will finally be at peace knowing that I have put you there," Anders continued.

Mads raised his hand, showing that he wanted to say something. Anders stared angrily at the vulnerable man under his blade. "One scream, one sound louder than a whisper and I'll impale you to your pillow before any words leave your mouth," Anders said in a dark tone. Mads nodded, and Anders removed his hand.

"I know an apology won't save me now," Mads said, his voice trembling and breaking. "I know what I have done, and I know that I must atone for it. I always knew that it wasn't you who had failed to guard my wife and children during their pilgrimage; but the one responsible for that failure fled after they were attacked on Hviten Path, never to be found," Mads explained.

"Y-you knew it wasn't me?" Anders asked, his whole world

falling apart with the words he was hearing. "I did," Mads replied. "Why?" Anders enraged, gripping his victim's shirt and pulling him up towards his face. "Why did you have *my* family suffer for the fault of another? Why did you have to pull the rug out from under *my* world? Why did you have to make me beg for death every day since then?" Anders asked angrily. Mads was silent. "Answer me, you slimy shit," Anders commanded.

"My councilmen told me that an example needed to be made to ensure that no other man under my command would ever betray their honor and allegiance to Hjalfar again," Mads began. "What?" Anders asked, incredulous to what he was hearing. "It's true. I chose you - the one man I knew that everyone knew I trusted above almost all others aside from my wife. I wanted it to be known that no matter one's station or status, one was never above their honor and duty," Mads said regretfully.

"So, you chose me? A man who, until that time, had never wavered in his loyalty? A man who had earned his way to his status through pure effort? A man whose life had such value to you?" Anders asked, growing increasingly enraged.

"Yes," Mads replied in a shaky voice. Anders' face was wet with tears. "You dragged me through the deepest depths of the Underworld simply to prove a point. Gods above and below. No, no, no... I don't care about your sob story. Knowing what I know now, I almost wish I had been the one to have murdered your family, you mangy fuck! I have never, and will never forgive you for what you did to me," Anders said. "I know," Mads replied, looking up at Anders.

"Do it," he said. "Take what is rightfully yours, I have no qualms or arguments remaining that could ever hope to spare me. However, before I leave this world, I must ask you one final favor," he continued. "And why should I hear anything more of what you have to say?" Anders said coldly. Mads looked deeply into his eyes, seeing nothing but the embodiment of the purest hatred.

"Because if there's one thing I've learned in all my years, it is this: the council of others is, more often than not, in benefit of their own ambitions. So, choose your allies carefully. Remember that," Mads said. "I already have," Anders replied in the same, cold tone. "Not carefully enough," Mads retorted. "What...?" Anders asked, confused by his words. Before the king could answer, a hand forced the blade into his throat. "Unni!" Anders raised his voice. "You were taking too long. We have to go." she urged, noting one of her teammates standing in the doorway.

Anders' blade sunk deep into Mads' throat, and blood flowed from the wound, drenching the pillow beneath it. He watched the life ebb from the eyes that stared at him for a moment and removed his knife, taking a deep breath. "Anders," Unni whispered from the doorway. Anders turned to face her with bloodshot eyes. Unni saw the toll it had taken on him and rushed over to him. She took him in her arms, where he sobbed for a few moments.

"It's over," she said softly. The words felt like a warm bath coming over him. He looked up into her eyes. "Thank you for everything, Unni," he said between sniffles. "I couldn't have done this without you," he said, grabbing her hand. "I know," she replied in her soft voice. "But we must go now, the other guards will be taking their shifts any minute now, and when they find the dead bodies, it will not end well for us," she said with urgency. Anders nodded, and she helped him up to his feet.

"Let's go home," she said, helping him to his feet. "Wait," he retorted, walking over to the desk and grabbing a feather and parchment. "What are you doing?" Unni asked. "Setting an example," he said, walking over to the small desk.

I, Anders Karlsson, ex-Synner of Odensby and all of her glory, have slain the king for dishonorable deeds he has done in the past against myself and other innocent people whom I held dear. Let this be an example to all of those who wish to hunt me down, for this shall be your end should you find me. Soon I will return to this place when I am ready to rule, and if a single hint of disrespect is shown to me, or any of my comrades, I will kill you myself, he wrote in shaky handwriting.

He pinned the message to Mads' unmoving chest with his knife, and proceeded out the door with Unni.

Daylight was on the horizon, and the outcasts observed the guards entering the main palace to take their shifts from the walls where their hooks were prepared for their escape. "One day, we shall return to finish the job. To rule Odensby," Anders said, looking out over the city. "One day, we shall take it all back for ourselves, and regain the lives we once had," he said, turning his head towards Unni. She smiled and grabbed the rope and began her descent. Anders took one last look over the dimly lit city.

And that day will come soon, he thought.

As he turned around, he noticed a dust cloud forming between the peaks of the Rhydian mountains.

That can't be a good omen, he thought.

He grabbed the rope, descended the wall, and went back into the comfort of the forest. They all mounted their horses, beginning the journey home to gather the others.

Daybreak arrived and Bashir awoke to the sound of a rooster just outside the window of Akmed's home. He rubbed his eyes when he got out of his bed, put on the armor that had been laid out for him the previous evening, and proceeded downstairs to meet with Ari, who was already gathering the others to prepare to march over the Rhydian Pass. "Good morning, my lord," Ari bowed.

"It is indeed," Bashir said, observing the red sun rising on the horizon. "A bloody sky in the morning bodes well for those who ride on the path to glory and honor, my lord," Ari said with a smile. "I suppose that is something you warriors say amongst yourselves, for I have never heard of such a thing," Bashir replied.

"It is, though many have forgotten it by now. It has been at least a decade since our last major fight, my lord," Ari replied. "I see. Well, that is not always a bad thing, is it? Many families have been spared the loss of loved ones, I'm sure," Bashir said, patting Ari on his shoulder. "Indeed, they have, my lord. Bring our king his horse!" Ari shouted behind him, while Bashir gazed out over the three-thousand battle-ready men under the red sky. "I had forgotten just how large an army can be," he said.

"And this was all I could muster in the one day it took, my lord," Ari said, gazing out over the mass of warriors. One of the soldiers brought Bashir's horse, with a fine, leather saddle, and a white and violet sash tied to its side. "Here you are, my lord," the soldier said, handing the reins to Bashir.

"Where is Hatal?" Bashir asked. "Hatal, my lord?" Ari asked. "The horse who carried me here," Bashir replied. "You don't want your favorite horse from your own stables, my lord?" Ari asked, confused. "No, I want the horse who is now worth at least twenty times this one," Bashir said, gesturing to the horse presented to him. "Have Hatal saddled with this horse's gear, and we'll be off," Bashir commanded. Ari clicked his tongue, and the soldier undid the saddle, and carried it over to the stables.

"Hatal is tired from his harrowing journey, my lord," Ari said gravely. "He is stronger than you think, and as I said before, he is worth much more to me than a fresh horse. He is a hero, for that is his name, or have you forgotten the value of a hero?" Bashir asked. "I have not, my lord," Ari said, bowing his head low. "See to it that you do not," Bashir said disgruntledly.

Moments later, Hatal was brought out from the stables, his new saddle fit perfectly. Bashir noticed the horse trotted happily, as if giddy with excitement.

I've always wondered whether horses felt emotions as we do. I guess that answers that question, he thought.

"He looks like one of the horses from the tales of old, my lord," Ari said, smiling as he watched the horse's trot. "He really is a fine horse indeed," Bashir replied, taking the reins from the soldier who walked him, patting Hatal's strong neck. Bashir placed his foot in the stirrup, and swung his right leg over to the other side. He adjusted his position, and looked out over the sea of men who did the same after him. "Men, we ride to Coltend! May our forefathers bear witness!" he shouted, and there was a roar in response.

Bashir stuck his heels into Hatal's sides, and led his men to the foot of the Rhydian mountains. On the way up the trail, he recalled the flight he had made, and could swear he saw a few of Hatal's large hoof prints in the dirt beneath him.

I fled for my life in fear of being hunted down and slaughtered like my son. Now I am no longer the hunted, but the hunter, he thought.

The sun was now stronger on their backs than it had been when they began their march as they reached the top of the Pass. "This sun will be our advantage, my lord," Ari began. "It will blind them, making them easy targets for our archers, avoiding the bloodshed of our own men," he continued. "Do not forget about the elven rebels, Ari," Bashir began. "They might not be as welcoming as we hope they are," he continued. "I understand, my lord," Ari said.

They reached the top of the pass, and turned the corner only to find a small camp placed in the middle of the way next to the body of an ice troll, a foul stench ruling the air. Bashir and Ari cast their eyes on the beast, and noticed the pile of stripped bodies - some of them missing limbs, while others were little more than mounds of rotting flesh. "That ice troll must have been the cause of that," Bashir said to Ari who was still observing the ice troll's dead body.

"The elves must be watching the encampment, my lord," Ari began. "It would be best not to get too close," he continued. Bashir dismounted his horse, and walked over to the troll's body. He noticed the point of an arrow sticking out of the beast's skull. He broke it off from its shaft, and wiped the rotting brain matter off of it. "It's of elvish make," he said, showing it to Ari.

Ari looked about him, hoping to see one of them. "In the name of King Bashir Ibn' Escea of Harut, come forth," Ari shouted.

A man from the camp came out from one of the small tents that were pitched on the far end of the pass. "That's him," Bashir said, pointing to Gorm who was still in full gear. "Have you returned to die like a dog to its vomit?" Gorm shouted. "Do not speak to King Bashir in that tone," Ari shouted back. Gorm turned his head to Ari who was still on his horse. "And who might you be to command me in that tone of voice? His personal, pox-ridden bitch? You don't scare me, boy," Gorm retorted angrily.

"I am Ari Vast, Commanding General of the Harutian Royal Guard, loyal servant of our great king," Ari replied. "Well, that's a fancy name and title for little more than a boot-licker," Gorm shouted back. "How dare you?" Ari shouted back. "Ari, until we have a location on the elves, do not attack, understand?"

Bashir said quietly. Ari sighed deeply. "Very well, my lord," Ari replied. "But he will pay for what he has said," he continued. "All in good time," Bashir replied.

"Gorm, was it?" Bashir asked. "That's the name I was given at birth, so yes," Gorm replied. "Gorm of *what*, might I ask?" Bashir said, trying to maintain some form of diplomacy. "Just Gorm," the man replied curtly. "Such disrespect for a king. Did your parents not educate you at all? Gods, for all I know, your name was probably written in the remains of a cocksneeze that dripped off your mother's face," Ari shouted, growing increasingly enraged at the man's disrespect for his king. Gorm furrowed his brow, and bared his teeth. "Silence, Ari! Compose yourself," Bashir snapped.

He turned to face the man once more, and began to walk towards him. "My lord!" Ari said, but Bashir simply raised his hand. Gorm, too, began to walk towards the man whom he had chased just a few short days ago. "There are elves all around us," Bashir began. "I know that," Gorm replied.

"They ambushed us just after we had arrived at the top of the Pass, and killed a few of my men. Then came that monstrosity you see lying before you, lifeless and numb to all things save decay," he said. Bashir looked down at the ice troll, admiring its crystalline armor.

"I see," Bashir said solemnly. "Where are the elves, exactly?" he asked. "Everywhere and nowhere you try to find them," Gorm said. "That's not very helpful," Bashir replied. "Their leader, Gwili, has taken it upon himself to make us his prisoners, and so we are simply here awaiting our deaths," Gorm said gravely. "Or perhaps something worse," Bashir replied. He knew what the elves were capable of, and knew exactly what happened to many unsuspecting travelers who crossed their paths.

Bashir looked up at the rock where Gwili once stood. "Perhaps up there, I shall get a better view of what lies around us," he said. "That's where he stood, so I guess it's a decent spot," Gorm said. Bashir made his way past Gorm, who uncouthly spat as he passed, and climbed the large rock. He was a little short of breath when he reached its peak, but noted upon a trail that he had never seen before. He looked carefully, trying to see if he could find any shapes or colors that did not occur naturally. His eyes caught the tip of a curved shape with a string tied tautly to it.

"Gwili," he shouted. "I know you and your men are here, so step forth and let us decide what is to be done," he continued. There was rustling amongst the small bushes that lie about, and one by one, the elves began to appear. Bashir descended from his vantage point, and made his way to the center of the pass.

"Not so well hidden after all," Gorm said with a grin. "Shut your trap," Gwili said, punching Gorm in the face. Gorm put a finger to his nose, and saw that the blow caused blood to run out of his nostrils. "*Heh*, didn't know you had it in you to beat an unarmed prisoner, you pointy-eared cuckold," Gorm said, spitting the blood that ran down the back of his throat.

"Gentlemen," Bashir said, holding his hands up in an attempt to prevent a violent breakout. "We stand here atop the pass on this magnificent morning, let us converse first before we trade blows," he said calmly. "Talk then hit? What kind of lame tactic is that?" Gwili asked.

"Politics," Bashir said with a grin. "Now, the situation from what I gather is as follows: Gorm wants my head for he wishes to regain his queen's honor, while you, Gwili, wish for their goods and armor, and I simply want to pass through to avenge my murdered son," he began. "Wow, your powers of deduction are truly superb, Lord Obvious," Gorm said with a bow in jest.

Bashir shrugged the offense off. "Now, this can go one of three ways: The first being we all kill each other until the last man, although I find it rather hard to believe that only a few men can take on the army I have behind me. The second is that my army and I pass through, while the elves deal with their prisoners in any way they see fit," he began. "And what of my honor as a knight?" Gorm said. "I care greatly about one's honor, and if you had only shut your mouth, you would hear the third way we could play this out," Bashir snapped. Gorm was silent.

"For the third and final option, I propose a duel between Gorm, and Captain Ari, seeing as how he is so willing to disembowel you," Bashir said, gesturing to Ari who breathed heavily. "Should my man win, the elves may do what they like with you and the remainder of your hunting party. Should you win, we would then strip you of your armor - giving it to the ever-so-patient elves - and take you as our temporary prisoners back to Coltend where you belong," he continued.

"And then what? You'll kill us anyway," Gorm said angrily. "I cannot believe you have already forgotten that I care greatly for one's honor," Bashir said, shaking his head.

"We would not kill you. Well, at least not immediately, anyway. You would have the chance to rearm and recover from your ordeal, gather your men and face us on the battlefield that is to be your great city," Bashir said, spreading his arms wide. "A fine way for a knight of honor to die, don't you agree?" he continued. Gwili remained silent, pleased at the fact that two out of the three options spelled success for him, while Gorm rued over the possibilities for a moment. After a small amount of thought, he finally looked back at Bashir.

"I accept the duel between myself and Captain Arsepiss," Gorm said with an evil looking grin aimed at Ari.

"Excellent! Ready yourselves, men!" Bashir raised his arms. Gwili whistled a bird call, and an elf brought Gorm's longsword, handing it to him. Gorm took it in his hand, and immediately felt comfort in it. Ari dismounted his horse and drew his large scimitar with intricate details carved into the pommel and ivory handle. He pulled the tie that held his shield, and grabbed it firmly. The two approached each other carefully.

"Let the duel begin!" Bashir commanded.

CHAPTER 14

Dissonance

On the night of the raid in Odensby, a raven landed in the tallest tower of the citadel in Valdis, landing on the perch designated for it. It waited a short while, squawking loudly to make its presence known to the one who would receive the message. The Masked One, who had already been waiting in the aviary, approached the raven calmly, retrieving the contents from the pouch on its back.

Everything is going according to plan, my lord. The apostate has also notified me that he has gathered what information he could. We will commence our attack soon, and prepare for your arrival, the message read.

The Masked One grinned, folding the letter once more. "You've traveled far, and have brought me great news, dark one. Here, a gift for your troubles," he said, conjuring a small treat which the raven graciously took from the palm of his hand. "Karak," he called out as he departed the aviary. The daemon crept crookedly up behind him, drooling all over the floor as it went. "My lord?" Karak asked in his raspy voice.

"Our newfound friends over in Hjalfar have done what I have commanded, I presume," the Masked One said, already expecting a positive answer. "According to my informants, they have already begun their assault on King Mads' fortress, my lord," Karak answered with a snort. "Then it is high time we made our move on Coltend, as that *man* has also informed me that their preparations are complete. We must move swiftly if we are to catch them off-guard before the news of Mads' death reaches them," the Masked One said.

"Even with their preparations completed, it will be quite a challenge to fully break Coltend's defenses, my lord. Their walls are thick, their steel strong, and their guards are well-trained. Can *he* really accomplish what you've asked of him?" Karak asked, genuinely concerned. His master did not turn to face him.

"I don't believe that Coltend will give itself up so easily, no. They will likely lose many people during their portion of the fight, but I will break any and all who remain," the Masked One replied. "With the horde we have created, it should not be too difficult to accomplish our portion of the task. I do, however, share your concerns for that *man*. After all, he has only aligned himself out of *fear*, as one should in the face of overwhelming power," he continued.

Karak chuckled maliciously. "Did you not give him a small portion of your power, my lord?" the daemon asked. "I did, though how well he uses it is entirely up to him. In any case, it is often good to make even the crudest tools feel useful. Even if he does fail, it will not hinder us too greatly," the Masked One said confidently.

"The crystals to control the horde are also complete, and the strength we hold in numbers alone will be able to overwhelm the capital entirely," the Masked one said proudly, walking into the nesting grounds.

He walked towards one of the massive doors that lined the

backside of the birthing chambers, and opened it. Countless cages, not unlike the ones in the spiral staircase, held their respective, restless creatures. He let off a burst of mana throughout the room to calm them down, establishing his dominance.

"Your servants have grown strong and are ready to serve your purpose, my lord," Karak said, recalling how many birthing chambers he had seen over the course of his time in Valdis. "Indeed, but this burst of mana won't last long, which is why I have brought you here," the Masked One replied. "You would have me assist you, my lord? I am truly honored," Karak said, placing one hand on his deformed chest, bowing low.

"While my powers alone would suffice, it would be greatly inefficient of me to do this alone. We can cover a much larger number in an infinitely shorter time if we work together. Thus, I need you to assist me in the embedding process, by taming them with a bit of mana, while I insert the crystals. This way, I can focus on proper placement to avoid killing them or hindering their performance," the Masked One explained.

"Ah," Karak said, finally understanding. "When do we start, my lord?" he asked with a grin. "In truth, we should have already begun. While most of them have already been completed, we just need to focus on the fire and ice golems that have already reached their maturation points. The outcasts started their attack on Odensby a little earlier than I expected, but it is of little consequence to me now," his master replied.

They began their work with a group of ten ice golems first due to their core's ease of access. The Masked One held multiple black crystals in tendrils of mana, suspending them over the golems in their cages. "Subjugate them," The Masked One commanded.

Karak's eyes glowed with an intense, violet hue, as his mana began to seep into the golems' cores. The creatures resisted the mana at first, but quickly succumbed to the sheer intensity of Karak's strength. The Masked One, fully focused on his own task, gently fused the crystals with their cores, and watched as their bodies now glowed with his mana.

"It worked! You truly are brilliant, my lord," Karak said with excitement. "Of course it did, but we still have forty ice golems and fifty fire golems more to do, so we had better keep up the pace," the Masked One said, immediately moving on to the next few. The two went from chamber to chamber, infusing and integrating the crystals to the golems' cores. One by one, they became tame and obedient, responding to any and all commands given them.

A few hours of work later, even the Masked One was a little drained from having drawn so much mana from the Underworld. He took a swig of the solution he had once given to his apprentice, and immediately felt stronger. "That makes a hundred of them, my lord," Karak said out of breath after taming the final group. He, too, was severely drained.

"Drink," the Masked One said, handing him a vial of the solution. Karak drank the remainder of the contents, accidentally spilling some out of the corners of his wide mouth. He wiped the spilled liquid off with his forearm, and handed the vial back to his master.

"Ah, the taste of death itself. I *love* it," Karak said, licking the remaining fluid off his forearm. The Masked One retrieved the vial, placing it into his cloak.

How long did that take? Four, maybe five hours? Dawn must be approaching soon, he thought.

"We must prepare to leave," the Masked One said urgently. "Take a crystal to aid you and gather the ones from the cages downstairs," he commanded. "Even the addia, my lord?" Karak asked. "Yes," his master said sternly.

I hate dealing with that overgrown ball of slime, the daemon thought.

"Very well, my lord," Karak said. He knew just how dangerous they were, and took a crystal with him as he went downstairs to the large cages. He released them one by one, hoping it would be able to control all of them at once. He noticed that even the largest of ochelons succumbed to his will, and he was pleased that it had worked as his master said it would.

Finally, he walked over to the addia's cage. "I know you're in there, so come on out," he said. He looked down at the crystal, still emitting the dark glow. He pointed it at the cage, breaking the addia's camouflage just enough for it to become visible.

Its dark, brown skin dimly reflected the light of the chamber, and its glowing eyes were fixated on the crystal. Karak unlocked the cage, and stepped back. The addia followed him as he walked back, as did the other beasts he had already unleashed.

Even though I am a powerful daemon, I must still be weary of these creatures. They are not to be underestimated, Karak thought, keeping his eyes fixed on the addia, as it could still very well be unpredictable.

The two, long tentacles that protruded out of the sides of its face were draped atop its long body. Its legs were muscular and shiny like the rest of it. Its paws with their retractable claws made it a truly terrifying beast to gaze upon. "You will follow me. All of you," Karak said in a commanding voice. The large creatures about him grunted and snorted in response, following the daemon outside to his master.

Meanwhile, Athar was outside preparing The Masked One's mount. An elder griffin, whose black feathers and beak shuddered the dimming moonlight, was led by the reins to the massive courtyard just outside the main tower. The Masked One approached him, with a few pairs of ochelons dragging massive crystals behind them to assist with the mass-broadcasting of the spell. "Your mount is ready, my lord," the young man said, handing the reins to his master. "A fine creature, is it not?" The Masked One asked.

"It really is, my lord. Although, I will admit I was a little hesitant to prepare it when I received your orders," the young man replied. "They're not as fickle as an addia, but they can surely be just as devastating when enraged," his master said, stroking its massive feathers. "My lord, am I going with you to Coltend?" Athar asked. "No. You must remain here and assist Karak in ensuring that no careless adventurer enters, as well as continue your studies," the Masked One commanded. "Very well, my lord. I will do as you wish," Athar bowed, returning to the citadel.

The Masked One pulled on the reins, bringing the griffin to flight. As he looked over the massive horde, he prepared to give his commands. "We will go through the mountains to the Rhydian Pass to Coltend Castle. You will not falter, you will not yield, and you will not surrender until our task is complete!" the Masked One said, his voice emanating mana.

The crystals inside the creatures' cores began to glow, dimming Karak's crystal. The creatures he led now turned to follow the ones behind the towering ochelons, rallying toward them.

"To war!" the Masked One shouted. There was a large mixture of roars and screeches in response. Athar looked about him at the army of trolls and ochelons, wondering whether they would be successful even with such a force. He watched them go off into the distant south, and when he could no longer see them, he entered the citadel, closing the doors behind him.

Meanwhile in Coltend, Leona lay fast asleep, and was suddenly woken by the sound of screams and swords clashing.

She quickly put on a thick robe, and tied its strings around her thin waist. Screams and cries for help could be heard coming from beyond her door. She unbolted her door, and opened it, the cries growing louder and louder as she proceeded down the cold stone steps. She cautiously gazed out from around the corner of the stairway that led to the throne room, and gasped at what she saw.

Bloodied bodies glistened in the torchlight of the vast hall before her. She did all she could to not unleash a projectile stream of bile at the mere sight of them.

What the hell happened here? There are bodies everywhere. Are we under attack? she asked herself.

She took another look at the large hall, and found hooded figures, clad in black robes running about, chasing the servants down the other hallways and out the doors. Their screams pierced her ears, and she felt a wave of fear for her own life come over her.

Suddenly, out of the left side of the large hall, a small girl burst into the hall at a full run, and came in Leona's direction. *Meliss!* she thought. Meliss ran as fast as she could, dodging a hooded figure or two along the way. When she was about to enter the stairway that led to the royal bedroom, Leona stepped out and grabbed her, pulling her close.

"Leo-!" Meliss began to say but was cut short by the hand muffling her mouth. "Shh, It's alright. I've got you," Leona said comfortingly as she could. She tried to hide her own fear, and be strong for both their sakes. "Thank the gods you're alive! What happened here?" she asked, hoping for an answer that she did not already suspect. Meliss caught her breath, but still shook with fear.

"I-I was finishing up some of the dishes in the kitchen when I heard a *clunking* sound coming from the hallway. When I approached the door to see what was happening, all I could see were the hooded people stabbing one of the guardsmen repeatedly," Meliss began in a hushed voice, her voice trembling as she spoke.

"By the Graces, who would do such a thing?" Leona asked.

"I... I don't know. They seem to have come out of nowhere. O-o-or maybe they were already inside the palace? I-I don't know. The only thing I *do* know is that they wanted to kill me, too. I ran as quickly as I could away from them, but no matter where I went, there were always more of them," Meliss explained, tears streaming down her cheeks.

Shit, that means that whoever's responsible for this attack must have known the guardsmen's locations and shift patterns. Fuck, fuck, fuck, fuck! Leona thought.

The hooded figures in the main hall were landing finishing blows on their prey, coating the ground in a sheen of blood. They finished off the last servant in their group, and began to search around for more targets. They caught a glimpse of Leona trying to hide from them, and began to walk towards the two women.

Here they come, she thought, putting herself in front of Meliss.

"I'll handle this," she said quietly, pushing the young girl to the side. Meliss was crying, and clutching Leona's robes tightly. The figures gathered and continued walking towards the pair, whispering amongst themselves words that couldn't be deciphered by either of the women.

Leona, taking the initiative, stepped out from her hiding spot. "I will not ask you who you are, for it is obvious you do not wish to be known, and asking you would simply be useless," she said loudly.

I can still hear people screaming in the distance. This will not end soon, will it? she thought.

"You must have come from within the walls, as any attempt from the outside would have already been thwarted. So as your Queen, I *demand* you tell me why you are doing this," Leona said sternly.

The figures stopped. Leona observed them, as though she had touched a nerve.. The hooded figures continued to approach her, and began to form a line, trapping the two. "Why do you slay innocent people who have been nothing but loyal to Coltend and its people?" she asked, growing increasingly enraged.

"You cowardly, spineless, maidenless *fucking cunts*! Answer my questions or I will have your balls *dragged* through miles of broken glass, just for me to cut them off and feed them to your mothers!" she shouted angrily. Meliss looked out from underneath Leona's arm, and saw the hooded figures continue to approach the two of them, unphased by her words.

Out of the back of the large hall, came a hunched, hooded figure. It moved slowly, like an old man just getting out of bed on a cold morning. It stopped when it had reached a point where the other figures stood midway between it and the queen.

"Oh, Leona. Empty threats in the face of death make you look weak. It is unbecoming of you," the decrepit figure said from under his large hood. "You ask us why we do this, and yet fail to see the obvious," the figure continued, grinning maliciously. "Enlighten me, then," Leona said.

"You see, there comes a time when all things must come to an end. You, me, the others around us here, citizens, civilizations, and lifestyles. They all end. Your time of reign, short as it may have been, has run its course, for a new power will rise in your stead," the voice said.

"If my kingdom and I are to be usurped in such a manner, I would at least like to know who *you* are. I care not about the rest," Leona said. The hunched figure drew back his hood to show a bald, gray-bearded, wrinkled man with gray eyes.

"Why, if it isn't Father *fucking* Mourtis, the sack-less, un-palatable bastard himself. Progenitor of the Church of Mideia, and *lover* of little boys," Leona said, coming to terms with who was behind the betrayal. "Yes, it is I," Mourtis replied, the malicious grin persisting on his face. "How could you do this? The Church and your faith should not allow you to take the lives of these innocent people," Leona said angrily.

"*Innocent? Faith?* What the *fuck* could you possibly know about either of those two things?" Mourtis asked angrily. "You who so readily lay with another man other than your husband, betrayed your loyalty to him and the others around you? Don't make me laugh. Your lack of consideration also happened to get Prince Bashaa killed, or have you already forgotten that?" he spat.

Leona's blood rushed from her face. "How *dare* you..." she said, furrowing her brow. "If you truly believed in the goodness of others and followed your faith, then you would have not committed such a heinous act. Not only did you betray your beliefs, but you also betrayed your country," he continued.

I'm going to make him wish he never said that. Fucking hypocrite, she thought.

"No, Leona, you know nothing of faith *nor* innocence. You also do not understand what is coming for the Continent, but I suppose ignorance is truly bliss," Mourtis said, shaking his head. "The faith you hold *so* dear is but a plague to this world; One molded into the perfect mechanism of mass population control through ignorance and fear. Do you also believe that if you come to the sermons, pay your tithes, and pray every night before you sleep that Mideia will save you from perdition? Well, I have news for you: perdition *is* coming, but Mideia is not its herald. No one has yet seen the *true* power that will shape the world, and its arrival will be magnificent. It is something I was loath to accept at first, but since having seen the truth, I know it is what is best for this wretched world," Mourtis said, spreading his arms widely.

"You don't believe that. You say that I do not know about faith, and yet, you cast yours aside so easily to believe that whatever is coming will benefit the world. I think that if that power is capable of such slaughter, then it will *not* benefit the world, but destroy it," Leona retorted.

"How could I not believe that the coming age will benefit the Continent? Mideia has done little with his own power, mighty as he may be, to better this land." Mourtis stated. "If he really cared, and was as almighty as we mortals have made him out to be, then how could he allow such terrible things to happen? How could so much be wrong with the world, and still have people who follow him in earnest?" he asked.

"Maybe because faith is all some people have. Maybe you cannot appreciate the good without the bad. Maybe, just maybe, it's what gives people hope," Leona replied.

Mourtis shook his head. "Over the years, I've found that faith is not what it once was," Mourtis began. "It is no longer a matter of believing in a supernatural force that controls all things. The faith in the Church of Mideia that currently exists is not real. It is bought and it is paid for through false piety, money, and power. Lots of it, to be exact, and with the coming of the new age, the *true* power will come and wipe away all sin. The culmination of the evils spawned from within this castle will be its own ruin." he said with a wicked grin.

"You have become a pawn. A fraud. One who has lived a bountiful life of debauchery and drunkenness, but alas, the royalty that once ruled Coltend has finally met its doom," Mourtis said threateningly.

"So that's it, then?" Leona asked. "You - the leader of the Church - are admitting to taking people's money and giving them false hope in something you yourself do not even believe in?" she asked. "People are more gullible than they look," Mourtis began.

"A *special artifact* here or there, and they lose their minds over it. Believing that they will be blessed if they manage to touch it, and trust me when I say that they will do and pay *anything* to do so. The poor, the middle class, the rich - anyone is fair game. Which essentially means that we - the Church - control everything. From what children learn in schools, to the outbreaks of wars - all of these things are controlled by what we convince people to believe. This is wrong, that is right. You cannot do this, or else you will burn in the eternal flames. Heh, I've always loved how people fear the unknown," Mourtis explained.

Does his corruption and hypocrisy know no bounds? He's an absolute lunatic! He's going to help destroy an entire country or more because of his delusions, Leona thought.

"But fret not, Leona. The Masked One has commanded that we eradicate all who could potentially stand against him. This removes you entirely from power as well as the ones who may try to revolt, while your ends will be swift," Mourtis explained. "The Masked One? I've always thought it to be a child's fantasy story," Leona said. "He is anything but just a story. He is very much a real figure, one who possesses great power and influence over all things, and I do his bidding willingly. Killing innocents is but a trivial matter," he shrugged.

Leona's tears began to well in her eyes. "You're evil incarnate," she spat. "Evil is but a point of view," Mourtis began. "What you may believe to be evil, I believe it to be for the betterment of humanity. What I may deem evil, you may deem worthy of praise. We all have our perspectives on life, but that doesn't mean that all perspectives can thrive at one time, nor that all perspectives are entirely correct, either. In the end, the beliefs and perspectives with the most power win, and so far, it seems as though we've already won," he said with his arms spread. "I don't think you've won just yet. You're just a hypocrite who's dug himself into a hole he can't climb out of," Leona said angrily.

She turned around and grabbed Meliss, who had been silent the whole time, and sprinted up the stairs. "After them!" Mourtis ordered. The three of the hooded figures chased after them. Leona's and Meliss' hearts were beating louder and harder than a battle drum.

"In here," Leona said, pulling the girl with her as she entered the royal chambers. She slammed the wooden door behind her just as soon as one of the figures had put its hand there to try and hold it open. She heard bone being crushed, and bolted the door. The screams of pain resonated from the door into the large room.

Leona let go of Meliss, and went to her easel. She grabbed a paintbrush, and stuck it into a tiny hole just behind the curtains of her window. "What's that for?" Meliss asked. "Shh," Leona put a finger to her lips. She pushed on the stone wall, and it began to move inward. Meliss' eyes opened. "Never would've known that was there," Meliss said, observing the walls fold in on themselves. "Only the king and queen know of this passage. Now follow me," Leona said, extending her hand.

Meliss took it, and Leona pushed the stone door back in place. They were off, down the unlit, narrow passageway. They moved as quickly as they could in the pitch black of the passage, and they used more of their sense of touch than their eyesight to find their way. A few moments later, they came to a solid wall.

"This is it," Leona said quietly. "Once we leave here, we

must find Thorsen, do you remember him?" she asked. Meliss nodded in the dark, and then realized it was pointless. "Got it," Meliss said quietly. Leona patted her shoulder, and pushed against the solid wall.

The stones moved, and the moonlight shone through the cracks it created. They arrived just outside the palace, where other hooded figures could be seen, scouring the streets for anyone they deemed unworthy of their revolt. Alarm bells could be heard in the distance, and a cacophony of screams and pleas for help ruled the night.

"Quickly now," Leona said, pulling Meliss along behind her. They hid behind a small shack on a nearly empty street, and waited for one of the hooded figures to pass. They held their breath as he walked past them, only a meter's width away without noticing their presence. He continued down the street, and in the moonlight, Leona saw that their course was clear.

"To Thorsen's house," she said. She led Meliss down the narrow streets from house to house, down to the commoners' part of town, where the giant's house was. They ran to the door, and Leona knocked vigorously. "Hallo?" a strong voice came from behind the door. "Thorsen, it's Leona, I must speak with you," Leona said quietly.

The bolts were undone, and the giant stood in the tall doorway. "What are you doing here at this hour of the night, your majesty?" Thorsen asked. "They've taken over, and killed most of my staff," Leona said shakingly. The stressful situation at hand was beginning to take its toll on her. "Who's done what?" Thorsen asked. "The Church," Leona replied.

"You mean the bunch of pious, spineless whoresons?" he asked angrily. "Well, if they didn't have spines before, they seem to have grown them quite quickly," Leona replied. "They would've killed us too, had it not been for her quick thinking,"

Meliss said. Thorsen looked at the young girl, and knew she wouldn't be lying about a situation like this.

"You must help us," Leona begged. "Of course I will," Thorsen said. "Come in, and shut the door behind you," he continued. The two women entered the large house, decorated with swords and trophies from past hunts. The women looked about them, and found a large stool that accommodated both of them.

They appeared to be only children in comparison to the size of the stool.

Thorsen returned a few moments later, with a leather jerkin and a great sword on his belt. "We must hurry if we're to make it out of here before dawn comes. With any luck, we'll slip by unnoticed. I can hear the contingency plan bells, which most likely means that more than a few people have escaped this horror. We should avoid joining them at all costs," he said. The two women nodded simultaneously.

He snuffed the candles that were lit and undid the bolts of the door. He peered out of the small crack he had made. "It's clear, but not for long, I assume," he said quietly. He motioned for the two to follow him, and soon as he did, a hooded figure appeared in front of them. He motioned for them to be silent, as he crept up behind the figure, snapped its neck, and lowered the limp body slowly. Meliss put a hand to her mouth to keep from screaming, while Leona put a hand around her shoulder.

"Come," he mouthed. The two followed him to the Western Gate, where there were a few more hooded figures standing guard. "It would seem as though some of the guards themselves were on the Church's payroll," he whispered. "By the Graces," Leona whispered. Thorsen counted the figures he could see. "We're not getting out of this without a bit of a fight," Thorsen said, handing the two women twin daggers he had strapped to his belt.

Meliss felt the weight of the large, gleaming dagger, and looked up at Thorsen. "I've never killed a man before," she said quietly. "Let's hope you don't have to," Thorsen said, squatting down to her height. "If it comes to it, where it's your life or your enemy's, you stick the pointy end of it into their gut or throat, pull it out, and rush to my side, alright?" Thorsen asked. Meliss' eyes filled with tears, but she nodded quickly, understanding the consequences if she didn't do as he said.

"Let's move," Thorsen whispered. The three came out of the shadows, and Thorsen drew his sword. The figures outnumbered them three to one, and Thorsen knew they'd put up a bit of a fight. He lowered his sword to his left side, letting it trail behind him just above the floor, allowing his first target to become overconfident. Leona and Meliss slowed their pace to be out of the way of the imminent strike, spacing themselves from the giant.

One of the hooded figures tapped another who stood next to him, and a grin could be seen beneath their hoods. Thorsen's eyes were fixed between their centers of mass, using his peripheral vision for tracking their strikes when they came.

And they came swiftly.

The first figure tried to strike from above, hoping to hit the giant's chest and slash his jerkin, but Thorsen swung his sword in a flash of moonlit movement. The sword looked like a bloodied glass shard as it sliced through the first man's arm, separating it from its previous owner. The second attacked from Thorsen's side, hoping to get in close enough to strike as his target recovered, but Thorsen was too smart for that. He quickly spun on his toes, and hacked the second target in half. Blood sprayed from the severed body, landing on the women's faces.

Two down, seven to go, Thorsen thought.

The other figures had been watching from a distance, and realized that Thorsen was not to be toyed with. One of them ran off, and the giant knew he would be back with something to hit him from a distance. Thorsen charged the other six men, parrying attacks and severing limbs from bodies, and heads from shoulders. Blood soaked him and the ground around him.

"There's still one left," the bloodied giant said to Leona. "Let's go before he gets back," he continued. Leona followed him, pulling Meliss along with her as Thorsen opened the guard door just as they arrived. The man who had run off earlier reappeared, pulling Meliss by the hair which tore her from Leona's grip. "Meliss!" she cried out. Meliss screamed in pain as she was overpowered and pulled away just out of Thorsen's reach.

"Stop where you are, or she dies," the figure said, tightening his grip on the girl's hair. Thorsen saw she still had the dagger in her hand, and that her attacker hadn't noticed it. "Alright, calm down," Thorsen said. "There's no need to harm the girl," he continued. "Shut up, giant," the figure said.

This bastard could end her life at any given moment. I can't close the distance quickly enough, even with my skills, Thorsen thought.

Meliss looked at him with a wide-eyed stare, fear clearly showing on her face. "What do you want with the girl?" Thorsen asked, trying to buy some time. "The fuck does it matter to you? Maybe I just want to have some fun with her, maybe I just want to kill her. Who knows?" the figure said, smelling Meliss' hair. "You detestable pervert!" Leona called out. The figure chuckled maliciously, putting his face closer to Meliss'. "I might have enjoyed this more if you two weren't here, but I guess this will have to do," the figure said, licking her temple.

Thorsen looked at Meliss who could only close her eyes

in disgust. "Meliss, it's going to be okay," he said calmly. "Oh-ho-ho, I don't think it will be. Not for her, anyway," the figure said, eyeing the giant. "Meliss, look at me," Thorsen said. Meliss watched the giant as he nodded, briefly looking down at the dagger she still held. He nodded once more, and she took a deep breath. Her hair twisted in her attacker's hands, and she stuck the blade deep into his upper gut, then cut downwards as she pulled the sodden blade out.

The figure loosened his grip on her hair, and put his hand to the wound. "You *bitch!* You dirty, sly, little bitch!" he screamed in pain. Two other hooded figures nearby heard the scream, and rushed to his aid. Meliss ran over to Thorsen and Leona, and they were out the door, running for their lives to the north. One of the figures opened the door, and had a bow in his hand with an arrow nocked in place.

He drew the arrow back, and loosed. The arrow whizzed through the air, and struck Leona in the shoulder. She fell to the ground, screaming in pain. "Get up, my lady," Thorsen said, helping her up. He saw the bowman preparing another arrow, and placed himself between Leona and the arrow.

As the bowman drew back the second arrow, Thorsen's eyes glowed with golden mana. The arrow, now soaring through the air, was met by a concussive blast of air from the giant's fingertips, shattering the arrow mid-flight. "What the hell? There aren't supposed to be any Synners here!" the hooded bowman shouted.

"You really thought so? My, my! I might know a rock with more intelligence than you," Thorsen jested, his eyes still glowing as he focused more mana to his legs. He bolted forward at an incredible speed, catching the bowman off guard, as someone his size shouldn't have been able to move that quickly.

Thorsen decapitated the bowman in a single strike so clean

that not even blood remained on his sword. Leona was in awe of the giant's prowess, but could only just keep Meliss' panic in check. The giant sheathed his sword, and picked up both of the women in his arms. "We're not going to make it if I don't do this, so I apologize in advance, my dear ladies," he said kindly, using more mana to boost his speed at an incredible rate.

An hour passed, and the trio found themselves in the safety of the nearby forest, where Thorsen was sure that no normal man would dare follow them there. He set Meliss down first, then Leona with added care. "It's not so bad, your majesty," he said, observing the shaft in her upper right shoulder. "I might puke," Leona replied with a groan. "Wouldn't be surprised if you did," he replied. "Just get it over with," she said between grunts of pain.

"Don't move," Thorsen said, pulling the shaft from her shoulder. She screamed in pain. He quickly put his hand over the bleeding wound, and his eyes glowed once more, *drawing mana from the Ethereal.* He condensed a small amount of it to his hand, searing the wound shut, leaving a small scar behind. "There, almost as though it never happened," he said, trying to cheer her up. Meliss watched the whole thing happen with wide eyes.

She had never seen a Synner in action before.

"How does it look?" Leona asked Meliss. "To be honest, it doesn't look too awful," Meliss said, looking at the new scar more closely. Leona nodded, and tried to move her shoulder. The knot in her gut from the pain was still there, but the actual pain in her shoulder dramatically lessened.

"Help me up," Leona said. Thorsen picked her up slowly, and set her down on her feet. Leona looked at the giant who had just saved her life. "You're a Synner," she said, finally understanding what had just occurred.

"I am, your majesty," Thorsen began. "Or at least I was until a few years ago, when I joined the Warrior's Guild," he said with a frown. "You must have had a really good reason to leave," Leona said, trying to better understand her savior. "I did, but it wasn't exactly my choice," Thorsen replied. He paused for a moment, remembering the course of events.

"Grundvollr was attacked by a powerful mage, leaving little more than a tenth of us alive. We who survived knew we could never go back, and King Mads had refused to give us aid. We were outcasts, even though we had all spent countless years defending Hjalfar. Mads had deemed us *dishonored and useless* by the fact that we were unable to take down the mage. As a result, we were banished from our own lands," Thorsen explained. Doing so took a visible toll on him and his usually cheerful demeanor.

"We never even so much as caught wind of such a terrible situation," Leona said. "I'd be surprised if you had heard of it. No one outside of the surviving Synners and Mads knew about it. He tried long and hard to keep our failure taboo for years to come. After having the rug pulled out from under our worlds, we knew we could no longer be Synners, and tried to live a normal life instead. Some of the others simply couldn't bear the fact that they had to be *normal* and such, so they took their own lives, or became bandits and outlaws. One other and I are the last living true Synners of Grundvollr, your majesty," Thorsen said, lowering his head.

"I am truly sorry such a fate befell you, my dear Thorsen," Leona said, putting a hand on his large shoulder. "I can assure you that if I am ever to be in power again, be it in Coltend or anywhere else, I will ensure that you are given the highest quality of living possible," she said. "Thank you, your majesty," Thorsen said humbly.

"You needn't call me that any longer, for I am no one's queen as it currently stands," Leona said. "You will always be my queen, my lady," Thorsen said with a warm smile. Leona smiled back, as he looked up at the sky through the canopy, and realized dawn was on the horizon.

"We must go," he said. "Where can we go where they won't find us?" Leona asked. "North," he replied. "North?" Leona asked. "Yes, to Fangsdalr, just to the east of where Grundvollr once was," Thorsen replied with a grin. "What lies there?" Leona asked. "Do you recall how I said that there was one other *true* Synner who survived the attack? Well, he has done what Mads would not dare to dream of," Thorsen replied. "And that is…?" Leona asked.

"He built a hidden Synner school, my lady," Thorsen replied with a smile.

CHAPTER 15

Codrean

After the battle for Codrean, we gathered our wounded and regrouped at the fortress. The wounded were tended to by Bernar and Garett, as well as a few other of the senior Synners. Any of our number that died during the assault were burned in a pyre to avoid the spread of disease that rotting corpses caused.

Meanwhile, I went over to speak with the Master, still covered in the Ochelon's blood from the battle. I found the Master in his study, accompanied by Anwill. The two were discussing something I couldn't quite overhear.

"Master," I interrupted, knocking on the door. "*Ah*, if it isn't the ochelon slayer himself! What can I help you with?" the Master asked, acknowledging my presence. "Might I have a word with you?" I asked. "Of course," the Master replied. The elf remained stationary. "I assume the subject of our imminent conversation is to be held in private," the Master said.

"No, Master. The only privacy here would be in consideration of *that* topic," I replied. "However, if you trust him as Bernar does, then Anwill may stay. After all, he might have information that could be useful," I continued. "I would trust him with my life, Thoma, so there is no need to worry. Please, sit," the

Master motioned to the chair nearest to the desk.

"Master, Anwill. What I am about to say here is not out of conjecture, but out of my observations over the course of my time here," I began. "I understand," the Master said reassuringly. I paused and gathered my thoughts.

Ah, I wish it didn't have to be this way, but here we go, I thought.

"I've heard Batch mention that after their training sessions that Irun has been scurrying off to study, although I don't believe that. Not one bit," I began. "What do you mean?" the Master asked, leaning forward intently.

"Well, you see, Master, Irun has never been one to study much of anything. I know this because we have shared quarters during our time here together, and I've never once seen him reading so much as a book before bed," I explained. The Master tilted his head. "Is that so?" he asked. "It is, Master," I replied.

The Master looked over at Anwill, who was visibly disturbed by the news. The Master looked back at me inquisitively, but it felt like he'd just probed my mind. "I can already guess what you are proposing, but I want to hear your reasoning for such a thing," the Master said.

"Well, Master, I don't propose we do anything yet, as we have no concrete evidence. However, I do think that we should try to keep a closer eye on him," I said hesitantly. "Given current events, and everything that has happened since our return from the council at Coltend, I have begun to see a pattern," I continued. "Forgive me for interrupting, but what exactly has happened since you've come back?" Anwill asked, trying to grasp the situation.

"To make a long story short, we have seen ravens leaving from the direction of the fortress, as well as another which flew just before the attack," the Master said. "And you believe this to be the work of one of your own?" Anwill asked. "Yes," both the Master and I replied simultaneously.

"These are dark times, indeed," Anwill began. He paused for a moment, as if preparing his next words carefully. "I believe you may have a point, young Thoma. While I was on my way here, I heard rumors about creatures stirring far to the North. Even along our own borders in Caegwen, there are plenty of portals that bring these bastards to our world, though none have spawned so close to our own school. Perhaps, and this is a bit of a long shot, those ravens being sent out were to update someone to keep tabs on all of you?" Anwill said.

You've got to be shitting me. They haven't had any spawn that close? And why would anyone want to keep tabs on us? What the hell is going on? I thought as I processed Anwill's words.

"The problem is: What if I'm right and he really is a traitor? I don't want to sit here thinking that someone I've basically grown up with could do such a thing," I said, my voice shaking a little near the end.

"I mean, I don't think I could beat him in a fight if it came to that," I continued with uncertainty in my voice. "You've unlocked the second stage of mana manipulation, taken down three ochelons, as well as a few dozen glicks and daemons. I think you'd manage," the Master said with a grin.

I felt a slight relief hearing the Master say that. "Thank you, Master, but I still have yet to unlock the full extent of the second stage," I said bashfully.

The Master nodded and smiled as gently as his face could allow. "Your time will come, Thoma. However, Anwill and I must discuss our next moves. You're welcome to stay, if you want to," the Master suggested.

"If it's not too much of an inconvenience, Master. Since the incident with Edryd and the injury I caused him, I've learned the value of situational awareness, and would like to gain as much as I can," I replied.

The Master gave me a look as if he understood what was going through my head while the probing feeling returned once more, but I said nothing.

"There should never be any shame in seeking out more information or bettering yourself in any way. After all, the pursuit of knowledge is not a gift granted to all. Some taste wisdom once and chase it their entire lives, while others enjoy the taste of rocks and windows," the Master said with a light chuckle at the end.

The Master returned to the map that was spread out on the desk. "As we were saying earlier, these attacks are becoming more frequent. It's not just near the school, either. Just a few days ago, another report was made of an attack near Coltend Castle. If these attacks are going to continue progressively get worse, we will require reinforcements," the Master stated.

"I agree," Anwill began. "However, Caegwen is much too far away, and we have troubles of our own with some of the outcast Synners in our own country, let alone the creatures on our borders," he said grimly.

I took in the words, though they sat like spoiled milk in my stomach.

He's right. If we tried to go to Caegwen now, we'd only end up wasting precious time and taking away their reinforcements. Wait a minute... I thought.

"What if we went to Hjalfar?" I asked shyly. Anwill and the Master both looked at me. I rose from my seat, and leaned on the desk, observing the map before me.

"I mean, we're practically a stone's throw away from the nearest Synner school once we cross the border. As far as we know, we haven't heard of any large-scale attacks happening there. If I'm right, we might find our reinforcements there," I said, pointing to the general location on the map.

Anwill observed the distance. "He's got a point, Master," he said, surprisingly agreeing with me. "Indeed, he does," the Master began. "However, we haven't had news from them in nearly forty years. While not hearing news of other schools is not unheard of, to go such a lengthy period of time without *anything* is cause for concern," the Master said grimly.

I observed the map once more, noting the distance between them and Odensby. "What if we simply went and asked the king?" I said. The Master looked at the map. "It's almost the same distance, not to mention the king might offer us some help, Master. He seemed friendly enough the last time we saw him," I said, hoping for a positive answer from my master.

"Hmm, we could always send a raven up there, too," the Master said, stroking his chin. "True, but you know how ravenries can be; sometimes it will be a week or two before they even see the message, let alone have a proper answer in short notice," Anwill said with a shrug. "It's worth a shot, at the very least," I chimed in.

"The issue here is what would become of Codrean," the Master said. "I'm not saying we should go in full force to Odensby. We would have to leave a few Synners behind to stand guard. How many are we in total, Master?" I asked. "Just over two hundred," the Master replied.

"If we were to leave here with a small party of about twenty, that would allow us to move quickly, while conserving plenty of resources and people to hold the fortress while we're gone," I said after a short pause. "You have got a good head on your shoulders, young Thoma," Anwill said approvingly. "I agree with him," he directed his words to the Master.

The Master thought about it, pacing about the room. "While we know that Irun has a higher potential for being the traitor than most, that still doesn't confirm he's the one to blame," the Master began.

"If the traitor remains among us, we risk any and all information getting into the wrong hands. If this person, or *these people*, are capable of charming an ochelon, we have to assume that they could also break any mana wards I put up to prevent them from gathering the information stored in this very room," he continued.

"So we're taking everyone with us? Abandoning the fortress?" I asked. "It may be our only option," the Master replied grimly.

"I must think it over," he continued after a short pause. "I am more than certain that we are all exhausted after the battle, and we all could do with some rest," he said, sitting back down on his chair.

"We shall continue this discussion tomorrow. *Oh*, and Thoma," the Master began. "Yes, Master?" I asked. "I would very much appreciate it if you were present for that decision," the Master said. "At first light, Master?" I asked, trying to hide the exhaustion in my voice. "Precisely," the Master replied. "I will be here, Master," I replied with a nod.

"And so will I," Anwill said with a smile. "I'm sure that you must have more pressing matters to attend to back in Caegwen," the Master said. "Nonsense," Anwill replied. "This is the best adventure I've seen in the last hundred years. Plus, before I left, I put *you-know-who* in charge of defenses," he said.

"Very well, then," the Master said with a nod. "Thoma, head down to the infirmary to notify your brother and Master Garett," he said. I nodded, and headed out the door.

The stairs that led from the Master's study to the infirmary seemed longer than they had ever been.

I can't imagine the Hjalfarian school falling so easily, he thought to myself. *I mean, if only about a hundred of us could take on such a hoard, the Hjalfarian school must have been under a heavy attack indeed. Either that, or something truly powerful overcame their forces. They were one of the oldest schools on the Continent, and had some of the most experienced Synners. It just doesn't make sense. Think, you fool, think,* I thought, furrowing my brow, trying to piece the facts together.

Continuing down the halls, making little sound as I did so, I realized that nothing was as it had been before. The walls seemed older and darker than they had looked just a few weeks ago. I felt the weight of the battle finally weighing down on me and my body.

Damn it, I feel like I'm carrying my brother on my shoulders after having trained all day, I thought.

I reviewed what had happened in the battle, thinking about what I could have done better, or more efficiently. I knew that jumping into the open claw of the ochelon was a stupid idea, and that it could have crushed me easily.

Won't be doing that again any time soon, I thought.

Walking down the final flight of steps that would ultimately lead me to my destination. The smell of blood and sweat began to fill the air. I stepped through the doorway and saw beds filled with wounded Synners. I had never had much contact with most of them, since the majority of the wounded were not in my immediate circle of friends, so I began to look for the ones I did.

I found Garett kneeling by one of the beds tending to a wounded Synner, whose chest had a ghastly cut in it. "Master Garett," I said quietly. "In a minute," Garett said, holding up a hand. I observed the wound being given the same treatment I had received from my brother.

I don't miss that feeling of wounds being seared shut with mana. It feels like a small horde of maggots on fire burrowing through your skin, I shuddered briefly.

Garett finished searing the wound shut with mana, and gently placed a hand on the woman's shoulder. "You'll live, lass," he said comfortingly. "Thank you, Master Garett," the woman replied in a weak voice. "No need to thank me. Just doing my job," Garett replied with a warm smile. "Rest, now," he said.

He rose from his kneeling position, and turned to face me. "Be quick about it. I have others that need tending to," Garett said. "The Master has called for you in his office at first light, Master Garett," I said quietly. Garett knew that couldn't be a good thing. "Anyone else invited?" Garett asked. "You, me, Bernar, and Anwill, Master Garett," I replied. "Anwill, the elf?" Garett asked.

I was puzzled at the question.

"Yes, Master Garett," I replied. He sighed and shook his head. "I don't usually trust elves," he began. "They're too old for their own good, and it creeps the living shit out of me. If the Master wants him to be there, I have no choice but to suck it up, I guess," he said with a sigh. "I'll be there, don't worry," Garett replied.

I nodded and made my way over to my brother, who was tending to Irun's wounds.

A broken rib or two was never as severe as an open wound, unless of course they had punctured a lung, I thought. "You got lucky," I overheard my brother say. "Lucky?" Irun wheezed. "The ochelon's claw could have impaled you. Would you rather it had?" Bernar asked with a shrug. "I think *anything else* at this point would be more comfortable than barely being able to breathe," Irun replied.

"So you would take death over a bit of discomfort? Seems like you can still talk enough shit to make it through this," I chuckled, approaching the side of the bed. "*Oh,* munch on a prick, will you?" Irun said with no small amount of sarcastic spice in his voice. He coughed and wheezed for a moment. "As funny as that was, I don't think it's a good idea to cause more damage than you've already got," Bernar said with a grin.

"Hurry up and fix me, then," Irun said impatiently. "Careful, now," I began. "Getting fixed in some places means having *itchy* and *scratchy* sawed off with a dull knife," I said, not bothering to hide the shit-eating grin on my face.

Bernar snorted with laughter and almost lost focus on what he was doing. "He's got a point. Careful what you wish for," Bernar said, desperately trying not to lose focus as he continued sending mana towards Irun's wounds.

"Your parents must have been something special for you two to be able to make jokes at a time like this," Irun said angrily. "Shut up and lie still," Bernar spat, flicking his middle finger on Irun's forehead. "Hey!" Irun exclaimed, laying his head back on the pillow. "There, all done. Although, I wouldn't recommend taking us on just yet. You'll need a good night of rest before it heals completely," Bernar said, arresting the mana's flow after a few moments.

Irun wriggled around, feeling almost no pain in his ribcage. "Thank you," he begrudgingly said to Bernar. "Next time don't be such a whiny piglet," Bernar replied with a nod. Irun rolled his eyes.

"Ungrateful little shit, he is," Bernar said quietly after taking a few steps away from Irun's bedside. "Yeah, he can be a real pain in the ass, at times," I replied. We walked down the rows of beds, passing Synners who had already been treated by both Garett and Bernar.

"I know you came here for more than just to check on Irun," Bernar began. "The Master has summoned us to his study at first light," I replied quietly. "Any idea what for?" Bernar asked.

"All I can really say here is that he did. He also didn't want people trying to spread rumors," I said with a raised eyebrow.

"Got it. I won't pry, then," Bernar replied quietly. "Let's go outside. We need to talk. That ingrate back over there was the last one for me for the night," he tilted his head in Irun's general direction. I nodded, and we promptly left the infirmary.

Under the dim light of the stars and the rising moon, not a soul to be seen about us, we walked towards the training grounds. "What did you want to talk about?" I asked after we had walked a short distance away from the main fortress. "I brought you here to ask you something," Bernar said.

This can't be good, I thought.

"Well, go on, then. Spit it out," I said with a mild anxiety creeping in. "I know you have very few memories of mother - and a lot of horrible ones about father - but I have to ask you whether mother had mentioned anything about our grandparents to you," Bernar said. "The fuck did this come from?" I asked. I was expecting something entirely different, though not even I knew what to expect.

"Just answer the damn question," Bernar said playfully. "Well, I know father's parents died a long time ago, leaving him a small fortune and a bit of land, what with being the son of a nobleman and all," I began.

I thought back as far as I could, struggling to unearth certain memories I thought had long since been forgotten. "I don't really remember mother saying much about our grandparents, though," I admitted, furrowing my brow in frustration.

"Strange, don't you think?" Bernar asked. "What do you mean?" I asked my older brother. "Neither of us remember much of anything about her side of the family, only that she comes from a long line of Synners," Bernar replied. "Alright, what are you getting at?" I asked.

"Don't you find it odd how little we actually know about our family?" Bernar asked. I looked at him with pure bewilderment written on my face. "Why *would* I find it weird? Mother wasn't the most open of people, was she? And father, being the shithead he is, isn't exactly the most approachable person, either. The only things I can remember are that, and how she looked on the day she left - never to return," I said, venom dripping from my words.

"Actually, I hardly even remember what she looked like, come to think of it," I frowned, realizing the image I had of my own mother was now blurred and askew from what I thought it should've been.

"Well, I remember a little more than you," Bernar began. "She was strong-willed. An unequivocally untamable force of nature, if you will, *and* she was an all-caster," he said. "She was?" I asked curiously. "She was," Bernar replied with a smile.

"Father always hated her for being a Synner, and as a result, he broke off their marriage a few years after you were born; ridding her from his life and ours all in one fell swoop. Just before she left, she begged him to watch over the two of us. At first, he didn't really agree to it all, but with a bit of mana, she managed to convince him. The reason he hated us so much was that we always reminded him of her, and the memories of her would always return in full force," Bernar explained.

"Holy shit, I had no idea," I said, taken aback. "Holy shit on a holy altar," Bernar added. "So that's why he never really talked about her, nor her side of the family. It also explains why he's a piece of shit, but maybe he was already like that before she left," I concluded.

"Exactly," Bernar began. "Another reason we don't know much about her lineage is that the two of us rarely ever saw her, and whenever we would, father would always be there to interrupt," he continued. "Because *of course* he was..." I said, looking away from my brother into the distance.

"Well, it can't be helped now, I guess. Either way, I'm glad to see you're also growing closer to the Master," Bernar said with a shrug.

"Over the last decade or so, the Master and I have grown close, and I can see he's beginning to trust you as he does me. To me, at least, he's like the father neither of us ever had," he continued, reflecting on the past few years.

I looked at him curiously. "Does it have anything to do with you knowing Anwill?" I asked. "It does, but that, as well as a few other things, will have to be a story for another time," Bernar replied. "Can't even get answers out of my own, damned brother. *Sheesh*," I said disappointedly.

Just as Bernar was opening his mouth to speak, a figure appeared in the doorway behind us. "Bernar, Thoma," the figure called out. "Yes, Master Garett?" I asked, immediately recognizing his grouchy voice. "Lights out," Garett said. "Right away, Master Garett," I replied.

I looked at my brother, hoping he would reveal the answer to the questions I'd asked. Bernar simply shook his head. "We'll discuss this some other time. Otherwise, that geezer will have us for a midnight snack," he chuckled as we walked back to the fortress. My mind was racing, scrambling to find an answer to my own questions

I'll be sure to take him up on this conversation again when this is all over, I thought.

Each of us went our own ways to our quarters, and I lay belly up on my bed, staring at the thatched roof above me. I glanced over at the scratched names in the wall beside my bed, listening to the soft snoring of my roommates.

It must be nice to not have racing thoughts during the late hours

of the night, I thought with an envious sigh.

I rolled over on my side, and pulled the blanket up to my neck to help stave off the cold air that the stone walls held. I closed my eyes, *placing myself back in the open field. I cast a few spells, each different from the other, and slowly but surely, my world went dark as I stepped into the dreamworld.*

Unfortunately, I awoke a little after dawn with a startle.

Shit, I'm gonna be late, I thought, realizing what time it was. I jolted out of bed, quickly grabbing my clothes and putting them on as quickly as I could as I dashed out of my room.

Shit, shit, shiiiit! I've got to hurry! He's gonna kill me if I'm late! I thought, feeling my stale joints groan as I darted up the cold, stone steps.

I reached the study with only a few minutes to spare.

Phew, that was a close one! I thought as I knocked on the door. It opened slowly, only for me to come face to face with none other than the Master himself. "*Ah,* there you are. Glad you could make it," the Master said calmly.

Yep, he's going to kill me, I thought, accepting my fate.

"Good morning, Master. I apologize for my tardiness," I said with a bow. The Master noted my composure with a quick glance.

I wasn't fully out of breath, but sprinting like I did first thing in the morning was anything but enjoyable.

"Now that we're all here, let us begin," the Master said, closing the door behind me, the latecomer. Anwill, Garett, Bernar and I all sat in the chairs provided for us.

"Gentlemen, we are at an impasse," the Master began as he watched all of us give him our undivided attention. "The attack on us here at Codrean has led me to believe that there may be yet another coming soon, and with most of our men and women wounded, and not fully battle-ready, we have no other option but to seek out reinforcements in case of future engagements," he said plaintively.

"As the situation currently stands, we are too far from Caegwen and Harut to request reinforcements, for they would have to travel over the Rhydian Pass just to get here, all the while having their own issues to attend to. Our only remaining option is to travel north to Hjalfar and request help from King Mads," the Master said, a tone of uncertainty lingered in his voice.

"The way there is anything but easy, and it may take us a few days to get there, but that is the least of our worries. The information contained here in the fortress is of the highest importance, and it has never been left entirely alone. Two hundred of us in total has always given us the advantage of being able to leave a few behind. However, given the risk of them being overrun and slaughtered by more of those creatures makes this call tougher than any we have faced before," the Master said with a frown.

Just then, a raven flew through the open window with a small pouch attached to it. The Master removed the contents from the pouch, reading them swiftly.

His face grew pale.

The others watched him stride back and forth behind his desk. We waited patiently for him to say something, but after what felt like an eternity, nothing was said. "What is it, Master? What happened?" Bernar asked. The Master, reeling from the news, slumped in his chair.

"There has been an attack on Coltend Castle. It seems as though after the death of King Truls, the Church has decided to take it for their own. There were some survivors, though exactly who's fallen during that attack is unknown," he said gravely. "The queen is dead?" Bernar asked. "I'm afraid so, but there is no confirmation in the letter," the Master replied with a sunken head.

I hope you're alive, Meliss, I thought fearfully, suddenly recalling her name from our first meeting.

Everyone present looked at each other, wondering what our next move should be. However, for a few moments, no one spoke, leaving the air both heavy and grim.

"The game has changed, and the decision is as follows: We either entirely abandon the fortress and take everyone with us north-east to Hjalfar to seek reinforcements and help take back the castle, or we risk leaving a few behind, the traitor possibly being among them," he said.

We all looked at each other, hoping one of us would answer the difficult situation presented. "I have summoned you all here to aid me in this decision," the Master began once more after a short pause. "We shall hold a vote, myself not included, for it would be an uneven number. All in favor of leaving the fortress with a few, hopefully trustworthy, Synners left behind, raise your hand," he said.

Nobody did.

"Well, that was simple," Anwill said. "Very well, then," the Master began. "I will take with me the most valuable of the books here - locked up in a chest that will be placed on a wagon directly behind me," he continued.

"What about the wounded?" Garett asked. "They will still need a few days to fully recover," he said. "They will ride in the center of our convoy on all other available carriages. We need to avoid combat as much as possible," the Master answered.

"The traitor will probably try to send a raven, Master," Anwill said. "As harrowing as that thought may be, at least there will be enough people around to see who it is," the Master retorted.

"Are we all in agreement on this?" the Master asked. Each

one looked at each other, ensuring we were on the same page. "We are, Master," Garett replied with a nod. "Then gather our supplies. We will ride to Hjalfar at first light tomorrow," the Master said.

I felt my stomach turn in a direction that shouldn't be possible.

CHAPTER 16

The Duel

Gorm and Ari's duel began under the bright sun of the early morning upon the Rhydian Pass. As the two men circled each other, Gorm was already beginning to feel the weight of his sword grow lighter in his hands with the adrenaline that coursed through his veins. His pupils were dilated and his heart pounded like a horse's hooves on a dirt road. Ari, too, was beginning to feel the same way, as he knew he had the support of his king and the army behind him.

I cannot afford to lose here. The already complex situation could bode ill for my family's life should I fail to uphold the strength and honor bestowed upon me, he thought.

Gorm, on the other hand, single-mindedly thought only of his desire to kill his opponent.

I must beat him. I must prove my worthiness as a commander, Ari thought. *He is a formidable warrior, and clearly knows what he's doing. I must be cautious, and strike when there is an opening. His defense is air-tight, and his presence of mind is astounding. I can feel the pressure of his murderous intent as if a weight was on my shoulders.*

He continued to watch his opponent, whose face was locked

in a state of pure hatred for him. Gorm was sizing him up, observing his footsteps, when he noticed a slight insecurity in Ari's footsteps.

Heh, he's scared shitless, Gorm thought.

"Begin," Bashir shouted, raising his arms. Ari quickly dashed towards Gorm, who stood his ground like a boulder stuck in the ground. Gorm judged the distance between himself and his attacker, and adjusted his guard to match his opponent's attack. The pommel of his sword was at waist height, while the point of the sword was tilted slightly forward. His legs were firmly planted on the ground at a comfortable width as he awaited the incoming blow.

Ari shouted loudly as he struck from above, his mighty blow carrying his full force behind it. Gorm raised his sword, deflecting the scimitar off to the side. He immediately stepped in towards his attacker and hit him on the nose with his large, wheel-shaped pommel. The blow drew blood from Ari's nose, who saw it as a wake-up call, forcing him to dodge an incoming slash.

That was foolish of me. I thought he would have moved differently, Ari thought.

He struck again from below, and Gorm easily deflected it, pirouetting out of the way of the following blow that just missed his shoulder. Again and again Ari attacked, but the blows either glanced off Gorm's sword, or hit nothing but air.

"Fight me like a man, you coward!" Ari shouted. "I will not fight an arrogant child as a man, because I would utterly destroy you. Right now, all I want to do is enjoy this kill," Gorm replied menacingly. "You can jest all you want to, but it will not save your life. I will not be killed so easily," Ari said angrily.

"Maybe not, but it will make for one hell of a show. Watching you struggle against someone much older than you is also incredibly amusing to me and my men," Gorm replied. "Struggle?" Ari questioned. "You have tried to strike me again and again, and yet you still haven't been able to land a meaningful blow," Gorm said. *That bastard,* Ari thought.

Ari angrily charged at him once more, striking quickly, desperately trying to find an opening, but Gorm's sword flowed through the air, parrying strikes as it went.

Time to teach the pup a lesson, he thought as he moved from defense to offense.

After dodging another overhead blow he had just dodged, he struck in rapid succession. Ari deflected the majority of the blows with skills he hadn't previously shown. Gorm decided to thrust, aiming at Ari's neck. Ari just barely managed to redirect the tip of Gorm's sword, scratching his armored shoulder.

Oh? Maybe he's not so bad after all, Gorm thought.

He struck again and again, but this time, it was Ari who deflected the incoming blows.

Gorm noticed Ari's focus begin to improve, demonstrating his true skills as the duel raged on. He attempted a side cut aimed for Ari's liver, but the blow was deflected. Ari responded with an elbow to the face, drawing blood from Gorm's nose. "Now we're even," Ari said. "Sure, but this is just going to make me enjoy killing you even more," Gorm snorted the blood that ran down the back of this throat, and spat it in Ari's direction.

He was pissed.

It was Gorm's turn to dash in for yet another blow, only to be deflected by the gleaming scimitar. Ari responded with a strike of his own coming from the left, which Gorm only adeptly deflected. Ari began a rapid succession of strikes from the left, and Gorm realized he had found Ari's weakness. Ari aimed a blow for Gorm's head, but he ducked out of the path of the sword, taking a few steps back, and swiftly avoiding another one aimed for his gut.

"You fight well, for a child," Gorm said. "You're not so bad yourself, old man," Ari retorted. "It is a true shame that even though you are so skilled, you will die," Ari said mournfully. "Is that pity I hear in your voice?" Gorm asked. "It is indeed. I have never met anyone who could match my blade so well," Ari responded.

"As much as I hate to admit it, you're much better than you let off at the beginning of the fight. Did you need to warm up a bit? Was that why you allowed me to strike your nose?" Gorm asked, genuinely curious. "I struck in anger, as I had underestimated you. However, I recognize your skills, and acknowledge you as a true warrior. I still think it's a shame you will have to die, as you would have made a great addition to our forces," Ari admitted. "That would never happen," Gorm quickly spat. "I could never work with *your kind*," he continued, disgusted at the thought of working under Harutian leaders.

"I take great offense in that comment, so I will fight you with everything I have," Ari responded grimly, entering his guard. "And I will repay your offer by dancing in your blood," Gorm responded maliciously.

Behind the duel that was taking place, one of the riders from Bashir's army spotted a moving object coming from the northern trail. He turned his head away from the ongoing duel to see if it wasn't simply his mind playing a trick on him. The object moved again, and he dismounted to investigate. He drew his scimitar, and cautiously went over to the large boulder, where he had seen the object move.

A glick darted out from behind the boulder, and charged him - its claw aimed for his face. The blow scraped his jaw, just missing his jugular. He stepped out of the way of the next blow, and severed the creature's head, spraying blood all over the ground. He made sure it was dead, and then looked down the northern trail once more only to find more coming their way.

"Glicks!" the man shouted, racing back to the others on the pass. A few of the other riders saw him running and shouting, and wondered what the commotion was all about. They followed the direction his hand was pointing in, and saw a larger number of glicks than the man had previously seen. "We're under attack!" the man shouted.

Gorm and Ari were still dueling, when Bashir noticed the commotion behind them. "My lord, an army of glicks approaches from the North," the man said, nearly out of breath. Bashir's eyes opened wide. "Stop the duel," he shouted. Gorm and Ari froze mid blows and looked at Bashir. "He must die, my lord," Ari said. "We have a larger problem than his death, Ari," Bashir said angrily. "Glicks are coming from the northern trail, and we will need all the help we can get," he continued. "You have an army behind you," Gorm began. "Why should you worry about whether or not we continue?" he asked.

"I have brought no Synners with me, and these men are not exactly trained to fight these bastards," Bashir explained. "Set your differences aside for now, and when the battle is over, you may get back to killing each other. Right now, we need to fight them as one," he said. "I will have your head when this is over," Ari said begrudgingly, looking at Gorm. "You're welcome to try and take it, pup," Gorm replied.

"Gorm, gather your remaining men, and stand with us," Bashir said. "Not like I have much of a choice," Gorm said under his breath. "Men, to arms!" he shouted. The elves that were guarding them from the nearby bushes slipped back, out of sight. "Cowards!" one of Gorm's men shouted at them, noticing the elves' flight. "It's no use. They don't get involved with human affairs unless there's something in it for them other than death or imprisonment," one of the other men said.

"Get in formation," Bashir called out to his riders. They made a line with their horses, facing the oncoming horde. Foot soldiers made their way up the pass, rallying behind the horsemen. "Wait for them to funnel together near that boulder," Ari shouted. The ground began to shake with the horde that approached them.

The glicks' screams and screeches grew progressively louder, and some of the soldiers began to shake with fear. "Stand together, and we may yet win this," Ari commanded. Bashir caught a single glance of the glicks, and made his way to the top of the rock where Gwili once stood. Meanwhile, Ari steadied himself and noticed Gorm was standing beside him.

"Not the most ideal of places, I know, but I'd rather be next to a strong swordsman than a soldier who has soiled himself," Gorm said with a shrug. "That's a fair point, but why take your enemy's side after saying you'd never work under Harutian command? A bit hypocritical, don't you think?" Ari asked. "Better the one you know will try to kill you, than the one you think might do it by accident. It's not that I don't trust my men, but I'd rather have a clean cut across my throat than get mauled by these nasty looking fuckers," Gorm said plaintively. "Good point," Ari replied.

The glicks were nearing the boulder, and the horses began to become uneasy. "Steady," Ari called out. Gorm gripped his sword tightly, lowering it to be almost parallel with his hind leg. The glicks passed the boulder in an unorganized fashion, causing congestion in their flow. The few who made it past the congestion were staggering about like chickens without their heads.

"Now!" Ari shouted, pushing off the balls of his feet. The riders charged the group, and took off with swords drawn.

Gorm and his men went after them, with a group of Harutian soldiers coming along with him and his remaining men. The horsemen met the glicks, and the pungent, green blood began to flow. The screeches let off by the glicks having their limbs severed by the riders was near deafening in the narrowed pass

The congestion of glicks nearest to the boulder only allowed a few to pass through at a time, but they were so large in number, that it seemed to be an unending stream of them. Gorm and the other soldiers cut down the stragglers missed by the riders, and all seemed to be going well, when suddenly, the glicks began to collectively tear the riders from their saddles.

It's like these bastards are being told to do this shit! What the hell is wrong with them? Gorm thought as he sliced into a creature's neck.

One of the glicks grabbed Ari from behind, trying to wrestle him to the ground. He threw his head back, knocking a few of the glick's rotting teeth back into its mouth. The glick released its grip on him, reeling in pain, and Ari got back to his feet to finish it off with his sword. Gorm saw the riders falling quickly, and called for reinforcements. He saw the glicks taking down the horses, beginning to eat them while they were still alive and kicking. He felt pity for them, but there was nothing he could do to save them now.

The battle raged on for the better part of an hour. Glicks took down many of the inexperienced soldiers, but fell to the ones who actually knew what they were doing. Gorm and his men were bloodied, beaten and getting tired.

They never stop coming, do they? Gorm asked himself.

Ari ran over towards him, killing a few glicks on his way over. "Seems as though we might die today after all," Ari said, severing a glick's head. "A pity that I won't be the one to kill you," Gorm said. "Nor I, you," Ari replied. They stood back-to-back, dealing with the creatures as they came.

The other soldiers were starting to learn the glicks' attack patterns, and more than a few of them were becoming adept at slaying the beasts. Off in the distance, a deep, rumbling roar came from behind the boulders. "That can't be good," Ari said. "Not one bit," Gorm replied, slaying the last monster in front of him.

The ground began to tremble even more than it had before, and the two men looked out over the small river of glicks and corpses. "Fuck me, not more of them," Gorm said. "More of what?" Ari asked. "Trolls," Gorm replied grimly. Ari's eyes opened wide when he finally saw them. "Gods be with us," he said to himself. "Retreat!" he called back. The soldiers began to move away from the boulder as the ground shook beneath their feet. The glicks began to pour in, as the trolls forced their way through the pile of the smaller creatures. "Get back, you idiots," Gorm shouted to his men and the Harutians around them.

They had almost fully retreated to the shelf in the pass, when one of the trolls smashed through the boulder, releasing the held back glicks. "Up to our necks in shit now," Gorm said, realizing that the horde was no longer being funneled. "Run!" he shouted. The trolls smashed through the rocks, and began to charge in behind the glicks. They covered more ground in less time than the glicks, and began crushing soldiers into little more than bloodied mounds of flesh. Screams of terror and fear resounded from the army, and some had dropped their weapons in fear.

There was little that could save them.

The trolls took care of the soldiers above, as the glicks began to overpower the soldiers with their numbers, and made their way down the pass, killing all who stood before them. Bashir was still up on his rock, watching the slaughter ensue. His eyes welled with tears for his fallen men, and he knew then that this may be their end. "It could be worse," Gwili said from behind him. "How could it be worse?" Bashir asked, feeling distraught at the thought of his men dying and his revenge on Truls failing. "My men have been squashed into bloodied pulps by the ice and fire trolls, while the glicks are overpowering the others like ants to sugar," he continued.

"You have not lived as long as I have, so you'd better believe me when I say that it can always be worse," he said grimly. The two watched the slaughter continue, listening to the screams of the men and women beneath them being trampled and mauled. A fire troll spat molten rock all over a group of soldiers, who melted away in an instant. "No!" Bashir exclaimed, watching his men smolder. The smoke from their burned bodies reached Bashir's nostrils, his breakfast shooting out through his teeth.

"Why do you not give us aid?" Bashir asked the elf. "Even if I had had my men place every arrow with the precision we elves are famous for, it wouldn't even have made a dent in this large of a force," Gwili explained. "So, you will abandon us?" Bashir asked, desperately looking at Gwili with bloodshot eyes. "It's nothing personal. Just know that I hope you die well," Gwili said grimly. He crept back down the boulder, and was off into the bushes, leaving Bashir alone atop the boulder.

Bashir turned away from the fleeing elf, to observe the battle. Many had fallen, and he could see his army on the uphill slope of the trail being overrun by glicks. "This is it; this is the force that will bring about the end of the world," he said quietly. He watched the battle for another moment, listening to the sounds of his men fighting to their deaths. He turned away and slumped behind the top of the boulder, placing his hands on his head.

I have sent my men on a suicide mission, he thought as the battle raged on behind him.

In my anger and hatred for Truls for slaying my son, I have now brought even more destruction upon myself and my kingdom. My son. My dearest Bashaa. I have failed to avenge your death, but I know that by the end of this day, we shall be together in the afterlife.

I pray that you will welcome me with open arms, even though I have failed to do the one thing I swore I would. I pray that you will forgive me for not only the failure of a broken promise, but as a failure of a father as well. I have done the best I could with the knowledge and power that I had. I pray that I may yet see approval in your eyes, for that is all a father could ever wish for from his son or daughter. I know that death comes to all things, and I hope that you witness mine with pride filling your heart.

There's no way for any of us to make it out alive, is there? he thought as he observed the battlefield once more.

Very well. If there is no escape for us, I have no choice but to accept our fates. Here and now, I will honor my forefathers. Tears streamed down his face, as he made his way down the boulder.

Let my sword sing my death song, and carry me onward into the afterlife, he thought as he descended from his elevated position.

He drew his scimitar, and spread his arms wide, facing and challenging the horde of creatures before him, letting out a cry that would have sent fear into the heart of the Undergod himself.

To my wife, I hope you find solace in knowing that I died well.

A few of the glicks saw him, and began to charge towards him. He cut them down, one by one, removing limbs from bodies, and releasing a river of green blood that flowed around his feet. He continued screaming loudly, hacking down the horrid creatures, not even watching their limp bodies fall. He was keen on killing as many as he could in the time he had left.

To my sons whom I will soon meet, I pray that you welcome me with open arms, embracing me in death as you did in life.

The glicks began to circle around him as he looked into their grim faces. They snarled and squealed at him, some flicking their scales in challenge. "I will make you wish you had never been brought into this world," Bashir said threateningly. The glicks flicked their scales in unison, and Bashir knew that this might be his last breath.

Just as they were about to attack, a loud screech like that of an eagle came overhead. The glicks looked up, and backed away from him, looking up at the figure in the sky. The glicks, no longer flicking their scales, stood down from his challenges at the sound of the screech.

Why aren't they coming at me? Do they have a master? Has he come here, to this place? he thought, looking up in the direction the screech came from.

The sun was now at its highest peak, and Bashir could only make out the silhouette of a winged creature in the sky.

Damn it all, I can't see a thing, he thought, his eyes watered from the bright light, forcing him to look away.

He could hear the flapping of its wings, even though the sound of the trolls and glicks about him were still bellowing.

Gorm watched the glicks around himself and Ari back away. "Was it the griffin that made them do that?" he asked his unlikely partner. "Not the griffin," Ari responded in shock, those being the only words he could say as he looked up. The griffin perched itself on the highest peak in the pass, looking down on the mass of corpses. Gorm looked up at the griffin, noticing a dark figure on its back that was holding a staff. The creature screeched one more time, and the rider got off of its back.

"It's him," Ari said. "Him?" Gorm asked. "There were stories of one who resided in a dark citadel in the North," Ari began. "He must be the one who brought these monsters here," he continued. Gorm looked up, and could only just see the figure and his staff. "How are you so sure?" he asked. "Because glicks and trolls don't simply decide to work together of their own volition. It's not in their nature to do so," Ari explained. "You should know that, by now," he continued. "I do," Gorm said, remembering his many years and everything he had learned during his time in the Guild.

The figure looked about at the devastation below. Bodies of both monsters and men strewn across the pass. They lay motionless in the sodden earth. He raised his staff, and struck it down on the rock beneath him, and a large sphere of dark mana rapidly spread out over the battlefield, blocking out the sun.

"You have fought hard and well," the rumbling voice said. "I have seen your valor, and have proven yourselves worthy warriors," he said. The remaining men looked up at the figure. "I now offer you a choice: Join me, and we shall take over the four countries of the Continent together. In addition, your loved ones and families will be spared. Your other choice is to oppose me and die," he said, spreading his arms as if ready to embrace them.

"Who are you to ask us such a question?" Bashir asked. "I am the one known as the Masked One," the figure replied. "I am but a herald of my master and his power. If you think I hold great power, then that means you know nothing of what power truly is. I am one who sees all and knows all that happens in this realm. I command this horde to do my bidding, but *he*... He is one *far* more powerful than I. Again, I will ask: Will you ally yourselves with me and my horde, or will you suffer the consequences of your choices based on ignorance and folly?" the Masked One asked.

He commands these beasts through his own power alone, and his master is more powerful than he is? Gods above and below... Bashir thought as he looked at him. It was evident that the Masked One certainly did have a power that was greater than an army.

Gorm and Ari now walked over to Bashir, and stood by his side. "My lord, should we believe him?" Ari asked. Bashir looked at the pair, unsure of what to say. "I don't like this one bit," Gorm said. "All the years I've spent in the Guild have taught me never to trust one whose promises sound too good to be true. By Mideia, I'd sooner trust Ari than I would that mage," he continued. Bashir gave Gorm's words a moment to sink in.

"We're dead men, either way, Ari," Bashir began. "Our lives have long since revolved around cheating death in each and every moment. However, it would seem today Death itself has finally caught us red-handed. Our wives, our children, even us - we all come to the same fate in the end. It doesn't matter if we thought ourselves to be good men in life, all that matters is what we choose to do in the present. The past cannot be changed, that much is certain, but right now... Right now, we have a choice to make. Do we abandon our values, our honor, and our countries we've held so dearly, or do we uphold our honor, and fight to the death?" he asked, looking at the pair of unlikely brothers in arms.

He walked over to the two bloodied warriors, and put a hand on either of their shoulders. "I know we may have our differences in opinions, beliefs, and other such matters. However, I must thank you two for being able to see past that, and work together as best you could. You have shown me that there is yet hope for this world, and that someday we may be able to work together in harmony once more," Bashir said. Tears welled in his eyes. "Gorm, I know you want to kill me, and I know Ari wishes to kill you. But I must ask the two of you to stand with me, in one final stand against this evil," Bashir said.

"I'm going to regret this, aren't I?" Gorm sighed heavily.

"Well, I suppose if we are all going to die today, then let's leave this world the same way we all came in: kicking, screaming, and covered in blood," he said, looking at his two unlikely companions.

"I see now the true meaning of valor," Ari began. "You may be an asshole, but you are still human. One filled with honor to fight for what you believe in and the honor you uphold for your country, not only your inherently selfish desire to kill me. I praise you for that, Gorm," he said. "I will see you in the afterlife, Ari. I hope that we can finish this duel when we get there," Gorm said, growing a slight grin on his face. "I'm sure we will," Ari responded in a surprisingly kind tone. "Let us end this, then," Bashir said.

The three of them looked up at the Masked One on his rock. "We will not bow to you, your power, or your promises," Bashir shouted up at him. "Fools," the Masked one said, keeping the dark sphere around them and commanding the remaining army to converge on them. The three drew their swords, and charged together headlong into the fray.

The Masked One watched, as they cut down the first few monsters that came at them. The three were soon overcome by the large force, and their bodies could not be seen amidst the chaos. He undid the dark sphere, not even bothering to watch the warriors' deaths, and placed his staff in its holster on the saddle. He mounted the griffin, the large wings kicking around small rocks beneath him as it took to the sky once more. The horde below him followed him down the far end of the pass.

He led the horde towards Coltend Castle, destroying every town and village in their path like locusts to a field. Bloodshed and fear reigned across the countryside, as the Masked One made his way with his large force of horrid creatures.

As the Pass finally cleared, an unrecognizably bloodied man

had managed to escape the massive horde, stumbling his way down the mountain. He went to the nearest town, where he procured the owner of what he recognized to be a horse stable. "Somebody help!" the stablehand cried out, noticing the man was covered in slash-like cuts, blood pouring profusely from them. "Please, you must help him! He's going to die!" the boy shouted as he ran to the front door of a two-story house. "By the gods, boy, what happened?" Akmed asked urgently, swinging the front door open. "Sir, you have to help him! Look at him!" the boy cried out, pointing towards the newcomer.

Akmed looked at the man, noticing his bloodied state. "Shit. Boy, fetch a pail of clean water and some rags and bandages. Move quickly!" Akmed commanded, rushing towards the man. He was too injured to stand any longer, and collapsed into the stable owner's arms. "Hey! Hang in there! If you can speak, tell me your name and what happened," he said to the wounded man. "A horde of... creatures. A-and... a dark mage... going to...Coltend. Send... raven... to warn... Synners... in Codrean," the man said weakly, coughing up some blood. "I will send the raven as soon as I get your wounds treated," Akmed nodded.

Nearly two hours had passed since the man had arrived at the town, and was only just now finished being treated. After Akmed completed the man's treatment, he wrote the letter, even though his Common wasn't exactly legible. "Sir, I have completed the letter, but I need your name to go along with it," he said gently. The man, covered in bloodied bandages, could hardly turn his head to look at Akmed.

"My name... is Gorm," the man said.

CHAPTER 17

The Journey North

As the moon set in preparation for the morning sun on the distant horizon, there was already movement within the fortress. I gathered my gear from my room and checked every piece to make sure it was in proper working order.

I was still wearing the clothes I had put on just before going to sleep, and in the cold before the light of day, I shivered at their touch. The others in my quarters did the same as they checked their loadouts.

Sword is sharp, my jerkin and boots are clean, too. I think that's about it for here, I thought, putting my gear on, and lacing my sword and scabbard to my leather belt.

"Got everything there, Ed?" I asked. Edryd scratched the few whiskers that grew on his chin. "I think something's missing," he said curiously. "What makes you think that?" I asked. "Well, you see, all of my equipment's here, but my pendant isn't," Edryd said.

"Not sure I've ever noticed you had one," I said, thinking back as far as he could. "Well, it's fucking gone," Edryd said frustratedly, rummaging through his belongings one more time.

"I'll help you look for it," I said, joining my friend in the pursuit of the pendant. "*Uh...*" I began. Edryd looked at him. "What?" he asked flatly. "I have no idea what it looks like," I said with a shrug.

Ed sighed and shook his head.

"It's my family's crest," he began. "My brother wore it during his time as a Synner. After he died, my mother found it in a small box under his bed. Not sure what it was doing there, as he never took it off, but that's where she found it," Edryd said grimly.

"I'm sorry," I said. "You've got nothing to be sorry about," Edryd began. "He died bravely, or so they tell me," he said distantly. "I have no doubts about that," I replied, trying my best to be sympathetic.

"I would if I were you," Edryd began. "What do you mean?" I asked. "Well, you see, he wasn't exactly the bravest of Synners, nor was he the most adept at casting spells. Mother used to say I reminded her a lot of him when he was younger," he continued. "Was that supposed to be a compliment?" I asked.

"Not sure, to be honest," Edryd replied with a light chuckle. "All I know is that I looked up to him, regardless of what my mother or friends thought. He might have had his difficulties with spells and courage in a fight, but he still did his job nonetheless," he said, looking as if he was recalling a few memories from his childhood.

"If it's of any comfort, you're not complete shit at casting spells, and you're pretty good with a sword. I think your brother would be proud of you," I said, trying to cheer my friend up. "You've only ever seen me cast during training," Edryd replied. "I have a hard time remembering that we have that power during a fight, so I simply stick to what I know," he continued. "Well, we could practice that one of these days," I said.

Edryd shook his head. "I fear that this journey may very well spell the end for some of us," he began. "What do you mean?" I asked, hearing the tone in my friend's voice.

I know he's got good instincts, so for him to say something like that... he thought.

"This whole thing of going to Hjalfar to fetch reinforcements is just..." Edryd began, but cut himself off. "Well, we did just suffer a massive attack on the fortress, and the knowledge held here in the wrong hands would bode ill for everyone," he said. "I know. Trust me, I've been thinking the same thing," I replied. Edryd looked at me and opened his mouth to say something, but his face paled, and words were interrupted by Irun who stood in the doorway.

"Need any help?" Irun asked. Edryd felt a small chill go down his spine. "*Uh*, sure," he replied. "What exactly are you looking for?" Irun asked. "My pendant," Edryd replied. Irun pulled an object out of his pocket. "This thing?" he asked. He held a small pendant of a metallic hawk's beak in his hand.

Edryd's eyes opened wide.

"You fucking snitch," he said, tearing the dangling pendant from Irun's hands. "*Whoa, whoa*," Irun said, taken aback. "I didn't steal *shit*. I found that on the floor of the training grounds about two days ago," Irun said.

"*Oh*, and you simply assumed you could take it for your own?" Edryd asked sarcastically. "Actually, I tried to figure out whose it was, but none of my other friends had seen anyone wearing it to know whose it was," Irun replied.

Edryd lowered his head. "I'm sorry. I thought you had wanted to keep it for yourself," he said. "I have no reason to keep trinkets or baubles that hold no mana in them," Irun said nonchalantly.

"By the way, why do you even wear that old thing?" he asked.

"It was my brother's from a long time ago. He died when I was about five years old," Edryd replied, examining the pendant for any damages. Irun didn't say anything in return but for a slight sigh under his breath.

I stood silently, observing the exchange between the two.

"Well, it's back in your hands, and that's all that matters now," I said calmly, stepping in between the two. "Hope it never leaves them again," Edryd said, putting the pendant around his neck. "At least now I know whose crest that is," Irun began. "If it ever goes missing again, I'll bring it straight back to you," he continued, a small, sardonic grin showing on his face. "Sure," Edryd shot back coldly. Irun raised an eyebrow at the remark, but said nothing, and the three of us left the room with our gear.

We made our way to the stables, where we found Batch already preparing his horse. "Early as ever. Did you even get any sleep?" Irun asked as Batch finished tying the last parcel to his saddle.

"Nope. Better to be ready early, than to have to rush to get things done," Batch replied. "Good point, but how slow do you have to be to not get any sleep?" Irun asked jokingly. "It's not that I didn't want to sleep, it's that I couldn't, you dim-witted chuckle-fuck," Batch shot back mercilessly. "*Oh-hoo*, someone's *extra* spicy today," I said in jest, obviously fanning the flames.

Irun was anything but happy about Batch's retort, as he had nothing to return it with, or at least that's what it looked like. "Alright, Batch, you've made your point," Edryd began. "Let the *dim-witted chuckle-fuck* get his stuff ready without taking his head off," he said between laughs.

We each walked over to our own horses, tying supply bags to our saddles which were mostly filled with apples, dried meats, and a few portions of dried fruits and nuts mixed together.

After we finished loading our horses, we walked them out

to the central courtyard, where there were already a few other Synners gathered. Garett was speaking with a couple of bow-casters, while Bernar was talking to Roburn.

"Decided to come along?" Roburn asked us. "Not like we had a choice," Irun shot back. Roburn chuckled. "Nothing like a good ride with *cheery* companions, *eh*, Bernar?" he said. Bernar scoffed and grinned in response.

"At least your little brother has decided to come along willingly," Roburn said. "Waking up before dawn to go towards Hjalfar, on a road I barely know anything about, with glicks and other horrible creatures potentially lying in waiting; I'd hardly call it willingly," I replied with a small chuckle.

"I'm actually somewhat glad you're coming with us," he began. "After that showmanship you put on during the most recent battle, I'd say you're more than ready for this trip," he said with a smile out of the corner of his mouth. I looked to my brother, hoping what I had just heard wasn't in jest, which he confirmed with a simple nod.

"I just hope he doesn't send anyone else to the infirmary this time," Edryd said playfully with a shrug. "I agree," Irun began. "That spell you cast on our way to Coltend was extremely risky. You might have missed and hit Ed with it," he continued.

I looked back at Bernar, almost asking for permission to choke-slam the shithead, but with the patience of a monk, he shook his head in response.

I sighed when I understood what he meant.

"I made my choice, and possibly saved his life in the process," I said coldly. Irun looked at him with a raised eyebrow. "You're not planning on doing that around me, are you?" he asked. "You're a bit of an asshole, so I might consider it," I replied with a shrug. Irun scoffed, and pulled his horse away, leaving the group.

"In his defense, he has been studying a lot, trying to prove himself worthy of going after a senior-level certification," Batch began. "Have you become his protector?" Roburn asked. "No," Batch replied. "I'm simply saying that he's got a lot on his mind. Maybe that's why he's being such a flaccid prick," he continued. Bernar laughed aloud, followed by the others.

"Fuck him, I don't care," I began. "He's got no right to take his bullshit out on us, and I'd rather see him gone along with it if that's how he's going to act around people he's been with most of his life," I spat. Bernar looked at me and knew I meant it. "Naught you can do about that now," Roburn said as I watched Irun lead his horse away.

He's changed over the last few months. Too much, I thought.

The Master walked down the steps from his study, with a small parchment in his hand. His gear was always kept in near perfect condition, and his sword was tightly laced to his belt as he stepped into the courtyard.

One of the stable boys awaited him with the reins in his hand. Daylight was on the rise, and the morning mist could be seen over the distant hills in the background. The Master walked past the other Synners who were gathered in the stone courtyard. He nodded to a few that he had come to know well over the years but maintained his pace.

He reached his horse, taking the reins from the stable boy who looked into his glowing yellow eyes as he did. "It is unlikely that we will return anytime soon. In the meantime, I want you to go home to your family, as you should be with your loved ones in these trying times," the Master said quietly as he handed the stable boy a bag of coins that was likely ten times the boy's salary.

"M-master, this is too much!" the stablehand exclaimed. "It's not just for you, silly. It's for your family, too," he said, scruffing up the boy's hair. With the last words, the boy's expression sank.

"But... I don't have a family to go home *to*, Master," the stablehand began. "Since I've started working here, you have all treated me better than I ever could have hoped, and for that, I am eternally grateful. You have all treated me like the family I never had. Some have even allowed me to practice some swordplay, and I have done my best to learn what I can," he continued.

The Master was visibly touched by this display of gratitude and placed a hand on the boy's shoulder. "Well, if you've no family to go to, would you like to come with us? You can ride with one of the carts, and I'm sure we could use your help with taking care of the horses," he said gently.

The boy was ecstatic with the Master's words. "You mean that, Master?" he asked excitedly. "I do. Go and gather your things. We're leaving in a few minutes. Hurry, now," the Master said, giving the command in a gentle tone. "I won't let you down, Master!" the boy said, happily sprinting off to gather what little belongings he had. A gentle smile grew on the Master's face, but quickly vanished when he remembered what he had to do next.

After having made sure all the others were prepared to leave, the Master mounted his horse, looking out over the crowd. He could feel the words he was about to say weigh heavily in his heart.

"I despise being the bearer of bad news, but I have received messages this evening that a large force of glicks, trolls, and other foul creatures have defeated a Harutian army destined for Coltend," he began. A few shocked gasps and murmurs could be heard throughout the crowd as we all looked at each other, likely wondering whether or not this was going to be a suicide mission.

"Not only that, but King Truls has been murdered, and now the Church has forcibly taken command of Coltend Castle. Therefore, our goals are now twofold: To protect Coltend from the oncoming horde, and restore order to the capital of this country. Perhaps a few of you will not like the idea, or maybe even decide to flee before the battle of our time, but believe me when I say that there is more at stake than simply saving a city," he said.

"As it currently stands, we must ride to Hjalfar to seek help, since the Rhydian Pass has been overrun with beasts, denying help from either Harut or Caegwen. I must know who will stand with me, and their fellow Synners to save our country and possibly others from this dreadful fate," the Master continued. A few of the Synners shifted in their saddles, glancing at one another in an attempt to see who would be the first to decline the challenge.

"I will not consider you as outcasts if you decide to leave now, but know that the odds of us *all* coming home are slim at best," he said, giving the crowd one more chance.

No one moved.

"Very well, then. We ride to Hjalfar," he said, the great wooden doors opening to the empty road ahead of them. The Master was the first to exit the fortress, followed closely by Bernar, Anwill, and Garett. I was ahead of the others in hopes of staying as close to my brother and the Master as I could. The sound of hooves echoed across the courtyard, taking over the quiet of the first light of day.

"It might be a hopeless cause," he said to Garett who rode by his side. "I might very well be leading them to their doom," he continued, barely loud enough for me to hear. "Perhaps not for all of us," Garett began. "This may be our final stand, but I am sure we will succeed in protecting this Continent to the extent of our abilities," he said.

"I admire your optimism," the Master replied, staring down the road for any potential threats. "So do I," Bernar chimed in. "I mean, this might not be the brightest idea we've ever had, but it's our only hope of not being completely overrun and having it stolen from us," he continued.

"Which is exactly why we must not fail," the Master said to Bernar. "I just hope the traitor among us, whose identity we have yet to uncover, will not pose too much of a threat to where it jeopardizes our mission," the Master said quietly. "We'll soon know who it is," Garett said. "Once again, your optimism is outstanding," the Master returned.

I was desperately trying to overhear what was being said, but failed to hear any further due to the thunderous sound of horses. We came to the crossroads and turned left, heading down the northern way. We rode with the sun to our right; the early rays of sunshine beaming across the blood-red sky.

I watched the sunrise for a moment, observing the sky and its gradual shifting of incredible colors.

A blood-sky on the morning of a voyage, that can't be a good omen, I thought.

I took it as a sign, and closed my eyes for a moment, remembering why we were heading north in the first place and tried to focus on our newfound purpose.

I watched the sky begin to disappear behind the ever-thickening trees. Birds sang in the high canopy of the woods, completely oblivious to the ones below them and our fate-deciding quest. I listened to their early morning songs, breathing in the woodland air deeply. I filled my mind with their songs, and my lungs with air in hopes of calming myself down.

If fate has already decided where and when each and every one of us will fall, then I have nothing to fear, because everything will happen the way it is meant to, I thought.

I have been trained to always be prepared to die, but never to go down without a fight, and that is exactly what I plan to do - slash, punch, kick, and scream my way to a glorious death, I thought with a slight grin on my face, as a fantastical scene played out in my mind.

Perhaps the gods will smile upon me as they did to the Lord of Codrean so many years ago. Instead of a physical gift, I would rather they give me the strength to face whatever comes, and if they deny me that, then I will die knowing I have tried my best to protect both myself and the ones around me from a horrific fate, I exhaled heavily.

I looked behind me at the other Synners who were possibly having the same thoughts as me. "I never would have thought it would come to this," Edryd began. "I had always thought I would die on some hunt, far away from here," he said grimly. "You won't die," I said firmly.

"You can't promise me that," Edryd replied. "Never have, never will. You're my best friend, and I know that no matter what happens, whether either of us dies, that our memories and reputation will live on forever," I said.

"Well that's comforting, I suppose," Edryd said with a false smile. "Don't get all emotional before the battle, you tits," Bernar interrupted the two. "It fucks with your head, and that is not something you want to happen. We haven't even reached Hjalfar yet, and you're already thinking about your deaths?" Bernar asked.

"Well, it's not like it isn't a possibility," Edryd replied. "It'd better not be," Bernar replied. "Don't want you to wet your hose again before you even draw your sword," he said. "That wasn't even me!" Edryd replied. "Sure it wasn't," Bernar said with a laugh. "Shut up, you two," Garett spat back.

I looked at my brother with an upturned lip and raised eyebrows. "Not a word," Bernar scowled at me, pointing his index finger between my eyes. "I didn't say anything," I replied, grinning brightly. Bernar squinted his eyes, and retook his place at the Master's side.

"What is it between your brother and the Master, anyways? I mean, I know they both have the same glowing yellow eyes and all, but what's that got to do with playing favorites?" Batch asked, finally joining in on the conversation.

"Couldn't tell you even if I tried," I replied. "You don't have the same eyes as your brother, and yet the Master still seems to take you closer under his wing than the rest of us," Irun added. "Look, I don't know a damn thing about the Master and his choice of favorites, alright?" I shot back.

"*Ooooh,* kitty's got claws. Should I be scared?" Irun said, mockingly. "They'll tear you from taint to throat, if you push me far enough. Whether you're scared or not is of no concern to me," I returned. "You wish you could take me in a proper fight," Irun said under his breath.

Oh, I don't wish, but I will *do what I must, you conniving shit-blossom,* I thought after catching what Irun muttered.

We continued on our journey, down the beaten path towards the borders of Hjalfar. We came to a choke in the river, which was teeming with aquatic lifeforms; trout, salmon, frogs and other such animals could be seen just beneath the surface of the crystalline water. The horses and wagons had no difficulty wading through the gentle current as everyone crossed safely to the other side.

"We have just crossed into Hjalfar," Garett said to the four of us behind him. "This land is full of dangers, many more so than Coltend, so be on your guard," he continued.

We began to observe our surroundings more closely, as the

landscape changed from a wide variety of trees into a pine forest. Birds and other beasts could be heard off in the distant reaches of the forest, far away from the road we were on, when something stirred in the distance.

Garett picked up on the moving figures through the trees, and immediately moved towards the Master. "Master, we're not alone," he said quietly, nodding in the figures' general direction. The Master peered through the gaps in the trees, and found the three figures off in the distance. "Let's go," he said, turning his horse towards them.

Bernar followed closely behind them and signaled for me to do the same, while Garett motioned for the others to stop.

Bernar, the Master and I rode through the trees, leaping over rotting logs and low-lying bushes that were in our path. The figures saw them coming, and rushed to find cover. The Master reached where the three figures once stood, and looked about him, finding little more than a few footprints in the disturbed mossy floor.

"We mean you no harm if you mean none to us," the Master called out.

No answer came.

Suddenly, a large man appeared from behind one of the larger pine trees. "Hallo, Master," the man said. "Thorsen!" the Master said astonished. "Where are the other two who were with you?" he asked. Leona and Meliss came out from behind a nearby shrubbery, dirtied and cold.

Your majesty, young lady," the Master bowed from his saddle. "Not so *majestic* any longer, master Synner. I am just a woman who has naught but her life," she said, returning the bow.

Bernar looked at her with wide eyes, remembering her beauty from the first time he saw her at the council.

What's the fucking queen doing here? Holy shit, is that who I think it is? She's alive! I hope she's not hurt, I thought, realizing Meliss was hiding herself behind Thorsen's large figure.

"You have no horses with you? How have you come so far from Coltend?" the Master asked the giant. "We failed to find any during our escape, Master, so I carried these two until I was sure we would be safe. Coltend has suffered a great treachery, Master," Thorsen began. He, too, was dirtied, and his armor was riddled with small specks of earth and moss.

"We're aware of the situation, but we only have minimal details," Bernar stated. "The Church decided that we were unholy and unfit to rule over Coltend, and so they took matters into their own hands by slaying nearly every innocent person who had failed to escape, or supported the royal family within the palace walls," Leona began. "I fear that by now they may have taken over the entire city.

"I didn't know priests knew how to fight like warriors," Bernar said. "Neither did I," Leona began. "They must have paid off most of the Guild to turn a blind eye to ensure their success in taking over the city," she said grimly. "I can think of more than a few who would readily accept such a deal," Thorsen added.

"This is ill news, indeed," the Master said. "I pray you are able to tell me how it all began," he said. "I was fast asleep in my quarters, when the sound of screams echoed up from the hall to my ears," Leona began.

"I went downstairs to investigate the cause of the screams, and found the majority of my staff strewn across the floor, with the symbol of the Church engraved in their foreheads, and their throats slit from ear to ear. I found Meliss fleeing from a few of the murderers, and we fled to find Thorsen, for he was the only one I could think of at the time who may have been able to help us. He gave us each a dagger, and we made our way towards the nearest gate, where we encountered some resistance. He fought bravely, and healed the wound that an arrow had made when it struck my shoulder," she explained.

"He healed it? How?" Bernar asked, visibly intrigued. "He did so with *mana*," Leona replied with a smile. "He is one of the last Synners of Grundvollr to have survived the attack that didn't turn to banditry," she explained.

Well I'll be... I thought, shocked at the news.

The Master, not as confused but still surprised nevertheless, looked at Thorsen who simply nodded. "It is true, Master," Thorsen replied proudly.

"You mentioned Grundvollr was attacked? When? How did we not hear of this?" the Master asked after a brief pause. "King Mads had declared that its fall should remain a secret, one that remained so for over forty years. He considered anyone who had survived the attack to be a failure and a disappointment, hunting and branding them outcasts as a result," Thorsen began.

"Only I and one other remained true to our lives as Synners for a time after, though he and I later went our separate ways," he said. "By the gods, I am sorry to hear that," the Master replied sadly. "As am I for having lived through it," Thorsen said.

The Master thought for a moment. "If Grundvollr has fallen, why are you heading North? We were going under the assumption Grundvollr was still active, but why are you going that way?" he asked.

"You see, Master, the fact that Grundvollr had fallen had stopped me from pursuing a Synner's life after a while, but it didn't stop the other one who had survived," Thorsen began. "He's hidden here in the southern part of Hjalfar, far away from Mads' reach and began a hidden Synner school," he said.

The Master and Bernar looked at each other. "Where is the school?" the Master asked. "Well, I'd be more than happy to show you, Master, but we have come a long way, and I fear the ladies might not hold out much longer at the pace we have maintained thus far," Thorsen said. The Master looked at Leona and Meliss, who were both equally filthy. "I will have horses brought for you," the Master said. "Thank you, Master," Leona replied.

"Bernar, take Leona with you back to the others. *Oh*, and Thoma," he said, finally acknowledging my presence. "Yes, Master?" I asked sheepishly. "You'll take Meliss with you. We'll get them some food and horses with the others," The Master said with a wolfish grin.

Fuuuuuuuuck, I thought as I realized what he was doing.

"I don't believe your horse will carry the two of us, Master," Thorsen said, judging the horse's size. It was a war horse, but Thorsen knew it would break under their combined weight. "I can hold my own," Thorsen said with a toothy grin. "Let's move, then," the Master said.

My heart nearly stopped beating entirely.

This can't be happening, he thought. *I mean, I'm glad to see her, and more than happy to have her ride with me, but I'm a nervous wreck. Think I'd rather face an ochelon again than trying to maintain my composure right now,* I thought, feeling my pulse begin to quicken.

She stretched out her hand with a warm smile as I was helping her up to ride behind me. She wrapped her hands around my waist and squeezed lightly.

He's got that shit-eating grin of his again, I thought as I noticed my brother staring at me.

My heart raced and my palms began to sweat as my body felt as if it was about to implode. "You're not about to spit your morning meal, are you?" Meliss asked me playfully. "N-no, I'm alright," I replied in a shaky voice.

Bernar helped Leona get behind him in the saddle. While I couldn't read his mind, I knew a nervous look on my brother's face when I saw it.

That's not to say mine was any better, to be fair.

The Master rode at a slow trot, with Thorsen jogging briskly beside him. Meanwhile, Bernar kept Leona in place, feeling her thin arms wrapped around his waist. We soon reached the others, where Garett had stopped the small army, and I saw the look on Ed and Batch's faces when they noticed who I had behind me.

Bernar helped Leona to the ground, where she was greeted by Garett and another Synner who offered her water and food. I helped Meliss dismount my horse, with a little help from Bernar, and she thanked him warmly. Just before turning to accept a meal offered to her, she gave me as warm a smile as she could muster.

I smiled like a child on the morn of his birthday in return.

Leona maintained her graceful composure, dirty, hungry, and disheveled as she was, while she drank the water offered to her. "Your majesty," Garett said, with a bow. "You needn't call me that any longer, for Coltend has fallen to our enemies and I am its queen no more," she said.

I couldn't take my eyes off Meliss, whose sole purpose in that moment was to ingest the food offered to her. She ate and drank her fill, and life returned to her in a flash. I tried to take my gaze off of her, but failed miserably.

She caught me looking at her and gave me a shy smile like she was embarrassed to eat. I returned the smile, and did my best to encourage her to eat her fill without saying a word.

You are a fucking fool, Thoma Fayren, I thought.

"As I had no knowledge of the hidden school, I'd like to ask you its precise location, now that we're in a more secure area," the Master said to Thorsen. "It is in Fangsdalr, Master. Only about a day's ride from here," Thorsen replied with a mouthful of bread.

"A hidden school? We'd best be on our way, then. Time is of the essence, after all," Garett said, not fully understanding why their destination was about to change. "Get horses for the lady and Thorsen, we must ride at once," the Master shouted.

Two of the extra horses were brought out for Leona and Thorsen, who immediately got into their saddles. "Meliss, you can ride with Thoma again," the Master said, with a grin just large enough to wrinkle the scar on his cheek. "Thank you, Master," she replied kindly.

I felt my face flush with blood so quickly that if Meliss had seen it in that state, she might have agreed with my earlier thought about exploding.

"We ride to Fangsdalr," the Master called out, turning his horse. Thorsen rode beside him, and they held an inaudible conversation. Bernar rode just beside us and next to Leona in silence, with a look on his face that clearly showed he was trying *not* to make a fool of himself.

His eyes darted at her periodically as he noted she had perfect riding form. The hems of her dirtied robes were draped over the sides, and gently flowed in the wind.

"I've never known a queen to ride with such ease," Bernar began, stumbling over his own words like a nervous child.

It made me giddy to see my once-confident brother shaking in his boots over a woman, just like my inexperienced ass.

"Thank you, though I'm not as adept as you Synners are," she replied with a warm smile. Bernar blushed, and smiled shyly back. "No need to blush," Leona said comfortingly. "I'm sorry, your majesty. I don't know why I am, truth be told," he said shyly.

Leona looked at him as if she knew he was around her age, but with far less experience in dealing with people who didn't carry a sword, or who weren't whores. She looked at his freshly shaved face, and newly braided black hair with an intent I couldn't read.

To his benefit, his glowing yellow eyes only added to his mysteriousness.

"You already know my name, and yet I didn't catch yours earlier," Leona said inquisitively. "Bernar Fayren from Kinth, your majesty," he answered. Leona was puzzled. "I don't believe I have ever heard of Kinth before," she said.

"*Oh*, it's a small village somewhere on the map, your majesty. Don't believe it holds much to be well known," Bernar said, dismissively. "Well, you come from there, so it at least held something of value," Leona said cheerfully. I was sure Bernar's heart skipped a beat or two, and after a slight pause, the two chuckled quietly.

"Meliss, the girl who's here with me, is from the Gramm Isles," Leona began, trying to continue the conversation. "I think you two might have something in common, for until I met her, I had only ever heard rumors about the place," she said. "Well, I just hope she and my brother get along well enough. After all, they are riding together," Bernar said, nodding his head backwards.

Leona looked beyond him and straight into my eyes. With a quick, darting glance, she realized whose arms were wrapped around my waist, forcing me to blush even worse than I already had.

"He's redder than a maple leaf in autumn," she commented quietly, yet playfully. "What is his name?" she asked.

"Thoma," Bernar replied. "He's just turned eighteen, and the horse he's riding is the one I gave him as a gift, your majesty," he explained. "You two get along well, I assume," Leona said factually. "We do. Quite well, at that. He's not as strong as I was when I was his age, about five years back, but he's got a good head on his shoulders, and a strong will; hard things to find in one person these days," he said.

"Am I included in that select group of people?" Leona asked playfully. "I believe you to be beyond that, your majesty," Bernar said with as low a bow as he could manage on horseback.

"You don't have to continue calling me *your majesty*, if you don't want to," Leona began. "I am no longer the queen of Coltend, and as it currently stands, I am simply a woman with the will to continue living, even if my old life of servants and banquets have come to an abrupt end," she said with a small frown. Bernar and I clearly understood what she meant.

She's made it clear that she didn't want to be treated as royalty, but as a person. A human being. I can't imagine what life must have been like for her until now, I thought, looking at the solemn expression on her porcelain features.

My brother, likely seeing the same thing I had just seconds prior, nodded his head in understanding. "I can respect that," Bernar said with a smile, which she returned in kind. I watched the two of them continue their cheerful conversation, telling tales of happenings in their lives, from daily habits to troubled times.

I just realized I haven't said much of anything since we set off again. Maybe she thinks I'm weird? Shit, what do I do? How the hell do you even talk to a woman? I'm scared, I thought, never once ignoring the fact that Meliss' arms were wrapped around my waist.

"I never got your name," Meliss whispered.

I froze.

Oookay, it's happening. Uhhh... think. Okay, we can do this! At least try to act naturally, I thought.

"Thoma," I replied. "Name suits you," Meliss said in her thick accent. "You're Meliss, right?" I asked. "How'd you know?" she asked with a hint of sarcasm. "I remember you from the first time you showed up to take our armor back in the room at Coltend Castle," I said.

"You had to strip yourself down to nothing but your birthday suit. I remember," Meliss said with a chuckle.

"Hell of a way to meet someone for the first time," I said with a smile. "I'm sure there are worse ways to meet someone for the first time," she said playfully. "Your accent... you're not from the Continent, are you?" I asked bashfully.

"No, I came to the Continent about a year after my father died. My mother got us a job at the Castle a little while after we had arrived. I've been there ever since I was a wee child. The Castle, Leona, and the other servants there have given me so much to be thankful for... I feel like I could never repay them for their kindness to me," she said, her tone dropping into a slight melancholy.

If only I could look at her right now, I thought.

I couldn't, and I knew that. Instead, I looked down at the small hands that fidgeted with each other. "Is something wrong?" I asked. "It might be a little much to say right now," she said hesitantly. "You've likely been through a lot already, so don't feel bad about getting it off your chest," I said as comfortingly as I could.

I felt her take a deep, shuddering breath, leaning her forehead against the middle of my back.

"I killed a man who wanted to kill me just before we fled the castle," Meliss began. "I don't know how to deal with it," she said shakily. I could almost *hear* the tears running down her cheeks.

For a moment, I thought about what she said. I'd never had never killed another *human* before, only monsters, so I could relate to what she was going through, but only a little. "Well, what I'm about to say might not be of any consolation, but I hope it helps put things into perspective," I began.

"I've been training all my life to kill monsters. Terrifying creatures who wished nothing more than to see me dead on the floor, even though I have done nothing to them to bring that upon myself. However, until a few weeks ago, I had never actually *killed* anything," I paused, doing my best to choose my next words carefully.

"I had to kill them to protect myself and the others around me, and the bloodshed I've seen has since stuck with me. The man you killed was no different from the monsters I've had to kill. He wanted to see you dead and he wanted to destroy an innocent life; making him no different than any monster out there. You did what you had to do to survive, and you should not feel sorry for ridding the world of such an evil person," I said calmly.

Meliss sobbed behind him, and tightened her grip around my waist. "Thank you," she said softly between her sobs. I looked down at the tiny hands, and placed one of mine on hers. The small hands responded by gripping my calloused ones tightly, hearing her sob just a little harder.

"I don't know what I can say that will make you feel better," I began. "The most I can say is that you did the right thing, at the right moment. If you hadn't, you wouldn't be here, and I wouldn't have gotten to see you again. To me, that would have been an immense tragedy," I said calmly.

Meliss' sobbing slowed down a little, as though my words

had actually worked their intended magic.

"I'm glad to be here, and I'm even happier that I'm here with *you*," she said quietly, turning her face to lean her cheek on my back. "Me, too," I smiled, but said nothing else, hoping to not ruin the moment.

The two of us rode on in silence, though I watched the conversation between his brother and the queen that seemed to be going quite smoothly; wishing I could do the same with the one riding with me at some point.

I wonder if I'll ever be as happy as those two seem to be with each other, I thought idly.

I looked up at the canopy, seeing the sun's rays scattered throughout our surroundings. Birds could be heard calling their mates off in the distant ceiling of branches above me, and wildlife on the ground shuffled the leaves around the trees, scurrying to find their breakfast of beetles and other such grubs to munch on. A weak breeze cut through the dense forest, making everything seem… *peaceful.*

This place makes me want to believe that there is no evil looming just around every corner. It's almost as if this were an entire world that has been separated and secluded from centuries of destruction by those damn monsters, I thought.

The Master still spoke with Thorsen ahead of him, and I strained my hearing to listen in on what they were talking about. "Master," Thorsen began. "Do you really think he'll be ready?" he asked. "He's stronger than he looks," the Master replied. "He may not look like it physically, but that boy has a willpower I don't think I've seen in a long time," he continued. "I pray you're right, Master," Thorsen said. "As do I," the Master said pensively.

What was that about? I wondered.

I knew they were talking about me, but as to what they

meant *exactly* was far beyond my comprehension of the short conversation.

We rode until dusk and stopped along the side of the road where we made camp beneath the trees. The rising moon's light cast little light through the canopy beneath it. The silver rays licked the ground they could find through the canopy, while our centralized campfire filled the remaining dark spaces around us.

For that night, Meliss and I were separated, having been given a tent for her and Leona to share until better lodging could be acquired. They didn't complain, but I knew it couldn't have been easy on them.

Nevertheless, we slept blissfully, as the forest that teemed with life around us, slept as well.

Just before dawn, we were awake once more, gearing up for another day of riding down the beaten paths towards Fangsdalr. Meliss appeared from her tent, as a few seniors helped her and Leona pack their things. She seemed to have recovered from her small breakdown the previous day, and greeted me with a warm smile.

She could melt ice with that smile, I thought, feeling the winged creatures in my stomach doing consecutive backflips.

"Good morning," she said brightly. "It's much better now that I've seen you smiling," I replied with a warm smile. I saw Meliss feel the blood rush to her face, as her eyes widened, and she turned her face away momentarily. "Ready to go?" I asked, trying my best not to call her out on her reddened features. She didn't verbally reply, only giving me a curt nod, before taking my extended hand to help her onto Celer's back.

She sat behind me as she did the day before, making me a little nervous. Although, I do remember that I could almost feel the warmth from her smile as she wrapped her arms around my waist again. It brought a subtle smile to my face that, unfortunately for me, was spotted by both my brother and Leona.

They, too, had just finished packing up and were now mounting as well. He smiled at Leona, who blushed ever so lightly, prompting a quiet, subtle chuckle from him.

Role reversal since yesterday? Huh, who would've thought? I almost said aloud, but bit my tongue to not ruin their little moment.

Within a few moments, the entire group was off, heading north-east down the path, with the Master at the helm. Batch and Irun had stuck together for most of the journey, avoiding mine and Ed's attempts to get them to join in on the conversation. My best guess was that the presence of both Leona and Meliss made them uncomfortable, but I had no real way of being sure.

We rode for a few more hours, observing the changes in terrain from grassy and forested plains to steep hills and mountains off in the distance. As we crossed over the bridge that had been built long ago that stretched over the Elv Avliv, everyone watched as the strong current flowed quickly beneath the bridge.

The water was perfectly clear with all forms of aquatic life, both in the water and on the banks, taking in the early morning rays of sunlight. Meliss observed the world around her, likely feeling as if she had returned to the Gramm Isles.

"I've heard tales of great, winged creatures that live deep in the mountains," Meliss said. "You mean to say that there are wyrms and wyverns living in this portion of the Continent?" Edryd asked.

"Well, I didn't say that, specifically," Meliss began. "I've heard it said that one of the greatest ones of... whatever those names were, fell from a ball of flame from the sky," she said.

"Interesting," Edryd said.

"Let's just hope none decide to drop in on us during our time here," I said. "Don't know what we would do if one did," Edryd. "Fight it with our fists? Hell of a way to go, if you ask me," I said sarcastically. Meliss and Edryd chuckled at the thought - terrifying as it was.

"What's it like being a Synner?" Meliss asked. "Well, you wake up in the morning, eat some unidentifiable goop that looks like something that came out of a troll's nostrils, then practice your sword fighting and casting abilities for most of the day," I replied.

"Then you fall asleep, hoping that the few bruises on your hands will heal the next day, only to find out your roommate has lit the room on fire with a mana-flame, and stupidly used a piss-filled bucket to try and douse it," Edryd chimed in.

"That was a *one-time* thing, Ed! For fuck's sake, I'm never going to live that down, am I?" I asked, my cheeks flushed with color. Meliss was giggling at the thought of the situation. "Once was enough to mentally scar me, so thanks for that!" Ed continued mockingly.

"But it's true. I always hope my bruises will heal the next day, and I tend to get a lot of them," Edryd said. "Only time that ever happened to you was when you failed to pay attention, dipshit," Bernar said, butting in on our conversation.

"Have you ever gotten hit in that way since I told you that?" he asked. "Not as often as I used to, I suppose," Edryd shook his head. "*Heh*, guess I'm not a horrible teacher after all," Bernar said with a chuckle.

"I don't know much of anything about mana," Meliss said shyly. "Well, it's not that hard to understand," Bernar began proudly. "All you have to know is that there are other realms outside of the one we currently live in, and each of those realms holds their own power. As it stands right now, we can only tap into two of them, one light and one dark," he explained.

"Which one do you *tap into*?" Meliss asked curiously as the terminology sat oddly in her mouth. "We mainly tap into the Ethereal - the lighter of the two realms. Although, that's not to say that there haven't been Synners known to tap into both. However, they are usually quickly seduced by the more voracious and easier Underworld - the dark realm. When that happens, they generally go against everything we stand for and are thereby outcast from the ranks," Bernar explained.

"You mean to tell me that there are evil Synners lying about the world?" Meliss asked. "Everything has a good side, and a bad side - from the greatest of kings, to the lowliest of servants," Bernar explained.

"In the words of the Master himself, *One must always strive to do good unto others. Unless, of course, that bastard has done something worthy of your wrath. Lean not into the temptation of the Underworld's power, but instead, rely on your own judgment, lest you find yourself counted among the most vile of the world.* I try to stick to that perspective," Bernar quoted his Master in a near perfect imitation.

The others and I laughed like there wasn't an impending doom waiting for us at Coltend Castle. The Master caught the sound of his voice being imitated and turned to see who it was. However, instead of getting angry about it, he grinned a little, wrinkling the skin around the scar on his face, and turned to face the road ahead of him once more.

The four of us continued to talk about our day to day lives, and Meliss shared what little experience she had had during her time as a servant to the queen.

Bernar, of course, was particularly interested in that part.

He watched Leona, as she was deep in conversation with

Thorsen just a few horse lengths in front of him, and smiled after learning all that she had done for the young girl.

Eventually, Leona joined in on our conversation and shared a few of her own experiences. Edryd and I took a little while to get used to someone from royalty to be so understanding and... *humane*.

It wasn't without reason that we had come to believe that royal families were often snub-nosed, ambulatory nutsacks with assholes for mouths. However, we soon became more comfortable with having her around, and no longer saw her as the queen, but as a person whose wit and personality were that of an angel among men.

I can see why my brother likes talking to her so much. Gods above, I hope he doesn't say anything stupid, I thought.

The sun began to set, and the bright orange rays were reflected by the rocks and trees around us, making everything look like it was coated in a thin sheet of gold. We could see the Elv Avliv beneath them shimmering in the golden sunlight - flowing as swiftly and surely as ever.

"I never thought I would live to see a sight like that," Leona began. "In all of my years going from room to room, servants or guards trailing closely behind me; an adventure such as this was something I thought could only ever happen in books," she said.

"I think I speak for everyone, especially my brother, when I say that we're honored to be able to show you this, even if it's not in the most perfect of conditions," I said, mustering any and all formal training I'd had during our week or so at the palace.

Leona looked at the others, who nodded in agreement, and smiled warmly. "It makes me glad to be in the company of such honorable, and fine people," she replied, her pale-blue eyes aimed right into mine. I blushed as I felt Meliss pull closer than before.

I could get used to this, I thought.

"We've arrived," the Master called out. Anwill, who had been silent the whole way, breathed a sigh of relief. He must have been contemplating what needed to be done, among other such matters like mortality and the fragility of life itself. "About damn time," he said to Bernar who laughed a little.

"An old man like you must hate traveling this far in one go," he said with a grin. "*Elf*, and that's bullshit," Anwill began. "I rather like traveling, it's just that I hate not knowing where I'm going," he said with a shrug. "Can't say I disagree with you, there," Bernar replied.

The Master rode ahead with Thorsen and Garett to the top of the path. The others were soon where the Master had once been, looking out over a few wooden houses, and a small fortress made of solid stone.

A single man stood atop the wooden palisade, wearing a black leather jerkin that had green scales sewn into it. His white, shoulder-length hair flowed in the breeze, and his glowing yellow eyes watched the oncoming party.

"Master Pyle Rumia," the Master called out. "The Master of Codrean," Pyle shouted back. "What brings you here to my humble abode?" he asked with his arms spread wide.

"We have traveled long and hard to find you," the Master began. "Thorsen has told us of Grundvollr's demise, and so we have come to you seeking aid," he said. "Magnar Thorsen is with you?" Pyle asked. "Hallo, my old friend," Thorsen shouted back in his thick accent.

"It is you! It has been too long," Pyle laughed heartily. "Indeed, it has been! It's good to see you're alive and well, friend!" Thorsen shouted up at him. "Come in!" Pyle shouted, motioning for the gates to the wooden palisade to be opened.

We rode inside, noticing that there were many more houses

inside than outside than they could have imagined. Pyle came down from the top of the palisade to greet us. Thorsen was the first one off his horse, and ran over to greet him. They were about the same height, and to the shorter Synners, it seemed as though two gods were greeting each other.

"You've put on some weight," Pyle said. "Being in Coltend's Guild will do that to you," Thorsen replied. "Master, this is the one I spoke of," Thorsen said, watching the Master dismount his horse. "We've met before, but possibly long before you were born, Thorsen," the Master said cheerfully. "It's good to see you, again," he said, greeting Pyle with a firm handshake. "I thought that after that incident with the Ochelon by the river you would never have come back," Pyle said.

"I have always meant to return, not only to visit Hjalfar, but to thank you as well," the Master said. "Nonsense," Pyle began. "I knew you'd find a use for what I had taught you, and it seems as though you have," he said, looking into Bernar's eyes. "Indeed I have," the Master said, looking over at Bernar, who dismounted and came over to the three.

"An honor to meet you, Pyle," he said, stretching out his hand. "Likewise," Pyle replied, taking the outstretched hand, and giving a nearly bone-crushing handshake.

"So, down to business," Pyle began. "What sort of aid do you seek?" he asked. "Well, we have traveled a long way to get here, so I think a place to rest and feed our horses will suffice for now," the Master began. "*Ah*, yes. My apologies, it's been a long time since we've had any visitors who came on friendly pretenses," Pyle said.

He put two fingers in his mouth, and let off an ear-piercing whistle. Out of the nearby stables, a group of stable boys came rushing out. The stable hand from Codrean rushed up from the cart he was riding in as well.

"Ready for your orders, Master Pyle," the boy said. "See to their horses, and make sure they are well taken care of. They have journeyed far, so I expect nothing but the best for these horses, understand?" Pyle commanded. A unified nod came from the boys, and they were off, taking the first few horses they could gather.

Thorsen, Pyle, the Master, Bernar, Anwill, and Garett walked together, discussing a few things just out of earshot of the others. "He didn't even introduce me," Leona said, somewhat discouraged. "I don't think the Master would want it to be known that you are here, lest someone spread the news that you're still alive," Thoma replied. "I suppose you're right. I hadn't considered that news to have possibly traveled so far, so fast," Leona said.

Bernar returned after a few moments, with a smile on his face. "Thoma, Leona, Meliss, and Edryd - I'm to show you to your quarters," he said, still smiling. "What of the others?" Leona asked. "According to Pyle, they will be more than adequately taken care of. Come, quickly," he said, taking Leona's hand.

Needless to say, most of us were surprised, including Meliss.

"Wonder what he's all worked up about," Edryd asked. "Can't say for sure, but it must be a good thing if he's smiling," I replied.

We followed him down the main street, where everyone openly carried a sword, living peaceful lives. There were no beggars nor any apparent signs of poverty within the palisade. "This place reminds me a lot of Codrean, ironically enough," Edryd said, observing his surroundings. Thoma smiled and did the same, taking note of everything he could find. "Everyone carries a sword, and yet there doesn't seem to be any sign of violence here," Meliss added.

"It's a lot like how we are at Codrean. We all understand that a real disagreement would likely lead to someone's death, which is why we speak the way we do to each other. Releasing constant tension through snide remarks and foul language, ironically enough, staves off physical violence quite a bit," Thoma explained. Leona pondered his words for a few moments. "That... actually makes a lot of sense. The court could do well to learn some tricks from you Synners," she concluded.

We followed Bernar into Pyle's house where the others, Anwill included, were seated around a large, wooden table cut from an ancient cedar tree. The size of the table made me think that it had been made from more than simply one tree.

I was wrong, of course.

"Come, sit, for we have much to discuss," Pyle gestured towards the vacant chairs. Each had their own distinct carvings of ancient and heroic feats performed by Synners of old.

The Master has one of these in his study, I thought back to the chair in Codrean.

"Ladies and gentlemen," Pyle began. "It has been a long time since I have had any visitors aside from traders and merchants, or other nefarious folk, so please forgive any inadequacies that you may find," he said. "I would like to first speak to Leona, who even though she has been unlawfully removed from her throne, still remains a queen to all of us," he said with a smile. "I am truly flattered," she said with a bow of her head.

"The others in this town do not know who you are, which is why I made no ceremony when I saw you, but I knew exactly who you were; the main reason I have decided to speak with you in a more *private* setting," Pyle said.

"Told you," I whispered to Leona who sat by my side.

"Keeping that in mind, I am more than certain that there are people here who would gladly sell you out to your attackers for a measly coin purse, but I will not allow that to happen,"

Pyle continued.

"The Master has also informed me that a large force of monsters has just gone through the Rhydian Pass, making their way West, and possibly, to Coltend. We have discussed all possibilities, and I've already agreed to the terms the Master and Anwill have presented. Hopefully, with yours and Thorsen's help, we will find a way to take back what is rightfully yours," he said cheerfully.

"But first, I would have you and Meliss tell your story, as I would like to hear how this all came to be so I can have a better understanding of what we're getting ourselves into," he continued, gesturing for her to begin her explanation. "Thank you, Master Pyle," she replied with yet another bow.

Over the course of the next hour or so, Leona and Meliss explained everything that had transpired over the course of the past week. Thorsen added in a few of his own points, and made mention of their tactics, in hopes of shedding some more light on the group.

After hearing the complete story, Pyle sighed heavily, and nodded his head with grave understanding. "Thank you for sharing that, your majesty. It must have been a harrowing experience, but I'm glad you made it out alive," he said, lowering his head in reverence. "We couldn't have done it without Thorsen, though," Leona replied.

"I know. He's one of the most trustworthy people I've had the honor of meeting," he said with a warm smile. "Speaking of which: Edryd, as I understand it, you are Thoma's best friend, but unfortunately, I must speak with him in private," he said with a thin-lipped expression. "That's alright, Master Pyle. I'll take my leave," Ed replied. "We'll retire to our chambers as well. It's been a long journey, and I would *very* much like a bath," Leona chimed in.

"I'm sure you would, your majesty," Pyle said understandingly. Edryd excused himself with a bow as he rose from his chair, leading Meliss and Leona out and closing the door behind them.

Out of the frying pan, I thought, feeling the anxiety begin to stir in my chest.

"Thoma, the others present in this room already know of what I am going to tell you, so there is no need for them to leave," Pyle began. "Well, I'm already nervous, but that's a little comforting to hear, Master Pyle," I said.

"There is no need to be nervous," Pyle began. "I mean only to ask you a simple question," he said. "And what might that be, Master Pyle?" I asked nervously.

"I know that you are a smart boy, not much older than I was when I was first told that my abilities could be enhanced even further than what I thought possible. I am more than certain that you have spotted a few similarities between myself, your brother, and the Master," Pyle said calmly.

"You three having glowing eyes is the answer, I suppose," I replied. Pyle nodded. "And I am more than certain that you know, by now, that it is because we have unlocked deeper stages of mana manipulation. But what if I told you that this could be unlocked for you, as well?" Pyle asked.

I looked at him, and tilted my head. "How, Master Pyle?" I asked. "Over the many years that Synners have been in existence, we have always had a few who sought out to enhance their abilities. Most failed, for lack of understanding what they were trying to do, while only a few managed to succeed. The Master is proof of one of the many experiments done in the past," Pyle explained.

"There are a total of five stages of mana manipulation as you know, the sixth being unobtainable by humans," he continued.

"Wait, there's a *sixth*? Why did we not learn about this when we began our training?" I asked. "That's because *that* level of mana manipulation would put one at the level of one of the many gods," Pyle frowned.

That's news to me. I wonder why that kind of information was hidden. He's probably thinking whether it was a good idea to tell me that, he thought. I thought as I looked at the Master who was vacantly staring off into the distance.

"While I am not as expertly trained in teaching mana manipulation as someone like Anwill or his people may be, I *am* offering you a solid test to lock in the second stage of mana manipulation. According to your brother, you've already reached the second stage, but do not have it completely under your control just yet," Pyle stated, his eyes staring at my core.

It's like I can feel him looking right at it, I thought, feeling an unsettling feeling.

"I will understand it if it takes you a few days to decide, but I must ask: Will you accept my offer?" Pyle asked.

I swallowed hard.

I looked at Bernar, who showed nothing on his face that might interfere with my decision. I then looked at the Master, who was still in his pensive state, and then at the others in the room - all with the same, emotionless expression.

If I accept his offer, there might be a chance I don't come out alive. However, there is also a chance I can more easily acquire the later stages if I unlock the second stage. Ahhhh, this is fine. This is fine! I'm totally not about to freak out, I thought.

"Well?" Pyle asked calmly. "I accept your offer, Master Pyle," I began. "However, I would like to know how I am supposed to unlock the later stages," I said, a slight mixture of nervousness and excitement seeping through my voice.

Pyle chuckled heartily. "By the gods, Bernar, your little

brother is a *monster*!" he exclaimed between laughs. "You should have seen him take on not one, but *two* ochelons," Bernar said. Pyle's eyes opened wide. "At the same time?" he asked excitedly. Bernar shrugged in response, pursing his bottom lip out a little. "This little bastard..." Pyle said, shaking his head as he lowered it, feeling the weight of the words he heard.

"Well, I suppose that concludes my business with you for today, although I would love to begin as soon as possible," Pyle said. "Thank you, Master Pyle. I will expect to hear from you soon," I replied, bowing once more. "And so you shall, Thoma," Pyle replied, returning the bow with a nod.

"Thoma," Anwill called out. "Yes, Anwill?" I asked, genuinely confused. The elf had not spoken much, if at all during the journey. "If we survive this, I will handle your training for the later stages in Caegwen," Anwill stated, watching the boy's reaction. "I can't wait," I replied, excusing myself from the room. Bernar followed me out the door, while the others remained inside, conversing amongst themselves.

Have I just made a mistake? I thought, breathing heavily as he felt his composure failing while closing the door.

"I know what you're thinking, birdbrain," Bernar said quietly, standing beside him. "It was a tough decision to make - more power means you become more of a target. I get that," he said. "But why did he ask me, and not any of the others?" I asked.

"There are things I wish I could tell you right now, but unfortunately, I'm under strict orders from the Master not to," his brother said. "You think it would have influenced my choice," I said briefly. "I don't think it would've, to be honest, although you would be more surprised than you could ever imagine," Bernar said with a grin.

What does he mean by that? I thought.

"Bernar," I began. "Yes, birdbrain?" Bernar asked. "Were

you the one who recommended me for second stage training?" I asked. Bernar thought about the question for a moment. "One day you'll understand that it is more than simply *more power*, to quote Master Pyle," Bernar began. "Not like I knew that before accepting my own second and later stage training, but I have come to learn it in the last few years," he continued.

"You dodged my question, you fuck," I said with a small grin.

"Of course I did, twit," Bernar spat back. "Did you really think I would answer that? No, no. The reasoning for you being chosen had little to do with me, if that helps your *birdbrain* piece it together," Bernar said.

"Can't beat that argument," I said, looking at the ground away from him. "No, you can't. However, I will say this: If you can fully unlock the second stage, the others will come more easily. I know you've dabbled in it already, but fully locking it in is another story entirely," Bernar explained.

I nodded, receiving a heavy pat on the shoulder. "Now go find Meliss, and get some, little bastard," Bernar said with a grin from ear to ear. "How did you...?" I began. "Leona mentioned that Meliss likes you to me this morning," Bernar interrupted.

My eyes opened wide. "Sh-she told you that?" I asked. "She did, but if you're not there with her, I don't know how much longer that *liking* of hers will last," Bernar said. "Run, dipshit, run," he said with a chuckle as he pushed his younger brother down the hall. I took a second or two to process all of that, and nearly stumbled when I turned around to go find Meliss.

I can't believe it, Thoma thought. *She... likes me? I mean, I'm definitely not the most handsome guy around, so why me?* I asked myself.

"Fuck it," he said quietly, and ran off to find her. He went straight to where he thought Leona might be, and knocked on the thick, wooden door. I heard some shuffling going on inside, but no answer came. "Leona? Meliss?" I asked at the door.

The shuffling stopped.

I took a step back, wondering if they really were the ones behind the door, or if I had just interrupted something else entirely.

Still no answer.

I turned around to leave, when I heard the bolt being undone. I turned around to find Meliss' eyes, peeping out of the small crack in the doorway. "*Oh*, it's you," she said quietly, excitement barely hidden in her voice.

I was puzzled.

"Who else would it be?" I asked. "Edryd was here a few moments before you knocked. He was looking for you," she said quietly. "He knew I was speaking with the others in Pyle's house, why would he come *here* looking for me?" I asked.

The two of us were interrupted by none other than Edryd himself. "*Ah*, there you are," he said from a short distance away. "So? What did they want?" Edryd asked, walking up to my side.

"The Master told Pyle about that situation we had over in Codrean. He wanted to see if I knew more about you-know-who," I lied. "What did you tell him?" Edryd asked. "The truth - that we still don't know who it is, and that we still have to be careful," I replied.

"Well, with any luck he'll be able to help us with that," Edryd said. He looked at the crack in the doorway, and found a pair of eyes watching the exchange.

"*Oh*, I'm sorry," he stammered. "I didn't know..." he paused for a moment. "It's alright, Ed," I said with a smile. "I'll, *uh*... I'll be going, then," he said, stepping away from us.

The sly bastard gave me a wink and a childish grin that could hardly be out of the corner of his mouth.

"Asshole," I said to myself with a small chuckle.

I looked back at Meliss, who watched the two's brief exchange. "Well?" She began. "Are you coming in or what?" she said quietly. I didn't really know what to say. Obviously, I wanted to go inside, but I was so incredibly inexperienced that all I could do was nod briefly, and cautiously enter the room.

You're acting like an idiot, cut it out, I thought.

"Listen, Thoma," she began, closing the door behind her, and bolting the latch. "This isn't my first time doing something like this, not by a long shot. Granted, it *has* been a while, but I'm not new to this," she said.

To say that I hadn't expected as much would've been a lie, but for her to come right out and say it almost sent me for a loop.

"Wish I could say the same," I muttered under my breath, trying my best to hide my surprise at her candor with an embarrassed smile. "You've never been with a woman?" she asked.

No way to escape that one, I thought.

"Never really got the chance," I began. "My days, up until recently, have been spent mostly in Codrean; where the female Synners there are more focused on their training, rather than messing up the sheets with someone," I said shyly.

Meliss noticed I was genuinely embarrassed by my own lack of experience. "Sorry. I didn't realize..." she said quietly. "It's alright," I said lightly. "No way you could've known that, right?" I said, trying to conjure a smile.

She nodded her head and, surprisingly, turned around, walking over to her bed, which was in the other half of the room. She began taking off her nightgown, slipping the shoulders off as she went; stepping out of it as she walked like it were some sort of practiced dance.

Naturally, I didn't know how to react, and felt that the only thing I really could do was stare at the ground. "Nothing to be afraid of. I'm not going to bite you… *hard*, that is," she said calmly.

I could've sworn I heard the sly grin beginning to grow on her face.

I finally looked up at her, noticing she stood before me wearing nothing more than her skin. She motioned for me to come towards her, and as if I were in some sort of trance, I did so. She helped me undo the laces and removed my jerkin, hose, and boots before motioning to the bed.

I sat down upon the soft, goose-feather mattress, and sunk deeply into it when I did. She approached me, spreading her legs to envelop mine, and kissed my forehead, pressing her chest into my face. She kissed down the side of my face, and I soon felt her soft, supple lips lock with mine.

"Lie back," she said sweetly, pulling her head back a little as she was pushing her hand against my chest. I slowly fell backwards, gazing into her deep, green eyes as she followed me down onto the mattress. She kissed me again, but this time, began to move away from my lips. She kissed her way to the backside of my jaw, down the side of my neck and all the way down my torso towards my hips.

Ah, so that's what that feels like, I thought.

Sparing further, and more personal, details, we were at it for more than half the night. At the end of it all, Meliss lay on my bare chest as I watched her head rising and falling gently in time with my breathing.

"You weren't bad for a first timer," she said playfully, turning her head to look into my eyes. "How was it for you?" she asked quietly. "Best I think I'll ever have," I replied honestly. She chuckled at my reply, but it faded more quickly than I'd thought it would.

"Thoma," she began. "What is it?" I asked calmly. "I don't

want to lose you," she said softly as I stroked her black hair that had more than a few strands strewn across my shoulder.

"I know this fight that's coming is something that can't be avoided, but if there were a way..." she trailed off. I sealed her lips with mine. "There's nothing more to be done," I began softly. "We're on a mission to get yours and Leona's home back, and that's exactly what we're going to do," I continued.

Tears began to well up in her eyes, as she tucked her face into my chest.

"But I don't want you to die. I don't know how you fight, or how well the others around you will protect you, but I'm scared I'm going to lose you. I finally find a person that's not a complete menace to the female gender, and he immediately has to go to war? I... I'm scared, Thoma. I'm terrified that even if the rest of the Synners succeed, that you won't be there at the finish line," she said, tears streaming down her face.

I know she's scared, but what am I supposed to say? I'm not immortal, and, to be honest, I'm probably more scared than she is, I thought, weighing her words heavily on my heart.

"I won't die, or at the very least I'll do my best to take as many of those bastards with me on the way out," I said softly. Meliss' small hand moved to the side of my face. "Can you promise me that?" she asked, gazing into my eyes.

I looked into hers, and pondered her question for a moment. "There is no way to know when either of us will die," I began. "All we can do is pray the gods don't let that happen sooner than it's supposed to," he said. "Then I'll pray to the gods to spare us both, and not have us suffer such a fate," she nodded her head with determination.

"I know I'm your first, and that makes this a little more difficult for you to comprehend certain things regarding relationships. You have to understand that even though I've been with other people, forced upon or not, you're the first one I've truly cared for," she said, moving her head back down onto my chest.

I'd never thought I'd hear those words come out of someone's mouth, so to say that I was shocked would be a blatant disservice to how I felt in that moment.

"It's true that it's a little difficult for me to understand what you're going through, but I promise that I will do my best to not let you down, or *uh...* you know, become *past tense*," I said jokingly, trying to make the situation seem a little less heavy. "I know it's in your nature to make jokes in dark times, but for fuck's sake..." she managed a chuckle.

"Hey, you laughed a little. Mission complete!" I said with a bright smile. "G'night, Thoma," she whispered, smiling a little as she said it. "Good night, Meliss," I replied, kissing the top of her forehead as she snuggled up more closely to me. She was soon fast asleep, as our little *adventure* had drawn more out of her than it did from him.

I won't let that happen to either of us, I thought.

Naturally, my mind began to race as it went over all of the possibilities.

I've decided that Fate was a cold-hearted bitch, that only took advantage of mere mortals for her own personal enjoyment. I promise I'll come back to you, Meliss, even if the gods themselves do not forgive my methods of getting there, I mentally asserted.

After coming to terms with that, I slept, *going back onto the plains, where he could train, and be free from all mortal worries.*

Dawn came, and Meliss had barely moved from her previous position the whole night. I was just waking up, though, only now realizing what had happened the previous evening. I gingerly tried to take my numbed arm out from under her head, but failed miserably as she woke up with my movement.

"Is there something wrong?" she asked. "Nothing could

possibly be wrong in this situation," I replied. "It's just that I always wake at, or before dawn - old habits. Well, that and my arm doesn't feel like it belongs to me anymore," I said in jest. "*Ah*, right," she said softly, lifting her head just enough for me to get my arm out from underneath her.

"The Master may be looking for me," I began. "Leona knows you're with me. If anything, she can tell him where you are," she said, her voice was raspy and sleepy.

Not a minute passed before there was a knock on the door. "I've got to go," I said with a light-hearted shrug. "I know," she replied, frowning slightly. I was out of bed in a flash - putting on my jerkin and boots as quickly as my sleepy limbs would allow.

There was another knock on the door. "Coming," I replied, getting my last boot on. As soon as it was on, I rushed over to her side, and gave her a kiss on the forehead. "One for good luck," I said. She pulled my head close, and kissed my lips. "Two's always better," she winked. "Go. You'll be late!" she smiled.

I rushed over to the door and undid the bolts, only to find my brother standing there with a smile from ear to ear.

"Someone popped their cherry," he said cheerfully. "Shut up, she might hear you," I replied. I couldn't hide the fact that I also had a smile from ear to ear, and probably the strong scent of whatever happened the previous night. "Hope she broke you in well enough," Bernar said, patting me on the shoulder.

"That's none of your business," I replied defensively. "*Whoa*, touchy, are we?" Bernar said, the grin still showing on his face. "I just don't want her to hear you," I said quietly. "*Oh*, right," my brother said, moving away from the door.

"The Master wants to see us," he began. "Not sure what he wants, but if he's only summoned the two of us, it must be serious," he continued. "Let's go, then," I replied. I closed the door behind me, getting one final look at Meliss, who was still in bed. I smiled, but felt that leaving her in that state might make me out to be an asshole in her eyes.

Wish I could stay there forever, I thought as he closed the wooden door, following my brother over to Pyle's house.

The Master was there waiting for us, along with Pyle, Thorsen and Garett, who sat in the same positions as they had the previous day. "Please, sit," the Master gestured.

"As I was telling the others, we must move sooner than we thought," Pyle began. "Friends of mine from the country have sent me ravens saying that the large force of monsters has been making their way to Coltend, destroying every town along the way. I have already notified the ones who have volunteered to help us, and we ought to be off within the next hour or so," he said.

"How many do we have," Bernar asked. "Counting the ones we've come with: A little over five hundred," the Master said grimly. "So, it's a suicide mission," Bernar said sardonically. "Not exactly," the Master replied. Leona walked in from a hidden corner of the room, holding a scroll in her hand. "Leona has laid out the plans of the city for us - drawn from memory," the Master said.

Bernar and I looked at each other in astonishment.

"Being that the army of Coltend would take far too long to send word to, assemble, and march to the castle, that option is one we do not have at the moment. However, that's not to say that all hope is lost, as deep beneath the city lies a network of sewers," Leona began.

"Coltend was originally an elven city, and a large portion of the city has been built upon the remains," she said, placing the map on the table, spreading it out as far as the parchment would reach.

"I know that place," Anwill began. "Legend tells us elves that it was the home of the Arwydus - the Formidable Ones in our native tongue," he said. He looked at the map carefully, recognizing a lot of the same stylistic architecture from his homeland.

"I believe there is a passage there that leads to one of the few Portal Stones," Leona said. "If we can muster enough mana, which I have nearly no doubt we will be able to do, we may yet be able to summon reinforcements from Caegwen," she said.

The others looked at her in surprise. "Your majesty," Garett began. "It would take an immense amount of mana to even open the portal, and so far as I know, we have but one full-mage among us," he said. Anwill looked over the diagrams of the inner workings of the underground passages. "I can draw an immense amount of mana, but to be able to hold it open, I would need someone to aid me in the Ethereal," he said.

"How would that even be possible?" Garett asked. "You humans have only but a glimpse of what you can do in the other realms," Anwill began. "If one of you were to volunteer to help me until all of the reinforcements were through, I will more than gladly show you how it can be done," he said.

Each one in the room looked at each other, wondering who would be the first to raise their hand. "Roburn might be able to help you with that," the Master said. "Roburn? That self-centered glick-herder?" Garett asked.

"Yes," the Master replied. "He may appear to be self-centered, but he is a formidable all-caster," he continued. "Seems as though we have little choice on the matter," Garett said. "I will begin his training at once, while the rest of you conjure up the plan," Anwill said, excusing himself from the room.

I looked over the map. "I think the real question here, for someone who has little or no knowledge of the last few hundred years, is: Why Coltend of all places?" I asked. The others looked at each other, and nodded. "It is where the Plant resides here on the continent," Pyle replied.

I swallowed the information like a dry tuft of fur. "Right, I get that, but monsters don't randomly team up to go somewhere," I said. "There must be someone leading them who knows it's there," he concluded. "The Masked One," Pyle replied.

I displayed a look of confusion and utter bewilderment to everyone in the room

"Who the fuck is *The Masked One*?" I asked with a raised eyebrow.

They sure had a lot of creativity with that name, I thought, not bothering to voice my sarcastic comment aloud.

"A long time ago, and far to the north of here, a dark power began to rise in a place called Valdis. Thorsen and I are the only two here who have seen his power firsthand," Pyle began.

"He was the one who attacked Grundvollr, slaying all in his path, and stealing our precious books of knowledge, as I'm sure you know every Synner school has a copy of them. We initially thought it was simply a random act of violence against the Synners, though only later discovered his true purpose. Thorsen and I traced him back to Valdis - a dark citadel that more than obviously was infused with mana from the Underworld. King Mads kept the failure of Grundvollr hidden from the rest of the world, and expelled us from our own country, striking the attack from our country's history as well," he explained.

I pondered what I'd just heard for a moment. "If he knows that the source is there and is bringing an army along with him to get it, why didn't he do this before?" I asked. "He wasn't strong enough to take on an entire city, until now," Pyle answered.

Seems like we're in some deep shit, Thoma thought.

"Alright, suppose we manage to make it to the Portal Stone and activate it, what then?" Bernar asked. "There are various openings placed around the city that would allow us to get in, hopefully without being noticed," Leona pointed at a few points on the map.

"Once inside, a small group will create a distraction outside the walls, while another will head directly towards the palace to thwart any attempt to open the passage to the source. The rest of us will keep the beasts at bay," the Master said.

"So much death," Anwill said quietly. "If we must die to protect the rest of the Continent - and possibly the world - from such a fate, then it is a sacrifice I know all of us here are more than willing to make," the Master said. "However, with a proper battle plan, I believe we will suffer minimal losses," he continued.

"Even the best battle plans go to shit after the first sword is drawn," Anwill said. "I know that, which is why we shall devise a secondary plan should the battle not go our way" the Master replied.

"So, shall we begin?" he asked. The others, me included, nodded in agreement and we began making preparations accordingly. A few hours of planning went by, and some food was brought in by Leona.

She knows how to cook, too? I thought, smiling as she brought my brother and I some food.

She sat next to my brother, nearly shoulder to shoulder, and continued their intermittent input on the plans being formed. A few more hours had passed, and the plan was finally coming together, and all that was really left was the execution thereof.

"All in favor, then?" the Master asked. "Aye," we replied in unison. "Very well, then. We'll ride just before dawn tomorrow. Anwill, find Roburn and teach him what you need to," the Master said. "Get some rest, gentlemen. We're going to need it," he said.

Each one went to their respective lodgings, while I returned to Meliss, who had cleaned the entire house before I arrived.

"You didn't have to do all of that, you know. But still, thank you," I said warmly with a bashful smile on my face. "You're welcome, but I was bored," she replied with a curt shrug. I walked over to her, pulling her in close by the small of her back and kissed her. "We're heading off to Coltend tomorrow at dawn," I said, my tone growing a little heavier than I had intended. Meliss nodded, understanding what I meant.

"Will you ride with me again?" I asked, moving a few, loose strands of hair behind her small ear as my eyes darted to each of her own. "*'Til the horse cannae carry us*," she replied in a singsong voice with a smile, undoing the clasps that held my jerkin shut.

I could've sworn I heard Bernar chuckle from just behind our door, though it sounded like he moved on towards Leona's room.

CHAPTER 18

Mourtis

Smoke rose from the East. The towns along the road to the Rhydian Pass lay razed to the ground from the massive horde that was being driven across the open plains and hillsides. The glicks massacred all who stood in their path, while the fire trolls set the houses aflame. Townsfolk slept silently in pools of their own blood and shit. Creatures gnawed on the remains that the horde left behind, leaving little more than piles of bones and tattered clothes lying about.

The Masked One left destruction in his wake as he made his way to Coltend Castle which was now in sight. The palace gleamed in the sunlight as it always did, though what lay within was less than the cheerful place it once was. He gazed over the griffin's mighty neck, observing the devastating force beneath him.

This will end quickly, he thought.

A few hours later he reached the eastern gate, and was met by a few hooded figures who stood watch atop the high walls. The Masked One flew up to the same height as the top of the wall, and watched the figures shuffle uncomfortably in the presence of their visitor. Their cloaks fluttered in the wind produced by the massive wings.

"Mourtis is expecting me," the Masked One said, his voice enhanced by mana so he could be heard clearly. "The city has already been taken, so what business do you have here?" one of the hooded men shouted. "You have no idea who I am, do you? This all came to fruition by *my* doing," the Masked One spat back. The two men began to tremble at the realization that he was the *true* orchestrator of the chaos beneath them.

"You insolent filth, I *own* you and everyone inside. Now, be good, little foot soldiers and open the fucking gates!" he ordered. The hooded man, to whom he directed his order, flinched at the brusqueness of the command, as well as the authoritarian tone this new master carried. "Y-yes, my lord," he said.

The man barked the order down to the ones beneath him, who speedily opened the gates. The Masked One landed his great beast, dismounting soon after as the horde gathered behind him. He peered inside the opening gates, and saw not a living soul aside from the hooded figures. No bustling merchants. No stable boys chasing horses back into their stables.

A dead city.

"Ah," he exhaled after having taken in the smell of death and decay that was in the air. "It's good to be back," he said to no one in particular. He passed between the gates, and spread his arms wide, letting off a disturbing cackle. The hooded figures who were now beside him began to tremble more than they ever thought possible. The Masked One looked up, and noticed the two atop the wall scour away from his gaze.

He grinned under his mask, and his eyes glowed their bright violet once more. *Mana flowed from the dark sphere in the sky, enveloping him instantly. He condensed* the raw mana to both his hands - outstretching them to pull the two who were above him. Dark tendrils of violet mana flew out like a shipmaster's whip, latching themselves onto the hooded figures, and tore them from the ground.

The two were suspended in midair for what they felt was an eternity. The Masked One lowered his hands, maintaining the spell without the need to keep his hands in the air. "Mourtis should have told you by now that I am not one to be trifled with, so why are you acting like children?" he began.

The two hooded figures squirmed, feeling their bonds tighten about them. "I will not have this kind of insubordination from anyone, especially not lowly foot soldiers such as yourselves. I *really* hope you don't have families waiting for you somewhere, because this example I am about to make of you... is going to hurt," he said with utter darkness in his voice.

The bonds were tightening, and beginning to tear into flesh. "Please, my lord, forgive us!" one of the men shouted. "Forgive you?" the Masked one asked, tilting his head to the side a little. "A parent might forgive their child for acting brashly, but as I am neither your father nor an admirable person, I never forgive," he said in a low voice, tightening the bonds even more. The two men screamed until their eyes burst from their sockets and their tongues exploded. They gurgled their own blood for a moment as they smashed into the stone floor. The Masked One looked at the others who watched their friends' harrowing deaths with pale faces and horrific expressions. "I think that will suffice," he said, moving deeper into the city, leaving the other figures with their heads bowed low.

He walked down the street, observing what had once been a bustling city, now smelled of death and decay. His enlarged figure cast a long shadow onto the ground beneath him that extended over the ruins. He made his way to the palace, and not a soul was to be seen along the way, save for rats and other such scavengers of the dead. Birds pecked at remains that lay motionless in the shadow of the small, thatched house which was once their home.

He didn't care.

A short while later he reached the palace steps. Another figure stepped out from behind the wall, and greeted him properly along with six others, all clad in the same, dark robes as the one in front of them. The leader held a wooden staff, with the mark of Mideia etched into it. The leader leaned heavily on it, as he slowly made his way forward.

"My lord," Mourtis began. "I have done all that you have requested, and might I say it is an honor to meet you in the flesh," he continued. The Masked One held his gaze. "The queen has managed to flee our little coup, however, one of my men struck her in the shoulder with an arrow. She will likely not survive much longer if infections take to the wound, my lord" Mourtis said.

"I ordered her not to be harmed. Do your men enjoy not following orders and suffering punishment?" the Masked One asked in a low voice. "Two of your men have already had a taste of how I deal with insubordination - although neither of them will be willing to disclose that information, unless you have a necromancer among you," he said. Mourtis felt a cold chill run down his spine. "The fact that she was harmed was none of my doing directly, my lord," he began. "I ordered my men to leave none alive in the palace, except for the queen. She should have been captured alive and remained unblemished. Seems as though my men are dumber than I thought," he said with a sneer directed at the others. "The culprit will be dealt with when we find him, I guarantee it, my lord," he said with a short bow.

The Masked One didn't say anything in return. He merely walked past the crooked old man and the others who followed him. The dark master raised his hand, and the beasts began to pour in from the gate, slaying the remaining hooded figures as they found them throughout the city.

"My lord!" Mourtis shouted after hearing screams coming from the direction of the gate. "Your stupidity and carelessness regarding my orders will not be tolerated. I recall giving explicit orders, and now, the queen is gone. As a result of your men's insolence, the only holder of the key to get me what I came for is now gone, wounded, and will probably *die* sooner than I can find her," the Masked One said angrily.

"I care not for your men in the slightest. I only needed them to extricate the ones who might have stood in my way," the Masked One said, as he slaughtered half of the other hooded figures surrounding Mourtis to set yet another example. "Now, show me to the throne room," he ordered. Mourtis caught up to his new master as quickly as he could, while the ones who followed him ensured none of the creatures would disturb them.

They Masked One pushed open the door to the palace with a large blast of mana. He moved at a much quicker pace than Mourtis who was struggling to keep pace. A few moments later, he reached the main hall with a trail of dust and frightened men behind him.

He looked about the large, silent hall, observing everything. He noted the stained-glass windows which allowed the morning light to enter, barely lighting the hall - the thick pillars catching a few of the rays. He walked down the hall on the carpet that reached from the thrones to the main entrance just a short distance from him. Dried blood and the smell of death ruled the air about them, and Mourtis had to hold his breath at regular intervals to keep himself from vomiting.

The Masked One continued down the foul-smelling hall, and

made his way to the throne. He glanced over its intricate craftsmanship, noting every detail etched into it. The cushioned seat held a slight indentation from the time when Truls sat there. *Heavy bastard,* he thought. He turned about, looking in Mourtis' general direction, as he sunk into the chair. He placed both of his hands upon the armrests provided, and leaned back.

"I have waited for this day for a long time. You see, Mourtis, like you I also have my orders to follow. However, my agreement with the Undergod only requires me to retrieve him a certain *something*. He never said how I should do it, when I should do it, or what I need to do to get it," he began. "May I ask what the point of you saying this is, my lord?" Mourtis asked, feeling his stomach turn at the potential backlash.

"Autonomy is a fickle thing," the Masked One began. "On the one hand, you have the freedom to do whatever you want, within reasonable expectations. On the other, you are given enough rope to hang yourself with. I gave you as much autonomy to do my bidding as the aforementioned agreement with the Undergod would allow. You, however, have taken your fair share of rope and tied yourself a fancy noose, Mourtis," he said darkly.

"My lord, I don't understand what you mean by that. Surely you don't believe that *I* wanted the queen to run away?" Mourtis lied. "What?" his master replied curtly. "I tried to get her to comply with your wishes. I tried to make her see that she is sinful, and that she should repent and offer up the key of her own free will to aid your success. I would *never* want to betray the trust you have given me," Mourtis lied again.

The Masked One cocked his head. "Oh? And what of your men who you were in command of?" he said, rising from his seat, walking towards the crooked man. "What are you saying, my lord? Do you think I ordered them to kill her?" Mourtis asked, taking a few steps backwards.

Mourtis spread his free arm wide. "Your invasion would not have been possible if it hadn't been for me and my men to bribe the guild, and the commander of the army not to march here, and now you wish me to be gone?" he asked in genuine surprise. "My invasion would have happened with or without your help. The only reason I even had to invade was to make sure that no force could tamper with what I came here to do. To top it all off, the queen and her key would still be here, were it not for your ignorance," the Masked One said angrily. "She must have fled through an unknown passage," Mourtis began. "None other than the royal families have knowledge of everything there is to know about the palace," he said shakily.

The Masked one continued walking towards him. "That is why you had had your minions try to gather all the information they could on the palace, was it not?" he asked.

"Why, then, did I teach you the spell to use during the Kings' meeting to provide me with information? Why were you in that room in the first place? Do you remember that? Can you answer me? Do you even *know?* Decisions, Mourtis, to abuse the blindness of human perception; something I have long since tried to overcome in my pursuit of knowledge. You keep making these excuses, trying to cover for your own subordinates, but failing miserably. The only thing you have done is kill a few useless people, and allow the *one* thing I actually needed from this gods-forsaken continent to escape," the Masked One said, his tone growing increasingly heavy.

"And since your men have failed in their endeavor, then they too shall die," he said, shocking Mourtis to his core.

"You... tyrant!" Mourtis shouted angrily. "You have treated me as little more than the scum beneath your boots for decades, and I have never wavered in my loyalty to you," he continued.

"I should have trusted my gut. I have always known, deep down, that you were little more than the monster others make you out to be. You will never find what you seek without my help," he said.

The Masked One's eyes glared even more intensely for a moment, then dimmed. "Mourtis, you have lined your pockets well enough with the coins of the poor and rich alike, so make your choice. Do not force me to change my mind about giving you a choice of death," he said threateningly. Mourtis shook, but held his ground. "I will take what I own and leave this place. I pray never to have to deal with the likes of you again in my remaining years," he said.

"You don't have *seconds* left if you continue speaking," the Masked One said coldly. Mourtis grimaced at him. He spat on the ground and turned on his heel, making his way down a passage that led to his quarters. The Masked One watched the slow man's figure disappear into the hallway followed by his remaining men.

He was soon alone in the large hall, and basked in the silence.

It's a shame he is such a shriveled weasel. Decades ago, he was much more valuable as an asset. I should have taken the information and killed him after all, he thought, angry at his decision to let the maggot live yet another day.

He turned to the throne, and began to reexamine its details. The armrests had been well worn over the generations of kings who had sat there. Wear and tear on the carpeting, near where the king's feet would normally be, was more than visible. He moved over to the queen's throne, her scent still strong enough to reach his nostrils.

She smells like a goddess among men, he thought, taking a deep breath through his nostrils.

He ran his hands along the throne, hoping to find something

out of place. His eyes flared a little brighter than normal, as he got on his hands and knees to see what was beneath the thrones, if anything at all. He noticed a small lump in the carpeting directly beneath the king's throne.

"Interesting," he said to himself.

His eyes glowed *as he drew once more from the Underworld,* casting the thrones against the wall with a blast of mana. The carpet didn't budge in the slightest. He could clearly see the small lump in the carpeting, and stepped away from it onto the stone floor. He tore the carpet from its lashes to the stone ground, tearing its bindings. Countless years of accumulated dust rose in the air about him, making things difficult to see.

There you are, he thought after the dust settled.

He stepped on the small stone that was out of place, and the stone floor in front of the stairs to the thrones began to open, releasing more dust and an earthquake-like rumbling in the ground. The paintings and hunting trophies on the walls fell to the ground with a large crash, but he continued to watch the stones move apart.

A stone stairway became visible behind the throne, covered in dust. He looked at them, wondering where they would lead him to. He stood at the top of the stairway, and took the first step. Dust rose about his feet, and he chuckled.

It must be here, he thought, continuing down the steps and kicking up dust in his wake.

His robes dragged across the steps behind him, leaving a cloud in his wake.

He continued down the steps, until all light from the hall above him had vanished, making the passage as black as a moonless night. Through his mask, he could smell the air becoming dirtier and denser than before.

For this to be so well hidden, I must be on the right track, he thought.

A few moments later, the stairs had ended, and his steps echoed in what he thought to be a large hall. His eyes didn't need a torchlight to see in the dark, and what lay in front of him was not what he had expected.

A library? he thought.

Books. Countless books. Leading nearly as far as his eyes could see on countless shelves. Every outlawed book and tome ever to be recorded or written during the time of the Continent, covered in ages worth of dust. Surprisingly enough, they were all very well preserved, due to the lack of fresh air reaching the large chamber. He looked about him, seeing gargoyle sentries placed at the end of every shelf - motionless.

This... this can't be, he thought.

His anger was so great that his eyes flared, casting a small mana-flame into the air above him. He screamed in anger and crushed one of the nearby gargoyles into a pile of rubble in his wrath.

It has to be here, somewhere, he thought.

He began to scour the shelves for anything that may seem out of place, pulling on countless books in hopes of finding some secret lever.

There was nothing.

A frustrated scowl grew on his face beneath the mask as he slammed a balled fist into the neighboring shelf.

Curse that old man, he thought. *I curse him to suffer a fate worse than death. To scavenge the dirt and earth for sustenance until the end of his miserable life, crawling like a wounded hound.*

He made his way up the stone steps once more, cursing and swearing as he went. He reached for the button once more, and the stones began to close, rumbling as they did. He paced back and forth, recounting everything that had happened over many years of his life, desperately trying to see where he went wrong.

He found no answer in his memories.

His eyes glowed intensely as he screamed in anger, outstretching his hands and releasing an unrelenting blast of dark mana across the room. It shattered the stained glass and other objects hung on the walls along its trajectory, when it finally reached the main palace door and obliterated it to thousands of wooden shards. With the door gone, he could hear the glick's screeches and the trolls' thundering footfall off in the distance. He walked over to the steps that led to where the thrones lay, and sat on the cold, bare steps.

I will find it, even if it takes me all of eternity. I wonder if my spy has uncovered anything that will be of use to me, he thought, gazing off into the distant hills that were now visible due to the lack of the large doors.

I will have it.

Just then, a small group of hooded men stormed through one of the doors to the right of the hall, desperate to find safety from the monsters just outside. The Masked One looked at them, and realized they may actually serve another purpose. "We're doomed," one of the figures said, not noticing the Masked One at the other end of the hall. "They'll find us anywhere we run," he continued. "If you don't shut your fucking gob, they will for sure," one of the others replied. "Osgar, I'm afraid Alf may be right," one of the others said. "Don't *Osgar* me, Wingar," Osgar began. He was the larger of the three, and his voice carried heavily across the hall. "Alf, do us all a favor and put yourself out of your impending misery," Osgar said.

The Masked One rose from his seated position. "You three," his voice rang out. The three hooded men were startled by the thunderous voice. "Who are you?" Wingar asked. "I suppose I could be considered the newest lord of Coltend, even though that is not really the title I wanted in the first place," the Masked One replied. "The beasts…" Alf began, his voice carried weakly. "Are of my doing," the Masked One interrupted. "So, it was you who brought those horrid creatures here?" Osgar asked. "I did, and I see they are doing my bidding well," the Masked One said.

The three looked at each other. "If we side with him, maybe he will let us live," Wingar whispered. "Why should we side with a man we don't even know?" Osgar asked. "Because he's in control of them, and we're running out of options," Wingar replied. Osgar shrugged, but said nothing.

"If you truly are the new lord of Coltend, and have brought these beasts with you, then the three of us here pledge our allegiance to you, great one," Wingar said with a low bow, motioning for the others to do the same. "You are members of the Church," the Masked One began. "What makes you so sure that I will simply take you in?" he asked.

Wingar looked at his robes, and saw that he bore the sign of the Sword and Staff sewn into them. "We *were* members of the church, but not avid ones, great one," he said. "And what would be the cause of that?" the Masked One asked. Wingar paused for a moment, recalling the events that had led up to that point in time.

"Osgar, my blood brother, Alf and I had seen what Father Mourtis was doing to the poor, and hated him for it even more after what he had done to us over the years. We three had been brought up in the poorer communities that were once here, and knew that the only way to make any form of living was to either join the Guild, or the Church. We took part in prayers and such, yes, but neither of us is religious in any sort, great one," Wingar began.

"Mourtis took us in, and from a very young age he molested us until we were each strong enough to be able to resist him.

One day, he gathered the three of us and told us that if we didn't let him have his way with us that he would cast us out, back into the streets to live like beggars. The three of us swallowed the harsh reality presented to us, and so we were forced into service until the day we die, or he dies, whichever came first, great one," he said.

The Masked One listened attentively to the story being told. "So, you are no friends of Mourtis, that much is certain. However, what makes you think I will be a better master than he was?" he asked. "Our chances of survival are stretched thin as they are, and we never wanted to take part in his treachery, great one. If he is not here with you, then he must be your enemy. And the enemy of my enemy is my ally," Wingar said.

The Masked One thought about what had just reached his ears.

If they hate him, they might aid me in unveiling Mourtis' secrets, he thought.

"Very well, then, I shall take you in on one condition," he said. "Whatever you ask, great one," Wingar replied. "If I sense even the slightest bit of deviation of loyalty coming from any of you, I will see to it that you are fed to the monsters outside alive," the Masked One said threateningly.

Wingar looked over at his brother, who simply shrugged. "Not like we have much of a choice now, brother," Osgar whispered. "We will be your servants, great one," Wingar said, bowing once more. The others followed suit, and the Masked One tilted his head backwards just a little in satisfaction. "Very well. Your first task as my new servants is to uncover Mourtis' journals, and any other documents that contain information about the palace itself," he commanded. "As you command, great one," Wingar replied with yet another bow.

The Masked One motioned for them to leave him, and

within a few seconds, they disappeared to Mourtis' quarters. Up the steps they went, through the hallways of stone, making their way to their harasser's quarters. They entered the room, finding books and scrolls strewn about the room. The bed was messy, and had countless stubs of wax from previously burned candles atop the nightstand. The smell was a palpable mixture of cinnamon and other unidentifiable herbs which lay smoking in a small tray in the corner of the room.

"I've always hated cinnamon," Osgar said. "Well, he's gone, and we have a task that we must complete unless we want to be fed to the beasts," Wingar said. "I never agreed to be with you two," Alf began. "I've just saved our lives for the time being, so shut the fuck up, and help me look for his journals," Wingar spat back. Alf shook his head, and reluctantly began rummaging through the scrolls and books on the floor. Wingar and his brother took to the bookshelves which had more books than they could count.

"Look at this," Osgar said, pulling a brown covered book from the shelf. "*A guide to little boys,* written by none other than the old, disgusting fuck himself," he said angrily. "We'll come back later and burn everything in here," Wingar said. "I hate him just as much as you do, but for now, we must put our hatred for that shriveled cocksneeze behind us," he continued.

The three went through the iterations of books, and began to think they would die to the monsters after all. Suddenly, Alf gasped as he was looking under the bed. "I think I've found something," he said to the others, who were no sooner on their hands and knees, looking under the bed.

"These must be the ones he left behind," Osgar said, taking one of the books and bringing it into the light of the small window. "I think we've found our salvation, boys," he said, reading the first page. Wingar got up and walked over to his brother's side.

"Look here," Osgar began. "It tells of how he first came into contact with one called 'The Masked One'," he continued. "That must be the one we encountered downstairs," Wingar concluded.

Year one of my service to the Church: It is probably not the best of ideas to make a deal with a devil from the Underworld, but I have no choice. Mideia has not allowed me to escape the clutches of evil itself, and I am beginning to fear for my life, Osgar began to read. Wingar's eyes opened wide, and he listened attentively.

I met the one in the mask along the road of my pilgrimage to the Hallowed Tree, where he offered me a chance to improve my life infinitely. Oh, how I long to have had the wisdom to simply continue on my path. The one in the mask told me of greater power than that of Mideia himself, and though I doubted him at first, I came to realize that there are many mysteries to our world that we have yet to discover. Of course, my consciousness wasn't fully devoted to the idea, but my heart told me that I should accept the offer.

I agreed to accept his knowledge, and in turn he asked me for my undivided loyalty to him, and to aid him in his quest for knowledge. Little did I know that this figure would probably someday be there at the end of the world, being the one who caused it to end in the first place. Over the past three months or so, he has harangued me for information on a source of power known only as 'The Plant', of which I know nothing about, as of yet, Osgar continued.

"Here, I found a few more years," Alf interrupted, handing two volumes to Wingar. "Read this one," Wingar said, handing it over to his brother.

Year twenty-seven: I have forsaken the idea of Mideia and his 'good will' towards all men, for it is now clear to me that it is the last thing he wants for us. I see now that he has forsaken us, leaving us to our own devices in the hands of evil itself. The Masked One - who, even after all these years has never said his real name - has given me the opportunity - through murder and cheating - to become the leader of the Church. I have no choice but to accept his offer, as refusing it could mean the end of me, Osgar read.

Wingar handed him another volume, and Osgar noticed it was far thinner than the others he had seen.

"Year forty: I can feel myself getting older each day, and yet even with all of my riches - stolen, inevitably, from the blind believers - I can see nothing but sorrow and misery coming to the world. The Masked One has continued to search for 'The Plant' itself, by taking matters into his own hands - he must believe that my service to him all of these years has been for naught. He has begun recruiting spies from all regions and classes of the world - from beggars on the street, to the Synners themselves - desperately hoping for a portion of information on its location.

It seems as though there may be no end to his never-ending quest for more power. I have begun to suspect that he has even been in contact with Volzuk - the Undergod - and have never feared so deeply for my very soul. He tells me that 'our' time is near, when in reality, I believe it to be 'his' time, for he seems to be one who is unlikely to share power with anyone other than himself, Osgar read.

"So, the old fuck *wasn't* fully on board with the idea of the Masked One taking over the world as we know it," Wingar said. Alf handed him the last volume from under the bed.

"Year sixty-nine: I have discovered its location, though I will not write it down anywhere unwanted eyes may find it. I cannot believe it, after all these years, I have finally fulfilled my 'contract with evil', and yet I am reluctant to share it with the Masked One. Imagine what he would be capable of with all of that raw power.

If there is a god more superior than Mideia, then he or she has most certainly died, abandoning us to this possible and terrible fate. Words cannot express my joy and fear once I found it, and now, in the twilight of my years in this world, all the joy has died. He is coming for it, Osgar read.

The final words hit everyone in the room as hard as a blacksmith striking the steel on his anvil. They knew what Mourtis had meant when he wrote the final words of his journal. They were now engraved in their memories, and the three looked at each other.

"What have I done?" Wingar asked himself. Osgar put a hand on his shoulder. "There was no way we could have known any of this before, and you did what you thought was right, older brother," he said. "I might have just sentenced the three of us to a painful death," Wingar said grimly. "We would have died anyway," Osgar said. "We've been fucked since the beginning of our lives - both figuratively and literally. No point in trying to escape fate, I suppose," he continued.

Wingar looked out the window to the distant, green hills covered in a dense forest, and scratched his well-shaven chin. "What do we do, then?" he asked. "We survive for as long as we can," Osgar began. "Think we've gotten the hang of it over the past few years," he continued. Wingar looked at his younger brother, and for once agreed with him. He nodded, and they put the journals back in their place, making their way back to the hall where the Masked One sat on his newly forged throne borne from mana.

"Well?" he asked. "We have found nothing, great one," Wingar said after a short pause. "The old man must have taken any information pertaining to it with him when he left," he continued. The Masked One grunted in response. "Go to the libraries, or the Church itself. Search everywhere you can. The creatures outside will not bother you so long as you do my bidding," he commanded. "We will, great one," Wingar replied with a bow.

He knows I lied, Wingar thought.

The three of them walked outside to head towards the Church, and encountered a number of glicks gnawing on the bones of fallen guardsmen and servants just outside the palace itself. Alf vomited at the sight, but the monsters paid him no heed, and continued about their disgusting business. Alf wiped the remaining fluids off his mouth with the sleeve of his robe, which smelled horribly for the duration of their search.

Meanwhile, the Masked One remained in his throne of dark mana, pondering about the chamber downstairs. He iterated over all of the possibilities, finding nothing.

Those fools had better find me something of use, he thought.

When he realized he was alone, he took off his mask, and set it upon his lap. He rubbed his knuckles in his eyes, trying to stave off the fact that he was growing weary. His mana-darkened skin gained from the royal ochelon's core twisted and wrinkled under the pressure, and he put his mask back on.

I will have it, he thought once more, leaning back in his dark throne.

CHAPTER 19

To Fate and Coltend

I once again found myself unable to rest at the thought of the battle to come, causing me to toss and turn, even with Meliss at my side.

I should have been asleep a long time ago, I thought. *Having her here, by my side and sleeping soundly, should have put me at ease but... Well, not much else to do but wear myself out a little more,* I thought with an internal sigh.

I kissed Meliss softly on the forehead, and watched a small smile grow on her face, squishing her face into the pillow. I put on my boots, and stepped outside.

I hope I can find a training area somewhere. I need to let off some of this pent-up anxiety, I thought as I walked a little way down the quiet streets, observing the homes built in the surrounding area.

This doesn't feel like a Synner school, rather like a secluded town that's long been isolated from the world, I thought.

Meandering for a few minutes led me to one of the training grounds used by the Fangsdalr Synners. Marks of previous training battles and torn earth riddled the ground in front of me.

This is perfect.

I closed my eyes, moving my arms in fluid-like motions, trying to focus my mind and body to be as one. My eyes darkened *as I began to pull from the Ethereal. Mana raced from the sphere in the sky, a little faster than usual, enveloping me entirely. The dark* left my eyes, as I realized my body was coated in mana.

"Close, but not quite right," a voice said from behind me. I turned to face the owner of the voice, to find none other than Pyle and the Master, standing a few dozen meters away. I dismissed the mana quickly, and bowed promptly. "I apologize for using the training grounds without permission, masters," I said humbly.

"*Oh*, don't worry about that," Pyle chuckled lightly. "We both knew you wouldn't be able to sleep, so we came up with a plan to help you. Although, I will admit, I wasn't expecting it to have taken you this long to get here," he said, smiling at me. I blushed slightly, gauging the words to be of a friendly origin, not a reprimanding one. "Will you help me, then?" I asked, bowing my head once more. "Why do you want to reach the second stage so badly?" the Master asked.

How the fuck do I answer that? I thought, frozen in place.

After a moment's silence, I finally raised my head. "Masters, I'm sure that you both already know what I am about to say. However, given that fact, I know that you mean to confirm the suspicions you already have," I began, hardening my will. "Go on, then," Pyle said, walking towards the boy.

"I know that the people I have cared about for so long are more than capable of handling themselves in the fight to come. However, Fate herself has decided to weave a golden thread into the tapestry of my life, as I'm sure neither of you have failed to notice," I said, a slight grin showing on my face. "We've both noticed and *heard* it, yes," the Master said.

I could feel the blood rushing to my face.

"R-respectfully, masters, there is little more I want to do in this world than make her as happy as can be. Not only that, but I want to make sure that I can keep both myself and her safe in face of the challenges to come," I blurted out.

Both Pyle and the Master looked at each other, and laughed heartily. "My, my, Thoma!" the Master exclaimed. "I knew you were a smart boy, but to hear you *so* whipped by a woman's charms... I might have expected that from your brother, but from you? Now *that's* going to make teaching you that much more fun!" he continued.

That was awfully uncharacteristic of him. How can he laugh this way, when we're faced with such a challenge ahead of us? Maybe this is how he really is? Why does he remind me so much of Bernar right now? I thought.

"It's true, Master. I just..." my words trailed off, cutting my retort shorter than I would have liked. "You fear you're going to lose her, don't you?" the Master said, surprising me immensely. "I do, Master," I said after a moment of consideration. The Master looked at Pyle once again. "He's all yours, Pyle," he said, gesturing towards me.

"W-wait! Does that mean you're going to teach me the second stage right now?" I asked, surprised at what was happening. "That's what you wanted, right?" the Master said, turning back slightly to get one last look at me, whose eyes began to shine brightly.

Pyle, on the other hand, grinned maliciously.

Uh-oh. What have I done? I thought.

Pyle put a hand on my shoulder, still keeping the malicious grin from before. "Before we begin, I have to ask: How high is your level of pain tolerance?" he asked. I shuddered at the words, sweat beading down the side of my face.

"D-decently high?" I said, unsure of my own words. "Good.

Since we don't have time to ease you into it, and given that you've already dabbled in it, we can speed this along by brute-forcing our way through the training," Pyle replied.

Brute... forcing? I thought, beginning to fear for my life.

"Don't worry, I won't push you so hard that you'll die, but it's going to hurt nonetheless," Pyle said, grinning even more maliciously. "I've only ever gotten to train two Synners like this, and that was well over a hundred years ago. I'm looking forward to seeing what you can do," he continued.

Fuuuuck... I thought.

Pyle took a few steps back, allowing some space between them. "First, I want to see how quickly you can cast an Exar spell," he said, *pulling mana of his own.* "What?" I asked. Pyle released his Exar spell, flinging me across the training ground. "Don't worry about your injuries, as I will heal them later. Now, try again," Pyle said. "Try what again?" I asked, dusting Myself off. "To counter my spell with your own Exar," Pyle stated plaintively.

What's the point of that? I initially thought, but decided to follow his orders.

Pyle prepared another spell, while I *gathered mana as quickly as I could*, only to be met by yet another blast. Picking myself up once again, I grit my teeth and smiled.

So, that's how it's going to be, huh? Okay, then. Have it your way, I thought defiantly. The expression on my face told Pyle exactly what I was thinking, and he grinned maliciously once again.

"Come at me," Pyle said, spreading his arms widely in defiance.

About two hours passed, and I was covered in sweat. Pyle, on the other hand, barely showed any signs of fatigue. "H-how... is that... possible?" I asked, desperately catching my breath. "Do you remember what you were doing just before we interrupted you? I said you had the right idea, but not quite," Pyle said, sighing slightly.

"What the hell does that even mean?" I asked. "Bernar, Anwill, and even the Master have said you were able to reach the second stage mid-combat. Why do you think that is?" Pyle asked. I thought for a moment, recalling the events that they were present for. "It was because I was in a life-or-death situation, I suppose. I don't really understand how I did it, but it just sort of... happened," I said.

"Do you remember how you felt in those situations? What was your body going through? What sensations do you remember?" Pyle asked. "I felt like my whole body was on fire, but that was just due to adrenaline, wasn't it?" I replied after a few moments.

"Almost, but not quite. In reality, your consciousness that you would normally send to the Ethereal became suppressed; meaning you subconsciously imbued your muscles and bones with mana, and continued circulating it throughout your body, instead of coating yourself in it," Pyle replied.

"I...did?" I asked, genuinely confused, looking down at my hands. "I said you had the right idea before, but that you weren't quite there. Try doing what you did at the beginning, but instead of wrapping the outside of your body, try focusing the mana into your muscles and bones. Only do a little to start, we don't want you to tear your body apart from the inside, do we?" Pyle asked.

My eyes opened wide in surprise, but I understood what Pyle meant. "I'll do my best," I replied. "Try it now. I'll watch over you and make sure you don't implode," Pyle said, grinning once again.

I closed my eyes and *reached into the Ethereal. As the tendrils began to wrap around my body, I focused my will, forcing the mana into my body.*

My consciousness returned to my body, and I could feel the mana coursing through my veins and muscles. My eyes, now glowing, had a slight mana-leakage that caused a steam-like trail of golden mana to leave them. "H-holy shit!" I chuckled. "You really got it on your first try? I was right to call you a monster," Pyle said, equally surprised.

He gave me an inquisitive look, almost like he was trying to figure out whether I was even *human* after all.

I looked at my hands and arms, noticing I could see the mana flowing inside of Pyle's body as well. "I can see your mana, too! *Oh*, even my voice is different!" I exclaimed. "Of course you can. Your entire body has been enhanced as a result of you properly infusing the mana into your muscles. Your vision, your sense of smell, everything. I'm still surprised you got it, on the first try. Normally, that would have taken a few weeks to figure out," Pyle said, still observing me carefully to make sure I wasn't overdoing it.

I began looking at my surroundings, and noticed that the trees had veins of green mana, whereas the earth beneath my feet had veins of brown flowing through it. The sky had wisps of white mana flowing through it.

"I've seen these colors before. That sphere of mana we pull from in the Ethereal..." I trailed off. "Precisely. The only difference is that in the Real, they are all separated into what those types of mana belong to. In the Ethereal, however, they all coexist and intertwine with one another," Pyle explained.

"Now, do me a favor, Thoma," he began. "What do you need me to do, Master Pyle?" I asked, enjoying the sound of my altered voice. "Try moving to the other side of the training yard as quickly as you can," Pyle said, trying to hide his excitement. "If you get it on your first try, I might need to have a word with your Master once we're done here," he said in jest.

I took a few seconds to gauge the distance between myself and the other end of the yard. I bent over slightly, and made sure my footing was sure. My eyes glowed more intensely just before pushing off the ground, a small explosion of dirt and wind trailed behind me. Within a second, I was already at the other end, where I skidded to a halt. "Holy shit!" I exclaimed, breathing heavily.

I've never moved that fast in my life! I thought.

"No… fucking… way," I heard Pyle say, his jaw dropping to the floor like a counterweight was pulling it down.

I steadied my breathing, and turned to look at Pyle. "Well, what do you think?" I asked. Pyle could only chuckle and scratch the back of his head. "I think, Thoma, that you have the makings of one of the greatest Synners of our time," he said.

I could feel the honesty in his voice, and acknowledged it with a bow. "Thank you, Master Pyle," I said humbly. "Of course! However, this is only the beginning. Now that you have learned to harness it, having mastery over it is another story entirely. Although, with your skills, I don't see that taking you very long," he said with a grin.

"One step at a time, as over-exerting myself right now would probably be a bad idea. Well, more than I already have, anyway," I said, feeling the bruises begin to form all over my body.

"Well, I'll heal you up and send you off to bed. It's already much later than I had anticipated, but I'm sure we'll be fine tomorrow," Pyle replied. "You say that, but I feel like I'm still going to be sore tomorrow," I said, shrugging my shoulders.

A few hours later, the sun began to rise over Fangsdalr, and with it came all of us gathering our things to prepare for the journey to Coltend. We set off at a reasonable pace, as time was of the essence, though over the course of the first hours of the morning, I could feel my legs being strained as I sat in my saddle.

I was right about being sore. Gods above and below, I haven't felt this since the early days of learning to ride a horse, I thought.

The promised days of rest in Fangsdalr would have been a much-needed revitalization of expended energies, however, fate had decided otherwise for all of us.

I looked around at the trees as we rode beneath them. The lack of sleep caused me to become mildly delusional to some extent, as the calling of birds and other such creatures nearly sent me into a trance.

Each branch seemed to mesh into the other, and the small bursts of sunlight did little to help my mental state. The chatter of the other Synners around me added to the cacophony that was my mind at the time, jumbling my thoughts into an ever-entangling web.

My eyes were heavy, and the dark circles under them sunk deeply, as my head was bobbing slightly in conjunction with the movement of Celer's stride.

Meliss noticed I wasn't doing all too well, and held me tightly. "Thoma," she said in my ear. I blinked, startled by the words in my ears. "*Oh*, I'm sorry," I said, trying to hide my surprise. "Are you alright?" Meliss asked. "I can't say for sure," I began. "Everything that has happened over the past few days has really taken it out of me, I think," I said in a raspy voice.

I yawned, and rubbed my eyes in an attempt to keep my sleepiness at bay.

"I understand," Meliss began. "When I was just a wee bairn, I'd often help my mother with her daily duties. It was exhausting, so I understand how you feel right now," she said reminiscently. "I don't mean any offense here, but have you always been a servant?" I asked.

"None taken," Meliss began. "Ma and I often took charge of

cleaning others' houses," she said, puffing up a strand of hair that had fallen near her eyes. "It was a low life, but we were happy in doing what we did," she said. I chewed her words for a moment, trying to create a connection between her lowly life and becoming a servant to the queen herself.

"I simply can't piece it together," I began. "What do you mean?" she asked. "Well, I mean, if you were simply cleaning other people's houses, how did you come to be a royal servant so quickly?" I asked. "It was Fulco who had brought us there," she began.

"He had seen us working on one of his neighbors' houses and ended up offering my mother and I positions at the Palace," she said. "Sadly, Ma couldn't handle the workload she was given and passed away about three winters back," she said grimly.

I lowered my head, holding her hand in mine. "I'm sorry to hear that," I said. "Thank you for your sympathies, but as you know, there isn't much to be done about it anymore," she said with a sigh. There was silence between the two of us for a few moments, when it was interrupted by Bernar, who had slowed his horse to ride by our side. "Not very talkative today, are we?" Bernar asked.

"We were just talking about the past, when I think I struck a nerve I hadn't intended to," I said grimly. "I'm alright," Meliss said comfortingly. "See? She's stronger than she looks," Bernar said with a warm smile aimed at Meliss who returned it.

"You know that this mission of ours may either make us heroes or force history to forget us, right?" Bernar asked me. "I do," I began with a sigh. "Although, I will fight against the darker side of our fates until my last breath," I continued, gazing off into the distance.

I hadn't really voiced those thoughts aloud before, but I knew they came from the bottom of my heart.

Bernar looked at me and seemingly knew what I meant. "I know you can handle yourself in battle, little bastard, but to you, Meliss: I intend to keep you by my side with Leona. With any luck, we won't be too bothered by any creature that comes along," he said. "That makes me glad to hear that," Meliss said warmly.

There was a short silence, as the three of us digested our short conversation.

"So, you and Leona, *huh*? Quite the woman you've gotten yourself," I began, breaking the silence. "Shut up, child of the ass," Bernar said with a grin, punching me in the shoulder. "Hey!" I exclaimed while laughing. Meliss laughed at our exchange. "I've always wished I had a brother. I think we would've been the same way," she said with a smile.

Bernar looked her up and down. "But you're a lady," he said with a smile. "And that has something to do with it? You have female Synners, do you not?" she said, pursing her lips

"We do, yes, but they're all brutes in their own rights. Oftentimes, they're even more aggressive than the boys," he began. "Also, why everyone assumes they can kick my ass is beyond me," Bernar said, rolling his eyes. The three of us laughed, and Leona glanced back towards the origin of the laughter.

She saw Bernar's smile, and I could tell she felt a small stirring in her stomach. She smiled seeing us getting along well with Meliss, and probably felt a happiness she hadn't felt in a long time.

She slowed her horse and decided to ride next to us, hoping to get in on whatever it was we were talking about. "I pray I am not putting an end to your happiness by being here," she said.

"Never," I said with a tired smile. "You bring joy and light to even the darkest of places, and I pray, for my brother's sake, of course, that you continue to do so," I said, glancing at my brother, who was trying to subtly motion for me to stop. Leona laughed when she noticed the exchange. "So, you know, then?" she asked.

I raised an eyebrow at my brother, who shrugged. "I'd say I know enough," I said with a slight grin. "And do you approve of what you say you know?" she asked, genuinely seeking my approval. "If what I *believe* I know to be true, then you have my blessing," I said warmly.

Leona smiled, and nodded slowly. "When we make camp, I'd like to speak to you alone, if that is possible, Thoma," she said. "Have I done something wrong, my lady?" I asked.

"No, of course not," she began. "I merely wish to speak to you, without anyone influencing what you may say," she said, looking at Bernar with a warm smile. "In that case, I look forward to our meeting, my lady," I replied.

She sighed lightly. "You needn't call me *my lady,* or even *your majesty,* any longer. You are now my friend. As I am no longer queen of Coltend, nor am I in the presence of other officials, there is no need for such formalities," she said.

"Thank you," I said, almost relieved. "I've always hated using formal speech, and I don't know how you manage to do so for countless hours on end around those bureaucratic fucksticks," I said with a chuckle. "You tend to get used to it," Leona began. "If you don't, you become an *unladylike figure* in their eyes, which, as a queen, is not something you want to be seen being," she said.

I was both grateful and sad that I knew what she meant by that.

Being unladylike in her position would probably create enmity amongst some of the officials, perhaps even leading some to question her capabilities as a ruler, I thought.

"Can't say I disagree with you, there," I said with a sigh.

"Come, now, let us speak of the more pleasant things in life," Leona said invitingly. The four of us rode on, telling jokes and stories and adventures we had had in our pasts. Meliss had very little to say, since she had been a servant girl nearly all of her life, but she enjoyed the tales of Bernar's drunken acts and my bravado to try and contain my older brother.

Leona shared a few of her own, which came as a surprise to all who listened, for none of us suspected her of being capable of such things. She took little pride in her adventures, but was happy to finally be able to share a few of them with people who didn't seem to worship or judge her every word.

We rode onward until the sun began to set to our right, transforming the land and trees about them into a golden-red river of windblown grass and trees. "Still not as impressive as the Elv Avliv at this time of day," I said. "That place was truly spectacular, was it not?" Leona asked. "It really was," Bernar said warmly.

I could've sworn I saw him blush as she smiled back at him.

Anwill and Roburn had been conversing the whole journey together, discussing what they needed to do in unison to open the Portal Stone that lay in the network of sewers. The Master spotted movement in the distance, and raised his hand, signaling a halt to the others who followed him. "Is that who I think it is?" Garett asked. "The one and only," the Master replied quietly.

"We have already seen you, Jehn," the Master called out. "No point in hiding anymore," he continued. The old farmer slowly moved out from behind the large oak that he hid himself behind. "Forgive me, Master," he called out. "Been awhile since I've seen any come o'er them hills," he said, pointing in the general direction. The Master glanced over at Garett, who simply shrugged.

"Who did you think we were, my good man?" he asked. "I *dunno*. Bandits mayhaps," Boone replied with a shrug. The Master looked around him, realizing just how far this man had come from his farmstead. "I take it you're out on a stroll?" the Master asked. "Nay, truth be told I were lookin' for ye, Master," Boone replied. "Looking for me? Whatever for?" the Master asked.

"Well, the reason be as follows: After ye'd saved meself from them damned abominations, I made my way to the market in Coltend. There, the vendor I were to sell me goods to asked me why some were fouled. I told him the tale, I did, and he were taken aback. He sent a letter off to the palace with a messenger of sorts, and no sooner was I summoned to meet with a man they called Father Mourtis. He questioned my house's where'bouts, an' I told him my farm lies about half a league from yer fortress," Boone said, gesturing in the general location of his farm.

"He then asked me to spy on ye for a pretty amount of crescents, an' that I were to report to him an' none else. I agreed, I did, for my family an' I needed the coin at the time, an' yet, I'm sorry for nay havin' told ye," Boone said with his head low.

The Master looked about him, to see if anyone within earshot stirred at the information being said rather loudly. "I understand, Boone, I do," the Master began. "However, I must ask you how you went about sending the reports," he asked.

"Why, I don't have the coin to make use of ravens, so I sent me son once every couple days to deliver the messages," Boone replied as though his reply should have been obvious.

"It's not him," Garett whispered. "But he did send messages nonetheless,' the Master replied. "So what do we do?" Garett asked. The Master paused for a moment, then looked at Boone, who was becoming a little nervous. "You are but a simple farmer, and you needed the coin, that much I can understand. However, I must ask you never to send messages to Father Mourtis, or any who wish to know of our whereabouts, understood?" the Master asked.

"*Oh*, not me, Master," Boone shook his head. "My hands and mouth are sealed shut like a bear trap," he said, motioning to his mouth. "I hope so, for all our sakes," the Master said. Boone paused for a moment, looking down at the ground around him.

"Master, there be one last thing I wish to tell ye," he began. "What might that be?" the Master asked. "Well, ye see, Master, during me last visit to the Market last week, I overheard a conversation between two hooded men who spake of a terrible thing comin' thataways," Boone replied.

The Master's eyes squinted subtly. "What sort of terrible thing?" he asked. "I *dunno* for certain, but sounded to me like some *dark mage*, or something o' the likes, were to be makin' its way there soon," Boone replied.

The Master looked at Garett, whose eyes were wide open. "Did they happen to mention when this *dark mage* would be there?" the Master asked. "The way they'd put it, sounded to me like it were to be sometime this week, Master," Boone replied.

"This is ill news, indeed," Garett said. The Master thought for a moment. "My good man, stay as far away from Coltend as you can until we return - if we return," he said gravely. "And my produce, Master - what am I to do about it?" Boone asked. Leona had been paying attention, and pulled the silver and emerald ring from her finger. "Take this, ser Boone," she said, tossing the ring to the bearded man.

"This... this be *far* too much, lady," Boone said, glaring at the ring. "The information you have given us is worth far more than that trinket. Consider it a form of thanks from all of us," she said with a smile. Boone tore his eyes from the emerald, only two find two more eyes as blue as the sky beaming back at him with a warm smile thrown in.

"Thank ye, lady," Boone said with his most humble bow. "I think you'd best be heading home, my good man," the Master said. "An' ye'd be right. The dark brings dark things, unless of course ye be one of those dark things creeping 'bout like some shade-walker," he said. "We can be, when needed to," The Master nodded, and raised his hand, motioning for all of us to move forward.

We continued down the path, and Boone went on his way to his farmstead, content with the priceless gift he had just received. Anwill rode up to the Master's side, trotting alongside him for a few moments. "That piece of information may prove to be more useful than we thought," he began. "With the passageways beneath the city, we may be able to infiltrate it and avoid many losses as a result," he said.

"That still doesn't guarantee that he hasn't already thought about that being a possibility, should one muster the courage to attack him," the Master replied. "Chances are there will be more than a few sentries placed beneath the tunnels, by his doing or not," the Master continued.

"Leona said that Coltend was an old Elven city, right?" Anwill asked. "If I recall correctly, she did," the Master replied. "Well, not many people outside the Elven Elders know about the old cities. Maybe, just maybe, whoever this *dark one* is doesn't know about them either," Anwill explained. "Even with that element of surprise, it might not be enough to completely retake the city," the Master sighed.

"That's why we're bringing five-hundred of us, isn't it?" Anwill asked. The Master grinned. "I have always admired your optimism, my old friend," he said. "I try to be as often as

I am able," Anwill began. "I pray to the gods, those who have granted us life and the ability to think for ourselves, to give us the knowledge to win this next trial," he said, staring off into the distance. "And I pray that the gods hear you," Garett chimed in.

We rode until the sun was just about to hide itself from the world behind the distant horizon. The others made fires and camps, while Bernar and I helped Leona and Meliss set up a pair of tents. Bernar helped Leona set up her tent, for she had no experience in doing so, and was failing miserably when she tried to do it on her own, eliciting a friendly chuckle from the two of us.

Meliss and I, on the other hand, made a single tent by conjoining the ones we each had, making it doubly spacious in the process.

Night came as quickly as it ever did, and a few of us, Batch, Edryd and Irun included, sat around a small fire we had started, telling tales of the days of old. Meliss and I slipped away after a little while, and were content to have some time to ourselves, away from peering eyes. That quickly came to an end, however, as we heard someone approaching.

"Thoma, are you in there?" Leona's voice came from outside the tent.

Shit, I completely forgot about that, I thought.

"Be with you in a moment," I said, kissing Meliss and proceeding out of the tent. Meliss lay back in the furs, and covered herself. "I suppose you have forgotten that I wished to speak with you," Leona began, noting the belt to my trousers being undone with a raised eyebrow. I looked down, and quickly tied it.

"Sorry," I blushed.

"It's alright," Leona began. "I've seen uglier and *smaller* things dangling between the legs of men with much higher social standings than you," she said with a small giggle.

I instantly felt comfortable, but I would be lying if I said that I didn't feel a little embarrassed.

"Come with me," she said, taking me by the hand. Bernar watched the two of us from a distance, and was clearly wondering what we could possibly need to say without him present. He shrugged, and joined the other Synners around the campfire, grabbing a mug of ale from one of the younger ones. "You can't handle much more than that, you're too young," I heard him say as he did so.

Leona led me a short distance away from the camp, and gazed up at the stars. "Beautiful, aren't they?" she asked. I looked up, and just as I did, one of them streaked across the dark sky, as the moon had not yet risen. "They are, indeed," I began. "I assume you want to talk to me about matters more important than the stars," I said shyly. Leona chuckled. "Way to point out the ochelon in the room," she said warmly.

"The first thing I need to speak to you about I believe to be the most obvious," she began. "My brother, you mean to say," I said. Leona nodded. "He is a good man, from what he has shown me, and I pray that our little... relationship doesn't affect you in any negative way," she said.

I laughed quietly to myself. "*Oh*, my dearest Leona," I said cheerfully. "If only you knew your worth to him and the world around you, you wouldn't say such a thing. Besides, after everything he and I have been through, I think having you by his side might make him an even greater person than I already know him to be," I said.

I could almost hear her blushing in the dark of the night. Had it not been for the soft rush of air from her nostrils which was indicative of blushing, I might have never known she had.

"With a compliment like that, it's no small wonder why Meliss likes you the way she does," she said. "I try," I shrugged. "You are an amazing boy of... wait, how old are you, again?" she asked. "Just had my eighteenth," I replied. "Ah, yes," Leona nodded, recalling what Bernar had told her earlier.

"Being the remarkable man he is, and the inquisitive boy that you are, has made you both invaluable to me," she began. "I pray that when this is all over, I will be able to grant the two of you a gift worthy of a king," she said. I shook my head in the dim light of the distant fire that could barely be seen shining on my face. "There is no need for that whatsoever," I said.

"Nonsense. I *shall* give you two the treatment you deserve," she said somewhat firmly. "Stubborn just like my brother. No wonder you two get along so well... Well then, I see no way of being able to turn you down," I shrugged once more. "I'm glad to hear that," Leona said, playfully nudging my arm with her elbow.

Leona looked back at the camp, probably listening to Bernar's laughter drown out the others'.

"There is, of course, one other matter I wish to speak to you about, to which I have told no one, not even Bernar, though I suspect he may already know," she began. I swallowed. I knew that whatever came next was of the utmost importance, and listened attentively.

"Thoma, what I am about to tell you only a few know of, and even fewer can find it," she began. "The castle is taken, this we know, but there is one thing that the invader probably hasn't figured out yet, though I suspect he will soon enough. *The Plant*, or *Gwynnleaf* as you Synners call it, lies there in Coltend, buried underneath layers of stone. Over the many years that the castle has existed, it has shifted its position under every kings' rule. Under Truls' rule, however, he moved it to a library beneath the main hall, where it was to be hidden in plain sight," she said.

"How is it possible to hide something like that in plain sight?" I asked, genuinely dumbfounded. "There is no sunlight down there that could reach the Plant, not to mention the lack of airflow down there. As it needs no sunlight or water to survive, we have been able to hide it from prying eyes by faking its death. The way we have always managed this is by painting the plants with mana-suppressant paste, making it appear dead. This paste can only be removed during the preparation, so it is highly unlikely that anyone outside of the preparers has seen its full glory," she explained.

I was trying to understand exactly what she meant by that.

"So you're telling me that even if the invader found the library, that they would believe the plants are dead?" I asked. "Precisely. Now, the purpose for us doing so is that the library beneath the palace is so vast, and has so many different routes to take, that it would be nearly impossible to find one that would let off a significant amount of mana to be found by a mage or otherwise," she explained.

I chewed on the information for a moment, and thought about all possible situations that may or may not come to be a reality.

"This may have come as a surprise to you, but the fact that it has been there, under so many people's noses for so many years has made it our best kept secret," Leona continued, as I digested the information being presented. "What if someone else had knowledge of its location - aside from the royal family and the Synner masters, that is?" I asked.

"Then we would all be in much graver danger than we already are," Leona said grimly. I frowned, but then turned my frown into a deadly looking gaze. "Then we must not let him have it," I said in a dark tone. "I have not trained for nearly all of my life to fight monsters, only to be overpowered by some intruder who believes himself to be better than everyone," I said.

I was just able to make out her smile in the dim light.

"You have a stout heart, Thoma, and for that you have my respect. You are brave, kind, and selfless when it comes to matters larger than yourself," she said in a warm tone. She embraced me, and the two of us looked back at the camp, from which the sounds of laughter were now dying out.

"Come, let us rest for our journey tomorrow," Leona said, taking my hand, catching me completely off-guard. Within a few minutes, the two of us were back in our tents with our respective lovers, Leona with Bernar, and I with Meliss. Naturally, there wasn't much sleep to be had in the dark hours of the night, but we still managed to get just enough sleep to where we felt rested the following morning.

The Master, aside from myself and perhaps a handful of others, was the first one to wake from his sleep. I later heard that he had had his first dream in many years that night, and I knew that it must have been some kind of premonition.

He was, after all, quite a strange man, and if something strange ever happened to a strange man, I knew it couldn't bode well.

I stepped outside after having put on my jerkin, hose, and boots, lacing my sword to my side as I looked out upon the ever-brightening horizon.

I observed the road ahead of me, and closed my eyes for a moment, trying to imagine the battle that was to take place in my mind, though emotionally and mentally preparing for such a fight was tougher than any of the others that had come before it.

I imagined myself locked in a duel to the death, but I couldn't quite tell who my opponent was. There were two others in the Great Hall, dueling with each other as though Fate itself had led them there. I saw mana being released, nearly cutting through the walls of the hall itself; swords sparking as we clashed, screams of anger and hatred also resounding from the walls.

The entire battle played out in my head, and I knew that there was always the possibility of me not surviving this upcoming trial. I tried to imagine the repercussions and consequential actions that would occur should I not, but my thoughts became blurred, as I heard someone approaching the Master, as he was standing a small distance away from me, probably doing the same thing I was.

"Master," Garett began. "I know," the Master replied. He turned to face the one who had disturbed him. "Wake the others who are still asleep. It's time to go," he said. Garett nodded, then made his way over to the other tents, leaving the Master to his own thoughts once more.

A few of the others were slowly getting up, readying their gear and horses as Garett woke them up. I watched as he looked at them, nodding to each and every one of them. He knew our thoughts, as they were likely similar to his own; we were about to ride into the challenge of our lifetimes.

I walked back inside the tent just as Meliss was putting on her gear as well. It was a gift from Master Pyle, after all, since he thought it might be a good idea to give her and Leona at least a little bit of protection. I noticed that she was having a little bit of a hard time, getting used to the buckles and straps that accompanied it.

"Here, let me show you," I said, reaching for the first buckle. "Once it's through, you've got to place the prong through the little hole after pulling it to a comfortable tightness," I said, pulling on the leather strap. She jolted a little at the movement, and was clearly surprised at just how close a fit the jerkin really was.

"Heavy thing isn't it?" she asked. "It *is* if you've never worn one before. Over time, though, it becomes a lot easier to wear and move in," I replied with a grin. "Chances are very good that it will save your life, if anything tries to get too close," I continued.

Meliss frowned. "Do you think it'll come to that?" she asked. I shook my head, and held her face in my hands. "Not if you stay by me, and if I'm not around, stay as close to either Garett or Bernar - you and Leona both, understand?" I said, looking into her eyes. She looked back into mine, and nodded her response. "We'll be alright," I said, embracing her tightly.

"Thoma," Bernar called from outside the tent. "Time for us to go," I whispered to Meliss. "On our way," I answered the call. Within a few moments, our tent was down and packed away, and we joined the others. Meliss saw Leona in the same attire as herself, and was instantly comforted that she wasn't the only one who had received the light armor.

"It fits you well, just as I thought," Pyle said, approaching Meliss. "Thank you, Master Pyle," she replied with a bow. He walked over to her, and grabbed the jerkin, shaking it about for a second to see if it was going to come loose. "A fine job on the lacings," he said, glancing at me. "I had help from Thoma," she said shyly.

"*Oh*, I know that," Pyle said cheerfully as he could under the circumstances. He reached for a leather-wrapped bundle, and handed it to her. "Here, take this. It's dangerous to go unarmed," he said with a smile.

Meliss unwrapped the leather package, and found a large knife in a leather sheath with intricate details, and the sign of the Synners near the mouth of it. She reached for the carved, wooden handle, and drew the blade from its sheath.

The blade had a curved tip with a false bevel on the curvature itself, and a long edge. "Thorsen has told me you know how it works," Pyle said. "Have to stick the pointy end in," she said. Pyle nodded. "Just know that it's not just the point of a blade that will save you. The edge will put in plenty of work if you use it in the right spot," Pyle said, putting a hand on her small shoulder. She nodded, and Pyle went over to meet with the Master and the others.

I faced her as I put the leather belt through the loops provided by the sheath, sliding it over to her left side. "Pat it once or twice so you know exactly where it is every so often," I said. She did so immediately. "More weight," she frowned. "Grams make kilos. Or, do *ounces make pounds*? I never remember the proper saying, but it's still true nonetheless," I grinned, knowing she could handle it.

"Mount up," the call came from behind us. "Ready?" I asked. Meliss had no words at the moment, but nodded her reply. I walked over to my horse, and checked my equipment one last time before putting the ball of my foot into the stirrup, throwing my remaining leg over to the other side.

I was glad to have gotten used to the height of the stirrups by that point.

I took Meliss' hand, and helped her up onto Celer's back. "My most honorable Synners and ladies," the Master began to say a short distance away from the others.

"Today's the day we reach Coltend, where a hoard of countless creatures awaits us, each eager to kill and devour our bodies. Fear may come over us, as it always does to any and all who enter a battle. But I ask you to enter with the will to fight that fear, and push through it like a plough to a field. To not have fear is impossible, but to have the courage and the strength to overcome fear *is* possible. We have done it time and time again on every hunt - solo or with a group. Together, I am certain we will be victorious, though the odds may seem impossibly stacked against us. Together, we will take back what has been taken from us and the others. Protect any and all living people who may yet remain there, trapped, hungry, and thirsty. Rid this country of this horde, and regain our freedom!" the Master shouted. There was a large, unified roar, and swords were raised in the air.

"To war!" the Master shouted, kicking his heels into his horse's sides. The thunderous sound of hooves permeated the thick forest of trees that was around us. Each one of us present, male or female, knew what we were getting ourselves into. We hardened our wills and calmed our minds as best we could, as we rode down the path to Coltend.

Off in the distance, a winged figure with burning eyes watched us as we rode in the direction of the castle. It soared through the air as it made its way towards its owner.

CHAPTER 20

The Library

Wingar shook uncontrollably on the floor of the chapel, while Osgar and Alf tried to calm him down. "Wingar, talk to me! What happened?" Osgar asked, trying to understand his brother's mental state. "We're doomed, and it's my fault," Wingar said. "He knows… he knows I lied," he continued. Osgar squatted down next to his brother. "How can you be so sure?" he asked. Wingar looked at him in despair. "I could feel it," he began. "I could feel his rage the moment the words left my mouth."

"What do you mean you could *feel* it?" Osgar asked. Wingar blankly stared at him, shaking his head like a nervous twitch. "I don't know how or why, but it was almost as if I could feel his will boring into my mind - looking for something," he said shakily. "That must have been so because you were nervous," Alf said.

"No!" Wingar snapped. "I know what I felt, and had you felt it as I did, you would've shat yourself the moment the feeling came," he said angrily. Osgar put a finger to his lips. "Shh, wouldn't want him to hear that, would you?" he asked.

Wingar fell to his side, and curled up into a fetal position, where he sobbed uncontrollably. "I'm sorry," he said between the hiccups that resulted from his weeping. "I... I don't know what we should do," he sobbed. Osgar looked over at Alf, who simply shrugged. "None of us do. For now, all we can do is play along with the lie that we know nothing about what he wants. Which, at this point, we are still uncertain of what that is, and what Mourtis meant by *he is coming for it*," Osgar said.

For once, the tables had turned: Osgar was now the reasonable one, while Wingar had taken Alf's place as being the one to fret.

Wingar's sobbing slowed a little as he regained his composure. "You're right, brother. We have no other choice," he said, wiping away a wad of snot. "We must find out what it is he wants, and how we can still find a way to uphold our end of the bargain," he continued. Osgar helped him to his feet, while Alf brought him some water from the nearby jug. Wingar grabbed the jug, and took a few gulps of old water that had clearly sat in the same container for far too long. He spat some of the bitter tasting water out, and instantly regretted having swallowed some before tasting it.

"Tastes like old socks," he said, spitting a few more times. "Well, if it got you out of your tantrum, then I suppose it was for the best," Alf said. Wingar looked at him angrily, but decided it was best they stuck together rather than get at each other's throats.

Wingar wiped his mouth with his sleeve, then looked about him at the empty chapel. The benches that faced them were empty, with the whole room smelling of old incense and spilled wine.

I remember this place, Wingar thought, recalling a speech Mourtis had once given there.

He spat in the direction of the sign of Mideia, and began

heading down the steps.

"Where are you going?" Osgar asked. Wingar didn't turn around. "To find something that will help us out of the shithole I got us into," he said. The two were soon behind him as they went to the second floor, where the scribes made copies of the books Mourtis had commissioned to be translated into common speech. A few benches were lined up along a lengthy table, where stubs of old candle wax had melted, wrapping themselves around their supports, and inkwells lay spilled and dried upon the dense wood.

"Look for anything regarding the history of Coltend, and read through the table of contents. With any luck, we'll find something that will be somewhat useful," Wingar said. The three began to scour the scrolls and leather-bound books on the shelves and table. Most of the books on the shelves were covered in dust - countless years without a single hand touching them had left them looking like they had been lost in time. Osgar went straight to the table, and began to read the first few lines of the works in progress. He went from page to page, all around the table, while the other two were scouring the titles of the books. "Nothing here," he said to the others. Wingar's stomach began to turn.

If we don't find anything here, we're really in for it, he thought.

"Keep looking," he said. Osgar shook his head, and went back to where he had begun. "There must be something in here," Alf said. Wingar heard it, but said nothing, continuing his search through the titles. After about an hour of searching, Alf sighed. "There's nothing here either," he said. Wingar continued anyway.

"Wait a minute," he said aloud. "What?" Osgar asked. "A book about Coltend wouldn't need to be translated," Wingar began. "Why would anyone want to translate a book about the secrets of the castle? So that potential enemies would know of every nook and cranny? It wouldn't make sense for anyone aside from the royal family to know the deepest secrets, but there must be information about them somewhere in case death takes the royal family before they could pass on the information," he explained.

Osgar looked at Alf, and then to his brother. At once, all three realized where the book might be. "I think we ought to pay a visit to Mourtis' room once more," Osgar said. The three went back down the wooden steps that creaked under their rapid movements. They exited the chapel doors, leaving them wide open, and broke out into a run back to the palace.

The Masked One heard their footsteps as they came through the previously obliterated doorway, and rose from his throne. "So?" he asked. Wingar breathed deeply. "We believe we may have found something, but we need more time, great one," he said. The Masked One grunted. "Time is the one thing that is never on anyone's side. Get me what I need, and be quick about it," he commanded. Wingar bowed, and the three were soon off again, sprinting up the stairs to Mourtis' quarters.

The cinnamon smell filled their lungs and nostrils, and Wingar spat. "Never get over that stench," he said. "We've got bigger fish to fry than worrying about the stench," Osgar said. Wingar nodded, and they began their search. He noted the journals that were still by the window, and shuddered, remembering the feeling that had come over him just a few short hours ago. He shook his head, and moved towards the back of the room, where there was a small, wooden nightstand with a drawer in it.

Wingar opened the drawer to the nightstand, creaking and whining as it opened. "What do you think is in here?" his brother asked. "I'm not sure, but if it hasn't been opened in a long time, then that could mean there's something inside he never wanted anyone to see," Wingar noted. The small drawer, now fully opened, contained only a single, black book. The pair looked at each other, while Alf still rummaged through the other books in the background. Wingar flipped through a few of the pages, his eyes opening wide.

"This... this book isn't translated into common," he began. "What does it say?" Osgar asked, trying to get a better look at the pages for himself. "It's hard to say, as this is in a much older version of Coltendian than we now know. If I'm reading it correctly, it says there's a... *library*?" he said the last word, questioning his own translation. "A library? That can't be right," Osgar said.

Wingar shook his head. "I think it is right, though. Look, there are more and more indications that it's actually a library. It talks about books and other such valuable things to the kingdom that are not often shared with the public," he said. "Do you think that's where whatever *he's* looking for is?" Osgar asked, hoping for a better answer than the one he had in his mind. "Only one way to find out," Wingar replied.

The three returned to the main hall, where the Masked One observed their cautious approach. "Great one, we've found this book inside of Father Mourtis' study," Wingar began. The mage cocked his head, and whipped the book out of Wingar's hands with mana, sending it flying through the air. The book landed in his hands, and he opened the book to read the first page. His eyes burned even more than they usually did. "Where did you find this?" he asked angrily. Wingar felt his stomach do a flip. "We missed it the first time we went up to Mourtis' quarters, great one. It was in his room all along," Wingar said calmly as he could manage.

The Masked One's eyes dimmed, and he inhaled deeply. "You

have done well, my servants," he smiled wickedly beneath his mask. "You have done well, indeed." Osgar nudged his brother, and raised an eyebrow. "We have done as you have requested, great one, and have held up our end of the bargain. Are we now free to go and live out the rest of our lives in peace - away from these creatures?" Wingar asked humbly.

The Masked One thought for a moment. "If you wish to live the impoverished life of the common folk, then by all means, you are free. However, should that not be the case, I offer you glory, gold, and power in exchange for your service," he said in a calmer tone than they were expecting given the recent display of anger. Wingar looked at the others, hoping to see how they would reply to such an offer.

Alf stepped forward. "I'm tired of always worrying about things. I'm tired of being anxious, and most of all, I'm tired of this world. If what you say is true, then I will join you, great one," he said with a bow. He walked over to the man in the mask, and knelt on one knee. The Masked One didn't move forward, but simply outstretched his hand. "Will you follow in your friend's footsteps?" he asked. Wingar looked at his brother who began to itch at the rough patches of beard on his slim face.

Wingar shook his head. "I can't believe you're considering it," he said. Osgar shrugged. "What? Avoiding a life of powerlessness and poverty is a bad thing, now? I don't want to be either of those anymore," he replied. "In exchange for your soul, brother? Think about it," Wingar said desperately, hoping to change his brother's mind. "My soul was taken long ago by that creepy old fuck, brother," Osgar replied gravely.

The Masked One observed the exchange, but was patient. He needed help - as little as he wanted to admit even to himself - and the more hands he had, the lighter the workload in the end. Osgar stopped itching, and turned to the Masked One. "I will join you," he said with a bow like Alf's. Wingar was emotionally struck. "Fine," he said, watching his brother walk off. "I for one will not sell my soul - what little there is left," Wingar said. Tears began to well in his eyes, blurring his vision. "I will not!" he shouted.

The Masked One simply nodded. "You are free to go, but this chance will never present itself to you again," he said. The threat was clear as the sun is at its highest point. "I pray to the gods both light and dark that we never meet again," Wingar spat. He turned around and proceeded out of the palace, never looking back.

His choice, his end, Wingar thought.

As he left, he noticed the creatures hadn't even noticed his presence, nor had his scent in their ghastly-looking nostrils.

My stupid brother thinks that the mage will truly let him have wealth and power? Is he insane? he thought, walking past the horde without so much as a twitch.

The Masked One looked down upon his two new followers. "You are wise to join me," he said in more of a majestic tone than he had intended. His eyes glowed their deep purple once more, as tendrils of mana wrapped themselves around the two men - solidifying into a dark form of armor with jagged edges. The armor barely reflected the light around them, and their horned helmets glowed the same color as the eye sockets. "This armor shall give you the strength of ten men, so long as you remain in my service," he said.

"You are no longer Alf and Osgar. You shall be named Dakzul and Kimzul, respectively, so that all may know that you are my servants," the Masked One said, raising his right arm. "Arise," he commanded. The two obeyed the order and stood at full height. They had gained a meter in height each, and they could feel the power of the armor surrounding them.

The Masked One could feel their awe through the armor, and grinned beneath his mask. "With the book you have brought me in hand, we shall rule the Continent together, discovering the secrets that lay about the land," he began. Suddenly, a dark, feathery figure flew through the shattered windows above them, and landed a few feet away from the three. Its wings morphed into arms, and its legs grew taller - revealing itself to be a daemon.

"Master, a force of Synners has come down from the north and are making their way here," the daemon panted. The Masked One's eyes flared a little. "Synners, you say? Now that is interesting," he said. "Ready the creatures for battle," he said to the daemon. "As you wish, master," the daemon replied. It transformed itself once more into the winged creature, and was soon through the window from whence it came.

Dakzul and Kimzul glanced at each other. Neither of them really knew how to fight, and with a small army of professional monster slayers on the way, Kimzul shuddered a little.

We've made a mistake in joining him, haven't we, he thought.

He felt the same way as Wingar had just a few hours earlier, and understood his brother's concern at once. The Masked One didn't react. He knew they weren't ready, but simply failed to give the slightest.

He opened the book once more, reading through it a little more carefully this time, though with immense speed. He went over to press the small stone that would open the passage behind the throne, but instead of clicking it once, he clicked it three times and slid it forward. Dakzul and Kimzul watched as the stones they had just been standing on began to move apart. "Gentlemen, we have our mission to complete first, and we must do so before they arrive," he said. "What exactly are we looking for, great one?" Dakzul said, noticing his voice was now distorted. "The Plant," the Masked One replied.

The great stones continued their rumble, moving away from each other, and revealing the stairway beneath them. The Masked One began to read the book once more while he led the other two down the steps and into the darkened library. His two servants were in awe at the sheer vastness of it all, and had a hard time processing the information their eyes received.

The Masked One turned countless pages, nearly completing the entirety of the book before even making it down the first flight of stairs. He noticed there were only gargoyles and tall shelves of books around him. "Gentlemen, welcome to the Library of Coltend," he said, a tone of grandeur ruling his voice.

Wingar was right, it is *a library,* Kimzul thought.

"According to this book, there is a plant located somewhere within this library. We must find it before the Synners arrive, so split up and report back to me when you do," he commanded. The three were off, down the vast halls that led to different sections of the library. "It's going to be like finding a needle in a haystack," Kimzul said - his voice, even telepathically, was distorted. "Only this needle is extremely powerful, important, and probably worth infinitely more than our lives," Dakzul replied. "Don't worry. We will find it, even if you two cannot keep your mouths shut," the Masked One snapped back.

They went on in silence, as the Masked One searched for even the slightest hint of mana, finding nothing. They turned down several different halls, when Kimzul noticed something. "Great one," he began. The Masked One turned to face him in a flash of movement. Kimzul was taken aback at the sensation the Masked One gave off when he did.

He's already here? Kimzul thought, noticing his new master suddenly appearing behind him. *He should have been a few halls over... how the hell did he do that?*

"What is it?" the Masked One asked impatiently. Kimzul gestured off to his left. "I've sensed a small draft of cooler air coming from this direction," he said. "Have you, really? Because I haven't," his master replied. "I am certain, great one," Kimzul replied.

The Masked One peered into the glowing eye sockets, and saw that he was not lying. "Very well, then," he said and started off in the direction his servant had pointed to. The hallway led them into a confusing labyrinth of more shelves and countless books that gathered dust from ages past. At the end of the labyrinth stood a large, iron door in their path.

This has to be it, the Masked One thought.

He *drew an immense amount of mana from the Underworld, and* put his hand on the door which grew extremely hot.

Heat bends iron like strength bends people.

He pulled his left hand back and cast the Exar spell, bending the door inwards, folding it in two. A rush of cold air filled the hallway, and the large room before them was silent. The Masked One stepped through, and felt not even the slightest tinge of mana. He looked about him, and saw a field of what appeared to be dead, leafy structures, each in their own pot.

It can't be that the ignorant bastards allowed these Gwynnleaves to die, he thought.

He opened the book once more, desperately searching for any information regarding their appearance. He quickly flipped through the pages to find the diagrams left behind by generations past.

The structure of these plants matches the ones depicted in the book, but it also says that it's supposed to be glowing and resonating mana. It can't have died - it was a gift from the gods themselves, he thought.

He walked over to the plant nearest to him, examining the first leaf he could find. He plucked one of the leaves, and instantly felt a small tinge of mana. He smiled wickedly. "There you are," he said quietly, looking at the small hole the plucked leaf had made in its stem. His two servants looked at each other, as both could neither feel nor see what their master had seen. "Great one?" Dakzul asked.

The Masked One turned to face them. "We've done it," he said in a dark tone. "I must contact the Undergod, and tell him of our findings. He will know what to do next," he said, still holding the plucked leaf in his hand. Both of his servants shook at the name. He stuck the leaf into the pouch that was on the inside of his cloak, and walked past them. "Come, for you shall meet *my* master," he said. The two behind him followed silently, and about as nervous as a whore in church.

Within the hour, they were back in the vast throne room that felt void of life itself. A featherless creature flew in from the front door, and perched itself on the Masked One's arm, where he made use of dark tendrils of mana to read its thoughts.

They're moving much more quickly than I thought. No matter, the horde outside will suffice to prevent their entry, he thought.

"You have done well, but continue to monitor *his* position," he spoke softly to the creature. The pair of servants didn't fully catch what he said, and shrugged at each other. The Masked One turned to them, gazing into their helmets. "Stand back, and do not speak unless spoken to," he said gravely. "Yes, great one," his servants replied. He walked to the center of the great hall and *drew mana from the Underworld*. He collapsed his hands together and slammed his palm on the ground, forming a massive summoning circle.

He poured more mana into the circle, and watched the glowing intensify tenfold. Within moments, a large, horned, skinless figure rose from the blast and grunted. The smell of sulfur and rotting flesh quickly filled the air about them. The Masked

One's servants flinched away from the blast, even though it did them no harm.

Gods above and below, that is a foul stench, Dakzul thought.

"Why do you disturb me once more, worm?" Volzuk's voice trembled the hall about him. The Masked One bowed, and the two behind him quickly followed suit. "My lord, I have sought this audience with you for I bring news," the Masked One said humbly. "So, you have completed the task I gave you, then?" the Undergod asked.

"Indeed, I have, my lord. However, there is one small issue that I will have to handle here before I can fully give you what you asked for," the Masked one explained, presenting the torn leaf. Volzuk reeled slightly at the sight, making the Masked One observe his countenance more closely. "What issue?" Volzuk asked impatiently.

"I have just received news that there is a group of Synners on the way here from the North as we speak. Their numbers are not great, by any means, but it is a needle in the side of our plans," he stated dismissively. The Undergod stroked the stringy flesh that took the place of a small goatee. "You once told me that you wiped out the Synners in the North. Are you now telling me that the ones from Codrean are the ones posing trouble?" the large figure asked.

The Masked One drew in a deep breath, knowing what sort of retaliation he might face, and exhaled heavily. "My lord, I *did* wipe out the Synners in the North, this is true. I made sure not to leave a single one of them alive. The Synners from Codrean, even never having posed much of a threat to us until now, have somehow found allies in the North. Who these allies are, I am still unsure of, but according to my informants, there are a total of five hundred of them on the way here now. Again, it is not a vast number, but each one is likely to be well trained, my lord," he explained. "We will be ready for them," the Masked One said with a bow.

"Pray that you are, for I fear much may come to pass that will hinder your judgment. End this quickly, and bring me what I require. I do not need to tell you what will happen should you fail," the skinless figure said menacingly. "I understand, my lord," the Masked One replied. Volzuk speedily sunk back into the ground, bringing the dark cloud of mana with him.

"Holy shit," Kimzul said quietly after watching the Undergod himself disappear. "You did well to keep that to yourself until he left. Otherwise, he might have killed you where you stood," the Masked One said. "So, he's real, utterly terrifying to look upon, and smells like a thousand dead corpses. Wonderful," Dakzul said to Kimzul. "I would advise against mocking him. He is more powerful than any other on this continent, let alone the realm," the Masked One began. He suddenly remembered the Undergod's recoil upon seeing the leaf itself.

Could there be someone more powerful than he is, or was it just not what he was expecting? the Masked one thought.

"Do not speak ill of him, for he hears and knows all that happens in this realm," he said, regaining his thoughts. "Yes, great one," the two replied. "We must prepare for the battle that will happen at dawn," the Masked One said, walking past his two servants. "Dawn, great one? Why dawn?" Kimzul asked. "Most battles are won in the twilight hours of dawn and dusk, as it is when one's guard is most frequently lowered" he explained briefly.

"B-but we, uh… we do not know how to do battle, great one," Kimzul said. "I know. Church folk and peasants seldom learn to fight with and against swords. That's why I have given you the armor and strength to fight them, even without properly knowing how. When in doubt, use your fists," the Masked One said. "But enough of that. We have other matters to attend to first which require careful planning. Synners are the ultimate swordsmen and strategists, and so we must ensure that nothing escapes us while we plan our defense," he continued.

"Yes, great one," the two replied in unison.

CHAPTER 21

The Portal Stone

Bernar idly toyed with the pendant around his neck as he rode beside me. It was clear that he was deep in thought, but exactly what was going through his mind was something I could neither read nor assume he would even tell me.

Every once in a while, he'd look at me with a slightly worried expression on his face. To be fair, it wasn't really like him to be worried about much of *anything*. This whole situation, however, was clearly different, as now we *both* had people close to us to worry about on top of everything else.

I wonder if there's anything else that's got him so worked up. Did the Master tell him something that he wasn't ready for? I wondered.

The forest around us grew thinner, and the wildlife that resided within the forest became increasingly sparse, almost as if they sensed what was coming. I heard a twig snap and glanced around nervously, almost waiting for something to jump out and attack us. When I found the creature to blame for it, I breathed a heavy sigh of relief to know that it was only a small rabbit.

"What's on your mind, Thoma?" Bernar asked, having pushed aside whatever was on his own mind. "*Ah*, it's nothing really. I'm just... worried," I lied.

I was actually thinking about how I might actually end up fucking *dying* during the fight that was coming, but I didn't want Meliss to hear me voice those thoughts after having promised her I *wouldn't die*.

Bernar glanced at me, weighing his words as if he were reading my mind. "Remember what I told you the first day we entered Coltend? *Don't think too much about it*. It's the mental equivalent of kicking yourself in the balls, and overthinking stuff like that will do you no good at the end of the day," he said. I felt my mouth grimace in response to his words. "Well, I know that, brother. It's just... I can't help it. I've never been in such a decisive battle before," I said with a heavy sigh.

Meliss had lifted her head up off my back to better hear our conversation, but nestled her forehead into the middle of my shoulder blades.

"*All* battles are decisive, shit-bird. They can be fought with weapons, emotions, or even against your own mind," Bernar began. "Even though it may not look like it, the outcome of even the smallest fight can change the course of Fate itself. I don't know if you know this, yet, but everyone is constantly fighting battles we know nothing of," he said, glancing at Meliss briefly.

"However, it's never a good thing to simply bottle them up. It's good to have people you can trust around you, and even better let those who care about you know that you're struggling with something. You might receive help from the most unexpected of places," he said, glancing over at Leona who gave him a kind smile.

I hadn't expected such a mature view to come out of my brother's mouth, but I knew, deep down, that he was right.

I took comfort in that thought and could feel Meliss' arms

tighten a little around my waist. "You'll be alright," she said in a low, sweet voice. "I hope you're right," I replied, rubbing her hand that was across my lap. "Leona knows her way about the castle. She'll know what to do and where to go. Trust her like she trusts you and your brother," she said comfortingly. "I'll trust her. I promise," he said, rubbing her hand with his own.

I held her words in my head for a moment as I stared off into the distant horizon. Off in the distance, I saw Coldend's palace begin to grow, the peak of it gleaming in the early afternoon sun backed by the Rhydian Mountains.

This might be the last time I get to see a sight like this, I thought.

We rode on in silence. Bernar watched as Leona rode by the Master's side, holding a conversation just out of the larger group's earshot. "He must have found it by now," the Master said gravely. "If he has, we'll have to move quickly to make sure he doesn't…" Leona began in a hushed voice.

"He is more powerful than you think," the Master interrupted. "He is ruthless, cunning, wiser, and possibly more powerful than I could ever have hoped to be," he continued.

Leona gave him a confused look, almost as if she were wondering where his sudden burst of anger came from. To be fair, anyone in his immediate vicinity did so, including Bernar.

"You shouldn't use such a defeatist tone, Master. I know next to nothing of doing battle. The one thing I do know is that if one enters a battle with the will to win, they *will* win. The reciprocate happens for thinking one will lose," she said.

The Master held a chagrined smile for a moment. "I am sure we will be victorious, even if it proves to be the most challenging fight of our lives," the Master began, but paused for a few seconds after completing his sentence. "I'm sorry. I'm not quite myself at the moment," he said.

"It's alright. Even with hundreds of years of battle behind

you, I wouldn't expect you to be. You are still *human*, after all," she replied. The Master raised an eyebrow briefly, but it seemed he was more shocked at her level of understanding. To him, it must have felt rather refreshing to have an outsider be so empathetic towards him.

"You're absolutely right," he began with a determined nod. "We have to focus on the task ahead of us," he said, trying to perk himself up from his moment of weakness. "And we must ensure he does not get away with it. Or, at the very least, not make off with a lot of what he came for," Leona said encouragingly.

The Master held a thin smile on his face for a few moments. "I admire your optimism, and I wish I shared the same thoughts," he said. Leona drove her horse a little closer to him, and took his hand. "We will succeed," she said firmly, gripping his calloused and scarred hand more tightly. The Master nodded in agreement, then gazed at the road ahead.

We were nearing the great, stone walls of the castle itself when Leona nodded her head to the Master, who signaled us to turn off the path, heading deep into the woods.

This must be the way to the passage under the city, I thought.

As we followed behind the Master, we did not say a word to each other. We all knew just how bad it would be if we were discovered sooner than we had hoped to be.

The trees seemed to cower at the presence of the evil within the castle. It was as though the wild knew our party's purpose, making our unbeaten path smoother along the way. When we reached a small, disheveled shack a few kilometers away from the great wall, the Master signaled a halt.

He dismounted with Leona and Thorsen at his side, following her towards the small, unassuming wooden door that could've been broken by a strong gust of wind. "This is the entrance," I heard her say as they walked over to the weather-beaten shack.

The thatching on the roof was rotten through, and the beams that supported the small, wooden house seemed to creak as they approached it.

"Wait here," the Master said, holding up a hand and signaling for my brother and I. We dismounted quickly and were soon at the Master's side, along with Thorsen, Pyle and Anwill. "Bernar, get the door," the Master ordered quietly. Bernar nodded his reply, and proceeded to the left side of it. He drew the seax from his hip as quietly as he could, and held it at waist height – prepared to stab anything that was behind the door.

As the door squeaked open, I held my breath as Bernar was taking the first few steps into the shack. A few moments of utter silence, and a voice came from within. "It's clear," Bernar said. The Master and Leona were the first inside, followed by Anwill, Thorsen, Pyle, and myself closely behind.

"Over there," Leona said, pointing to a small rug that lay covered in years of mold and moss. Bernar quickly tore the rug from its resting place to find a hidden, wooden door that seemed to lead to an underground passage. He grabbed the iron ring attached to it, and pulled the trap door open. I could hear air rush into the exposed hole, though it quickly expelled a foul stench from within.

I saw Bernar flare his nostrils and spit, shaking his head to try to rid himself of the smell. "I think we've found it," he wheezed, rubbing his nostrils with his forearm. Anwill approached, and gazed downward into the hole.

"This must be it," he said. "There are markings on the walls inside of elven make," he said, gesturing toward one of the only visible walls in the dark, to which the Master nodded his understanding. Pyle and I, on the other hand, went outside and signaled for the others to dismount, tying their horses to the nearest tree.

I helped Meliss hop off first before leading Celer to the closest tree I could find, tying a quick half-hitch around its trunk. Edryd did the same and walked over to join us. "Guess this is it," he said. "Watch your ass down there," I began with a wry grin. "Don't wanna have to use my *Whip of Doom* anywhere near you again," he said in jest. "You say that like I haven't learned my lesson," Edryd replied, punching me in the shoulder.

Irun and Batch came up to us after having secured their horses. "I say we hold a competition of who slays the most," Batch said with a slight air of arrogance. "I agree," Irun chimed in. "After all, we still don't fully know who's the better swordsman of us four," he continued.

I shrugged. I knew Irun was a good swordsman, but I still felt either myself or Batch could give him a run for his money.

Maybe even Edryd, if he actually cared enough to try.

"It's the quality of the kill that counts, not the quantity," I said, double checking Meliss' gear to make sure nothing had come loose. "Sure, it is," Irun sneered.

We started off towards the small shack. "Remember what I told you about staying near to Leona and the other masters," I whispered. "I remember," Meliss replied. It comforted me to know that while she was good at following directions, she also placed great trust in all of us to keep her and Leona safe

Garett and Roburn joined us without a word as we entered the desolate shack. No furniture, and no sign of previous owners could be found within; aside from a few cobwebs that were in every corner of the walls. The Master looked at the six of us as we entered the shack.

"Alright, here is how this will work. Thorsen, Thoma, Bernar, Pyle and I will enter first, while Meliss and Leona stay close behind us. Garett will lead the archers in a superficial attack to draw the Masked One's attention away from the Palace itself.

We'll follow this passage while Roburn and Anwill will remain closely behind us to open the Portal Stone once we reach it," the Master said.

"So, I'm to be bait, Master? Wonderful," Garett said, visibly discouraged. "Just stay out of their range as much as you can, and pick them off as they come," the Master replied. "Will do, Master," Garett replied with a nod and proceeded outside to summon the bow-casters. "Here we go," I said quietly.

Thorsen was the first one down the small ladder that was attached to the opened hatch. There was no light inside of the tunnel when he reached the bottom, and he could barely see even a palm's width in front of him.

"We need torches," he called out to the others as loudly as he dared. "Here," the Master said, throwing a pair of strange looking half-faced mask down to him. "What am I supposed to do with this?" Thorsen asked. "Just put it on already," Bernar said playfully.

Thorsen shrugged, and did as he was told. "I couldn't see shit before, and now I can't see a fucking thing," he said to Bernar. I knew the feeling all too well and grinned at my brother.

"One moment," the Master said. His irises glowed more intensely *as he drew from the Ethereal realm* and waved his hand downward, infusing the wooden mask. I could almost hear Thorsen's blinking as the mana began to flow into the mask. "I-I can see everything!" he exclaimed. He let out a small chuckle. "Wish we had these while I was still a Synner," he said to himself.

"Alright, everyone, get your masks on," the Master ordered. He didn't need any himself, nor did Bernar and Pyle, but the others and I quickly followed his command. We reached into our leather pouches, and each of us put on our odd-looking masks, tying the leather laces around the back of their heads.

Batch went outside, and signaled for the others to have them on hand. After having learned the spell from my brother, I infused my own, then went over to Meliss who didn't fully understand what was going on. "Hold still," I said. My eyes filled with mana, waving my hand over the mask Meliss had put on.

I heard her take a sharp breath that was filled with both surprise and awe.

"What the...?" she trailed off, able to see everything in the dark shack as clear as day. I grinned, remembering what it felt like the first time I saw what it could do. "It's... amazing," she said in awe. "Let's go. We're going to be late, and we don't know what we'll meet down here," Bernar said to the pair of us.

We descended into the tunnel, and the other sword-casters followed them in. Thorsen led the way, as he was the largest and most frightening to look upon should any creature get in their way.

I observed the walls and their fine markings. They had been engraved in the stone walls as though time had not noticed them, and the mossy floor lay damp beneath my feet from the humidity.

Now this is what I call walking into the past, I thought.

The masks provided more than ample sight in the darkness of the tunnel, and Meliss, like the others, was in awe. "I've never seen anything like it," she said quietly. "This tunnel was one of the sewers of the Arwydus, the ones who resided in these lands many years before the castle was built," Anwill explained in a hushed voice. "Quiet, now. We do not know what lies ahead," the Master whispered.

The others and I took the warning seriously. Formidable creatures adored being out of reach from the sun's strong rays, and their senses had adapted over the ages accordingly. We went on in utter silence, and the only sounds we heard were that of Meliss and Leona's footfall on the soft, mossy ground.

We went through various passageways for what seemed like forever and an age to reach our destination. Although, in reality, it didn't even take two hours of walking. Suddenly, Thorsen reached a large area that was ridden with moss hanging from the walls, and a small pool of water in its center. The area was as still as a graveyard, and could have easily been confused for one.

"Anwill, is that what I think it is?" he whispered. Anwill stepped forward to investigate. In front of the pair was a large, circular stone with runes engraved in it, and writing only he could understand around its circumference.

He smiled.

"It is, indeed, my enormous friend," he said, lightly patting Thorsen on his shoulder. We soon followed behind them and entered the large area, seeing the stone which had nearly put Anwill in a trance. "Here lies one of the greatest mysteries of old. Folk in my homeland often spoke of such things, though even *I* am too young to remember them," he continued.

Thorsen looked at him curiously. "How old are you again?" he asked. "Eight-hundred and eighty," Anwill replied calmly. Thorsen was visibly shocked to hear that, his eyebrows lifted far above his already widened eyes. "I-I must be a child in your eyes," he said jokingly. "...But you are. An *oversized* child, perhaps, but a child, nonetheless," Anwill replied with a grin.

I decided to keep my mouth shut, since I didn't want to know how he probably saw my brother and I.

"Time we got to work, Roburn," Anwill said, gesturing towards his partner. "And you're certain this will work?" he asked skittishly. "I am not certain of anything aside from death," Anwill replied. Roburn shrugged. "Well that's... *comforting*," he muttered under his breath.

He stood beside Anwill, and took his hand. "Just like we practiced," Anwill said. Roburn took a deep breath, and nodded. Their eyes went dark *as they stepped into their own Ethereal realms simultaneously.*

As they did so, I closed my eyes, trying desperately to *feel* the mana exuding from the Elf and my senior. It was a difficult task, to be sure, but my brother stepped up beside me and put a hand on my shoulder. "Do you want to see what they're doing?" he asked quietly.

I was stunned at his question, to say the least. There was so much more to the realm of mana manipulation that I simply didn't understand, but after having experienced and gained access to the second stage, I wanted more. I *needed* to know more.

"I didn't even know that was *possible*," I said plaintively, trying to hide my obvious excitement. "Activate your second stage, and I'll help filter the mana for your augmented vision. If done correctly, you should be able to vaguely see what they're doing in the Ethereal overlapped here in the Real," he said quietly.

I nodded my head, and closed my eyes, *drawing my own mana from the Ethereal realm*, before nodding to my brother that I was ready. He saw the mana-leakage from my eyes beneath my mask and smiled. "You little *monster*," he said with a light chuckle before putting his hand on top of my head.

I watched as the mana began *to paint an incredible depiction of what was going on in the other realm.*

Anwill drew a vast amount of mana, returning a part of his consciousness to infuse the hand that clasped Roburn's. *Roburn raised his left hand, and the other that held Anwill's in the real, completing the connection between them. Roburn began to forcefully pull on the mana from the Real and send it back into the Ethereal, forming its own, secondary sphere in front of him. Anwill's consciousness began to be forcefully pulled through the channel Roburn created, and spat him out in the Ethereal with Roburn.*

"It worked!" Roburn exclaimed. "Yes, it did, but do not lose focus. We need to activate the stone," Anwill said. *The pair stretched out their arms, pulling an incredibly vast amount of mana.*

Anwill condensed the mana to his core, holding it there as compactly as he could. The mana became so bright and dense that it began to create a mirrored version in the Real. *Anwill glanced at Roburn, and gave him a nod to* sever the connection, and aimed the hyperdense mana at the large stone.

Bernar undid the spell on my eyes immediately, since it was no longer needed. I watched Anwill struggle with the quantity of mana I had just seen him pull.

How the hell is he even controlling that much? I thought, feeling my heart begin to race.

"Hera fi Arwydus karuwa," he said through gritted teeth, commanding the mana to do his bidding.

The command pulsed out from his core, rapidly enveloping the large runestone in a golden coat of raw mana. The rune in the center began to turn slowly, as though it were kicking off the rust and grime of bygone ages.

"Hera fi Arwydus karuwa!" Anwill said again, thrusting another burst of mana into the stone.

The rune spun more quickly in response.

"HERA FI ARWYDUS KARUWA!" he shouted loudly, commanding the mana with as much willpower as he could muster. The spinning rune finally gave into his command and spun at full speed to the point where the symbol of the rune became one, solid, figure.

"You have heard me thrice, O' mark of bygone ages. Seethe with my will, and heed my command: Open," he said, his voice imbued with mana. A bright burst of mana suddenly exploded from the stone, nearly knocking Roburn off his feet.

Thorsen quickly stepped in and caught him before he fell, avoiding contact with any bare skin that was showing. Roburn's eyes were still the obsidian ovals they had been over the course of time, and sweat began to drip from his brow.

"Hold on just a little longer," Thorsen whispered. We *all* stood around them, observing the largest display of mana any of us, not including the Master, had ever seen.

The swirling mana around the stone glowed brightly, illuminating the dark area that we were in, nearly voiding the need for the masks. Suddenly, a single figure appeared, and passed through the opened portal.

"Anwill?" the figure asked. The others could not see his face, while Anwill was desperately struggling to keep the portal open. "I've summoned you to help us face those who would try to destroy this world. I deeply apologize for the abruptness, but I cannot hold this much longer," he said.

The figure slightly tilted his head, and stretched his hand outward behind him, holding the portal stable with only one hand and minimal effort. "What, and I cannot stress this enough, the *fuck?*" I quietly said to my brother. "Your guess is as good as mine, little brother," Bernar replied, watching Anwill nearly collapse to the floor with exhaustion.

Roburn, on the other hand, remained unconscious in Thorsen's arms. "Make sure he wakes up and gets some food in him. He's going to need it," Anwill said through clenched teeth.

The strange figure glanced around the surrounding area for a few moments, then turned back to face Anwill. "Long has it been since any have summoned us from this stone. What are you facing, and how many are there?" the figure asked. "We've surmised there are about ten-thousand of all manner of creatures, though our numbers might be off," the Master chimed in.

"If what you say is true, then your situation is not favorable for the ones you have here," the figure said after pausing for a moment to consider something no one knew of. "It's worse... we believe they're going after the Gwynnleaf," Anwill grunted.

The figure nodded and cast a spell to hold the portal open in his place as he walked back through it. Not a single soul present could even imagine just how powerful this person was, let alone what other forms of mana manipulation he might know.

The figure reappeared with a small army that filled the space behind him. He closed his hand, as the portal shut down behind him. Roburn's eyes finally returned to normal, and he panted heavily in Thorsen's arms. "We've done it," Thorsen said comfortingly.

The area grew dark once more, as the figure approached Anwill. His features could clearly be seen through the masks' enhancements to be akin to Anwill's. His ears held the same, ringed earrings, and his large, green eyes glowed in the dark. His armor was thick and intricate engravings were set in an unknown metal, as was the curved sword at his side.

The figure had a cloak that nearly reached his ankles secured by two brooches that held viper-like eyes engraved in amethyst, wrapped in pure silver. "Do not fret, children of men, for we mean you no harm," the figure said calmly. The few hundred elves behind him were all clad in the same armor, save the cape.

Male and female elves composed the army, although due to their fine features, it was difficult to tell which was which. Even their eyes glowed the same green as their leader's, though the two by his side stood out, with one having gray eyes and the other a pair of deep red.

"What is your name?" the Master asked. "I am called Nenvalur

Aralamin, and I bring with me the aid you and your mage have sought," the elf replied, gesturing to the ones behind him. "I am at your service," Nenvalur bowed. Thorsen shook his head, trying to wake himself from what he thought to be a dream.

Nenvalur nearly stood at Thorsen's height, and looked him over. "My, you're a large one, aren't you?" he said, dropping his formal tone a little.

No one, not even Anwill, had suspected such a comment coming from the elf. "I am as my Hjalfarian Blodt has made me," Thorsen said with pride. Nenvalur grinned "And such a heritage it is. Honestly, if the ones behind you had your height and strength, there would be no need to summon us," he said playfully.

We all immediately felt more comfortable with him and his presence. Granted, we hadn't spoken to the others he'd brought with him, yet, but the friendly display Nenvalur gave us certainly helped quell any nervousness.

"Tell me, how may we assist you? From what I gather, you said the Gwynnleaf was at risk?" Nenvalur said, while Anwill nodded in agreement. "It might very well be, unfortunately," he began. "Leona, the former queen of the land you are in, and the Master of Codrean, here, may be more able to give you the details you will need," he continued.

Leona and the Master stepped forward, greeting the elf with a bow. "There is no need for that," Nenvalur began. "I am a simple warrior, not some king that requires such formalities to boost his ego," he said with a warm smile. He looked about him, and only then noticed that nearly all wore strange masks. "This will not do," he said, shaking his head.

He motioned to the ones behind him, and a few of them drew torches, igniting them with mana-flame. The large area soon became bright enough to where there was no need for masks any longer.

"So, what is required of my warriors and I? Support? Security? *Slaughter*?" Nenvalur asked, cutting straight to the point. "All of the above, I suppose," the Master began. "Above us lies a great force of creatures that have invaded the castle - taking control of it and possibly slaying all who live within it," the Master said.

Nenvalur rubbed his clean-shaven chin. "And to top it all off, they're probably going after the Gwynnleaf. *Ah...* This is a terrible situation all-round, isn't it?" he asked, sucking wind through his teeth. "Very well, then. Tell me where we must strike, and it will be done," he said with a shrug, indicating that mere monsters were of little nuance to him and his men.

"There is another thing that I believe to be of the utmost importance," Leona began. Nenvalur shifted his gaze. "And what might that be, Queen of Men?" he asked. "The source of the Synners' prowess with mana manipulation lies here," Leona said. Nenvalur raised an eyebrow.

"You meant to say *one* of the sources, I presume?" he asked nonchalantly. Leona was taken aback, as was the Master. "I'm sorry?" Leona asked, hoping to confirm what her ears had just heard.

"It is true that a source of great power lies within Coltend, which many of us here were already aware of. Gwynnleaf *is* that source for many on the Continent. However, there are other sources which we elves have closely guarded in secret over the ages in which mana has existed," Nenvalur explained as though he would to a child.

The Master nodded as though it confirmed an old theory of his. "So, there *are* other sources. I had always suspected as much, but this... this news is..." the Master trailed off. "That is correct," Nenvalur replied. "Naturally, I am not at leave to tell you much more about them. Simply know that they exist, and that we must preserve the one hidden here," he said nonchalantly.

"Of course, to do so will mean that my men and I require a layout of the castle itself, for as I have stated previously: it has been a long time since any of us have been here. Things have certainly changed in the past two millennia," Nenvalur said. Thorsen approached him, and handed him the map that he had been entrusted with. "Ah, thank you, Giant," Nenvalur said with a smile. The giant returned the smile.

"Thorsen's the name," he said. "Thorsen, like one of the many gods' sons? A most fitting name if ever I've heard one," Nenvalur said with a grin. He observed the map, holding every minute detail in his infallible memory.

"We need you to attack…" Leona began. "The ones nearest to the Palace itself, and work our way outwards, giving you a safety bubble around your real target. I understand," Nenvalur finished her sentence.

Leona looked stunned. "Rightly so," she said. "Very well, then, but we must move at once. Nightfall comes and even worse things than a simple attack tend to happen in the dark hours of the night," Nenvalur said.

I wonder what he means by that, I thought.

"The spawning of crying, eating, shitting, meat-bags for cores, obviously," Nenvalur said cheerfully.

Did he just read my thoughts? Also, what the fuck? I thought with an internal laugh, standing silently and wondering whether my suspicions were correct.

"I did, young man," Nenvalur said, staring directly at me. "I meant what I said in jest, of course. There are much *fouler* things than children, though they are rather high on my list," he said pensively. "Come, we must move quickly."

Nenvalur's elves who held the torches merged with our group, heading through the tunnels for a few kilometers, until we began to feel the rumbling of the hoard above us. I noted that the sound of their muffled bellowing could only just be heard if one were to listen attentively.

"We must be inside the castle walls by now," Leona said, hearing the rumbling coming from above. Thin wisps of dust fell from the ceiling of the tunnel. Nenvalur and Thorsen led the way, while Meliss held my arm tightly.

"Thoma, I think we're one man short," she whispered.

I felt a chill go down my spine.

"Who?" he asked quietly. "I can't say for certain, but I've just had a weird feeling since the portal opened," she replied. I dared not turn around in case anyone had overheard what Meliss had said. We went deeper and deeper into the tunnels, making various turns along the way, when we reached a fork in the passageways.

"I believe this is where we split up," the Master said. "I've said it before, and I'll say it again: Dividing a force is dangerous in war," Pyle warned. "*Dangerous* but necessary. We knew it would come to this, and now it has," the Master replied simplistically. Pyle sighed lightly, but nodded his agreement in the torchlight.

"Leona and Meliss, you will accompany Pyle, Bernar, Thoma, Edryd, Batch and myself down the northern passage, while the others will accompany Nenvalur, Thorsen and the elves to the southern entrance," the Master said.

"It will be an honor to see you fight, Thorsen," I heard Nenvalur say quietly. "Likewise," Thorsen replied. "When the battle is over, and should we all survive it, we are going to reconvene at the palace, understood?" the Master asked. There was a unified clanging of hands slapping the scabbards of their swords.

Meliss shook nervously. "This is it, right? We're doing this?" she asked me quietly. My thoughts halted for a moment as I tried to find the right words to say. To be honest, I didn't know what to say, other than what I had been trained to do for most of my life.

"Breathe deeply, and draw your blade once we're topside. Stick close to me and the others, and no harm will come to you, got it?" I asked calmly as I could, though I was also beginning to break into a nervous sweat. Meliss nodded, and focused on her breathing.

"Time we showed these bastards what we're *really* made of," Batch said to Edryd. "I just hope you know what that is, because it better not be a steaming pile of shit," Edryd replied with a grin, which was returned in kind.

Bernar walked over to me and put a hand on my shoulder. "I hope you've learned a thing or two, you lanky fuck," he said. "So do I, you perennial dingleberry," I retorted. Bernar chuckled quietly. "That's the best one I've heard you use as a comeback, ever," he said. "I've been saving it for a special occasion such as this," I replied with a wink.

"Must you always use derogatory terms between the two of you?" Leona asked, but Bernar merely shrugged his initial response. "He's my little brother, and has to continuously be reminded of that fact. Such is the way of being the older brother," he replied. Leona shook her head, but grinned as she turned away from them. Bernar and I winked at each other, and looked forward. "Cheeky little shit," he muttered.

I heard the comment and was instantly comforted.

"Let's move," the Master called out as loudly as he dared, and no sooner were we off, each to their destinations, and some to their fates.

CHAPTER 22

Traitor

The Masked One and his two new servants had made their preparations as best they could as the sun began to set. "Dakzul," he began. He was reviewing a map of Coltend of violet swirls of mana that levitated just above the stone floor.

"You will take the western facing side of the palace, while Kimzul will watch the northern side. I suspect they will attempt a diversion of some sort, so be on your guard for anything that may seem suspicious," he said, pointing to certain areas on the map with a tendril of mana. "I will command creatures to aid you, while I begin preparations to transport the plants back to Valdis. Any questions?" he asked.

Dakzul shook his head, but Kimzul gazed at the map. He was no strategist, and felt something was missing, but said nothing. "Kimzul," the Masked One said, breaking his train of thought. "None, great one," Kimzul quickly answered. "Then go now to your stations, and await further instructions," the Masked one said.

He waved his hand, and the two bowed before him, and made their way to their destinations. The Masked One disintegrated the map he had made, and proceeded up the nearby stairs that led to the royal bedroom.

He saw the hand Leona had crushed in her flight still wedged between the door and the frame. It was covered in small, white maggots that bore deeply into the dead flesh.

That must have been interesting to watch. Greedy bastards, he thought.

His eyes glowed intensely, and a blast of violet mana came from his fingertips, splintering the door, and twisting the metal hinges. He stepped through the now empty frame into the room. The large bed was just as Leona had left it on that fateful day - the sheets and red covers were in a wrinkled mound near the center of the bed. The easel in the corner of the bedroom stood as a silent guardian. If it had eyes, it would have been terrified to see the large, cloaked figure in the room gazing at it with genuine interest.

The painting on the easel was that of a dense forest, with a flowing river running down the center of the painting. There was a fawn drinking from the river that gleamed in the small rays of sunlight that seeped through the canopy. He stepped away from the easel, proceeding to look out the large windows.

He moved the curtains aside, and before him was a vast field of houses and shacks, with the wall that protected the city itself beyond them. He looked out beyond the wall, and into the direction of his dark hall.

So many months and years. So many nights alone that now are under the threat of being wasted. I've always wanted to know the secrets of this world, and now that I will soon have one of the greatest ones in my possession, it so quickly comes under threat.

However, I find myself feeling more unsatisfied than I had originally thought I would be. The Undergod has granted me more power than I thought possible, and because of that, I know I will likely never be able to break free from my debt to him.

Oh, the knowledge I have acquired over these many years. Had I continued living my life as it was, I probably wouldn't have seen even a third of what I have.

He chuckled quietly.

Fate is a worthless, fickle bitch who doubts what one can achieve through pure and unrelenting displays of power. I have challenged it time and time again, always overcoming the odds. But now that this massive step is ending, I can't help but feel a sense of unease. Have I miscalculated anything? he sighed.

If I play my hand correctly, I could become a god amongst these worms, but I do have to be cautious. One false step and it could spell the end for all of my ambitions. I must be patient, he thought.

He closed his eyes, and imagined himself in front of a sea of people - both regular and Synners alike - as they all bowed down to him.

He smiled wickedly as he opened his eyes. "One day."

He left the royal room, and made his way outside of the palace to find Kimzul, who stood atop the stone wall that guarded the city. He levitated himself to his servant's side, the afternoon sun beaming warm rays onto his mask. "Status," he said. "Everything is calm, and there have been no signs of their approach, great one," Kimzul replied, gazing off into the distance with the aid of his helmet.

The Masked One looked out in the same direction. "Something isn't right," he said quietly after a moment's pause. Kimzul heard him say the words, and instantly felt a chill go down his spine.

Off in the distance, a rider appeared out of the dense forest, coming along the path to the Northern Gate. The horse's hooves could be heard from a distance in the silence atop the great wall. "Great one," Kimzul began. "I see it," the Masked One said before Kimzul could explain what he was seeing.

The horse was snorting heavily under the stress of galloping at such a high velocity. The caped rider pushed the horse as hard as he could, as though he were fleeing from something.

Kimzul scoffed. "It's almost as if this was the only one of them who had the courage to come and fight you, great one," he said. "Then let's give them a warm welcome," the Masked One said with a tinge of evil in his voice. The glow in his eyes intensified as he cast his hands backwards, releasing tendrils of mana down to the great gears that turned to open the massive gates.

The gates opened, and out of it sprinted an ochelon on its fours. It rapidly picked up speed, digging its claws into the dirt beneath it to gain more traction. The rider pressed on, continuing to push the horse as fast as its legs would carry it. The ochelon saw its prey, and its blackened eyes focused directly on its target, gaining even more speed.

Suddenly, the rider lifted the hood of its cloak, and the Masked One looked upon the rider's face.

He made it. He actually got away, he thought.

He raised his hand, and the ochelon came to an abrupt stop, skidding along the dirt for quite some distance. The rider rode past it, and it followed him back to the gate. Once inside, the rider dismounted his tired horse, and led it to a nearby barrel of water. The Masked One floated down from the walls to greet the newcomer. He opened his arms in a welcoming gesture as his cloak fluttered in the wind. "Welcome to the once *impenetrable* Coltend Castle," the Masked One said.

"It is an honor to finally meet you in person, master," Irun said humbly.

"I have waited so long for this day, I can hardly believe it's here," he said, keeping his head low. "As have I," the Masked One began. "Your services in Codrean were more than adequate.

Inside knowledge of an enemy's movements is always a great advantage to have," he said. "Now, tell me of their movements towards the castle," the Masked One said.

"They have gathered reinforcements from a hidden Synner school in the North, as I'm sure you're already aware. By now, they might have already made their way here to the castle, master," Irun began.

The Masked One shook his head. "I have not yet seen such a force," he said. "That's because they've split up into two groups, one from the North, and the others from…" Irun began, but was interrupted by a call coming from the top of the wall.

"They're coming!" Kimzul shouted from above. The Masked One levitated himself and Irun to the top of the wall to observe the attackers' approach. They saw a group of horsemen coming down the same path as Irun had taken a few short minutes before.

The Masked One cast his tendrils to open the gates once more, raising his hand to summon glicks and ochelons to fight the riders. The horde left the gates screeching and bellowing as they always did whenever they moved in for a kill, and they watched the riders off in the distance get into their formation.

"They are no match for such a horde, great one," Kimzul said. Irun looked at the tall, armored person towering over him. "Forgive me, master, but *who* or *what* the fuck is this… thing?" he asked.

The Masked One didn't turn to face him, instead, he held his gaze on the charging creatures. "He is my new servant. Once a member of the Church, he has seen the error of his ways, and pledged his service to me, just as you have done from the Synners," he replied.

Irun, naturally, was confused.

So, a crunchie gets an awesome suit of armor, while I'm stuck in this smelly, leather jerkin? That's a fair way to treat an ally, he thought.

The Masked One turned to face him so quickly that it startled Irun. "You ought to be taught respect, you little shit," he said angrily. "I-I apologize, master. I meant no disrespect," Irun stuttered, frozen in place. "I could have decided to let that ochelon kill you, even after all of your service to me. You want armor of your own? Here, take it, you little ingrate," the Masked one said.

Irun knew he was angry, but began to feel the cloud of mana enveloping him. The mana solidified into the same type of armor as Kimzul's, but it was far less intricate and glorious, leaving more than a few spaces open for a possible attack.

"You already know how to fight, so I don't have to give you as much protection," the Masked One began. "You ought to thank me for not transmuting you into some sort of giant prick with legs and an anus for a mouth," the Masked One said. Irun swallowed. "Thank you, master," he said humbly. The Masked One watched as the battle raged on in the distance.

Arrows flew through the air at Garett's command, and struck their targets with superb accuracy and precision. Irun, too, was watching carefully. The Masked One turned to his spy. "They split up, didn't they?" he asked. "As I was going to say before, master, the others are to arrive by way of an underground passage," Irun said. The Masked One grabbed him faster than a snake to its prey. "What underground passage?" he asked. Irun began to shake uncontrollably, as fear made speaking more difficult than ever before.

"Th-there's a passage that begins from far outside the castle, and leads directly beneath the city itself. Something of old elvish make," he said shakily. "And why am I only hearing about this now? Didn't I tell you to inform me of anything and everything that they were planning to do?" The Masked One asked, glaring at Irun.

"I-I-I didn't know they were going to use an underground passage, master," Irun began. "By the time I realized what they were doing, we were already at the entrance to the tunnels. Prior to that, I was not informed of how we were going to enter the castle. At that point, I figured I was close enough to be able to make my escape over here to you, master," he continued. The Masked One could see no lies in Irun's eyes, and released him. Irun stumbled back a few steps, and breathed a sigh of relief.

"This is not good news, indeed. There must be countless entrances and exits to this *underground passage* strewn about the city," the Masked One said grimly, briefly glazing over the city's rooftops. "We must be on our guard for any sign of movement that isn't one of the creatures below. It doesn't seem like they will follow their usual convention of attacking at dawn, so be prepared for a night raid," he continued.

Irun paused for a moment. "What am I to do when they arrive, master?" he asked. "I will send a small portion of the horde to support you when the time to fight against your old comrades comes," the Masked One replied. Irun digested the words.

I've always known that one day it might come to this, he thought.

"Very well, master," he replied.

The sun was lowering itself on the distant horizon, and a night fight wasn't exactly the best of situations one could possibly be in, even if one could see in the dark. The Masked One lowered himself and Irun to the base of the wall, gently landing on the stone floor. The Masked One had a much longer stride than Irun's who struggled to keep up with his new master.

"Are you ready to fight your friends, possibly to the death?" the Masked One asked. The question struck Irun square in the chest. He hesitated for a few moments. "I've never really fit in with any of them, or at least it never felt that way. I've always felt a bit more estranged around them than anything else, master," Irun replied. Saying the words out loud for the first time gave him a small amount of relief.

"That's... not at all what I asked. Does that mean you're willing to fight them? It's a simple *yes* or *no* question," The Masked One said, dumbfounded by the answer. "I... I think I'll be alright, master," Irun replied after a few moments of consideration. "I pray you do not hesitate as you just did when you meet them in battle," the Masked One said, observing his demeanor.

"I won't," Irun replied. The Masked One scoffed behind his mask, barely audible to Irun's ears. "Very well, then. You will be the vanguard of the force that I will send to draw them out of their newfound hiding holes," he said. Irun nodded, then realized it was stupid of him to do so, for his master was not even looking at him.

"Where should I start, master?" he asked. "If what you say about the underground passage is true, and their secondary force is coming from the north, I'd tell you to begin somewhere on the northern side of the palace itself. If you have a better idea of where they might come from, I advise you to take this with you," the Masked One said, pulling a crystal from one of the pouches in his cloak.

He threw it over his head to his servant, who was trailing behind him. Irun nearly let it drop as it fell from the air, but managed to recover it. "Go. Now," the Masked One ordered. "Yes, master," Irun replied, scurrying off down one of the many roads void of human life.

He eyeballed the crystal for a few moments, realizing he knew nothing of how it should be used. The Masked One realized it as well, and cast a spell of violet mana into it. Irun was taken aback at the sudden glow of the crystal itself, and felt the ground beneath his feet begin to rumble. "Do not allow anything to destroy it," the Masked One said with caution. "If any harm should come to it, the monsters around you may very well turn on you or each other - as is their natural way of doing things," he continued. Irun nodded, still feeling the ground beneath his feet tremble.

The screeching, cackling monsters came *en masse* towards him. He drew his sword - more out of habit than anything else at the sight of them. They came to a halt a few meters away from him, as though awaiting orders. He observed them closely. He had never seen such creatures at such a close range, other than when they were attempting to disembowel him.

Their jagged teeth and scaly skin flared at the sight of him. "Damn glicks," he said quietly. He turned his back to them, making his way towards the northern end of the palace with the small horde following closely behind him. The sun was setting on the distant horizon, and they were all now in the shadow of the great wall that had failed to keep the creatures at bay. The houses shook as they went past each one, the smell of rotting flesh of the ones who had lived in them filling the air.

Did I really make the right choice here? I mean, my mother died as a Synner, and a damned good one at that. I don't think I've lived up to her reputation, but I'm fucking trying my best, he thought as they went past the derelict houses.

Not much of a choice left but to follow through, I suppose. Gods fucking damn it all, I don't want to die. I have to go through with this. Mother, have mercy on me when I see you again, he thought, kicking himself for the choice he had made.

I have to press on, and meet whatever Fate has in store for me now.
He led his small band of grotesque creatures to the general

area of the northern gate, and waited for those moving between the trees to begin their assault.

And so it begins, he thought.

CHAPTER 23

Unexpected Company

My heartbeat could almost be heard throughout the tunnels that lie beneath Coltend, and my palms and brow were exuding sweat. They knew they had to be close to the exits that the tunnels would eventually lead to. My hands began to shake a little due to the adrenaline coursing through my veins even before the battle had begun.

I have to get my shit together. I can't afford to become a liability now, he thought.

Bernar and the others were walking ahead of him, while Meliss was at my side. She, too, was a nervous wreck, and whispered countless prayers to the gods that the need to fight for her life would not come. I glanced over at her, and saw that she was nearly in tears.

I put my hand on her shoulder, and she looked at me with no small amount of fear in her eyes. "You alright?" I asked, already knowing the answer. She paused for a moment, then nodded her response. "Other than shaking like I've got an internal earthquake underway, I'm fine," she said quietly in the dimly lit tunnels.

By fine *she means fucked up, insecure, needy, and emotional, right? I've been shaking so badly, I hardly noticed her own this much,* I thought, trying my best to keep my own fears under control.

"We're going to be alright," I said as comfortingly as I could. She nodded again, squeezing my waist a little more tightly.

Thorsen was still at the helm of the small party that was wandering in near darkness, when Nenvalur heard a sound. Anwill heard it as well, and looked over at him. "Think we've been noticed?" he asked quietly.

Nenvalur shook his head. "Nothing's been down here for centuries, it seems. The odds of someone or something wandering down here of their own accord are astronomical," he replied. I overheard what the two had said, and felt Meliss shudder. "We should hurry if we wish to maintain the element of surprise," Nenvalur said to Thorsen, who simply nodded and picked up the pace.

They went on for a few minutes without interruption - except for a few rumblings above them - when Leona pointed at a sign on the wall. "Here, take a look at this. I can't read it, but I recognize it. I believe we are heading in the right direction," she said. Anwill went over to her side, and read the inscription that was barely visible. "Quite an eye you've got there, my lady," he said with a grin.

"I have been searching for it ever since we entered. When I was younger, I used to sneak into the library to take a gander at the books that were *unsuitable* for a queen," she said, returning the grin. Anwill pursed his lips while widening his eyes. "Well, I'm glad you did. Nenvalur, I believe she's right," he said. Nenvalur stepped forward, and read over the sign. "Indeed, we are. Let's get to this battle already. My sword is thirsty," he said more cheerfully than anyone had expected.

This elf is a nutbag! My favorite kind of person, I thought with a subtle grin.

Nenvalur and Anwill took point alongside Thorsen and they soon came to yet another sign, signaling that they truly were on the right path in the network of tunnels. A few minutes and a few signs later, they came to it. An open area like the one that held the portal stone, where near the back stood a large, wooden structure supporting the inner walls lay before them. Between the large beams of the frame, there was a metal door that had intricate designs laid into it.

"This must be the entrance," Anwill said. Nenvalur observed the detailed workings on the door itself, infusing a little bit of mana to light up the carvings. It was a beautiful display that shone a dim light in the darkness. "Unless Coltend has such smiths that could craft something akin to the smiths of my homeland, this *has* to be it," he said.

There was a crumbling sound coming from the right. Nenvalur and the others turned as quickly as a hummingbird and saw the walls begin to move.

"Sentries!" he called out, drawing his sword. I heard the call, and quickly brushed Meliss aside, where Leona took her and maintained a safe distance. Three gigantic stone figures emerged from their resting places in the walls, crumbling the stones around them. The Master *allowed mana to flow* into the sky, as he cast a glowing ball of light to the high ceiling, revealing the golems. "I've met one of these before. It's an earth golem," Thorsen said.

"Where the hell could you possibly have met something like this?" I asked, staring up at the golem's mouth. "I had encountered one of them before in the Rhydian mountains by chance, and barely escaped with my life. Three of them are going to be nasty business," Thorsen replied.

"Fucking hate these things. Without the right elemental attunement, you can't really damage them," he said, his great sword gleaming in the light from the sphere above them.

Elemental attunement? The hell does that mean? I thought.

"Keep the others back to avoid unnecessary losses," the Master shouted. Bernar spread his arms to help the ones behind him remain in the safety of the tunnel. I could see the sentries still recovering from ages of sleep, one of them even shaking their head to wake themselves up from ages of slumber.

While they had no ears, their massive, black eyes allowed them to see much more than a normal human could. "They must have woken up because of the mana I used," Nenvalur said with a slight discouragement in his voice. "Inconvenient, but not impossible to overcome. To battle!" the mad elf shouted.

Inconvenient? Who the hell is this guy? I thought.

The stones that composed their bodies had moss and other such things growing on them, with the peaks of the stones just barely sticking out, and the only sounds they made were those of the rocks grinding together as they moved. Anwill, the Master, Thorsen and Nenvalur were the only ones who were to stand against them.

"Oh, don't bother trying to slash them. Their skin is *far* too tough to be affected, even with mana-infusion and the right attunement," Nenvalur said, watching the sentries carefully as they began to move towards the small group. They all began to draw mana as quickly as they could from the Ethereal, preparing for the fight ahead.

"How the fuck are we supposed to beat them, then?" Thorsen asked. "Last time I saw one of these, we knocked it off the side of the mountain," he continued. "It's been awhile, let me think how we're supposed to do this in such a small area," Nenvalur replied. He had also faced sentries before - many times over, in fact - although each time it was along one of the many paths through the Rhydian mountains.

The first sentry moved in for a crushing blow aimed at Anwill, who expertly dove out of the way. The thin layer of mud where he had once stood was cast into the air by the blow, and the ground shook. "Get underneath them, if you can! They don't bend well, so if you just dodge their feet, you might have a better chance at surviving," Nenvalur said after recovering from the first blow from the sentry nearest to him.

The four of them began to fan out, each one going in their own direction towards the living stones themselves. Another blow aimed at the Master and Thorsen came in at a sweep, forcing both of them to jump over the large fist that came for them. "Good thing they're somewhat slow," Thorsen said. "Slow, but still deadly if you don't focus," the Master shot back.

Anwill circled the sentry nearest to him while keeping an eye on the other two that were in the area. Another pounding blow shook the ground and made some of the stones from the roof fall to the ground about them, adding a new enemy to the arena. They dodged the falling stones, as best they could, though one of them hit Anwill in the shoulder, nearly crushing the bone beneath his elven armor.

"We've got to hurry, or else this entire network will come down on our heads," he shouted. "I have an idea," the Master said. He moved closer to one of the sentries, grabbing a stone along the way. He threw it at its head, and it instantly began to swing at him. "Move," he shouted while both he and Thorsen dodged the incoming blow. It struck the wall at its side, causing more rubble to fall from the ceiling.

"On me," he said to the others, who came to him, dodging other blows along the way. The sentry nearest to the Master tried to crush them with his enormous stone foot, and he stepped out of the way. "Cast Exar at their heads, make them come this way," he said.

"Are you insane?" Anwill asked. "Perhaps, However, if we can turn their blows against one another, we might just win this. Let them do the work for us," the Master replied, dodging yet another stomp. "That should do it," Nenvalur said, approaching the Master and Thorsen. Anwill came soon after, and the four bunched together. I and the others looked on anxiously, some of them were praying for a positive outcome.

They drew an immense amount of mana once more. "Now!" the Master shouted, and they cast their spells to get the attention of the ones who threatened them. Large bursts of blue and violet mana emitted from the small group, reaching their targets. The sentries replied with their own tricks - clasping their hands together, and smacking down towards the ground.

The four of them rolled out of the way of the unified blows, covering themselves in mud. The Master saw his plan had failed miserably, and he sighed. The sentries began to turn on them, more aggravated than before.

The barrage of blows came in quick succession, and the four who battled them were hard pressed to get out of the paths of the blows in time. I looked on, and for an unknown reason, it reminded him of when he had beheaded the ochelon in my last battle.

I've got an idea, I thought.

He sprinted out from the hallway, and into the open area, dodging Bernar's hand that tried to hold him back. "Thoma! No!" he shouted. I didn't even look back, and caught the Master's eye. "What are you doing?" the Master asked. "I've got an idea, but I'll need your help," he said.

My eyes began to glow as he cast the Exar spell repeatedly, forcing my target to turn towards him. "Come at me, you overgrown pebble!" I shouted with my mana-infused voice.

"He knows they don't have ears, right?" Nenvalur muttered,

Anwill could only shrug his reply. My target turned on him with extremely violent intent, barely managing to escape the sweeping blow that came much more quickly than anticipated.

"It *turned* to him?" Nenvalur asked, surprised at the response the young boy got. "It probably has to do with the fact that the second stage of mana manipulation still leaks enough mana to be heard in one's voice. Maybe that's what did it," the Master suggested.

"That still doesn't explain how quickly it responded to his command," Nenvalur said. "He's right, it makes no sense. I've never seen a golem move like that before," Anwill chimed in.

I went between the legs of the one who had attacked me, and was soon behind it. The others were dodging their own blows right and left, but the Master carefully observed what I was doing as best he could. I cast the spell again, directing the blast behind the golem's knee, forcing it to kneel. I used its leg as a step, climbing up its back as quickly as I could.

I grasped the stones near the nape, and held on as tightly as I could as my impromptu mount began to rise. Once it was at its full height, I adjusted myself to where I could just see over its shoulder.

"Now you want to ride the damn thing as if it were a giant horse? Fuck me," Anwill said. "I have a plan! Just trust me!" I shouted. The Master had caught onto my plan, and was already behind the one nearest to him. "Nenvalur, take the third," the Master shouted. "Understood," the elf replied, not entirely sure what was happening but deciding to trust the Master anyway.

They cast as I had done, and their respective sentries kneeled, leaving Thorsen and Anwill in the center of the three sentries.

"Now what?" Anwill asked - he still hadn't understood my plan. "Draw their attention and move before they strike. Once they strike, the three of us will aim Exars at their heads, forcing them to swing at the source of mana! That will keep us low enough to the ground to quickly escape without injury, and kill them at the same time," I replied.

"You're a few marbles short of a full bag, that's for sure," Anwill said, shaking his head. "I trust him. Nenvalur, get ready," the Master shouted. "I hate being bait," Anwill muttered, shaking his head. He and Thorsen cast their spells at the sentries' heads, adeptly dodging the incoming blows. The three of them struck the ground, lowering their heads in the process.

The others and I managed to hold on to their mounts as their blows landed, sending bits of rock and clouds of dirt into the air. "Now!" I shouted the moment the blow landed. The three of us cast our spells at each other's golems, in hopes of forcing their swings on one another.

The sentries felt the blast to their head, and each one swiped its large arm at the other's head. I timed my dismount according to the swing, barely managing to get out of its way as it knocked my sentry's head clean off, smashing it into the distant wall.

Did the others' die as well? I thought as I landed on the ground.

The sentry I was on began to fall like a large tree towards Anwill and Thorsen, who were observing the coordinated attacks. "Look out!" Anwill shouted, knocking Thorsen out of the way of the falling monsters. The wind caused by the body falling rustled his hair that was thick with mud, as it passed over a few centimeters away from his torso.

The two of them recovered as quickly as they could, and were quickly back on their feet. "That was too close for comfort. Thank you," Thorsen said. The five of us began to laugh heartily at our accomplishments.

More stones began to fall due to the rumbling from the golems' attacks, and I noticed a massive chunk coming right for me. I got out of the way, and shielded my face from the dirt and mud it kicked up.

"Well, that was fun! A bit risky, but fun nevertheless!" Nenvalur exclaimed. The Master and the others were also visibly pleased that my plan had worked. "I-I just did what I thought would work. After my fight with that pair of ochelon back home, I realized that these massive creatures don't see well from behind, even if they are sensitive to mana. I wanted to capitalize on that observation, is all," I replied shyly.

"*Pair* of ochelons? For one your size, I'm surprised you could even take *one* on. That was an amazing plan, young man. I'll be sure to pass that onto my own warriors who lack the necessary elemental attunements when I return," Nenvalur began. "*Oh*, t-thank you," I replied with a nod. "What is your name, if I may ask?" the elven warrior asked. "My name is Thoma Fayren, sir," I replied, putting a hand to my chest and giving a curt bow.

"Fayren, *eh*? A strong name for a Synner. It's an honor to meet you, and thank you once again for your bravery. You will always be welcome in my home," Nenvalur said with a slight bow. I returned the bow, and made his way to the others in the tunnel who were cheering as loudly as they dared.

Wait, where the fuck does he even come from? I thought.

"You're one ballsy, little shithead, you know that? You almost up and fucking died on me... *us*!" Bernar said, embracing his younger brother. "I agree, you almost gave me a heart-attack," Meliss chimed. "Well, I'm sorry I scared you, but I didn't die. Those sentries took my place," I chuckled, raising my hands placatingly.

Suddenly, the entire cave began to tremble, knocking massive boulders loose from the ceiling.

"We need to go! Everyone, follow us!" Anwill shouted. The Master tore the large door from the archway they had seen earlier with mana, and cast it against the wall. "Move!" he shouted. Everyone present rushed into the doorway as the stones fell from the roof above them.

Leona was nearly crushed flat by a large stone that fell, but Bernar had pulled her out of the way just in time. Nearly all of us managed to get through, though a few were killed during our escape.

The beams that supported the walls caved in behind us, cutting us off from the other passages that they had come from. "Is everyone alright?" the Master asked, shielding his face from the cloud of dust the cave-in caused. A few limbs could be seen crushed beneath the rubble, and knew there was nothing to be done.

We very quickly realized just now nearly we'd escaped with our lives.

"This is all *your* fault! Don't you know to stay in your fucking lane?" one of the Synners said, approaching me. I glanced over at the one who had said it, while Roburn put his hand on a woman's shoulders, stopping her in her tracks as he shook his head. "Not worth it, Rosie. There's no way he could have predicted that would happen," he said calmly.

Rosie? With a mouth like that? She's the embodiment of irony, if ever I've seen it, I thought, turning to face her.

"Even if he *could have*, does that mean that we can all just run off and do our own things? What the fuck happened to orders, chains of command, and other such things, *eh*?" she asked. Roburn shook his head. He knew her temper had always been a fiery one and realized what she said made sense. "She's got a point, you know," Roburn said, agreeing with her.

I didn't really know what to say. All I could think of was some sort of logical explanation to what had happened.

"I know she does, but nothing they were doing seemed to

be working. To be entirely honest, I don't think my killing the sentries had anything to do with the cave-in. They were embedded in the walls to begin with, so it's more likely that our presence there as a *whole* is what caused it, not just the golems' attacks," I said, turning away to face my brother.

"*Tsk*. What would *you* know? Cocky, little shit," Rosie said under her breath.

"Did you think I wouldn't hear that?" I snapped, asking the question with my mana-infused voice as I looked over my shoulder. I could feel my eyes glowing even more intensely than they had been before.

She was stunned, her jaw bouncing up and down, trying to find an answer to my question.

"I-I didn't..." Rosie stammered. Just as the word left her mouth, the entire remaining area began falling apart, with stones beginning to fall from above. I still hadn't released my second stage, and while my vision was still enhanced, I noticed the stone was falling directly towards the pair. I used his *Whip of Doom* to quickly transform it into little more than dust.

"Next time, a *cocky, little shit* like me might not be there to save you. Might want to learn to live up to your name, *Rosie*," I said with a glare, returning my eyes and voice back to normal. As I looked around at who was left, I realized just how bad things had really been.

About a fifth of us are gone. Damn it, I thought after I did a brief headcount.

I had to acknowledge a fact that was hard for me to swallow: It could have been worse. The alternative solution to our problem, if we had stayed there and fought with them any longer, would have led to more of us getting killed beneath the rocks. I knew the whole situation hinged on our successful infiltration, but I hadn't expected so many of us to die before the fighting had really started.

Needless to say, my heart tried to sink to depths I didn't know I had, and for a few moments, I allowed it.

We all did.

Nenvalur, only having lost one of his own, sent a silent prayer to the gods to guide them safely into the afterlife. The Master surely felt remorse for the ones he had lost, but he knew, just as well as the rest of us, the cost of our sacrifices and how their losses would not be in vain.

"Only one way out now, and I'm sure that the ones above us will soon notice the gaping hole in the city, if they haven't already. Let's go," the Master said after having allowed us a few moments of silence for the fallen we were forced to leave behind.

He cast a new ball of light that led us down the hallway. Sobbing could be heard from a few of the Synners who had lost their friends in their flight to escape the rubble, but there was no time to mourn the dead.

We're already on borrowed time as it is, I thought, holding Meliss a little more tightly.

A few minutes passed before we reached the final doorway that led to the surface. We paused for a moment to ensure everyone had made it. Meliss looked at the others, and the feeling she'd had that something was wrong grew as she tugged on my jerkin twice. "Where's Irun?" she asked. The others looked about them to see if he was with them.

"He was with us when we entered the passage, but he wasn't saying anything. I was too scared to even think about talking to anyone, lest I awake some sort of ancient daemon in here," Edryd replied. "Did he get crushed by the rubble?" I asked. "Can't say for sure. I didn't speak to anyone either, but if he's not with us, chances are he got crushed," Batch replied gloomily.

I felt a slight turn in my stomach.

I never grew very close to him, but he was still mine, Batch, and Ed's roommate for more than half our lives. I don't want to believe he's dead, but the alternative isn't much better, either, I thought.

Meliss put a hand on my shoulder. "Sorry for the loss of your friend," she said. I felt another turn at the word *loss*. "Thanks," I replied quietly, losing myself in thought, while Batch was nearly in tears at the thought of our friend being crushed by the caved-in ceiling.

The Master walked over to Nenvalur and the others. "Alright, here's what we must do," he began. "Most of my Synners will go with your warriors to create distractions for the creatures above, while the rest of us head to the Palace to deal with the Masked One," he said.

Nenvalur nodded. "Sounds like a plan to me," he said. "Haven't had a good fight in… what, two hundred years? It's about time I've gotten some action," he grinned.

"I admire your attitude," Anwill began. "Let's hope it lasts the night." Nenvalur chuckled, and slapped his hand on Anwill's shoulder. "You're still young, and have got a lot to learn," he said cheerfully. "Anwill's considered *young* to him?" I asked Bernar.

"It's always something with them. Damn, it's hard to imagine what it must be like to be that old," Bernar replied. The Master observed the exchange, and allowed a grin to form itself in the corner of his mouth. "Everyone ready?" he asked.

No one said a word against his question, but we all had our answer written on our faces, regardless.

"Let's move," he said to the others. Nenvalur and his group drew their swords as he quietly opened the door. He peered out of the small crack he had made into the twilight before them.

No moon, yet. As unfortunate as it is, at least the fires from within the city will give us just enough light to see, I thought, staring at the dim orange glow in the sky through the crack.

"Seems to be clear, but we should all have our eyes peeled as best we can in the dark," he said cautiously. "Once in position, remember to make a lot of noise to create distractions," the Master said. Nenvalur grinned. "Don't worry. We've got that covered," he said with a wink, beginning to push the door open.

They flowed out of the doorway, and I could hear my heart beating louder than my steps. My palms were beginning to sweat and my breathing was steady, but heavy as the anxiousness kicked in. The smell of smoke was thick in the air, and I knew that this battle must have taken more lives than we imagined.

I hope at least some of the people here managed to get out safely, I thought, glancing over at Leona's tear-filled eyes.

Her city was burning, and even though we were trying to do something about it, a lot of damage had already been done, taking an unknown number of lives along with it.

"Go right," Thorsen whispered once we were all out in the open. The party was separated into groups of twenty, and each group found cover behind the nearest building. The Master - followed by me, Bernar, Thorsen, Leona, Meliss and a few others from Nenvalur's group - allowed only one of his glowing eyes out from around the corner of the house we hid behind.

"Listen up," he whispered to the others. "When I give the signal to Nenvalur, we're going straight to the palace. Thorsen, I believe you know this city like the back of your hand, so I'll leave it to you to lead us there as quickly as possible. Leona, Meliss: you two stick close to me, understood?" he asked.

The two women nodded in response to his question in the dim light of the fires that were strewn about the Castle. The Master raised his hand, and moved it like a blacksmith's hammer strikes hot steel on an anvil. Nenvalur and the groups that followed him moved quickly in the darkness to their positions just to the right of us.

Thorsen took point once more, and moved as quietly as his armor would allow, while the others trailed closely behind. Down the alleyways and streets that would carry them down the most direct path to the palace.

We went from cover to cover, house to house, avoiding being seen and ruining our element of surprise. Garett's distraction had clearly worked its magic, since many of the foul creatures seemed to be gathering near the Palace gate. However, the smell of burning buildings, flesh, and death present throughout the city was still more than palpable to all of us.

Suddenly, an uproar came from our left, and we all turned to see what it was. "Horses," the Master whispered, his eyes glowing a little more than normal. "That must be Garett initiating phase two. We've got to hurry," Thorsen concluded.

We pressed on as quickly as stealth would allow, and finally made it to our destination just outside the entrance to the palace. "Here we go," the Master said. His hand cupped mana, swirling it in his palm just before he cast a green ball of light high into the sky.

Nenvalur looked up at the signal, then back down to the horde of glicks before him, making sure that their attention was solely on the ball in the sky.

Curiosity killed the cat, and now it will kill them, I thought.

"Charge!" he shouted. He and his warriors charged out from their hiding spots with swords drawn. The glicks took a moment to register what was happening.

They were never very bright to begin with.

Nenvalur's sword sliced into the scales of the first glick, spraying the green, death-smelling blood up into the air. He shouted his war cry. "Mae eich enaid yn fy!" he shouted as his sword went deep into the enemy's body.

The others shouted their war cries, making as much noise as they could. The Master observed the battle for a few moments, ensuring that the creatures around us heard the commotion, and headed towards it. Nenvalur and his group began to sprint down the streets at high speeds, forcing the glicks to give chase and leave the rest of us alone.

Once the Master was certain their plan had worked, he signaled to the rest of us that it was time to move forward into the next stage of the plan. I held Meliss' hand as we went, her palm was feeling just as sweaty as mine, though her breathing was much louder. "We'll make it," I whispered. She said nothing - not for lack of trying, but simply because she was out of breath.

The Master signaled yet another halt. "The entrance is close, so listen carefully," he said, gesturing just ahead of him. The distant fires shone a dim light on his face as he turned to face us.

"Thorsen, you and the others will watch our backs, while Bernar, Thoma, Meliss, Leona and I will enter. Ladies, you will stay close to Thoma and Bernar at a safe distance, as I will face the Masked One," he said.

"Alone, Master?" I asked, not bothering to hide the concern in my voice. "Yes, young Thoma. *Alone*," the Master replied. I grimaced, but nodded my understanding. He signaled for everyone to move, who began following closely behind him to the main entrance of the palace.

Where our fates had been weaved into a tapestry that none except for the Master understood.

CHAPTER 24

The Battle for Coltend

When the sounds of battle outside made their way to the Masked One's ears, he immediately felt his frustration boil to its maximum limit. He crushed one of the gigantic skulls in the Great Hall, reducing it to dust in synchrony with his hand.

They're here. I must summon the others, he thought.

He used one of the crystals he kept on him to transmit his commands to all affected creatures. "Return," he said, his voice echoing in their minds.

Irun - who encountered Garett and his men after they had expertly slain the creatures that the Masked One sent for them - felt the urge to return to the palace itself. One of Garett's warriors came for him with sword in hand - ready to strike. He redirected the blow away from him and got out of the way of the horse at the same time.

Time to go, he thought

He sprinted towards the palace, constantly glancing over his shoulder to ensure the rider who longed for his life wasn't coming after him.

She was.

He moved much more quickly since his enhancement from

the Masked One, but he had only gone a few meters before he heard the hooves approaching him once again. He turned to face the rider and was almost too late to do anything about the sword that was aimed at his head. He rolled out of the way just in time and was quickly back on his feet.

"Fight me, you coward!" the woman shouted. "You will die if I do," he countered. She scoffed at his words, and dismounted. She drew the black-hilted sword from her left side and made her way over to him. Irun swept his sword back, in line with his hind leg, and awaited the first blow.

She charged at him with her sword trailing behind her. She turned on the ball of her right foot and leaped into the air, sending her into a spinning motion. Her sword struck down at Irun who quickly raised his sword. The blow glanced off his blade, but she wasn't one to be caught off guard.

She recovered from the parry, and swung her sword at Irun's side. He parried, and countered with an overhead blow. She slid the overhand strike off to her left, and struck Irun's helmet with the pommel of her sword - removing it.

Irun staggered back a few paces, and recovered. His nose was bleeding from the powerful blow. The woman saw the distorted face of her attacker. "Irun, is that you? What are you doing here? Why are you helping the enemy?" she asked. She was confused, and it showed blatantly on her face. Irun spat some of the blood from his nose that had dripped into his mouth and sighed.

"I will not be the pet of a master who does not want to share knowledge with us, Isla," he replied. She furrowed her thin brow. "You think that the Master is keeping things from us? You're not even a senior yet, and here you already think you've learned it all," she said, tightening her guard.

"You cared for me and I've always cared for you, even if I

could never fully admit to it. I have never forgotten the words you said to me after my brother died, and how kind you were," she said, tears beginning to gather in her eyes. Irun could say nothing in return. "But this new form of yours... I can't. I can't do it anymore. It seems as if the Irun I once knew never even existed in the first place. You're the traitor Edryd told me about, after all!" She shouted.

Irun grew enraged at the sound of his old friend's name. "Ed told you it was me? That son of a bitch..." he said angrily. "I'll make sure that he knows his place in the world once we're done here," he said menacingly.

"You... bastard! You've betrayed us all!" she shouted, raising her sword. Irun said nothing, but spat once more towards her. She was visibly enraged at the gesture, and attacked wildly with her emotions raging within - making her attack sloppy. Irun parried the blows as quickly as they came until their swords locked, and they glared at each other.

Schluck.

The pain in her lower abdomen caused her to grunt. She looked down and found a dagger stuck in her gut, and warm blood began to soak her jerkin. "I... I didn't want you to be the one to find me first. Thoma was supposed to be the one to come for me... I'm... I'm sorry," Irun said quietly. He drove the dagger upwards, severing intestines and spilling them onto his hand. She barely made a sound.

"I hope you live forever to remember this moment as your own, personal hell," she whispered, choking on her own blood.

Shlick.

He withdrew the dagger from Isla's gut, and she fell to the ground, wriggling like an earthworm for a few moments and gurgling blood. Irun watched as her life ebbed away, and cleaned his dagger. "I'm sorry it had to come to this," he said quietly. He turned his body away from her, but his eyes and heart weren't responding to his mind's commands. He sheathed his dagger, and made his way back to the palace to find his master.

A few moments later, the sounds of another battle could be heard off in the distance.

I guess the glicks really did fail to do their job, he thought.

He shook away thoughts of the consequences of his failure, and continued on his way. He saw a small group of people off in the distance who were also making their way to the palace. He recognized the giant that was with them, and turned into one of the service entrances to the palace.

Irun ran into the main hall, where his master waited patiently for his return. He breathed heavily as he approached his master. "There you are," the Masked One said. "Forgive me, master. I ran into some trouble along the way," Irun said. He wiped the blood that still dripped from his sword.

I'm sorry, Isla, he thought

"You're not dead yet, which means we still have work to do," the Masked One began. "You have failed to find where they would come from the tunnels, and as a result, we might have lost the progress we made," he continued. Irun spread his arms. "Five hundred Synners are hardly a swarm against ten-thousand, master," he said angrily.

"But one Synner does what ten normal soldiers would do in half the time, or have you already brain-dumped the training you have spent the majority of your life going through?" the Masked One asked angrily.

Irun lowered his head and sighed. "We will still win this, master," he said. "*Oh*? Do tell," the Masked One said. Irun paused for a few moments. "If we can just take the damn things from below and be off with them, then we have already won without shedding our own sweat and blood," he explained.

"Do you honestly believe that I have not already surmised as much? By all the gods both light and dark, you truly are worse than Athar," the Masked One snapped back. Irun grimaced and said nothing in return.

"Your failure is why I have summoned you and the others here. You three are to go down and fetch whatever you can carry, for we must make haste. They've come sooner than expected, and we have been caught unprepared. Use mana if you must and are able to do so without dropping whatever you carry," the Masked One said.

The boy was frozen in fear. "What are you waiting for? A biff to the back of the skull? Get down there and fetch me those fucking *Gwynnleaves*!" he shouted angrily. Irun quickly proceeded down the steps and into the library. The Masked One had paved the way through the labyrinth of tunnels with blasts of mana, giving his servants a straight shot to the area in which the Plants lie.

Irun desperately tried to catch up with the two enlarged beings that were on the same mission. He ran as quickly as he could to catch up to the two who were already halfway there. "He's really pissed, isn't he?" Dakzul asked in a hushed tone.

"Shut your fucking trap, Alf," Kimzul snapped back. "Just because he calls you by a new name doesn't mean I will. If we're going to survive this ordeal, we've got to follow his orders," he continued. Dakzul silenced himself, and walked briskly alongside his armored friend.

Irun was confused. "Wait a minute, who are you?" he asked. "We were once men. *Servants of the Church and the True God Almighty* as Mourtis would have it," Kimzul said, imitating Mourtis' voice as best he could with his own distorted one.

"As it stands, we have decided to follow the Masked One. He

has given us power in exchange for our service," he continued. Irun tried to wrap his head around the concept, then realized that he was only a little different from the two of them.

"So you mean to tell me that if there is a fight, you two don't know how to do battle?" he asked. "Like I said, we were servants of the Church. We were not taught to do battle, but to *preach the word of God to all infidels,*" Kimzul said mockingly.

"*Infidels?* Meaning who, exactly?" Irun asked. "The ones who believe in anything supernatural other than the *one true god*. How did you think that you Synners came to have your name? That, my small friend, was the work of the Church," Kimzul explained.

Irun spat. "I'm not a Synner anymore, so don't call me one," he said. "*Oh*, I'm sure of that. If you were, you wouldn't be alive and on this side of the battle, would you?" Kimzul asked rhetorically. Irun blew wind between his teeth and said nothing.

They went down the newly made tunnel to the Plant's location, where the two armored men grabbed armfuls of vases. "You can use mana, right?" Dakzul asked, trying to steer the conversation into a much more amicable tone.

Irun shrugged. "We're taught how to use it from the very beginning, in tandem with sword skills, although, I don't think I know of anything that would help me carry anything my arms can't," Irun said. "That's mighty helpful," Kimzul muttered.

"Grab as many as you can. We're going to have to make a few trips anyway," he said. Irun looked at the Plants in their vases. "But they're all dead. Why on the Continent would he want a dead source of power?" he asked. "According to him, they're not dead," Kimzul replied.

Irun closed his eyes, and shook his head. "Very well, then," he said. He grabbed four of the vases - the other two had at least ten in their enlarged arms - and they made their way back through the tunnel.

The two set their bindle on the floor beside the Masked One's newfound throne, and stepped back, as Irun set his measly bundle of vases on the floor. "Weakling," the Masked One muttered just loud enough to where Irun could hear it. He did hear it, but said nothing, and turned to follow the others down the steps once more. The Masked One watched the three descend into the darkness, and sat on his throne.

I know you're here. Come out already, will you? he asked the empty hall through his thoughts.

Meanwhile, just outside of the main hall, Edryd slaughtered creature after creature. He severed another limb from one of the horrid things that came for him, and the green blood flew into the air as the thing writhed on the ground before him, screeching in agony.

He breathed heavily for a moment, gathering information about the others about him. Nenvalur, Roburn and Anwill were in a line, carving a path deeper and deeper into the horde, leaving a trail of foul-smelling corpses in their wake.

I wonder how Thoma and the others are doing, he thought.

Another three glicks came to kill, and Edryd cast a fireball at the one in the center, consequently setting the other two alight. They writhed and screamed as their blood boiled, rupturing their skin and making a popping sound as the internal pressure grew too great for their scaly hides.

"*Heh*," he allowed himself.

He charged in behind the others alongside Batch who was just as soaked in gore as he was. "How many so far?" Batch asked. "I've lost count," Edryd replied as he stuck his blade into yet another one. Batch severed the head of the one who faced him, and accidentally got some of its blood in his mouth, forcing him to choke and spit the contents.

"It tastes worse than it smells," he managed to say, desperately fighting to keep whatever was in his stomach where it belonged. "Surprised you're not dead from it," Edryd said, cutting into yet another glick's gullet, nearly severing its head. "Not yet, but... *hurrok*... I'm pretty sure I tasted it," Batch returned.

Nenvalur's sword song transformed him into a whirlwind of wet steel and shouting. He twisted his sword so eloquently and cut so deeply that it made him appear to be a single, blood-spilling storm. He shouted his war-cry as he went, and carved a deep path on his own.

Anwill cast almost as quickly as Nenvalur's blade could strike, scalding one, then another with his balls of flame and spears of lightning. He moved his hands together, keeping a small space between them while compressing a large amount of mana.

The hair on his arm stood up, and the air surrounding the sphere of mana cracked and rumbled. He released the spell, which turned out to be a continuous Kyr spell, chaining lightning between multiple enemies, and charring those affected.

No squeals came from the ones who were.

"There are too many of them!" he shouted to Nenvalur who was a small distance away from him, carving his gory path. "Keep fighting no matter what!" he shouted back. Roburn severed limbs from their owners, giving himself a small amount of breathing room.

The small gust of fresh air from the evening's wind was like a splash of river water to the face. "Rosie, are you okay?" he asked. "I'm fine, there just seems to be no end to these bastards! Where the hell are Batch and Edryd?" she asked.

"Ed's behind us, and I think I saw Batch with him," he stated. "We should regroup with them," she suggested. "You're right, we'll do that once we can clear more of these bastards out of our way," he said, casting an Exar to push a number of them away. He breathed deeply, and caught the scent of horses being carried through the wind. He turned to face the direction of the smell.

Garett and the horsemen who remained had come at last. They had fought their battle at the Northern Gate from a distance, minimizing their losses as best as they could. He led his horsemen into the horde with their swords drawn. "Leave none alive!" he shouted. With that burst of courage, Garett and the riders cast, hacked, and infused their remaining arrows to dispel the ones around the small group.

The space between Roburn, Rosie, and the other creatures was enlarged, allowing the ones on the ground a moment to rest - even if it was only for a few seconds.

Garett approached Nenvalur and Anwill, who regrouped as the horsemen did their work behind him. "Gentlemen," he said with a grin. "My men and I have discovered something as we made our way here," he continued. Anwill and Nenvalur glanced at him with genuine interest.

"We have spotted a number of ochelons guarding some massive crystals. They have some of their own, embedded in their skin, but I believe that our enemy is using the bigger ones to control the others through mana, as this is definitely not a natural partnership among monsters," he explained. Anwill stepped forward. "I hope you know where the rest of them are located," he said.

"My scouts informed me earlier that there were at least twenty or more were stationed at each of the gates. I suspect they were to act as deterrents to any other army that might seek to give aid. Given the direction from which the glicks are coming, I'm assuming they must be somewhere in what remains of the market to the west. We must head there immediately and destroy them if we are to survive this," Garett replied.

Nenvalur was panting heavily atop a pile of corpses he stood on, but still showed plenty of vitality. He swung his sword quickly, sending the remaining blood on it flying towards the ground. "Let's get to it, then," he said, starting off in the direction in which Garett had gestured. "Give me a moment to recover," Anwill said, also panting heavily. "All of that casting has made my mind quite exhausted," he continued as he rubbed his forehead.

"Here, take this," Nenvalur tossed him a small flask. "It should help with the fogginess, though I would recommend abstaining from using mana for a little while until your will has recovered," he said.

Anwill popped the cork, and drank the contents. His head twitched and his neck writhed. "*Ugh*. It tastes like goat piss," he grunted. Nenvalur patted him on the shoulder, smiling wryly. "I'm just hoping you don't know what that tastes like from personal experience," he said with a chuckle.

"Master Garett, please take point. We'll follow as closely as we can," Anwill said, drawing his sword. "Don't dally along the way," Garett said with no small amount of caution. "We don't know what to expect once we get there." Nenvalur removed his gauntlet, and put his sweaty fingers into his mouth and blew a whistle.

The remainder of the attack party heard the call, and quickly rallied on the four of them. Roburn's shoulders were burning, his hips and legs also feeling like they weighed a ton from all of the fighting. Garett glanced over his shoulder, to see that the ones whom they fought had been almost entirely wiped out.

"I'll ride ahead and scout with a few others until you arrive. We'll have to surround whatever's there and use up the last of our arrows to provide covering fire," he said.

He kicked his heels into his horse and urged it onward to the

Eastern gate. As he rode, the others fell in line behind him, and the sound of their hooves trailed off into the distance. "We'd better hurry," Roburn suggested. "We can't waste our energy sprinting, but I think a standard jog will do the trick just fine," he continued. "Let's go," Anwill said, still trying to get the bitter and salty after-taste out of his mouth.

The three of them started out at a good pace, as Edryd, Batch and the others were close behind them. Their footsteps made no sound, but the sheathes and armor rustled lightly as they went down the gentle slope that led to the western portion of the castle itself. The riders ahead of them left a trail of bodies in their wake. "Look at that, Garett's made us a gorgeous path to follow," Nenvalur said cheerfully.

Anwill shook his head. "That confirms it, you're a loon. I don't know how you can fight that hard and long, and *still* be so cheerful," he said. "When you spend most of your life fighting battle after battle with the creatures, then suddenly come to a halt for a couple hundred years and end up missing the battle rage, then you can call me a loon," Nenvalur replied to the comment.

Still a fucking loon to me, Anwill thought.

"I wonder if anyone made it out before the invasion," Edryd said, gazing down the now-emptied streets. The desolated houses and huts along the way gave no signs of human activity, and were as quiet as can be. The massive horde could still be heard in the distance, and their bedlam echoed down the empty streets.

"How many do you think that we've slain so far?" Edryd asked Batch. "Perhaps two thousand? Maybe more? These bastards might have the advantage of numbers, but when one of us can do what ten men can in a fraction of the time, and the fact that they aren't the most intelligent of creatures, gives *us* a bit of an advantage over them," Batch replied.

Edryd chewed on the words as he trotted alongside his friend. "Think Thoma and the others have met the enemy, yet?" he asked. Batch shook his head. "I don't know, but I suspect that by now there is something going on up there," he replied. Edryd cast his gaze towards the palace, and could see bright shafts of violet, red, and green light coming from the shattered windows and into the night sky.

Batch noticed Edryd wasn't saying anything, and looked off into the same direction. He, too, saw the flashes from the window, and knew Edryd was worried about him. "Hey, we've got our own shit to deal with. That lanky fuck is fine... I think," he said. "I hope you're right," Edryd said. He knew he had to focus on the task at hand, but couldn't help but worry about his best friend.

The war-party trotted on for the next few minutes until Roburn spotted Garett's horse tied to a post. "They're over there," he said to the others. Nenvalur spotted the horse as well. "I wonder why they've dismounted," he said pensively. "We're about to find out," Anwill replied. The group went silently up to the horses, and saw that the others had not yet dismounted, but were holding back a good distance from where Garett's horse was.

"He must be scouting the market for a vantage point," Roburn concluded. "He tends to do that before entering a fight," he continued. "Let's see what he has to offer us," Nenvalur said. Anwill raised his closed fist, and held it high in the air, telling the ones behind him to come to a halt.

He gestured to Nenvalur, Roburn, Batch and Edryd to follow him, as they crept up to Garett who was lying flat on the ground that overlooked the market. "Ah, there you are," he whispered. The small group crept up low to the ground, then laid themselves on the ground beside him. He motioned slightly over the ridgeline of the small hill. "See those giant bastards over there?" he whispered. The group laid their eyes on a group of ten, monstrous ochelons gathered in a circle.

"Those massive crystals must be the ones he mentioned earlier. If I'm correct, the smaller crystals are for individual control, while the large ones are for amplifying the broadcast of that spell. Hell, We don't even have to kill the ochelons themselves, for they might prove useful to us once the amplifying spell has worn off - saving us energy and men in the process," Garett said. Batch noticed a vacancy in their circle. "Master Garett, I think there may be something else there with them," he whispered. "Ah, yes, that would be the addia," Garett sighed.

"An addia, master?" Edryd asked.

"There are few of them left roaming the world that we know of, but they are extremely dangerous, and just so happen to have the ability to blend in with their surroundings. I spotted it within the first few moments of taking a look at them, but it must have picked up our scent with its long tentacles," Garett replied.

"The creature has tentacles and can make itself invisible? Fuck me, that's not even fair," Batch whispered. "No, it's not, but there are ways of making it visible again," Garett said. "How?" Anwill asked. He had never encountered one before, so he was almost entirely oblivious to knowledge of the creature itself.

"Easier said than done, I'm afraid. My archers must infuse their bows with as much mana as they can muster to char its skin, thereby disabling its cloaking abilities," Garett explained. "Once we do that, however, we will have lost the element of surprise, if we haven't already," he continued.

Nenvalur understood Garett's predicament best. "Where do you need us?" he asked simply. "I need you and the others to surround them as best as you can without spreading yourselves out too thinly. That way, we can at least try to keep some of them from escaping and reaching the others in the palace. My archers and I will take care of the addia from here. Nevertheless, it will take a few minutes for us to join you. During that time, you're on your own," Garett made plain.

"Are you and the others ready to go?" he asked. "I believe so. We'll return to the others and discuss what needs to be done to dispel whatever binds them and the other vermin," Anwill replied. "Make it quick. We're running out of time, and the longer we wait, the more at risk we and the others will be," Garett cautioned.

The small group retracted themselves from the ridgeline and made their way back to the others who awaited orders. Garett went on to explain his plan to his archers, and they began to move on foot to their vantage points on the roofs of the nearby houses.

Anwill explained the plan to the other Synners who were waiting for them, and they began to make their way down the streets, fanning out between the houses as they went. Once all were in position, Anwill held a small flame in the palm of his hand, and used the glint of his sword to signal Garett that they were primed for action.

Garett saw the signal. He and the others nocked their arrows, *drawing from the Ethereal, directing the flowing mana to the palms of their hands,* where it began to seep into their arrows, making them glow a fiery orange. They drew the strings to their cheeks, and tilted their bodies back a little to increase their range.

They had the high ground, but even their bows - powerful as they were - needed a little help in ensuring the arrows hit their mark. Garett loosened his grip on the bowstring, sending the first arrow soaring into the night air. The others loosed their arrows together a fraction of a second after Garett had loosed his. The air flooded past the feathers on the arrows themselves, making them hiss.

Thwack, thwack, thwack, thwack...

The arrows struck their invisible mark, and in an instant, the addia was engulfed in mana-flame, revealing itself to its attackers. It writhed and bellowed deeply, swinging its long tentacles at its own body to try and douse the flame that burned it. Anwill sent up a large ball of light into the air immediately after. "Now!" Anwill shouted, as he began to charge.

Edryd, Batch, Roburn, Rosie, and Nenvalur were at his side, roaring as they sprinted towards their targets, striking fear into their enemies' hearts. The large group of numerous monsters met their attackers in a messy fashion, charging wildly at their armored enemies.

They clashed.

Swords sectioned their enemies, talons met their marks, and the bloodbath ensued, sending all kinds of putrid odors, insides, and blood into the air. Edryd and Batch's strength was beginning to wear thin, but the knowledge that this was one of the most decisive moments of their lives motivated them to continue landing their blows. Anwill was still recovering from the first fight, so he resorted to using his somewhat rusty sword craft.

If he was out of practice, it didn't seem so, for the carnage he caused was nearly as effective as Nenvalur's rampage. The uproar caused by the attacking Synners was one that would be remembered for ages. Even after having lost more than a few during their first encounter, the power they commanded over the horde was astonishing.

Garett and his men made their way down the streets to reinforce the ones below them. As they were a stone's throw away, one of the flanks broke, and glicks began to pour out and head for the palace. "Shit," Garett let out. "Run!" he shouted. They broke out into a sprint, and drew their swords. Within a few moments they met the enemy where the ranks had broken, sealing the hole. The others began to cut and slice their way towards the ochelons, who were stationary.

"Why haven't they attacked us yet?" Batch shouted over to Edryd. "They're waiting for us to get closer, maybe. Squash us one by one; you know, weird, troll shit," Edryd replied.

That's not happening. Not on my watch, Batch thought.

He cut more quickly than before, carving a path through the horrible creatures. "Batch, no!" Edryd shouted.

He's going to get himself fucking killed. Damn it, Batch! Edryd thought.

He cut his way through, going after Batch as quickly as he could while Nenvalur, Anwill and Roburn were now completely swarmed by creatures, forming a small circle to fend them off.

"We can't hold them much longer! We must break the crystals!" Roburn shouted. Nenvalur caught a glance of Batch and Edryd making their way over to the ochelons.

"Damn it! Those kids are being reckless. Follow me," he shouted. He made himself a trail of severed limbs and writhing bodies as he made his way over to the two boys at twice the speed they were going. Anwill and Roburn followed as closely as they could, but were a bit slower than the master swordsman.

Batch reached the ochelons, though they didn't seem to acknowledge his presence. He staved off a few more glicks who dared not get too close to the looming, stationary giants.

"Batch!" Edryd called out a few meters away. Batch was distracted, wondering what made the ochelons behave the way they were; their heavy breathing caused their broad, muscular shoulders to rise and fall slowly.

Batch turned his attention to the addia, who hadn't noticed him yet. It was too busy tending to its seared hide, gurgling mucus in its throat, then using its tentacles to smear it over the burned areas. He watched it closely, as he had never seen such a horrible creature before.

Its large, muscular legs and broad paws made it a formidable enemy, even to the most experienced of Synners. The two tentacles added to the danger, and its large eyes saw everything that would try to flank it. "Damn, you're ugly," Batch said. The addia gurgled more of the icky goo and opened its eyes to make sure it had enough.

It saw him.

It flared its tentacles and let out a roar that would have shed the skin off of Batch had he been standing any closer. The addia reared on its hind paws and began to charge him. Batch was nearly frozen in fear, and somehow managed to get out of the way of the first flick of the beast's long tentacles. "Batch! Keep moving! Don't try to fight it!" Nenvalur called out from the addia's left side. Batch heard it and understood why he had said it.

Alright, you slimy piece of shit. Eyes on me, he thought.

Another whip of its tentacles came for him, and he rolled out of the way yet again. He saw Nenvalur moving out of the corner of his eye and vanishing behind the beast. Its retractable claws came out, and shone in the moonlight.

Another blow came for Batch, only this time, he was too slow to react, and the creature struck his side, sending him straight into one of the legs of the ochelons. One of the metal prongs that was used to pull the crystals punctured his leather jerkin, burying itself into his arm and, ultimately, shattering the bone. Edryd saw it all happen much more slowly than reality allowed, hearing Batch's scream echoing in the void of his thoughts.

The addia came for Batch at a charge, and picked him up with its tentacles. He screamed in pain, as it had grabbed both of his arms, stretching them as far as they would go as they raised him into the air. Edryd had only just now made his way to the circle of ochelons, and watched his friend being held by the two long tentacles.

"Batch!" Edryd cried out, but it was too late. The tentacles ripped Batch's arms from their sockets, and his body fell to the ground, landing on his neck.

Crunch-thud.

Edryd looked on in awe, as tears filled his eyes for the loss of his friend. The fire in his belly grew hotter and hotter, as the purest strain of rage imaginable began to fill his entire being. "You slimy fuck! I'm going to pull those tentacles of yours out through your ass!" he shouted as he charged the addia. The creature heard his shout and immediately turned on him, whipping the lifeless arms at him. He slid under the limbs, feeling a few warm drops of his friend's blood speckle his face.

"Fight me fairly, fuck-face! How *dare* you use my own friend against me like that!" he shouted again, continuing his sprint. A single tentacle came for him this time, but he was ready for it. He jumped over the sweeping attack and swung his sword downward. It met the slimy flesh, severing the tentacle in two.

The addia reeled in pain, and wildly swung another tentacle at him, that met the same fate as the first, as he jumped both over Batch's body and the tentacle in one bound. Its steaming blood soaked the floor and body beneath it, making it bellow and screech in pain.

"Doesn't feel good, does it?" Edryd shouted. He didn't care if the beast could understand him or not, but it gave him courage. Nenvalur still crept behind it, hoping to get in close enough to wound its leg. He was in range for a strike, when its eye caught him sneaking up on it, and flicked its tail towards him.

He stepped out of the way, and sliced the sharp tip off with a single blow. It screeched and moaned in pain for a moment, and as it did so, Nenvalur landed a blow to both of its hind legs at the same time, striking the tendons. The creature's rear fell to the floor with a heavy *thud* and it struggled to keep its other half balanced.

Edryd walked over to it, knowing it still had its claws that could still kill him with a single blow. He breathed heavily, his eyes were fixed on the glowing ones that were opened to their widest, and glaring back at him. It leaned on one leg, and sent a forceful blow aimed for Edryd. He swung his blade to meet the blow, and severed its paw in half.

"Just die already!" Edryd screamed, looking directly into its eyes. Blood poured from the wound on its paw, and before the addia could even think about trying to strike it with its newfound stump, Edryd spun around and jabbed his blade under its chin, puncturing its hide and brain. Its glowing eyes twitched for a moment and blood could be heard gurgling in its throat.

"Fuuuuuuuck!" Edryd shouted with tears in his eyes, ripping the blade out of the creature as violently as he could.

He withdrew his sword that was covered in its warm blood, and walked over to Batch's lifeless body. He fell to his knees in the puddle of blood that had now drenched the stone floor about the body, and sobbed.

The battle raged on around them - glicks and Synners alike dying around them, the ochelons still motionless. He wiped the snot that ran down from his nostrils, shutting out everything around him. "I'm so sorry, Batch... I'm so sorry I couldn't get to you in time to save you. I should have been faster, stronger... I..." he said between hiccups. He bowed and ran his fingers over his friend's still-open eyes, and leaned on the body.

Nenvalur approached him, and put a hand on his shoulder. "You will see him again in the next life, of this I am certain. I have also lost many of my friends in battle, but I know that I will see them again. Our mana can never be created or destroyed, only transformed. His mana has simply returned to the Ethereal, where he will embrace you once more, when the time is right," he said comfortingly to the sobbing boy. "You've honored him by slaying the beast that took his life, making them even in death," he continued.

He helped Edryd to his feet, and put a hand on his shoulder. "Come on, we have a castle to save," he said, patting Edryd's cheek. Edryd wiped the tears from his eyes, and nodded. Anwill and Roburn arrived, covered in guts and other entrails. "Holy shit!" Roburn said, looking at the fallen beast. He saw Batch's body on the ground, and bowed his head. "We'll meet again, my friend," Roburn said quietly, understanding death better than most.

"Anwill," Nenvalur said. "We need to use mana to either pull these crystals out or break the big ones, so I will need you, Roburn and Edryd to do that with me," he explained.

"My mind is still a little weak, but I'll manage. However, I do think breaking them will be easier than trying to rip the crystals out," Anwill replied. He glanced at the young boy's body on the ground, and understood what had happened.

"Edryd, can you cast?" he asked. "I'll do my best," Edryd replied. The tears had stopped coming down his cheeks and into the few whiskers of beard he had, but the image of his friend being torn apart was still fresh. "Good enough for me," Anwill said. "I can help, too!" Rosie shouted from a distance. She was covered in blood, but seemed to have her wits about her.

"Shit is that Batch?" she said, noticing the body on the ground.

"It was, yes," Edryd replied solemnly. "Damn… I'm sorry. We'll mourn him later, I promise. What do we need to do?" she asked.

I've never seen her be sweet like that before, Roburn thought.

"We'll need to make use of the Inar spell, in more than one direction at the same time, think you can manage?" he asked. "Yes, I can do that, but what about you, Ed?" Rosie asked. "I think I can do that, though I've never tried it before," Edryd replied. "No time to learn like the present," Roburn said. "On me," Anwill said.

They equidistantly positioned themselves around the crystal, and *as the four of them drew from the timeless realm, they split the resulting nebula of mana to each of their hands.* They aimed at the large, glowing crystals that were still bound in chains. "Ready?" Nenvalur asked. The mana gathered in each of their hands, as they signaled to each other that their preparations were complete.

"Now!" he shouted. Edryd closed his eyes, contracting his fingers and pulling his arms inward towards his waist. The five, massive crystals shattered, as the ones embedded in the ochelon's cores were also torn out, drawing blood as a result. They fell to the ground with a loud *crash* and they shattered into pieces.

"It worked!" Roburn shouted, but as he did so, the ochelons woke from their trances. Grunts and snorts were heard, and it sent a chill down the four men's spines. "Let's hope the old man was right," he said.

The ochelons looked around, confused as to where they were, finally noticing the battle raging beneath them. Their rage unified them, making them one single force of mass destruction, as their large arms swung down and struck the glicks beneath them, sending more than a few of them flying into the air.

Garett saw that his plan had worked, and smiled. "Retreat to a safe distance!" he shouted. The order was passed down from Synner to Synner within earshot, and the ten ochelons went to work, slaying every glick they could lay their arms on. The smaller creatures fled as quickly as they could, through the western gate in hopes of safety from their new, larger enemies, but were met by the ones who remained outside.

The four who were in the circle did their best to avoid being seen by the massive ochelons, who spat fire and ice onto their targets. They encountered little resistance in their flight to regroup with the others on the far end of the market, and they hid themselves from the sight of the ochelons, who chased the remaining glicks as they fled out of the destroyed gateway.

"We've done it!" Garett shouted. "Victory! We have victory!" he shouted again. Everyone cheered and embraced each other. While Edryd felt glad that they had won the battle, he had suffered an even greater loss than most even knew of.

Meanwhile, the battle in the main palace hall was taking place, sending tendrils of mana far outside of the palace.

CHAPTER 25

Weavings of Fate

My heart was nearly in my throat, as I stared at the entrance to the Great Hall.

This is it. This is what we've fought so hard for. To those of you who've lost your lives in the cave, your sacrifices will not be in vain, I thought as I swallowed dryly.

The Master pointed to the steps that led to the entrance of the palace. "Form a line over there at the top of the steps. Let nothing pass. If you do, then one of you will have to stop it from getting to me," the Master said, gesturing to Thoma and Bernar.

"How long will you need in there?" Thorsen asked quietly.

"As long as you can give me," the Master replied. "Once I'm inside, I have no doubt that he will want to summon reinforcements to overpower us. Nenvalur and his men can only hold off so many, so cast a ball of light in the air when you hear them approaching to aid you," he continued.

"Where do we stay if you're going off alone?" Leona asked.

The Master grinned. "I suspect you're already in better hands than mine, my lady," he said, glancing at Bernar. Leona blushed - not something she had expected to do in such a situation.

"Time to go," the Master said.

We crept behind the stones that held the trees and other such plants in the garden beside the entrance to the palace. In the dark, we were greater obstacles than we would be if we had any light.

Luckily for us, the architects had placed the ornaments in a perfect line.

We reached the base of the steps from the left side and the Master gave the signal for Thorsen and his men to form the line. He took point, while Bernar, Leona, Meliss and I trailed behind him.

I saw the Master take a deep breath, as we stepped into the vast, long hall where, at the end of it, we saw the Masked One sitting on a throne made of mana as if he was waiting for him.

"All of you stay behind the line, right here. Do not move, even if things go South, do you understand me?" the Master asked us, who nodded in agreement.

He stepped inside the dark hall, and looked around him. The glory of the hall had more than lessened; rather, it had been destroyed. The red carpet that lined the central corridor of the hall was thrown over to the side, the thrones in little more than splinters and piles of velvet on top of it.

"You have a true taste for destruction of all things beautiful," the Master called out. I saw the Masked One rising from his seat, and I could almost *touch* the sheer quantity of mana he exuded.

If he's got that much of a tangible feeling from here, why the hell is the Master taking him on alone, then? Has he suppressed his true power all this time? I wondered, struggling to focus as the Masked One took a step forward.

"*Beautiful*? What could possibly be beautiful about this place for overweight wretches who only seek to take from the people without ever giving anything back?" he asked.

He came down the steps from his throne, walking slowly

towards his enemy, to which the Master responded in kind. Meanwhile, Bernar, Leona, Meliss and I scooted off to the right side of the hall.

"It is not that I don't care for the people, nor what they've suffered at Truls' hand, but you have taken away their artistry and craftsmanship," the Master began. "By the looks of things, you seem to have thrown a tantrum of some kind," he continued, glancing around at the broken skull fragments strewn across the floor.

The Masked One tilted his head. "*Oh*? Tell me, then: What can I also take away from you, then? Your Synners? Your homeland? Power? Your *brother*?" he asked with a low chuckle wreathed in malice.

I could tell the last question stung like a wasp striking the Master's heart, because his facial expression was unlike any I had seen him wear before.

Is that pain? Shock? Whatever it is, this mage has apparently struck a nerve. Speaking of which, is he wearing the Nethersong Mask? How the hell did he get that? the Master thought.

"Ardrin... is th-... is that you?" the Master asked, trying to see any details he could that would prove him right. "In the flesh," Ardrin responded, bowing his head and spreading his arms. "It's been too long, Taegin," Ardrin continued.

What the...? I thought, too stunned to speak.

"How... How is it possible? I thought you were dead!" Taegin replied not as the Master of Codrean, but as a long lost sibling instead. Ardrin began to laugh in what started out as a low chuckle, but grew into manic laughter like his mind was breaking. "There are numerous ways to overcome death, and one of them is to make a deal with a devil," he replied.

The Master, or rather, Taegin shook his head defeatedly. "I care for many things, and even though you have turned into little more than a pawn of the Undergod, I still care for you... brother," he said, the words leaving a bitter taste in his mouth.

The Masked One laughed wickedly.

"Ah, Taegin, you have always had the larger heart of the two of us," the Masked One said. "Not something difficult to attain, seeing as you've never had one yourself, Ardrin," Taegin replied. "Do not call me by that name, as it died long ago," Ardrin said angrily, flaring his mana as he took a few more steps toward us.

Since I could hear their conversation from where he stood, and his eyes opened wide. He looked at his brother, who shrugged. "You knew?" I finally asked. "I've known since I trained in Caegwen. He just never gave me or any of the others permission to ever call him as such," Bernar replied.

Needless to say, I was dumbfounded, though Meliss and Leona were entirely oblivious to what they had been told or not, in this case.

"Anything else you'd like to surprise me with?" I asked sarcastically. "I don't believe I'm the one who should tell you anything else right now, curious little horseshit," Bernar replied with the same grin. I shook my head, and tried to turn my attention away from the discovery.

Taegin and Ardrin approached each other, then stopped a few paces apart. "You've grown taller, even if it's more than apparent that it was not of natural causes," Taegin said, noting his brother's increased height. "This is the sort of thing you could have had for yourself, had you gone down the same path as I did," Ardrin replied.

"You mean burning two Synners alive because you were bullied a little bit? That was murder and childish, but I don't think I have to tell you that," Taegin said. Ardrin shook his head. "That wasn't murder, that was an eye opener," he began.

Taegin showed no change of emotion on his face.

"Come now, brother. Did you honestly expect our old master to teach us how to draw from both or even *all* the realms? To finally be able to bridge that gap in power to smite our enemies?" Ardrin asked. "You mean the ones you have now taken as your allies," Taegin snapped back. "Precisely. You see much, and possibly know even more, Taegin, but you failed to see our true potential, as you always have," Ardrin said.

"Enlighten me, then," Taegin said calmly. Ardrin began to pace back and forth. "The gift we received from the gods; it doesn't give us the ability to control mana. Instead, it gives us an easier time controlling what we are already capable of. There are other uses for it, of course, but over the course of time, many of those uses have been lost," Ardrin said. "You're talking about what happened to Nexis, aren't you?" Taegin asked.

The Masked One nodded. "Indeed, brother. But now all of that will be meaningless. We were given this gift to rule over the weak. To take over this Continent and the others of our world, while the Undergod does whatever it is he has been planning to do all these years," Ardrin explained.

"And let the rest of the world crumble and fall to the monsters of the Underworld? What would there be left to rule once they've had their fill of humans?" Taegin asked. Ardrin spread his arms wide. "The rest of the world without the weak to look after and care for, of course," he said.

"Naturally, there would always be the monsters roaming the lands, but that doesn't mean that we couldn't one day eradicate and eviscerate every last one of them. You know me, brother; all I've ever wanted was power and knowledge. Through *his* instructions and benevolence, I have gained plenty of both," he continued.

Taegin shook his head in opposition.

"You're wrong," Taegin began. "The Undergod himself would never allow that to happen. He needs a foothold in this world to slowly but surely make his way back to face the ones who made him as such. With you doing his bidding, you're only a steppingstone, nothing more," he said.

Ardrin lowered his head a little. "I see that there is no convincing you that what he has promised me will come to pass," he said. "And what might that be? Becoming ruler of the world? Everlasting life and power?" Taegin asked. "At last you see *some* of the potential gain from all of this. This realm will be mine in its entirety... eventually," Ardrin said, somewhat relieved that his brother had finally begun to see things as he saw them.

"Join me, Taegin. Together we can do what the Undergod has planned. You know the ways of the Gwynnleaf better than anyone. Just imagine the knowledge we could uncover together!" Ardrin said invitingly, extending a hand out to Taegin as he walked forward.

No, he wouldn't accept that... would he? Sacrifice the entire continent and potentially other realms for knowledge? I thought, feeling my heart begin to race.

"There is only so much we can gain from it without angering the gods," Taegin retorted after a short moment of consideration. "Would you not want to strengthen the Synners as a whole? Imagine an entire continent of Synners ridding us of all these creatures! Once this realm is mine, that could become a reality, brother!" Ardrin shouted.

Taegin shook his head once more. "No, brother, I will not and cannot join you. Not after what you've done. You are merely his pawn, and once his will has been done in this realm, he will no longer have need of you and discard you. He will not give you what you seek, nor will he give you what he has promised you. Instead, he will take everything from you, even your very soul; if you still have one," he said defiantly.

"Then I suppose our paths diverge once again. Mine to glory and god-like power, and yours to the Synners and all those loyal to you to your dooms," Ardrin replied. Taegin lowered his head, and sighed deeply. "I am sorry to see that there is no changing your mind, though I should've known better than to try and change your mind," he said, readying himself and taking a few steps back.

"Then you have chosen death? So be it," Ardrin said, taking a few steps back. Taegin drew his sword, and his eyes glowed intensely.

As did his brother's.

A large spike of mana shot out from across the palace floor, meeting a ward that the Master cast to counter it. Sparks of what looked like lava fell to the floor from the impact, sending a shockwave across the Great Hall. "*Ohoho*, well done, brother. I see you have not grown weak in your old age, but instead quite powerful," The Masked One jested. The Master was a little rattled at hearing the word *brother*, gritting his teeth in response.

Taegin still couldn't accept his words from earlier, as tears began to well in his eyes. "Ardrin, put an end to this madness! What deal did you make? How can I help you get out of it?" he pleaded. "Have you ever considered that maybe, just *maybe*, I wanted to bait you out so I could kill you before you became a threat to our plans?" Ardrin replied, tilting his head and raising his hands slightly.

"You bastard," Taegin retorted. "*Nah-ah-ah*, you don't get to say that about us. We're twins, after all, so mind your tongue," Ardrin said menacingly. "You won't stop, then, will you?"

Taegin asked, already knowing the answer to his question.

"You've always known the only way to stop me when I set my mind to something," Ardrin said. "If only you knew the true extent of the power I have gained over these many years as a result of that drive... you wouldn't be standing where you are," he said.

"We'll see just how well it compares to my own upgrades," Taegin replied, returning to his fighting stance and positioning his sword accordingly. His eyes began to glow even more intensely, while his older brother prepared a large amount of mana.

Ardrin grunted as he cast three fireballs in a single flick of his arm. Taegin dodged the first that nearly struck Leona and Meliss, which Bernar and I blocked with a wall of mana we cast. I don't know how the Master hadn't flinched when blocking his, but it felt like Bernar and I just stopped a bull from charging.

I can't let a single one of those get by me, I thought, sharing the same, determined look with my brother.

We'd always had an unspoken sort of understanding with one another, and we knew that this battle was going to mostly be about protecting those two behind us. However, our thoughts were cut short, as another three spikes barreled down the hall, slamming into the wall once more.

Ardrin contorted his hands like claws, and two ghostly hands attempted to strike his brother, who cut at them with his mana-infused sword, forcing them to disappear. The two vanished momentarily, exchanging blow after blow that I could hardly follow along with, even with my second stage active.

As I was observing the battle, I saw three figures coming from the stairway in the ground nearest to the Masked One carrying vases, but barely recognized one of them. I immediately felt rage surging within me as my adrenaline kicked in, and my hands began to shake like a hunter's.

Irun, I thought.

Behind me came a call from Thorsen. "They're coming!" he shouted as he readied himself to face the small horde of glicks. "Thorsen, hold them off for as long as you can! Meliss, Leona, Get somewhere deep inside the castle and stay there. Bernar and I will handle the newcomers," I called out, knowing my brother was still heavily focused on the wall of mana protecting us.

"I don't want to leave you," Meliss said. "You'll be okay so long as Thorsen can hold the line. Leona, please take her somewhere safe," I replied.

The two women agreed, and scurried off down one of the nearby corners to hide themselves. "Whoa, whoa, whoa! We can't just leave them to go off on their own! What if they run into some monsters we didn't know were in here?" Bernar asked urgently.

"If we don't, then the Master will be outmatched, and all of this will have gone to shit," I said quickly. Bernar sighed. "I fucking hate it when you're right," he said. He looked over at the three newcomers, his eyes stopping on Irun's distorted figure.

"Is that who I think it is?" he asked. "The shit-sucking traitor himself. Gods above and below, I had really hoped it wasn't going to be him," I replied, my hatred beginning to stir. Bernar must have felt it immediately, because he gave me a concerned look, then shook his head.

"Well, I'll leave him to you, while I take on the other two," he said. "I was hoping you would say that," I replied angrily. "Don't let your emotions make your fighting sloppy," my brother said with an air of caution. "If they allow me to kill the bastard, then I'll let them devour me, if need be," I said, focusing my attention on my target. "Fine. Let's move," Bernar said.

The two of us stormed across the Great Hall of the palace, veering our attention from the battle that ensued between the twins to our targets.

"Irun, you slimy turtle shit!" I shouted, hoping he would stop putting whatever Gwynnleaves he had in the portal *and* fail to notice Meliss and Leona who had run off down that side of the hall. Luckily, Irun lowered his vases to the floor, and turned to face my all-too familiar voice.

"Thoma Fayren, the Lanky Synner," Irun grinned. "I've waited for this moment for a long time, now," he said. "You mean the day you die you traitorous fuck? Didn't know you wanted me to tear you from taint to throat so badly," I shouted from across the hall.

Irun chuckled. "Dakzul, Kimzul. Take care of the larger of the two, leave the lanky one to me," Irun ordered. The two, armored men said nothing, but made their way towards Bernar. "Heavily armored pricks without swords? This should be interesting," Bernar said, a slight bit of amusement in his voice. I heard my brother, but said nothing in return since my focus was on my once-called *friend* and the two, undetected women.

I saw Meliss and Leona halt about halfway down the hall, frozen in fear, and likely praying nothing would come after them. Thorsen and the others were having it out with the small horde of glicks that attacked them just outside the Hall, but during that time, their line had not been broken.

Suddenly, one of the Synners to Thorsen's right fell to the floor with a large gash in his neck. "Hold the line, damn it!" I heard him shout in his thick accent.

A glick somehow managed to slip past the line, unnoticed by the others, making its way into the castle beneath the cacophonic noise.

The others it saw in the large hall were too occupied to notice, and it caught onto their scent. I heard it rustling its scales and followed it into the corner where Leona and Meliss had run into, hiding behind a set of pews and a little beyond my current reach.

Damn it. I can't get to them in time, I thought, mentally kicking myself.

As it went down the hall, I watched Meliss pull the knife that Pyle had given her out from its sheath. hallway where it spotted the two, fleeing women. It screeched and flared its scales when it noticed them, the pair hearing its scaly feet smacking the cold, stone floor.

"Some horrible thing is coming. I won't hesitate like I did last time," Meliss said, showing the blade Pyle had previously given her. "Get behind me," she said, pushing Leona to the side. Leona staggered backwards, and landed her ass on the floor. "What the hell are you doing?" She asked. "I'm going to save your life," Meliss replied with a determined look in her eye.

Meliss gripped her dagger tightly as the horrifying creature charged them. It raised its claw just before reaching the young girl, who stepped in when the claw was at its highest peak, jabbing the blade into the creature's gut. It screeched in pain as she withdrew the dagger, covering her in the foul-smelling blood.

It staggered backwards for a moment, but attempted another attack. Meliss responded by jamming the blade into the soft meat just under the glick's jaw, piercing brain tissue. It became limp, as blood poured out onto the floor and all over her hands. "*Ugh*, that... *hurngf...* that smells rancid," Meliss said, holding back her puke.

"I can't thank you enough," Leona breathed a sigh of relief. Meliss was still processing what she had just done, staring blankly at the creature's body below her. "Hey, Meliss. We need to keep moving in case another comes along," Leona said, leading her by the arm.

Meliss responded with a grunt, but had a hard time tearing her eyes off the creature, delaying her turn to sprint off to the safety of the royal quarters.

Gods above and below, that could've gone so much worse, I thought, having seen the whole ordeal through my peripheral vision.

Bernar and I formed a line with Taegin, who was deep in battle with his brother, and drew our swords. My black-hilted sword was practically singing, yearning for blood as it left my scabbard. Irun drew his as well, though with the upgrade to his armor, his new, jagged sword only dully hummed as it was drawn.

The two giants broke out into a run towards Bernar, who got into the Ochs guard. He raised his blade up to the height of his right shoulder, with his left hand on the pommel, and tilted the point at a small angle towards the armored men, *drawing mana* and infusing his blade with Recia; igniting the mana that coated his blade.

I let my sword trail behind me just above the ground as I began to sprint towards Irun, who did the same. When we were nearing striking range, I spun on the ball of my left foot and leapt, sending me into a spin to create momentum for my attack into Irun's blade.

He countered the attack with one of his own that just missed my neck, hitting nothing but air. I rolled off to the side, and as I recovered, Irun moved in for a killing blow that I only just managed to catch on my blade.

"You're not using your second stage? Are you trying to say that I'm not worthy of it?" Irun asked. "Exactly right. The only thing you're worthy of is a swift death, as I have no time to trade words with a witless worm," I said through the bare of my teeth. "So? Why not use it on me? In your eyes, I'm sure I've done enough to earn it, right?" Irun asked mockingly. "Not yet. Tell me why you did it? Why did you betray us?" I asked through gritted teeth.

"I began this journey long before you unlocked your second stage. Once I'd heard that you had, it only fueled my jealousy of you. The Synners have grown weak, and are increasingly stingy with their techniques. I wanted more power to live up to someone's reputation, so I turned to the Masked One. Does that answer your question, or do I need to spell it out a little more?" Irun replied in a simplistic tone, staving off more of my attacks and eventually blade-locking me into a stand-still.

"Your arrogance and lust for power will be your downfall, even if you do not die today," I replied, straining against the pressure Irun was putting on my blade. We pushed away from each other with our blades, but I swung my sword down from the left, something Irun had never seen me do in training.

I struck Irun's shoulder from beneath the gap that his pauldron failed to protect, forcing him backwards. "You sneaky little shit. I'll have your head!" Irun said, taking a few steps back and harnessing the pain for only a second before I was upon him once more.

I felt Taegin *draw from the Ethereal* and cast a spell at the same time, creating an extended Kyr strike. Ardrin cast one of his own, and the two met halfway, creating a sphere of pure mana in the center of the two castings. Taegin and his brother both struggled to maintain their flows of mana, as they were equally matched.

"You will never win this battle, brother!" Ardrin shouted. "I *will* have more power and knowledge than you've ever had, and there is nothing you can do to stop me, now!" he continued.

How the hell is he supposed to land a blow? Ardrin has blocked just about everything he's had thrown at him, I thought.

I heard him scream as he forced the spells upward, ultimately striking the ceiling of the palace itself, blasting a hole the size of a giant clean through it. He momentarily sheathed his sword, turning his hands at opposing angles and thrusting forward with both his arms and his weight. The mana he gathered for this spell resulted in a sphere of pure, scarlet mana streaming towards his brother. Ardrin did the same, causing the two spheres to collide halfway, creating a sizable explosion of mana that nearly struck them both.

Meanwhile, Bernar was sidestepping and strafing the incoming attacks as much as he could. I soon realized that the two he fought had little or no experience in battle.

If it weren't for their armor, he'd have made quick work of these bastards by now, I thought.

I sent Irun flying backwards, giving me some room to breathe. I was watching Bernar fight the armored giants, but noticed there was an expression on his face that was almost... *calculating* something.

Whatever it was, it was both reassuring and horrifying to know that he even *had* that capability.

There must be some way for him to get at these oversized shit-beans, I thought.

"Alright fucksticks, play time's over," he said. His adversaries laughed with their distorted voices. "Having a hard time getting at us, are you?" one of the giants asked. Bernar furrowed his brow. "*Awh*, look! You made him angry," the other replied. "Shut it, Alf," the first one spat.

Alf? That's a human name. Wait, those two aren't daemons? Are they just men in fancy suits of armor? Damnit, Bernar, I hope you've figured that out, too, I thought.

I was nearly caught by another flurry of Irun's strikes which I just barely managed to dodge. It seemed my brother was also mildly distracted, as he was nearly pommeled by a rapid succession of incoming hammer strikes that cracked the stone beneath where he had just been.

Irun swung almost as quickly as I did; deflecting, parrying, and attacking as quickly as our muscles could manage.

He's had an upgrade. He was never this good when we trained. I might actually have to use the second stage, but I could die if I lose focus for even a split second, I thought.

Another blow came from above, and while I had blocked the majority of the blow, the sharp point managed to cut into my forehead, spilling blood into my right eye.

Shit, I can't see a fucking thing through my right eye. I've got to do something to clean it, I thought as I deflected more blows aimed for my sides.

Irun prepared a crushing blow for me in hopes of flattening me against the stone floor. I quickly stepped out of its way, putting some distance between the two of us, using the backside of my gauntlet to wipe away some of the blood.

"Are you even trying to kill me, Thoma? You know, for someone as *blessed* as you are, I expected so much more from you," Irun asked mockingly as I caught my breath for a few seconds. I spent the next few moments searing the wound with a bit of mana and holding my sword steady as I did so to show that my guard was not being let down at all.

"*Oh*, you *want* me to try? Alright then," I replied, grinning wickedly. Irun was taken aback as he watched my eyes begin to show signs of entering the second stage.

I've never seen him like that. That's more like it, I thought as I watched mana race down his spine.

Through the second stage, I could see where there were

slight amounts of mana-leakage from his rapid transformation. It was like there were side effects to having been changed so quickly, and as a result, I began to notice weaknesses in his defense, and took note of them.

"You know, I'm sorry we never grew close. We might have prevented this whole situation," I began. "*Pfffft.* What makes you think that *you* could have done anything to stop me?" Irun asked, but I could only sigh in immediate response.

Doesn't look like there's anything I can say that will even begin a real conversation, huh? Fine. Have it your way, then, I thought, getting to my feet.

"I'm only going to warn you of this because I once considered you a friend," I began, *drawing much more mana from the Ethereal and infusing it into my muscles.* "*Friend?* What could you possibly say to me?" Irun asked, preparing to launch an attack aimed at my clavicle.

"*Speed blitz incoming,*" I said maliciously, my voice oozing with an intense amount of mana.

Irun dashed towards me, swinging his sword directly towards the base of my neck, looking to decapitate me in one, clean strike. However, after his sword was left wanting, and finding nothing other than air, I felt his panic. I suddenly appeared behind him with a menacing look on my face, the shadow of the night hiding my features, showing only the glow of my eyes and glint of my sword.

I could tell he was scared by the look on his face when he turned to react to my initial swing.

It made me smile.

I began swinging my sword at a much more rapid pace than before, leaving Irun minimal time to react. He was barely managing to get his jagged blade at a bit of an angle to deflect an incoming blow from above. "You think your speed will help you?" Irun said with false motivation, probably trying to shield himself from the fear that began to creep in.

I didn't reply. I didn't have to. I simply continued berating Irun with attack after attack.

Meanwhile, I saw Ardrin was growing impatient at his brother's ability to block and counter every spell he tried. He yelled as he cast the same spell he had used on the ochelon to remove its soul from its body. Taegin had only fractions of a second to conjure a mana barrier that was only just able to block it, stopping the claws a few centimeters away from his body.

The two of them struggled for a few moments, but Ardrin began to gain the upper hand. He used all of his might to push one of the tips of the claws into his brother's shoulder at the joint, causing Taegin to scream.

Master! I thought for a split second after hearing his cry cut through the sounds of my own battle, distracting me from Irun's incoming attack which sent me flying backwards into the nearby pillar.

Taegin seemed to be faltering in his defenses, like something was draining his mana right out of his body.

"You cannot defeat me, brother! Surrender and I will let you live!" Ardrin shouted, forcing the claw in a little more deeply. Taegin looked tempted to simply let go of it all, and give up as his strength waned.

I deflected another set of blows from Irun, who seemed to grow increasingly frustrated with my lack of care for our fight since entering the second stage.

"I will never surrender to you, brother. Even if it means my death," he said with all the strength he could muster. He used the last of his might to cast the scarlet claws into the ground. The tip of the claw that was in his shoulder nearly severed his arm entirely as it crashed into the stone floor beneath him.

I could only watch as Taegin began falling forward, the blood rushing from his shoulder, being too weak to stand from the blood loss. Ardrin turned away from his younger sibling towards mine and Irun's battle as if he was going to help.

Just as Taegin's body hit the floor, Bernar cast an Exar spell aimed at his two foes' heads, blowing their helmets clean off their shoulders. The two armored giants staggered and grouped together from the forceful blast, but failed to recover in time, as he had already leaped into the air. His airborne strike sliced both of their heads in half with a swift, spinning motion that sent blood high into the air. He landed like a cat jumping off a high shelf, as the two fleshy chunks struck the floor beside him.

"You two definitely succeeded in pissing me off," he spat. He turned to see how the Master's battle was faring, as he noticed a slight lull in the mana flowing through the air, only to find the Master lying on the floor - motionless. "Taegin!" he shouted as he dashed to his aid. He slid on his knees, and turned his master's body over, noticing the wound.

"Does it look as bad as it feels?" I heard Taegin ask weakly. "It's only a flesh wound," Bernar said as he turned to see that the line outside had kept the creatures at bay. "Pyle!" he called out. Pyle heard his call, and saw Bernar with the Taegin in his arms, bleeding profusely. His eyes *intensified their glow as mana rushed from the sphere in the sky*, pouring into and around the open wound.

Meanwhile, Ardrin saw the beheaded pair lying motionless on the floor. "Why is everyone around me utterly useless?" he asked aloud. I heard the comment, but didn't have time to think much about it as I landed a pommel strike to Irun's nose, breaking it in three different places. "You fucker!" Irun shouted, swinging aimlessly through teary eyes. Ardrin saw this, and sent out a tendril of his dark mana to aid his companion, leeching my strength.

Irun must have seen it coming, because he *began drawing copious amounts of mana from the Underworld*, landing a crippling strike on my guard, knocking me to the ground.

Damn it, I'm losing consciousness, and I don't know why, I thought as I felt my eyes begin to cease their glow.

He's gonna get away at this rate, I thought, realizing what was actually happening.

For whatever reason, I thought I saw hesitation in his eyes. I might even have called it *remorse*, but whatever the real emotion was, one thing was certain: Irun wasn't going to kill me.

While I tried a recovering maneuver, the pommel of Irun's sword smashed into my face, nearly rendering me unconscious. "Irun, it's time to go! Move your ass," Ardrin called out as Irun looked down at me.

"Seems like you won't have my head after all, Lanky," he said, spitting blood on my chest. I didn't flinch, as my rage was now only fueled by the gesture. I could only watch as Irun walked briskly over to a freshly created portal.

I struggled to get to my feet, feeling my knees tremble and muscles groan in response to my commands. I looked up through blurry eyes, struggled to get to my feet, and headed after Irun who was now more than halfway there.

You're not getting away that easily, I thought.

I was on my feet, yes, but I was bent over like a drunkard and struggling to keep my balance. My blurred vision didn't help much either, but I knew what I had to do. I *drew from the Ethereal*, and re-entered my second stage, drawing my free hand over my shoulder then flinging it forward to cast my *Whip of Doom*. The jade tendril wrapped itself around Irun's forearm just before I flicked my finger to ignite the mana.

I admit I almost chuckled when I saw the chunk of his flesh

soaring through the air with a trail of blood following behind it.

Irun screamed in agony as he watched his beloved forearm fly near his face. I could just see him clutching his new stump tautly as Ardrin seared the wound shut, dragged him towards the swirling, violet portal and threw him inside.

Disoriented as I was, fell to my knees, exhausted from the ordeal and the spell the Masked One cast on me earlier. "One day, Irun," I mumbled weakly as I watched the pair go through the portal that shut quickly behind them. My eyes were heavier than they had ever been, and I could feel the exhaustion hitting me like a fully loaded wagon.

Can't... let him get... away, I thought briefly before collapsing unconsciously onto the stone floor.

EPILOGUE

Aftermath

I opened my eyes only to find myself staring at a ceiling I didn't recognize.

Where the hell am I? Whose bed is this? Why does my face feel like it's been kicked in? I thought as I touched my face.

There was still some minor swelling from the hit I took, but it had mostly subsided. I touched the fractured jawbone that had caused the tissue around it to swell, wincing at the pain, which in turn reopened the cut above my brow.

All fucked up. Wonderful, I thought.

I looked about the room, trying to gather information on where I was.

Looks like an infirmary, and I'm not alone, I thought, my ears beginning to notice the sounds of pained groaning around me.

Judging by where this would be on the map we looked at, I'm somewhere between the kitchen and the service room, I guess, I surmised.

The room was full of other Synners who were also wounded, but they were either fast asleep or picking at their own wounds. I began to search my own body for unknown wounds as frantically as the pain and lingering effects of the draining spell would allow.

"Calm yourself, will you? You're going to hurt yourself if you keep moving like that," a familiar voice said from the doorway. I lazily carried my line of sight over to the origin of the voice, and found a pleasant looking face.

"Hullo, Muluss," I mumbled. My jaw ached and I winced again. She stepped over to my bedside, sitting down beside me and holding my hand. "Try not to talk, you stubborn bastard," she whispered. I couldn't smile with my lips, but I did so with my eyes.

She put her right hand on my chest. "The Master would like to see you, if you can stand," she said softly. I closed my eyes and nodded slightly. Meliss helped me up from the bed, as I swung my legs lazily over the side. The white, linen sheets and soft pillows seemed to pull me close - never wanting to let me go. I felt lightheaded as I stood, nearly fainting from the rush of blood. I glanced down and saw that my clothes had been changed.

Instead of my leather jerkin, I was shirtless, but had some linen pants that were loosely tied around my hips. My many cuts and bruises from the battles showed, and the scar on my back from the cave showed in its entirety.

"Gods above and below, you're eighteen years old, and you've already been through all that?" she asked, observing wounds both past and present, including the latest addition on the bridge of my nose.

I could barely open my mouth before Meliss put a finger to it. "Sorry, I know I told you not to talk, but these wounds... a bit excessive, aren't they?" she asked. I could only perform a light shrug, which I hoped explained enough. She handed me a shirt, helping me to get it safely around my face and other wounds.

I took a step, but the linen pants I wore decided not to go with me due to their lack of a drawstring. Meliss couldn't help but chuckle a little. "It's kuld," I muttered, trying to tell her it was *cold* in the room. She patted me on the shoulder lightly, letting me stand on my own for a moment as she went over to the nearby chest to grab a large towel.

Well, it's something, at least, I thought.

I wrapped it around my waist, sticking the corner into the fold at my hip and rolled it over on itself.

There, that's not going anywhere, I thought.

I began to walk, but every step I took made my jaw ache more and more. I grunted as I took my first few steps, and then decided it would be best to suck up the pain once and for all. The two of us walked slowly for a few minutes, though to me it felt like an eternity.

Everything hurts. What the hell did I get hit with yesterday? Two days ago? Three? How long has it been? I thought.

My arms were sore, my hips were weak, and my jaw continued throbbing. We came to a small flight of stairs, and went even more slowly than I had thought possible for humans to walk. "This is humuliuting," I mumbled. "Didn't I tell you to keep quiet?" Meliss asked. I grunted and took another step.

It took us the better part of fifteen minutes to make it up the stairs until we finally reached where the Master was being kept. I saw him with a large bandage on his left shoulder, while Pyle - who sat at his side - kept watch over him. The room smelled of dried blood, as the used bandages were only recently removed from the room.

"Welcome back to the land of the living, Thoma. We weren't expecting you to wake up this afternoon, let alone the following day of the battle," Taegin said. "Same to you, *Mustur*," I mumbled as I slowly walked inside. "Gods above, lad, you look like hell. Bernar, help your little brother, will you?" Pyle said, noting my swollen face.

Bernar walked over to me, *drawing mana to* his palm and infusing it into the swollen area. "That's much better, thank you," I said, feeling more relief than I had expected. "You really should learn to do this on your own. It's not fully healed yet, but it should allow you to talk a little more freely for now. Speaking of which..." Bernar trailed off. "I think it would be best if we left them alone," Pyle said, glancing at Meliss. "I will return when you summon me, Master," Pyle said as he stepped away from Taegin's bedside.

"Come, Meliss. I wish to discuss something with you that I think you'll be excited to hear," Pyle said as he approached her. "What's this about?" she asked me. "I have absolutely no idea. I just woke up, remember?" I said, putting my hand on Meliss' shoulder.

"You'll be fine, so go with him. I'll be here whenever you get done. After all, I'll need help to get back down those damned stairs," I said playfully. I watched the two leave the room, as Bernar took their place in the doorway. He grabbed another chair from the corner of the room, and sat opposite me.

"Bernar told me of what happened to Irun, and I have to say from the bottom of my heart that I am sorry to discover he really was the traitor among us. As I understand it, you two were never very close. Even so, it must have been difficult to fight an old friend," Taegin said grimly.

I merely shrugged, knowing there was little more I could do at that point.

"He was always a little bratty, but I still considered him a friend, nevertheless. However, I had a hard time controlling my anger when I saw how mutated he was from the dark mana," I muttered, my wound still aching a little. I winced again, and a small drip of blood ran down the side of my face which I wiped off with the sleeve of my oversized shirt.

"Be that as it may, I wanted to give both of you my thanks for aiding me with the others. If you hadn't, I most likely would have died," the Master said humbly. "Which one of you two was it that made the call to tag into the fight?" he asked.

"Thoma made the call," Bernar began. "I was originally against it, because it would've left Leona and Meliss alone, but he saw something I guess I didn't," he continued.

"I see," the Master said. "Well, I thank you for making the decision, Thoma. I'm still alive, though it will take some time to fully recover my strength, as the claw that pierced my shoulder drained me of a small portion of my core," Taegin continued.

"Your core? What the hell was that claw made of?" I asked.

"It wasn't an ordinary claw of mana. That was the claw from the *Nethersong Mask,* one of the many gifts from the gods all those years ago," Taegin explained.

My eyes fell to the side of the bed as I sighed. "Regardless of the outcome, you two have fought valiantly in a battle that was definitely not in our favor. With that said, I grant you the rank of Adept, Thoma. Although, I do apologize that it's taken this long to get you the experience you needed to get there," he said with a small grin that wrinkled the scar on his face.

That's one above senior, and two away from master, I thought, hardly believing the words as they sounded in my own head.

"It's about time you got your rank-up. I always knew it would be coming soon," Bernar said, smiling full of pride. I allowed myself a small grin out of the corner of the better half of my face.

My eyes opened wide, and even though it pained me, I bowed from my chair. "Thank you, Taegin... I mean, *Master,*" I was barely able to say for the lump in my throat.

"*Ah*, so you *did* hear that part of the conversation. There is a lot more to that, but I'll wait for Pyle to heal you completely,"

Taegin smiled, breathing deeply as he adjusted his position in bed, wincing at the pain.

"However, I did want you to be the first to know that with your new rank, you will aid New Bloods and Juniors for their basic training, since we will have need for many more trainers. Since you're still new to teaching, Bernar and I will handle Senior ranks and above once we return to Codrean; which I hope is soon. The food here is good, but I'm tired of sitting in bed all day," Taegin said playfully.

"There is, of course one more thing I would like to tell you, but again, we must wait for your jaw to fully heal. I will have Pyle tend to it so we can have a much deeper conversation than the one we've just had," he explained. "You will have lots of questions, I imagine," he continued.

I didn't fully understand what he meant by that, and so I simply nodded.

"In the meantime, you are free to go where you please. We've won the battle for Coltend, but I am sure that it will not be the last for the Continent," Taegin said gravely. "Do you think he will try again soon?" I barely managed to ask.

He sighed heavily, as if a weight had been put on his chest. "My brother Ardrin, as you now know him, will most likely have returned to his fortress to rebuild his forces. Since Garett destroyed the crystals that controlled them, the creatures turned on each other, nearly wiping the entire force out in the process," he began. "His fortress, I assume, is likely in the North, but we have yet to fully confirm that," he continued.

I pondered the words for a few moments, digesting the information given to me.

"In any case, you have to have your jaw taken care of, so I suggest you go and do that immediately. We still have much to discuss," Taegin said. I nodded my head, and rose from my seat.

"I'll keep an eye on him until Pyle gets back," Bernar said to me just as I was leaving the room. Just then, I realized the predicament I was in, and the lack of assistance I now had to face it.

Ah, yes, my arch-nemesis of the day: Stairs. Should I wait for Meliss to come back? No telling how long she'll be gone for, is there? Damn it... I thought, embracing my demise with a deep, heartfelt sigh.

With every step taken, I could feel my jaw throbbing in response. I found myself praying to all the gods that Pyle would repair the damage Irun had caused with the blow to my face.

I've already taken his hand, but I will have that bastard's head one day, I swear, I thought, wincing through each step.

After more than a few minutes, I was back down on the ground floor. I was still wrapped in my towel, and barefoot on the cold, stone floors of the hallways I now limped down to find Pyle. I went as quickly as pain would allow me to, down the emptied halls and into the main hall, where the battle had taken place the previous evening. I cast my gaze to the horizon through the destroyed door and saw that it was nearly dusk.

I think that's the fastest passing of time I've ever seen, I thought.

I noticed that the path to the library was now closed, and that the throne on mana was gone as well. The shards of the previous thrones still lay about the hall as though they were the representatives of days of glory past. I saw a severed hand in a small pool of dried blood near the top of the steps that would have led to the thrones had they still been standing.

I slowly went over to it, and picked up the cold, lifeless hand, staring at it for a few moments. My eyes glowed, and I ignited the hand with a directed Pyrus spell, turning it to little more than a pile of ashes and smoke. I dusted my hands, and made my way over to the servant's area, where I was certain to find Pyle, and consequently, Meliss.

I came to the wooden door of the room, and poked my head through the crack. Meliss was telling him of how she had used her previous experience when fleeing the castle to strike down the glick that had come for her and Leona. Pyle was enjoying himself at the tale, he always did love a good story, and congratulated her for her accomplishment.

"I am curious to see what you might accomplish with a sword in your hand. You might not be as adept as those of us who have done it our entire lives, but you will still learn a vast amount of skills, nevertheless," Pyle began.

Meliss' eyes grew wide. "Do you mean that? Do you really think I could learn sword skills? What about mana? Can I learn that, too?" she asked eagerly. "Whoa, whoa. One question at a time," Pyle gestured, trying to calm her down. "Why do you want to learn so badly?" he asked. Meliss pondered for a moment, as I listened intently from the doorway

"Even though I've been a servant all my life, since this incident began, I've had to defend myself twice from both man and monster," she began, looking away as she spoke. "If it weren't for the knife you gave me, I wouldn't be standing here right now. I've learned, very quickly, that I never want to feel that kind of fear or helplessness again," she said, reverting her gaze back to Pyle's glowing eyes.

"You do know that courage is not the absence of fear, right?" Pyle asked. "What do you mean?" Meliss asked, visibly confused. "Being courageous, brave, or whatever you want to call it, doesn't mean that you do not *fear* whatever it is in front of you. It simply means that you accept the possibility of things going to shit, but you know that you're going to give it your best, regardless of the outcome," he explained.

Meliss took a moment to digest the words, and nodded her agreement after toying with the jeweled stubs in her ear lobes.

"In that case, I would like to learn to become both courageous *and* skilled with a sword," she said determinedly.

I knew she would say that, I thought.

Pyle chuckled heartily. "I'm glad to hear that," he began. "Even though you might still be a little too old for me to train from the very beginning. That's not to say it's not possible, you just likely won't be as adept as others your age. If you're capable enough, I might be able to begin and still have you graduate with some of the others from Fangsdalr, should you wish to become one of us, that is," he said.

Meliss looked down at the ground. "I've recently put eighteen winters behind me. Is that too old to be trained?" she asked, genuine concern ruling her tone. "It *is* a little on the older side," Pyle began. "She could always train with us at Codrean," I interjected. Meliss' face lit up when she heard my voice more clearly than earlier that day.

"*Ah*, you actually managed to make it down here," Pyle said playfully. "I was worried I'd have to send Meliss to carry your ass down the stairs," he jested. "I'm broken, not dead, Master Pyle. The Master sent me here to get my jaw fixed," I muttered. Meliss grabbed me a chair, and pulled it up beside her for me. "Thank you," I said quietly.

"So, you think the Master would let her train with you there at Codrean?" Pyle asked, as he poured mana into my jaw. "I think he wouldn't mind, but I'd have to ask and confirm that," I replied. I could feel the fracture closing, and the swelling dissipating as more mana flowed into my wound. "There, all done," Pyle said, proud of his work. "Gods above and below, that is *so* much better," I said, moving my jaw around.

"In any case, we might be able to train you as one of our own if the Master agrees to it, and you're up for the challenge," I said. Meliss' eyes held both excitement and seriousness that I had never before seen. "If he lets me, I'll do whatever it takes," she stated confidently.

Oh, *dear. Leona and Bernar are going to kill me,* I thought.

"Well, we will also have to have a discussion about Fangsdalr, since the traitor gave away its position," Pyle said solemnly. "I'm sure the Master will be more than willing to accommodate. We've lost many of our own as well, so it wouldn't be too large of a stretch to supplement our forces with yours," I said suggestively. "You might be right, but time will tell," Pyle concluded.

A short silence fell amongst the group, each one digesting the information presented here. "*Oh,* fuck! I just realized I haven't seen or heard from anyone else since I woke up. Where are Ed and Batch?" I exclaimed. "Edryd should be just outside the main hall," Pyle began. "The turd survived? *Heh,* I knew he would," I said with a grin. Pyle and Meliss glanced at each other with knowing looks.

"Wait, what about Batch? Wh-what happened?" I asked, fearing the answer after noticing the pair's exchange. "You should probably go find Edryd," Pyle said. "Meliss, take him with you and go find him," he continued.

Meliss led me to where Edryd was sitting on a bench in the light of the setting sun, while Garett, Roburn, Anwill, and Nenvalur were telling their tales of the monsters they had slain the previous evening. I greeted them with a wave, and they acknowledged my presence, continuing their conversation. Edryd was sitting with his hands folded together, and leaning his elbows on his legs, staring off into the distance as he sat in silence.

"Hullo, Edryd," I said. Edryd looked up at me in surprise. "I thought you'd be out for a lot longer," he began. I noticed something was amiss and decided to prod him for the information. "Well, I would have rested longer, but I heard that you were out and bout, so I came to check on you," I said.

Edryd shrugged. "We won the battle, and managed to turn the fuckers on themselves, but not before the addia tore Batch's arms off in front of me," Edryd said, choking on the last few words. "It was... effortless for that addia - killing him, I mean," Edryd said.

The words struck me like a troll's fist, and my eyes lowered to the ground.

"Damn it, Ed. I'm sorry you had to see that," I said empathetically, putting a hand on my best friend's shoulder. "Batch was a good person, and he died the way he always wanted to," I continued. Edryd lowered his head, trying to hide his tears.

"I believe we all must see such things at some point in our lives," he began. "Makes us stronger for whenever it comes around again, I suppose," he said with a shrug. "I avenged him by killing the fucker that took his life, but I still wish I could have saved him," Edryd said as his eyes began to water. I put a hand on his shoulder. "You did what you could, and I don't think anyone could have done any better under the circumstances," I said comfortingly.

"You don't know that," Edryd said grimly. "Perhaps I don't, but what I do know is that death comes for us all - be it sooner or later. All we can do is keep that in mind, and when our friends' or our own times come, we greet it as though it were an old friend; embracing the harshness of reality, for that is ultimately all we humans can do," I said.

Edryd wiped off a tear that dripped down his cheek and sniffled. "I guess you're right, as usual. Thanks," he said. I patted his shoulder, and left him and Roburn to their silence. I made my way back inside the palace, and found Leona in the main hall, picking up a few of the pieces of the smashed thrones. "I take it they have sentimental value to you," I said quietly as I approached her.

Leona sighed. "They do. As little as I had liked being the queen of an overweight madman, I still cared deeply for my subjects. I have sent messages out to where I pray the majority of them have escaped to before Mourtis closed the city entirely," she said. "Might I ask how many you believe made it out?" I asked. Leona shook her head. "I can't say for certain, but word of the Church's rebellion would have spread about the city within a few minutes, so there's no telling how many survived the attack," she explained.

"I pray that most made it out, but after seeing the state of the city itself, I fear less than half made it out alive. We will only know how many within a few days just how many of them there are left," she continued. I grimaced in solidarity, but handed her a shard that held the queen's insignia engraved in the wood. She took it, and smiled warmly at me as a token of her gratitude.

"I pray that you and your brother will visit me often, here at the palace," she said. "After having spent time with you and the others, your senses of humor... well, not only has it rubbed off on me a little, but it would be a tragedy to lose friendships like that once you depart," she said, furrowing her brow.

I shrugged. "I suppose we could pass by and visit from time to time. It's always nice to have an outsider to talk to about things different from sword maneuvers and spell-casting," I grinned.

Leona bowed gracefully, and I returned the bow. "I suppose I should get back to formally addressing you, now that you're back here at the palace," I said. Leona waved her hand. "*Oh*, nonsense. So long as there are no official members of any kind, you needn't use formal speech with me. We are friends, now - something I have longed for since I first became queen of Coltend," she said. I blushed, and bowed once more.

"I'd best be off to see the Master now that my jaw has healed. If you need anything from either myself or my brother, let us know," he said. "I don't believe I will need anything for now, other than a cup of wine, and a warm bed for the night," she said.

I knew what that entailed, but decided against saying anything.

"Very well, Leona. I'll see if I can't have *someone* get you a glass of wine," I said with a wink. It was obvious whom I had in mind to fetch the aforementioned glass and Leona blushed in response.

I bowed, then made my way back up to the Master's quarters. Bernar had remained at the Master's side, and was tending to the wound in Pyle's stead. "I see Pyle has done his work on you," Taegin said, noting my newly scarred, though less swollen face. I grinned. "Indeed, he has. I really should learn how to self-heal. I've noticed a trend in me getting hurt... a *lot*," I said, recalling the past few weeks' adventures.

"Feels like the hands of a goddess running over you, doesn't it?" Bernar asked. "Mind is always in the gutter," I said under my breath. "What? You might have different ways of comparing things that touch you, little turd, but I prefer to compare mine to women," Bernar said with a grin.

"Not all things can be compared to women, Bernar. I thought your mother would have taught you such a thing," Taegin began. I looked interested as soon as the words had left Taegin's mouth. "Did you know her? My mother, I mean to say," I asked.

Taegin sighed, and looked upwards. "I know her well," he replied. My eyes opened wide, while a wrinkle began to form itself in the corner of Bernar's mouth. "She is an extraordinary woman, warrior, and friend. She is as wise as she is beautiful, though I think she takes a bit too much from her great-great-grandfather's side of the family," Taegin began.

I looked at him with utter confusion on my face. "How do you know so much about her? Did you know her before she abandoned us?" I asked, not bothering to hide my curiosity.

Taegin furrowed his brow. "*Abandoned* you? Is that how you remember it, or did your insolent father who hated both her and her profession lie to you? That obese sack of shit only married her because he was forced to do so by his own parents to have closer ties to Synners that could protect their farmlands from monsters. He told you a lie, and I suspect many more like it about her. She is the exact opposite of everything he said she was," he said sternly, as though doing so would instantly rid any negative ideas of my mother.

I stared deeply into Taegin' eyes, thinning the gap between the lids of my own. "How well do you know her, exactly?" I asked. Taegin raised an eyebrow to Bernar, who shrugged. "Don't look at me; I haven't said anything," Bernar said, upturning his bottom lip and shaking his head.

Taegin closed his eyes and breathed as deeply as the wound in his shoulder would allow him to. "Bernar has known this for quite some time, now, but the two - better yet, *three* of us - decided to keep it from you until we figured you were ready," he began.

"Thoma, believe me or not, I am your grandfather, and my great-grandfather was the Lord of Codrean - the one who first encountered the gods," Taegin said, as matter-of-factly as he could. "Wait… you're saying that…" I began. "Your mother is, in fact, my daughter. Yes," Taegin cut me off.

My jaw could've split the Continent in two with how hard it dropped.

"Did… did I hear that correctly?" I stuttered. "You mean to say that not only are we directly related, but that we are the

Lord of Codrean's direct descendants?" I asked, only receiving a nod from the Master. "Which also makes Ardrin my great-uncle?" I asked again, with the same response. "Damn it, that's uh… that's a lot to take in," I sighed.

"I have two more questions: What is our real last name, and where is our mother?" I asked, wanting to get straight to the point. Taegin looked at Bernar, who could only purse his lips as his reply. "I'm surprised your brother was this good at keeping secrets," he said in a slightly playful tone.

"To answer the question about your mother, she's been in Caegwen since you were about three-years-old. Also, how did you know your last name was a fake?" he asked. "Given our heritage, it would stand to reason that if mother wanted to hide, the first thing she would do is hide her family name, and by default, mine and Bernar's as well. So, what is it?" I asked, noticing Taegin's features twitch.

Whatever ran through his head just now means I just touched a nerve, I thought, watching his expression shift ever-so-slightly.

"Pelantyr," Taegin replied.

"As in *Nexis Pelantyr*? Author of *Dissection*? That's a lot to chew on at once," I said, slumping into the chair to digest the information.

"Told you he would handle it well," Bernar said. Taegin pushed his lips to one side and raised an eyebrow. "What? I did, and you know it," Bernar continued, while I was still processing what I had heard.

"Once we have returned to Codrean, I plan to train you up in your second stage, and then send you off to find her in Caegwen like I did with your brother," Taegin began.

So that's why Bernar knew Anwill, I thought.

"What has she been doing in Caegwen all these years? Was it too much to ask for her to visit at least *once*?" I asked sardonically.

Both my brother and Taegin looked at each other, almost as if saying something without words.

"She has been searching for some of the artifacts that the gods had given us all those years ago. The night she left Coltend, and the night that I brought you under my wing, she called it *her sacred duty*, but I just think she wants to bring back the powers we once held as a family. A few of them have long since gone missing. Where, why, and which ones are still unclear, but others were stolen - one of which my brother currently holds in his possession. If I know him, I am certain he is searching for the others as well," Taegin said.

"I see. Well, if you're already sending me there, I would like to take Anwill up on his offer of learning more about mana manipulation stages," I suggested. "I could let him know, yes, but I feel like she might want to take part in that, as well. However, I'll let you figure that out for yourself," he said, recalling a conversation he had with Anwill about this very topic.

"There are, of course, still a few things I want you to learn before going off to Caegwen, so it will be some time before you actually depart," the Master continued. "Of course, Gran-... Tae-... What the hell do I even call you now?" I asked, genuinely confused. "In front of others, *Master* will suffice. Between the three of us? Call me whatever you want," Taegin smiled, wrinkling the scar on his cheek once more.

"I see. Well, *grandpa*, Pyle has something he wants to discuss with you about Meliss and what remains of his Synners, if you're feeling up for it," I said.

It feels weird calling him that, I thought.

"We'll be leaving for Codrean in a few days, perhaps weeks depending on how much work we need to help with, here. We will have plenty of time to talk to him about what the next steps will be," Taegin said.

"Sounds like a plan to me," I said excitedly. "I'll inform him and try to get some more rest, as I'm still feeling a little queasy from whatever happened during the battle," I continued. "As we all should. It's been a long few days, though I feel they will only grow more difficult from here on out," the Master said gravely.

I swallowed dryly, clenching my fist.

"We'll be ready for them when they come," I said with no small amount of bravado. Taegin looked at me proudly. "An Adept, indeed. Now, go get some rest," he said. I looked out of the window at the back of the room, realizing the it had gotten darker since the beginning of the conversation.

"Right. I'll take my leave, to be able to process all of this... information. I bid you goodnight, and I will, *uh*, see you tomorrow," I said awkwardly. Taegin smiled and nodded slowly. "Goodnight, Thoma," he said.

"See you tomorrow, fuckstick," Bernar said with a grin. "Until tomorrow, you slimy turd-blossom," I shot back. He chuckled, but remained at Taegin' side and returned to his work on the wound which was not yet fully healed.

Just as I was about to exit the room, I halted in the doorway, feeling the shit-eating grin starting to grow rapidly on my face. "*Oh*, and Bernar," I called out as he turned to face me. "Someone would like a cup of wine brought to them when you are done here," I said with a wink.

Taegin glared at Bernar, who blushed slightly. "Like you didn't know that already," Bernar said sardonically. Taegin looked at me for an answer, but I could only shrug indifferently before stifling a chuckle as I walked out of the room.

I made my way back to the infirmary, where Edryd and the others were also getting ready to sleep. Meliss approached me with a set of linen sleeping clothes. "Back to square one, I guess.

Only this time, you're bringing me clothes, not coming to take them off me to wash them," I said. Meliss blushed. "Back to square one," she said with a smile.

"What did the Master say?" she asked, but I knew there was only so much I could tell her at that point in time. "Only that I am to go to Caegwen with my brother sometime soon," I said nonchalantly. "Will you at least stay with me awhile in Codrean if the Master allows me to be trained with Master Pyle?" she asked.

"Of course I will! He still has things to teach me before I head off, anyway, so we'll have a good amount of time to spend together. Besides, I think he'll like the idea of having Pyle around at Codrean," I said comfortingly.

"That's all I need to know, then," she smiled, wrapping herself in my arms. I kissed her goodnight, and stroked her hair as she fell asleep.

Caegwen, huh? I thought as my mind began to drift back to that grassy plane from what felt like forever ago...

And to a new power that I'd only scratched the surface of.

THOMA WILL RETURN IN "THE SYNNER: ECHOES IN THE SNOW"

AFTERWORD

Author's Notes

Well I'll be, you actually made it!

While I'm entirely unaware of whether you enjoyed this story, I would like to thank you from the bottom of my heart for even having considered this book out of the other possible choices you might have had. It's an incredibly humbling feeling, but I'm glad to have been a small part of your literary journey.

This story holds such a special place in my heart, because I know for a fact the next time we meet, it will be even better. I know I said that Thoma and the gang would return, and as of writing this Afterword, I have just finished the second installation in the series.

I would be lying if I said that it was easy to write.

Either way, I had originally written the initial draft for this story back in 2015, but after nearly two years of world building and writing, I "finished" it in 2017 just before I joined the military.

Like I said in the Preface, I sat on the story for about 6 years, but there was a reason for that. I knew for a fact that I had to mature both as a person and as an author before I could truly do this story justice. It gave me perspective, and a lot of experiences I might not have had otherwise. I knew that I had a daunting task before me, but I'm certainly glad I pushed through and got this first part out.

Here's a little trivia for you: All the chapters with Thoma in it were recently converted to first person. I did that for a reason, but it will truly make itself apparent much later on. You'll see what I mean, eventually, since I already know how this story ends.

Nevertheless, welcome, New Blood. I can't wait to show you what the next part of this story holds. It's gonna be a wild ride, I promise.

PS: Who was your favorite character and why? Come find me on socials (@nooburai) and tell me about it!

Made in the USA
Monee, IL
30 December 2024

72350814R00333